Praise for Marcia Rose's previous novel, *Nurses*

"A fast-paced, unabashedly soap-operatic tale of love and betrayal in a hectic Manhattan clinic."
—*Kirkus Reviews*

"*Nurses* may be fiction, but there is no truer story of urban American nursing."
—JANE CARPINETO
Author of *RN*

"Funny, heart-wrenching—always entertaining—*Nurses* is an ode to unsung heroes as well as a great story."
—*Press* (Middletown, CT)

By Marcia Rose
Published by Ballantine Books:

ADMISSIONS
CHOICES
CONNECTIONS
SECOND CHANCES
SUMMERTIMES
ALL FOR THE LOVE OF DADDY
SONGS MY FATHER TAUGHT ME
A HOUSE OF HER OWN
HOSPITAL
LIKE MOTHER, LIKE DAUGHTER
NURSES
A TIME TO HEAL

A TIME
TO HEAL

Marcia Rose

BALLANTINE BOOKS • NEW YORK

A Ballantine Book
Copyright © 1998 by Marcia Kamien
Published by The Ballantine Publishing Group

http://www.randomhouse.com

Library of Congress Catalog Card Number: 97-90966

ISBN 0-345-40226-X

Manufactured in the United States of America

First Edition: May 1998

10 9 8 7 6 5 4 3 2 1

This book is dedicated to the real-life Harry K., beloved of many, missed by all.

The author is grateful for all the research help from head librarian Virginia Chapman of the Killingworth Public Library and, especially, the tireless and efficient Elizabeth Ellis.

All the characters in this story—with the possible exception of Margaret Sanger—are the products of the author's imagination. If they remind anyone of real people, or seem to be terribly familiar, the author is grateful. But they are all fictitious.

Prologue: Shining Stone and Her Daughter, Bird

Pequot Territory, at Massapoag near the Konektikut River, Summer 1637

Shining Stone straightened her back and stretched a little, blinking. It was hot in the meadow, and sweat had begun to run into her eyes. After a third long day of medicine gathering, she was weary. They should have started back yesterday, but the sunny days and evening rain showers had fed the yarrows, making them thick and heavy with healing blossoms. She wanted to pick as many as she could carry. As *they* could carry. Her daughter, Bird, now twelve summers and nearly a woman, had made the journey with her. Bird had often come with Shining Stone, even as a small child, walking flatfooted and uncertainly; but this year, the time had come for her to begin to learn the arts her mother knew so well—healing, birthing, and burial rites.

Bird learned, as she did everything, swiftly and with grace. Shining Stone gazed at her daughter with great pride. The girl, unaware of being watched, was busy pulling and picking, bending and straightening, pliant as a reed in the wind. Her long braid swung back and forth as she looked for the small pale flowers of the pipsissewa. Bird was a fine-looking woman, although not exactly beautiful. She was tall and broad-shouldered, with high round breasts and strong legs. She could walk or run long distances. And her hands, with their long narrow fingers, were deft at all her tasks: making baskets, sorting

1

shells, or tanning a deerhide. Or gathering plants for the medicine bag, as she was doing now.

Many young men in the village nodded at her, preening a bit when they walked by the wigwam. Each one hoped she would say, "I want *him* for my husband." It would do them no good. Shining Stone had already chosen the man who would be Bird's betrothed. White Wolf, the son of the sachem, was the man she wanted for her daughter. Ah, what a fine match that would be. Bird was the daughter of one of the village's most respected families, one of the most important families in the whole tribe for that matter. Shining Stone was a well-known healer and witch. Her husband, Great Eagle, was the *pawwow*, the shaman. Together, they were high in the order of the mighty Pequot.

The Pequots, as everyone knew, were the most feared nation hereabouts. They numbered in the hundreds of hundreds of hundreds, and every other tribe quaked in their presence. Alone, they had conquered all the peoples in this part of the world—all but the Narragansett, those wily weasels, and they would soon fall, too. Shining Stone smiled at her fierce thoughts. She was no warrior; she was *moigu*. It was good to be *moigu*—healer and witch—in the tribe whose name was a shortened form of *pekawatawog*—the destroyers.

The day was beautiful, sunny and clear, with a fine golden light shining over the meadow. Shining Stone looked about her, breathing in the beauty of her country, where the spirits were kind. She and Bird had found hellebore, bearberry, sassafras, snakeroot, elderberry bark and fruit for good sweating, squawroot for ease in menstrual cramps and childbirth, stoneseed to stop the moon cycle of a woman. Now the medicine bag slung across her chest was heavy and full, like a pregnant woman come to term. It would not do to be greedy and rob the earth of all her children. Some must be left for the animals and some to make seed and a new generation of plants.

"Come, Bird," she called. "We have enough, and I wish to see Wild Goose before nightfall."

Bird obediently straightened and joined her mother. "I dreamed last night of my brother. Wild Goose was swimming with many golden fishes, and then they turned to stars and began to fall down, out of the sky."

Shining Stone frowned. That was an odd dream indeed, and she was not sure what it meant. But she felt a quiver of apprehension, and said, "Let us hurry, Bird."

When they set out, three days ago, her son had been almost fully recovered from a festering wound on his foot. He had stepped on a broken shell on the beach the day before and, boylike, had continued the hunt for oysters and clams with his friends, rather than go home to have his foot wrapped in poultices. He had paid dearly for ignoring the gash in the sole of his foot. Within a day, the foot had turned red and then swelled to almost twice its size. He became feverish, his eyes rolled back in his head, and he muttered phrases nobody could understand.

His father had stayed all day with the boy, to pray over him. Communing with the spirits was all very well and good, but Shining Stone knew that the poultice she had used on Wild Goose would work better in the end. Still, there was Bird's strange dream. . . . Shining Stone was uneasy and she quickened her step.

"Mother, I dug up many of the secret roots. The old roots had given birth to many new ones," Bird said, hurrying to catch up with her.

"Good." Shining Stone knew that Bird was referring to dogbane, turnip, and wild ginger, which were important, because, boiled or ground and eaten, they became a strong medicine that could keep a woman from becoming pregnant. Shining Stone's mother had told her of these roots, just as she had been taught by her mother and so on, back to the beginning of time. Because she had this knowledge, Shining Stone had become famous. No other knew all that she knew. Ordinary women knew that squawroot could bring on the menses, the same way it brought on labor when it was time for the baby to be born. But squawroot did not always work. Shining Stone's medicines did.

"You remember well, Bird. And I have watched you, so I know that you have good hands as well as a good mind. You were born with the healing spirit and you will be a famous witch."

Bird flushed with pleasure. "Oh, I hope so."

They marched on in silence for a few minutes. Then Bird said, a bit timidly, "Mother?"

"Yes, my daughter."

"My dream made you scowl. Please tell me, have I dreamed an evil omen for my brother?"

Shining Stone waited a moment before answering, considering her words. "I do not know what that dream means. For your brother to be in water is good, for as we all know, water has great healing powers. But to be in the middle of many fish, that is not good. We know that a sick person must be isolated from the healthy or his sickness will leave his body and go into another's. So I do not know the meaning, whether it is good or bad. I only know that I would like to see him and touch him and know that all is well." And she pushed herself to go a little faster. Bird hurried with her, not complaining.

"Tell me a story, Mother, of when you and father were young."

It would help the time to pass, Shining Stone thought, and keep her from thinking too much about Bird's dream.

"When your father, Great Eagle, was only a small boy, he fell upon the ground, shaking and quaking, and foam appeared from his mouth. Everyone who saw it was in awe. How many spirits must be inhabiting this small body for it to twitch and dance this way! And when it stopped, he remembered nothing of it and wanted only to sleep. The people said, 'The spirits have chosen him.' . . ."

"And then, when he got older—" Bird prodded. She loved this story and never tired of hearing it.

"As he got older, he knew ahead of time when the spirits were coming, as he does now. He sees the air quivering. No one else sees that. And they always come."

Bird's eyes were round with wonder. "I wish the spirits would speak with me, Mother."

"Hush. You don't know what you say. It is not pleasant. Think of Little Fern, your father's mother, your grandmother. She spoke often with the spirits and everyone came to her to be cured of their illnesses. But the spirits became angry with her and told her that her family was evil and wished her dead. That caused her to walk into Massapoag where she drowned.

Her father's brother, too, was said to speak with spirits, and one day when he was sixteen, he walked away from a hunt and disappeared. He never returned to his family. So don't wish for what may hurt you."

Stubbornly, Bird said, "If it's so dangerous, then why do we choose our shamans this way?"

"Silly girl, we don't choose them. They are chosen by signs from the spirit world. It is a difficulty they are given and they accept it."

They walked on in silence, skirting the tall plumed grasses that grew in the swamp. There was no trail but it didn't matter. They knew the way well, and the squawking of gulls told them they were very near Massapoag, the Great Water, where they had set up their summer village.

Bird looked over at her mother, admiring her. She was dressed, as was Bird, in a knee-length skirt of deerhide, wrapped around and fastened with a belt. Her mother's belt was intricately woven of tiny beads of many colors, and her headband was very fine, birdskin sewn with beads. Bird's clothing was much simpler, as befitted a younger woman. Her good luck amulet was of stone, while her mother's was a beautiful long tubular bead, carved from an iridescent quahaug shell, purple like the most valuable wampum. It was very old and had been pierced with a very thin stone, which took many days—not perforated with a white man's metal nail, like today's wampum. "This amulet is very special, Bird, and when you reach your womanhood, it will pass to you." That day would be quite soon, Bird thought, and was pleased.

Suddenly, Shining Stone stopped walking. Bird also came to a halt.

"That smell," Shining Stone said. "Do you smell it?"

Bird sniffed the air. "Meat cooking," she said.

But her mother shook her head. "No. No, it is . . . something else. Something bad. Come. We must hurry." She pushed through the tall plumed grasses, panting a little. Bird became frightened and her heart began to thud quickly in her chest.

"Mother, what do you mean? What something bad? What do you know?"

"Nothing. I know nothing. Just let us hurry!"

"They are cooking food to take to the sachem's great celebration." Her brother had been angry to be left behind, Bird remembered. He wanted to go to the sachem's fort on Pequot Hill to be with the others who were celebrating. Uncas and his English friends had slunk away from Pequot territory with their tails between their legs, and so a feast was called. Horrible Uncas! Furious because he had not been named sachem, Uncas had separated from his tribe, taking other angry young men with him. He called this group by the tribe's ancient name, Mohegan, and lived apart from the rest of his people, making treaty with the English. They had threatened war upon the Pequots, but thought better of it and went away. The sachem then sent word that he would host a great feast at his fort and invited the entire tribe. Of course, everyone of importance would be there. Oh, how Wild Goose had wept and argued—but he was still unable to walk and his swollen foot would have slowed them all. So Bird's father had also stayed behind to pray him better, along with those too old or sick to make the journey.

The smell of cooked flesh was terribly strong now, and it was mixed with another smell, something evil. Shining Stone dropped her bundles and ran up through the shifting sand to the crest of the dunes, Bird close behind her. When they looked down, Bird felt her heart leap into her mouth. Where was her village? Where was everything? Only two or three wigwams were standing. The rest had been trampled into piles of saplings and reeds scattered over the scorched ground. Only the stone hearths in the center of the dirt floors were left. No sleeping platform had been left intact; all was smashed and strewn about. And everything had been torched: the sleeping mats, the blankets, the hides ready for sewing! The very sand was blackened and burnt. Even the ceremonial longhouse, the holy place, was broken and crushed. Sobs of fright and shock came out of Bird's throat, but her mother clapped a hand over her mouth to stop any sound.

"Hush," she whispered in a voice that was almost not a voice. "Listen for our enemy." Bird felt rooted in place, unable to move, unable to breathe, but she obeyed and listened. Not a living soul stood upright or walked about. Her father! Her brother! Her elderly grandparents! She crouched behind the dune, feeling empty inside of her body, while the tears she could not stop poured silently down her cheeks.

Shining Stone heard a great buzzing in her ears and a pounding, like the sound of the surf. After a moment, she recognized it as the heavy beating of her heart, a heart fractured with woe and grief. Gone, all gone, all! Gone! She struggled to take it all in, to make sense of what her eyes saw. Their village, almost totally destroyed. But why? And by what enemy? No warriors had stayed behind; nobody had been left but the ill and the very old. Why kill them? It made no sense.

She became aware of moans and weak cries, which meant someone was still alive down there. Her own wigwam had been spared. It still stood, smoldering a little around the edges. Then she saw the bodies of her husband's old parents, flung outside the wigwam. Maybe her son still lived, and her husband. Perhaps they had been taken captive. If so, she would free them, and then she would put a curse on those who had taken them. A curse that would kill them slowly, painfully! A cleansing anger rose in her chest.

"Come," she said under her breath, in case an enemy waited and listened nearby. "We will go down there now. Stay behind me." Together, they crept slowly down the dunes, stopping every few steps to listen. But with every step, Shining Stone was more certain that the enemy had left, long ago. *Kill like cowards, run like cowards,* she thought.

She moved quickly, sliding down the side of the dune, her heart pounding heavily, and raced to her wigwam. *My son!* She prayed silently. *My husband. Let them be alive!* Pausing for a breath, she bent and entered her home. And her heart stopped. So much blood! So many terrible wounds! They had been killed together; her husband's dead arms still encircled his son's body. And then she saw that his head had been hacked away from his shoulders and lolled sideways like a broken bird. A wave of darkness swept over her and she closed her eyes to keep it from taking her.

A terrible cry came from behind her. Bird, who had crept in

after her, moaned. "Oh, no! This cannot be!" Her daughter began to rock back and forth on her knees. Shining Stone fell to her knees and held the girl tightly. "Remember this," she said. "Your whole life long, never forget this terrible day." Dead, all of them dead, and no wise and respected man to conduct the burial rites for the poor souls, slaughtered like animals, no other women to weep, no one left to visit, saying, *"Kutchimmoke,"* "be of good cheer," nobody to stroke the cheek and head of each mourner. Shining Stone held her daughter, and together they wailed their grief.

After a time, Shining Stone stood up and Bird stood with her. They went out to the beach lit with the blood-tinged light of the setting sun. Shining Stone shivered. Her entire body wished to run away from this place. Nearby, she heard a thin whisper of pain. She moved toward the sound, Bird right behind her, so close she could feel the girl's breath on her shoulder.

"Aie!" They almost tripped over him—a slender young man lying curled up under a dune. Shining Stone knew him. He was one of the men who often came by their wigwam hoping to attract Bird's attention. His name was Thunder-cloud. There were so many terrible wounds on him, she did not know how he still lived. When she knelt by him to see if she might be able to save him, he opened his one remaining eye. He tried to speak, but she could hear nothing until she bent her ear next to his mouth. "Run," he was saying, "run from this place . . ." He had to stop and a thin trickle of blood came from his lips.

"Tell me everything you can, little brother," Shining Stone urged. "You are badly wounded, and I must know who did this thing before you die. Tell me, it was the Narragansett, wasn't it?" But he was mouthing, "No."

She sent Bird for water to wet his lips. Two and three words at a time he told of the attack. By the time the sun had sunk below the horizon and the first faint stars had appeared in the sky, Shining Stone knew the whole story. It was worse than her worst imagining. Uncas had done this terrible thing together with the *Yenguese*, the English. They had only pretended to leave Pequot territory. In the night they had turned and, at daybreak, had gone silently up the Mystik River to where the Pequots were celebrating at the fort, leaped upon them, and slaughtered them all.

"The Destroyers are destroyed," Thundercloud said. "Two days ago. The sachem, too." Some of the Mohegan warriors had left the Mystik fort, looking for more Pequots to kill. Thundercloud had run the many miles to warn those who had stayed behind. "But they were already here," he whispered. More blood flowed from his mouth. Shining Stone took his hand in hers, willing the strength from her body into his, if only for a moment.

Next to her, Bird said, "But Uncas is a Pequot and Pequots do not slaughter their own." Shining Stone answered her, "No, Uncas calls himself Mohegan, not Pequot. I call him renegade. He has turned on his brothers and sisters and he has destroyed the Pequot people." Tears poured from her eyes as she spoke.

Finally, Thundercloud breathed his last breath, and his head dropped. Bird fell to her knees, weeping and wailing.

Shining Stone put her arms around her daughter. Her heart had turned to stone. "We will weep later, my daughter," she said. "But now, you must stop. They shall not have *us*. If there are to be any Pequots in the world, we must leave at once. We will go to a secret place I know, near winter camp. Perhaps others have escaped and that is where they will go."

They gathered only a few things, their medicines, two pots, and blankets. Then they climbed the dunes, and began to run. When it was fully dark, they stopped to sleep. At daybreak, they arose and continued their journey, always looking over their shoulders, starting at every rustle in the woods. They found a stream where they drank and picked currants from the bushes to eat. Then Shining Stone said, "Let us follow this stream to her mother." She meant the big river called Konektikut that was born far north and came roaring down through Pequot country, emptying into Massapoag to become one with the great water.

By sunset, they were far upriver. "Will we be at our secret place soon, Mother?"

"Yes, quite soon. We will come to a turning in the river, and there we must turn away from the water and climb up through the forest."

The next morning, Shining Stone found the hidden trail. They climbed up and up, through woods thick with growth and filled with the whispers of many animals. They would have food enough, Bird thought. She noted the many strong saplings, which they would use tomorrow to build a new wigwam.

At last, Shining Stone pushed through a thick grove of birch and said, "Here."

The flat clearing in the midst of the forest was well lit by the sun, cooled by the surrounding trees, and from there, you could hear, far below, the rushing river, and closer, a nearby brook. On the far side of the space stood a mighty hickory. The tree's shaggy bark made it look like a great gray bear; its wide spreading branches hung almost to the ground with their load of ripe nuts. Bird thought, such a large and friendly tree must be a good omen.

"We must be strong," her mother said. "We cannot go back. We have left forever *Manitook*, God's country, and will make our home in this new place."

Bird put her arms around her mother, to comfort her, although she felt empty and without direction. She hardly knew who she was. Who could she be, a girl without a family, without a village, without a tribe? She was so small and the world was so big.

As they stood there, clinging to each other, a half-grown fawn wandered out of the woods and stared at them with big soft eyes, then bolted. They both laughed a little. Shining Stone wiped the tears from Bird's cheeks, and from her own. She took her daughter's hand and they walked about the clearing.

"Here we will have the wigwam and there, a small garden, and we will make traps to catch rabbits. You see that big tree, Bird? That tree will be our mother and father. It will shelter us. Soon, others will make their way up here and then, we will begin.

"Yes," she said decisively, looking deep into Bird's eyes, so that Bird would know to remember her words forever. "This is our place. Here, we will stay."

SECTION ONE

Annis
(Little Bird)
Rebecca
(Wounded Bird)
Morgan
(Water Bird)
Todd Wellburn

1

August 1868, in the hills above East Haddam, Connecticut

It was a hard birth. The baby was broad-shouldered with a large head, and Annis was old—near thirty. But she welcomed the pain because it would give her a son. She was sure it was a boy. For months, he had been kicking and pounding inside her, growing strong. Her dreams were all of tall pines and herons and feathered lances. She knew how to read dreams and other signs. She was descended from a long line of witches and healers, and had the right to call herself *moigu*. It would be a boy.

Annis squatted on a blanket she had spread under the great shagbark hickory that shaded the house, and silently urged her son to use his strength to move into this world. The late afternoon heat sat like a panting animal on the earth. The cicadas screeched shrilly. The only other sound was her own breath, puffing and grunting. The sweat ran down her body. No breath of air stirred the long dry grass at the edge of the clearing. Not even the leaves of the aspens quaked. At last, as the sun started to sink beneath the earth in a blaze of red and purple, the child slid out, and began to howl. He was dark, dark and red. She would name him Red Sunset in the old language.

Annis picked up her baby, wiped him off, blinked, and looked again. Not a boy, not a son. The signs had been wrong. How could that be? No question about it, though. She had a daughter, another girl. But what a girl! So dark and fierce with her lusty cries and her thick thatch of straight black hair. Very different from Becky, who was a tiny thing, like the fairies in the stories Pa used to tell. Becky was pink and white with thick coppery hair that fell in ringlets to her waist. A little beauty, everyone said. What they meant was: Not a bit of the Indian in *her*. Well, she was the spittin' image of Pa, an Englishman who'd come across the wide water to see what he could find in the New World. And what he'd found was Annis's mam—Margaret to the townsfolk, but her real name was White Bird.

Her mother's parents had turned away when Margaret brought her Englishman up to their encampment. They were pure-blood Pequots. They might take on Christian names—it was easier for trading—but they never took on the Christian god, and they would never accept a Christian for a mate. After the massacre, which the *Yenguese* called the Pequot War, a very few of their people had escaped, and some had made their way to this place. Though the Pequot were not entirely destroyed, they all knew they had to keep their own ways and keep to their own. Margaret's family was highly placed. They were directly descended from the famed Bird, the *moigu* who could stop the cramps just by looking at you and bring bloody knives out of the air, exactly like a shaman. Well, and why not? Bird's mother had been *moigu* and her father a well-known shaman, killed by the traitorous Mohegans in his own wigwam, while he tended to his dying son. The direct descendents of a shaman and a *moigu* did not approve of her *Yengue*, with his strange copper hair and milky skin and tiny orange spots all over his face.

But White Bird had fallen in love and didn't care. She disdained the men of her tribe, many of whom had succumbed to the evil rum and lay about drunk. She deserved better than that, she told her mother. She was already a famous healer. She could have any man she wanted, and she wanted her Englishman, Arthur Armstrong. With him, she had a daughter—that was Annis—and a son, Tristram. But Arthur had died on a trip upriver to Vermont. Leastways, he never came back to them. White Bird came back up here with her two children and bent her head before her parents. They took her back, for the sake of their grandchildren and because, by then, their only other child, White Bird's sister, had been taken from them by the spirits.

Annis remembered her pa only in little flashes of memory. What was vivid was the recollection of her mother's terrible grief, a torrent of sobbing and crying to the gods that seemed like it would never stop. Such all-consuming love Annis had known only once—and him she had sent away. Sent him away and expelled his child, which was already clearly a male, from her womb. She was already married to Todd Wellburn who had gone off to fight in the Great War, somewhere far away. How could she show Todd a son when he'd been nowhere near her for so long? So she had used her herbal skills, dosing herself with an infusion of powdered snakeroot in warm water. She made it from the black cohosh that grew in the open fields, which was stronger than the blue one from the deep woodlands. She cooked it carefully, making herself a tea, and drank it straight down. In an hour or so, the cramping began and soon enough, the tiny creature slid out, its little arms and legs curled up so innocent and sweet. Then she dug a hole and, wrapping him in a nice bit of linen she'd been given by one of the women she'd midwived, she buried him. She thought she might die of her sorrow. But Becky needed her mam, so dying was out of the question. She never did forget that half-formed little boy, though. Nor his father, neither, come to that.

If Todd hadn't gone to the war, it never would have happened. But everyone was going, so he went, too. "Don't want to miss the fun," he told Annis, and off he went with the First Connecticut Volunteers, marching away in glory from Hartford on the 20th of April, 1862. He signed up for three months but it was five years till she saw him again. Oh, he had someone write her a couple of letters for him. So she knew that after Bull Run, he'd signed up for three years, like so many of them did, the fools. Then a year or so later, she got a letter written by "a real fine lady" from a prison camp down South. And that was all she heard. He might have died, but she was sure that he hadn't. If he'da died, she would have dreamed a sign, for sure. She was certain sure he'd come back, and so he had, near a year ago now.

Annis looked across the clearing to her house. Standing on

the porch, waiting like she'd told them to, were Todd and Becky. Rebecca's name was Wounded Bird, in the old language. That's all of the old language she knew: family names, and the names of herbs and plants that she needed for her work. In her family, all the womenfolk were called some kind of Bird in the old language. Her Indian name was Little Bird and Becky's was Wounded Bird because a sparrow with a broken wing fell to the floor of the cabin and fluttered around, all the time she was giving birth. And this child, this new daughter? Her name could wait until Annis was given a sign.

Hoarsely she called to her family, "Come look! We have another girlchild!"

Todd came at a lope, only the smallest gimp now in his gait. He favored the wounded leg very little. She had done well to put it into the anthill, where the insects ate away the putrified flesh and left it clean and ready to heal. When she'd first seen him, late last summer, he'd come hobbling into the clearing leaning on a stick. You could smell him coming, his leg all swole up and purple with putrefaction, his face bearded and furrowed with pain. She hadn't even known him for her own husband. She'd crept crabwise to the door of the cabin, grabbing up the hunting rifle, thinking to blast this sunburnt intruder straight to perdition.

He'd yelled at her, "What's the matter with you, woman? Can't you see it's your husband what's been fighting Johnny Reb these past years?" Well, she still wasn't sure, not till he pulled her into a heated kiss and she knew his smell and taste at once, in spite of the gamy leg and the layers of grime and filth on him.

Now he took the newborn babe from her, studying it. "Looks Injun, don't she? Too bad it's another girl, though. I coulda used a boy to help with the trapping and skinning and such. And here we had such a nice name for him. Morgan. My ma's family was all Morgans." The infant stirred in his grasp and turned toward him, her mouth opening, looking for milk. Todd began to laugh. "Hell's bells, girl, I ain't the one you want!" The baby began to squall. He turned to Annis, and said, "She's a feisty little critter, just like her ma. I say, who cares if she's a girl, hey, Becky? Girls are necessary to the human race, now ain't they? She'll do just fine. What the hell, we'll call her Morgan anyways. Morgan Wellburn, now there's a name to reckon with."

"Morgan le Fay," Annis said, reaching for the baby, to nurse her. The tiny mouth rooted about for a moment and then clamped on the nipple and began to suck. Nothing namby-pamby about this one. "I recall Morgan le Fay from an old story my pa used to read about King Arthur and all his knights. She was a witch!" She made three spitting motions, for luck, although her mouth was dry as dust. "And so what? Ain't my family a perfect passel of witches? Who knows what spirits speak with Quare Auntie?" Annis spat again and looked around. The old woman usually wandered in the woods, hiding from other people. But every once in a while, she came into the clearing, shouting at the top of her voice, be it night or day.

"Now you mind my words, Rebecca," Annis said, pulling her other daughter down to sit next to her. "These here are your ancestors I'm telling about. And my old grandmother, she called her grandmother *moigu*, 'cause her granny came from the Mohegans and *moigu* is the Mohegan word for witch. Or medicine man. It means both, the same word, woman or man. You paying attention?" Becky smiled at her and said "Yes, Mam," but Annis doubted that her beautiful daughter would ever be *moigu*. She was biddable and would follow instructions, but she didn't have the second sight nor the healing power.

"Don't start in with that Injun spook talk, Annis. This baby's my child, too, and she's no moygoo."

"Don't be daft, Todd. A witch ain't bad," Annis said. "A witch has power. This here Morgan le Fay I speak of, she was a *white* witch. My Daddy read us that whole story, about Arthur and the sword in the stone and all. Nothing wrong with a white witch, nothin' at all. They called my mother a witch 'cause they were scared of her. But they came to her, anyway, when they were sick or in labor. She was born with the power, same as me, and—"

She broke off, staring past Todd's shoulder. Wouldn't you know it. Here came Quare Auntie, out of the woods. She certainly didn't look any better than the last time Annis had seen her. She was covered in dirt and her shaggy white hair hadn't seen brush nor plait in a long time, maybe not for years. She had an ugly red sore on one leg and even though she was still at the edge of the clearing, you could smell her: a mixture of dead animal, excrement, and rot. Annis wanted to shout, "Get gone, you horrible old woman! Don't you come anywheres near my baby!" But of course, she didn't. Quare Auntie might be took by spirits, but she was Annis's mother's own sister. How old was she? Hard to tell. Sixty, or near that. It was a wonder she'd come this far, living as she did all alone, wandering in the forest. So it must be true: that the spirits she spoke with protected her.

"Who is that?" Annis called out, and Quare Auntie answered, "Small Sparrow." Annis had forgotten that was her name, it had been so long since anyone had used it. Once she must have been a dear small girl with bright button eyes. Annis tried to imagine her grandmother putting a fond hand on Small Sparrow's head and telling her how pretty she was.

Quare Auntie crept from the edge of the clearing, looking all around her, suspicious like, gesticulating and shouting, "Git back! Git! Begone, I says!" She turned all the way around, shouting at invisible creatures.

Todd froze, and Becky burrowed into her mother's shoulder. Keeping her voice nice and even, Annis bid her aunt welcome. "Why have you come to visit us this evening?" she asked.

In a completely normal voice, Quare Auntie said, "Why, a spirit told me in a dream to rise and come to the new baby. I'm to put my hand on her head and name her."

"Now how do you know it's a girl?" Todd demanded. "Come to that, how in tarnation did you know Annis was birthing? You watchin' us, Auntie? You always nearby, spyin' on us? That what you do all day?"

Quare Auntie paid him no mind—that was her way—just marched herself over and put her hand on the infant's head. "I name you Woman of the River," she intoned, using the old language for the name, "and you will follow the river to your destiny."

Suddenly, she noticed a birthmark on the baby's shoulder, and recoiled. "A bird! An eagle! She should have been a boy!"

She bent close to Annis, narrowing her eyes, and shouted, "Whore! Your shameless rutting by the river has poisoned this child! Oh, yes, I saw you, you and your black-haired lover!" Annis's heart begun to pound. Quare Auntie had been watching them? Watching her with Nattie Marcus? Bile rose into her mouth and she swallowed hard. So what if she had? She was just an old woman who saw things nobody else saw and heard voices nobody else heard. And who was able to move about as soundlessly as the spirits who surrounded her. Annis shivered.

The ragged old woman smiled at her, revealing her greenish teeth. Then she backed off, singing, *"Black is the color of my true love's hair . . ."* She was leaving. Good. Enough of this black-haired lover talk. Besides, the stench from Quare Auntie was worse even than the stink of Todd's wound had been when he'd come home. Quare Auntie broke into wild mirthless laughter and, turning, walked to the woods. She stopped to cry out something in Pequot, then changed to English. "Listen to me, little niece: our family ends with this child. This child will change everything! Take care with her!"

Annis had taken heed to the way Quare Auntie pretended she didn't see Becky, like Becky wasn't there. She hadn't come out of her hidey-hole the day Rebecca was born; she hadn't had any dream to come name her. What did it mean? A chill chased down Annis's spine. Of course it meant something; everything that happened meant something. Was Becky fated to die soon? Is that why Quare Auntie couldn't or wouldn't see her? Then, sudden like, Quare Auntie gave Becky a long hard look, and hissed like a snake. A moment later, she melted into the trees.

They all fell silent, even the babe, who stopped suckling and lay quiet in her arms. Annis couldn't bear to look at Todd, although she felt his eyes glued on her. Finally, he said, in a dangerous quiet voice, "Black-haired lover, Annis?"

Still without looking at him, Annis said, "Oh, don't be daft, Todd. It don't pay to listen to Quare Auntie, you know that! You recall when she came by, talking of your dog lying dead near that grove of white birch?" There had been no dead dog in the grove. Of course, a week later, that dog had been killed in a fight with a raccoon. But Todd was not one for believing in signs and portents. He thought it all Injun nonsense.

"Was she always crazy like this?"

"Far as we're concerned, she's not crazy. She talks with the spirits. The women in our family are known for that." Todd spat into the dust. Annoyed, Annis said, "And how about that Moses in the Bible who spoke with God and made water flow from a rock and turned a stick into a snake? You believe *that*!"

"That's different!"

"It ain't a bit different. You think on it, Todd Wellburn. But right now, help me to my feet. I'm wanting my bed."

She handed the baby to Becky and took Todd's hand to help her up. Her body was a bit sore, on the inside, and she wouldn't be getting too close to her husband for some days. And she was dead tired. But she was hungry. This morning, when she felt the child inside her shifting, and her bulging belly began to tighten, she'd put a stew on to cook over a low fire. Later, on her way out of the house to have the baby, she'd had Becky bank the fire, to keep their supper warm.

She leaned on Todd's arm as they made their way across the clearing toward the sturdy stone and log house that sat just in front of a small orchard of crabapple and cherry trees. It was true twilight now, the sky a soft blue filling with fluffy gray clouds. Low in the sky, the first star of the evening was already bright. Maybe nightfall would bring a breeze and rid them of the heat that had built up all day. Her great-great-something-grandfather had built their house, and he'd built it good, with a fireplace you could stand in, two rooms and a loft for sleeping. The two windows had thick wooden shutters for the bad weather—they were flung wide now, of course—and the front porch ran across the width of the house. On that porch, Annis had rocking chairs she'd got in barter for birthing Mrs. Carter, whose husband was a joiner down in East Haddam—one chair for each Carter child, four in all. Her butter churn was there, and her loom. They lived real good up here in the hills. They had pigs in a sty over one end of the clearing, and a shed and a hay rick and a chicken coop where she put the birds in at night to keep them from wolves that prowled. Their horse, Josie, was cropping grass inside her paddock, and they had a cow for milk and butter. Yes, it was a good life. Everyone around knew where to go if you wanted to have a baby, or you didn't want to have a baby, or you were in labor and about to have a baby. They came for Annis's other cures, too, for the dropsy and rheumatism and burns and such. Some women wanted to know did she have something that would stir up a man's sleeping passion. If it was doctoring you needed here-abouts, there was only one person you wanted to tend you and that was Annis Wellburn. For all that, they called her The Squaw behind her back.

As Todd helped her up the porch steps, she noticed him dragging his leg. "Becky, hand me that baby," Annis said. "And then get your Daddy some yarrow leaves to chew on . . . or, wait. No, I don't want that. Make him a tea of boxberry, you hear me? You drink that, Todd, it'll kill the hurt in your leg."

Then, she just had to climb into her nice soft bed, she was that weary. Becky had made everything neat and clean, she saw, and had put a little posy of yellow flowers in a glass by the bed. Becky was a sweet child, though too pretty by far. Her looks were her curse. Annis had seen how men looked at her, and her still just a child! Worse, Rebecca enjoyed the attention, not understanding what it meant. She would dimple and smile and get a little blush on her cheek. Annis had tried to warn her that she ought to take care. But when Becky said, "But why, Mam? Why should I not say thank you if Mr. Cartwright tells me I'm a pretty little thing?" Annis had no ready answer. All she could do was keep the child tight by her side. But with a new baby to see to, how could she keep an eye on Becky all day and all night?

Well, never mind. She'd think about Becky later. Now was the time for the new one, Morgan. Annis had to study her child and wait for a sign of her Indian name. Woman of the Water was meant for her secret, sacred name. She needed a nick-name. Especially since she looked so much like her mother's family, with dark shiny button eyes, high cheekbones, and a full head of straight shiny black hair. Now that the flush was fading from her, Annis could see that her skin was almost the same milky white as Becky's. Not olive like that other's had been, the little boy's. . . . She blinked back tears. She must stop such thoughts. It was done and gone. She had made her choice; she had known what she was doing.

Once again, she pulled her attention to the mite cradled in her arms. "What is your name, little one?" she murmured. She thought about Quare Auntie. The old woman might smell to heaven, but she lived with the spirits and they had told her to lay hands on the baby and give her a name. If the river was her destiny, and if she must be named some sort of bird . . .

"I know your name now, my daughter," Annis said, putting the baby to her breast. "Water Bird. My beautiful Water Bird." She *was* beautiful, but she had an Indian face, and Annis knew that an Indian face could bring much grief. She, too, would be followed by shouts of "Squaw" whenever she went down from these hills into the town. Everyone in the town was English. Most Pequots had long ago fled or had died of the pox, and those left were either "praying Indians," or—like Annis and perhaps half a dozen others—lived isolated in the hills.

Annis dozed, dreaming of Indians dancing around a fire on the beach. Todd came tiptoeing in, but she knew he was there. She opened her eyes, letting wisps of her dream still cling.

Todd said, "Well, never you mind, next time, we'll have our boy." Wasn't that just like a man, thinking she'd eat herself up over the baby not being a man-child. She shook her head, amused. "I'm not having any more babies, Todd, not at my age." He gave that some thought. Then he grunted and said, "Well, then, I guess I'm gonna be teaching her everything I'd teach a son." His eyes slid sideways, to see what she'd say.

"We'll see."

He cleared his throat and fidgeted a bit. "Our little Becky, she made me a tea took the pain right out of my leg," he said. "Maybe she'll grow up to be a healer like her mam."

He meant it for a compliment, but Annis shook her head. "No," she said, "Becky knows how to make medicine, if I tell her exactly what to do, and she knows what each medicine is for. But the healing spirit? No, Todd, it sorrows me, but she ain't got it." She paused and looked down at the dark-haired infant suckling at her breast, so hard, so fierce, so strong.

"Not Becky," she said. "But maybe this one. Maybe Morgan."

2

October 1880

"There she goes," Annis thought, as Morgan went running off to meet her pa. She could hear him coming through the woods, crashing through the underbrush, making enough noise to rouse the dead. He'd gone down into the town this morning to trade. She hoped he'd got the material she wanted, the red check gingham. Both girls needed dresses something fierce, Morgan especially. Annis couldn't keep that young'un in her clothes. No sooner did she put something on Morgan's back than it was too short and too tight. Not that Morgan wanted a new dress. She'd as soon dress like a boy. She always said she wished she *was* a boy.

Annis blamed Todd for that. He favored Morgan, and Morgan doted on her daddy, hung on his every word, wanted to follow him everywhere. Well, he did talk to her—more than he ever did to anyone else in this world. But Morgan wasn't no son, no matter what Todd had said the day she was born. Morgan was a girl—a woman, nearly. It was time for her to learn from her mam, the same like Annis had learnt from hers.

Annis bent once more to the basket of wet wash and picked out a shirt, snapped it till it hung straight, then laid it across a bush to dry. When she straightened, a twinge in her lower back reminded her she was thirty-eight, near thirty-nine. Soon she would be an old woman, wise and respected. That made her laugh. Elders nowadays were not treated with the awe and reverence she had given hers. She felt fortunate if Morgan obeyed her once in ten times. She finished with the wet wash and brought the empty basket to the front porch. As she went inside, she caught her reflection in the piece of looking glass Todd had been given in trade for a rabbit. It was missing one corner but that didn't matter none. She'd never had a looking glass before. For years, she had plaited her hair kneeling by the pond out back. Pausing to admire her image, she thought: still slim as a girl, and back as straight as ever, for all it ached from time to time. Todd thought her beautiful. He never said so but she knew. He still came to her at night eager and stiff as a boy. She studied herself. Was she beautiful? Not to the townfolk, that she knew. But her long hair was shiny and dark, and it hung in its thick braid down her back to her rump. Her skin was dark, yes, too dark. The cotton dress she wore was no different from any of them down in the town, fitted at the waist with long flaring skirt. 'Course she had tucked it up into the band of her apron, to leave her legs free for her work. The women in East Haddam did not do that. So she did look different. Well, and she *was* different, being part Indian and all. It gave her certain powers white women did not have. And yet, they looked down on *her* for a savage. Didn't make no sense.

She fingered the amulet that hung around her neck on braided string. It had been carved from shiny purple clamshell, and her mother had given it to her when she became a woman, saying that it had belonged to their kinswoman, Bird, the *moigu*. Dangling from her belt was a leather medicine bag that had been her mother's, too. She often touched the medicine bag, like it was a charm. But she didn't touch it for luck. It was the sign of who she was. She was Annis Wellburn, the healer.

Her potions and spells were considered magical by folks in the countryside, and they came long miles to have her doctor them. She was known to have a way of bringing a bad fever down and for healing sores that nobody else could make better. They sent for her regular when a birth was starting, wouldn't have any other. Annis smiled to herself. They kept asking her for receipts for her medicines. She could tell them exactly where to go to find the right herbs and plants, but it wouldn't help them none. Because not a one of them had the healing spirit. The healing spirit had come down to her from her mother and her mother's mother and her mother's mother's mother, all the way back to the beginning of time. She could look at a sick person, just look into their eyes and feel of their limbs, and pretty well know what had got ahold of them and what was likely to help.

Her mother and her grandmother, they had taken her out every day and taught her the healing arts, singing her songs to help her remember all the names of the plants and what they cured. And at night, her grandfather told her the stories—of Great Eagle, the *pawwow*, the shaman of the Pequot tribe, and his son Wild Goose, massacred by the evil Uncas and his Mohegans, who deserted their brothers to fight side by side with the Yankees. He told her about the shaman's wife, a great *moigu* called Shining Stone and her daughter Bird; how they came home from gathering herbs and plant leaves for Shining Stone's medicine bag, and found the camp on the beach destroyed, everyone dead.

Annis remembered how her grandfather wailed, saying, "That was the end of the mighty Pequot, daughter of my daughter. They killed the sachem and one thousand of his people, gathered in his fort on the Mystic River. Those who were left were few, and scattered, and frightened." The end of the tale recalled how Shining Stone and Bird had been forced to flee to a secret place, in the hills far up the Connecticut River.

"And this is that same place," her grandfather would say. It didn't matter how many times she heard the same story told in the same words, that last phrase had always put a shiver down Annis's spine.

But Morgan was not interested. Morgan longed after the impossible thing, Annis thought sadly. She'd tried to make the child proud of her Pequot background, but Morgan only wanted to look like her fat, bad-tempered friend, Lizzie Bushnell, the minister's girl. Morgan couldn't see that Lizzie was plain as a mud fence, with doughy skin and pale, almost white hair. Colorless. Like a ghost. Or, Annis thought with amusement, like a bad-tempered rabbit. But Morgan wouldn't hear a word against Lizzie, who sat on the bench next to her at the schoolhouse down in the town. Annis was all for taking Morgan out of that school, but Todd would have none of it.

"She'll learn to read and write, like any respectable girl," he said. "She's not *all* Injun, remember."

She knew that. But she also knew that Morgan had the healing gift, even though Morgan chafed at the learning of it. Morgan had got a mind of her own and was not about to pay heed to her mother. Annis sighed. She knew the girl had the head to learn. She was only missing the will . . . And Annis needed to teach the girl all the medicine she knew. Because now she knew that Becky never would learn. Never.

At the sounds of breaking twigs from the edge of the clearing, Annis turned, a welcome on her lips for Todd and Morgan. But the words died, when a scrawny female figure emerged, blinking, into the sunlight. She had a smudged face and filthy matted hair, and a tattered something was tied around her waist with grapevine. Her breasts were bare, covered with dirt, and beautiful. She stank.

"Good day to you, Becky," Annis said loudly in a calm, uninflected voice. The waif did not answer, but looked about fearfully, muttering to herself. "There's no danger here, Rebecca, you're home. Nobody here will hurt you."

She did not respond, and when, a moment later, Todd and Morgan came out of the shadow of the woods, dragging a load of goods on a litter made of tree branches lashed together, Becky scurried back to the shelter of the trees. This time, though, she stayed within Annis's sight. She was probably hungry; that was the only reason she ever came home, lately. As Becky stared at Morgan, Annis felt herself tense up to protect her younger daughter. There was no telling what Becky might take it into her head to do.

A couple of weeks ago, Becky had come by, saying, "Hungry. Food," in the way she had. No please, no thank you ma'am, no hello how be you—just the demand. When Morgan brought out bread and meat for her, Becky had snatched it from the child and started in ranting. She had gone on about how evil spirits lived in Morgan; she could see them plain as day coming out of Morgan's nose and ears and mouth and out from between her legs. Todd, who was nearby, had come striding out, fierce and angry, and slapped her across her face. Becky hadn't cried:

There seemed no tears in her since the spirits came and got her. She'd spat at him and ran off into the woods.

Today was the first they'd seen of her since then. Try as he might, Todd couldn't find her hidey-hole—he who could smell the track of an animal before ever he saw it.

"Becky, hello," Morgan said, very gently.

"You keep your distance! You hear me? I see what you're thinkin'! You think I don't know? You just stay away!" Becky was yelling at the top of her lungs.

Morgan ran up to Annis. "What's wrong with Becky, Mam? Why does she say such things? Why does she hate me?"

"She doesn't hate you, Morgan," Annis said. "She's been taken by spirits, just like Quare Auntie. It's like she can't hear us any more, only her spirits. If this was the old days, she might be thought holy. To talk with the spirits, Morgan, that's powerful medicine. But times has changed. Folks are mostly scared of spirits. Nobody gives sacrifice to them any more. Nobody goes out into the wild to dream about them. So maybe all the good ones have gone away and what's left has got your sister. But to tell the truth, I dunno. I just don't know."

The child was leaning into her body, for protection. For a minute or two, Morgan was silent. Then, she said, "Will I be like Becky when I'm older?"

"I don't know that, neither," Annis said. "Would you want to?"

"No! At school, they all make fun out of my sister! They say she's crazy! They imitate what she does! I hate it!" Morgan burst into tears. "So I have to know. Are the spirits coming after me?"

Annis shook her head and said, sadly, "I don't know, Morgan. Becky was close to your age now, when you were born, and she was so good with you that we called her Little Mother. I never dreamed this would happen. Those children at school, they may call her names all they want, but we know it's the spirits, Morgan, don't we?"

Making a choked sound, Morgan tore away from her and ran into the house. Annis heard her climbing the ladder into her loft as fast as she could go. As if she could outrun the spirits!

Well, best tend to what needed tending. Annis called out, "You want food, Becky?"

"Yes. Bring me food."

"No. You come get it."

"Can't." She cowered, in the shadows, looking real fearful at her pa, who was standing with his load of supplies from town still in the dirt behind him. He knew not to make any sudden moves or she'd skedaddle. "The demon will git me!" Becky said, her voice quavering.

"There ain't no demons here."

Becky pointed at her father. "The demon lives there, between his legs. I seen that demon, the snake demon! Ow! It bites! It hurts!" She put her hands between her legs and pantomimed pain. "Boy brought his demon to my cave," she said, still staring at Todd, "and he let it out to bite me. But I bit the demon, I did! And then I pushed boy over and ran and ran and ran." She stopped speaking and, for a wonder, she smiled. "I got me a diff'rent cave, I did. Nobody can find me."

"Becky, lookie here, I'm turning myself around so no demon can get to you," Todd said in a honey voice. As he turned, he said to Annis, "Damn them, why do they try to force her to lie with them, when they can see she's got no way to think straight? It riles me terrible to think how they can even *want* to!"

"Down in the town, they talk about her, Todd. I've told you that. The Wild Girl they call her. You remember how when she was but twelve, how every man stopped whatever he was doing to stare at her. And don't think the girl didn't know it. She'd toss her hair and let her hips sway from side to side. I had to smack her to teach her to behave. But she did love that staring and smiling. Trouble was, if she so much as looked their way, they were lusting after her."

"Well then, they should be shamed!"

"Indeed they should," she said dryly. She'd never told Todd what happened the year Becky was thirteen; that would be seven years gone now. She was feared that Todd would take his rifle and go down into the town and kill four people and get himself put into jail and maybe hanged. For sure, hanged. Then what would she do without her man?

So she kept her mouth shut. But she never forgot it, not a

minute of it. They had gone into town to get kerosene and
molasses and flour and material for dresses, she and Becky.
Even then, Morgan was happiest with her daddy. Annis went
into the general store and, it being a fine day, she let Becky
stay outside on the porch, sitting on a rocker. 'Course, it gave
her some worry, knowing how the girl batted her eyes at every
man. But, Annis had told herself, it was broad daylight and the
main street. So she went into the store, thinking to be but a
minute or two.

The shopkeeper's wife was eight months along with her
fifth baby, so it took a bit longer than usual, while they arranged for Annis to come down to midwife the birth. Mrs.
Griswold told everyone she wouldn't think of having a baby
without Annis Wellburn. Her first one had a been a difficult
birth and she might have died if Annis hadn't been called.
Annis had felt of her belly and knew the trouble. The baby
was turned rear end first and couldn't push out. Annis stood
the woman up, held by her sister and mother, and swayed her
from side to side while she gently urged that baby with her
hands to turn around. Well, he did, and before you could say
spit, there was a fine big boy for Mr. and Mrs. Griswold, yelling for his dinner. Mary Griswold said Annis Wellburn was a
genius. But it was just the Pequot way, the way of all the Algonquin people.

Anyways, it was fifteen, twenty minutes before Annis came
back out onto the porch, and Becky was gone. A strange queasy
feeling came over Annis. Something had gone awry, she knew
it; she could *smell* it. Sure enough, when she rounded the back
of the general store, she could hear a commotion in the stable,
along with a lot of shushing and hushing.

She ran to the stable, pushed open the big door, and climbed
the ladder to the loft, where the noise was. But she was quiet
as quiet—on Injun feet, Todd would say. And there was her
beautiful daughter, an innocent only thirteen years old, pushed
down on a hillock of hay, her skirts flung up over her head, writhing and crying out, as a man braced on his two arms pushed
his instrument rapidly in and out of her. Annis had noticed all
the young boys sniffing around Becky, but neither her attacker,
nor the three others in the hayloft, all red-faced and erect with

excitement as they waited their turn, were boys. They were grown men.

Annis gave out a war whoop, and threw herself on the man's back, the one raping Becky. He yelled and rolled off Becky, turning with angry face to fight her. And they stared at each other in disbelief. He was none other than Josh Griswold, the man whose wife was carrying their fifth child. He was supposedly haggling with the itinerant horse trader, Amos Webb. One of the men waiting for his turn was that same Amos Webb, and there was George Spencer and William Chesley, too. Supposedly good, church-going citizens of the town.

The men all stood dumb as statues. Annis ignored them. She marched over to where her daughter lay with her clothes over her head, hauled her up by her arms, wiped the tears from her face, and pulled down her skirts. Then, she gave those men a tongue lashing they weren't likely to forget any day soon. She took the weeping Becky home with her and put her in a tub of hot water and scrubbed her good. But it didn't do no good. Since that day, Becky was feared of men. Now she was scared of everyone—her pa, her sister, creatures only she could see. For some years now, she'd taken to muttering to herself or suddenly hollering at her spirits, having long angry conversations with them.

Since Becky had took herself away to wander in the forest, there was always some man or another thought if he could find her he'd lie with her and who'd know? Who'd believe a girl not in her right mind? It'd be so easy, those men reckoned. But them as thought so had another think coming. Becky was fierce and fast and she always got away. Leastways, Annis hoped she did.

"You come onto the porch, Becky, and you eat," Annis called. To her surprise, Becky came right over. You just never knew what she might do. The girl attacked the meat and bread like a wild animal, wolfing it down, stuffing it into her mouth with both hands, and when Annis offered her water, she drank as if she hadn't had drink in a month. She even let Annis put her into the big copper tub and scrub her down and wash her hair. She sang the whole time. Not a tune a body would know, just a jumble of words without meaning, but she seemed at peace, for a change. That was a blessing.

After she'd filled her belly and was clean, Becky curled up in a corner and fell asleep in two heartbeats. Annis knelt down beside her, smoothing the girl's long coppery hair, gazing down at her. In sleep, the tight terrified look disappeared. Becky looked like a regular beautiful young woman, even if there were still some tangles in her hair and she was all scratched and bruised from living out in the wild. Sometimes the spirits went away for a spell, leaving the old Becky, sweet and biddable and eager to learn. Then, without warning, back they'd come, filling her head. And she'd turn on you; maybe grab a knife and tell you she'd kill you if you came closer. Or she'd head out into the woods, babbling six to the dozen in a strange language.

"Do you love Becky the best, Mam?"

Annis whirled around, startled. "What are you talking, girl? Of course I don't love Becky the best! And next time, don't come creeping up on me on cat feet, you hear?"

Morgan's lower lip began to wobble and her eyes filled. "Mam, I didn't creep up on you, I didn't. I made noise, only you didn't hear me."

"No need to cry, now. I didn't mean nothing by it. No, it's just that I worry over Becky, that's all, 'cause she lives on her own in the woods."

"But she has her spirits, Mam."

"Yes. She has her spirits." Annis knew spirits were real, that they lived in everything: the water, the trees, the earth, and the plants that grew out of that earth and the animals that fed off that earth. Some were good and some were bad. But Becky's spirits . . . they seemed altogether different, somehow.

Just then, Becky waked, and the minute she saw her sister, she began shrieking and screaming and calling her evil and vile. Annis had her hands full, just to calm her down. Todd came in just then and saw what was happening. He said, real quick, "Annis, I'm takin' Morgan out with me, to check the traps and maybe do some hunting. We'll be gone a day or two."

"Yes, yes," she agreed, before Morgan could say a word,

"you two go find me a turkey and I'll make us a feast." She couldn't look at her younger daughter, she felt so bad pushing her off that way. Still, it couldn't be helped. Poor Becky needed her mam, but Morgan was sturdy and strong. She'd always find her way.

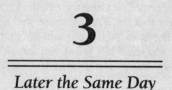

3

Later the Same Day

Morgan felt bad that Mam loved Becky more than her, but being out in the woods with her pa sure helped make it better. She felt . . . grownup, being alone with him. When they were all home together, he was always moving around, busy doing something. If she asked, "What are you doing, Daddy?" he'd always say, "Working, Morgan, and you ought be doing the same." But as soon as he was out in the woods, he was different. He'd explain everything real careful and treat her like she was already fully growed. Well, she was twelve: That was pretty big. She could read and write and do her sums, and she was good at it. The biggest change in Pa when he was in the woods was he'd talk. Being out in the open seemed to free him up and loosen his tongue.

Tramping through the woods, he'd be talking to her, making conversation. He almost never made conversation, so it was a treat. Today, as they checked the traps and went after guinea hens and rabbits, he started talking about his time in the Great War. Morgan loved her daddy's war stories. She thought they were much more interesting and full of danger than fairy tales in a book. And they seemed more real than her mother's tales of long-gone ancestors and spirits and such. She knew

Pa's stories by heart, but that didn't take any of the pleasure out of it.

"Yessir, we was sure it'd be over in one shake of a lamb's tail, the day we marched out of Hartford. Oh the crowds, Morgan, all a-yelling and cheering us on and waving the flags, the flag of Connecticut and the good old stars and stripes, both. Our drummer boys drummed right smart and the bands were all toot-tootling so fine, it fair lifted our feet off the road. They cheered us mightily, Morgan, all the townsfolk. They filled the streets until there weren't no more room and the rest climbed up on the rooftops to cheer us. We kept a-marching all the way to New Haven, led by our brave Captain Daniel Tyler, and there our ship lay at anchor, just waiting for the First Connecticut Volunteers to climb aboard and sail to glory!

"The sun shone bright the day we left New Haven, and the flags was snappin' in the wind, and when we sailed into Washington, D.C., President Lincoln and all his cabinet were on the banks of the Potomac River to greet us. Imagine, Morgan, the President his own self! They had everything we needed, right there—tents, rounds of ammunition, baggage train, food . . . enough for twenty days. Well, it might take one-and-twenty days to show the rebels who was boss, we figured, but surely no longer than that! It was good to be young and strong and be marching to war, Morgan!"

He paused a moment, and Morgan rushed in. "And that's why you signed back on for three more years when you were only supposed to be gone three months. 'Cause you thought it would be over pretty damn soon."

Pa laughed. "Now, Morgan, it's one thing for a man to say 'damn' but it's another kettle of fish for a little girl. But no, we all signed back on because President Lincoln, he asked us to. He needed five hundred thousand loyal Union men to keep up the good fight. By then, we was called the First Connecticut and we was first to say we'd stay." Again he paused, his eyes far away. But after a moment, he continued, just like she'd hoped he would.

"They beat us at Bull Run and they took Virginia for the Confederacy. Oh, that was a fearful day. When we heard the bugle blow retreat, we shook our fists and cursed, but a good soldier follows orders. It was a-raining cats and dogs, not a man but was soaked to the skin—and even under the skin, some said. I know I ain't never been so wet, not before nor since. And then we ran out of food. We had nothin' to eat for three days. We thought we was goners. Well, we lived—leastways, most of us did—but then we knew we'd been just a-dreamin', to think we'd win so quick. Johnny Reb was no faker. He was some fighter, and we were in for a long long war." He spat, to show how he felt about the war.

They were following a well-worn path in the woods, with Morgan putting her feet in his footprints, careful-like. Her daddy caught many a fox with his clever traps. You could trade fox furs for a lot of flour and salt and material for clothes. All of a sudden, he stopped dead, and, of course, so did Morgan. He stood like a statue and she did the same, just as she'd been taught. Pa thought he heard an animal nearby, a deer, maybe, or a wild turkey. Just thinking about it made Morgan's mouth water. The sun was low in the sky and she was getting hungry. She eyed the guinea hens hanging on his belt, but she didn't want to say she needed to eat and sound like a baby. Maybe he could read her thoughts, like Mam could, because, shaking his head at the elusive animal, he said, "About time to make camp for the night. My stomach's a-growlin'. Your ma packed us some johnnycake and jerky, and maybe a clever little girl I know will find us some mushrooms we can cook up with the fowl, for our dinner."

He turned and struck out along a crooked little trail Morgan never would have seen if he hadn't taught her how. "I know a nice spot," he said. "We camped there last year one time, Morgan. I hear water, there's a little stream yonder. And see that big old white pine? Remember that? You said it looked like a shaggy dog and so it does." He was dragging his right leg a little—the one that had been wounded—which happened when he got tired. She was happy to stop. The sun was red-orange in the western sky and she didn't like to be out in the dark, not even with her daddy. Her ma had told her about how the spirits liked to come out at night, and she didn't want to be bumping into any spirits, not after seeing what they did to her sister.

After they had settled down, and the mushrooms and wild onions and chunks of guinea fowl were stewing over the fire, her pa sat with his back to a tree, massaging his leg. Morgan kept her eye on the stew. "Tell more, Daddy. About the war."

"Where was I? Oh, yes. Bull Run. Lesee . . . Now, General Lee of the rebels was certain sure he was winning the war and he got bold, Morgan. He wanted Washington, D.C., and, after that, he figured he'd just march north and take us over. He did beat us at Antietam, Morgan, I'm sorry to say. That's in Maryland, right close to Washington. They sent us hither and they sent us thither, chasing Johnny Reb. After a time, we scarcely knew what state we might be in. We marched, and we bivouacked, and we waited for the bugles and the drums to tell us what to do. Charge. Stand fast. Take cover. Retreat. One day, in a woods just like this here one that we're walkin' in today, only this was, I dunno, somewhere in Maryland or maybe Virginia . . . Anyways, I was slopin' along, rifle at the ready, looking to see could I spot the enemy. And bang! There the enemy was, smack in front of me. Damned if he didn't shoot me. Twice! And he got me, too, in the shoulder and the leg!" He spat and stopped talking.

"And they took you to a hospital, to get better," Morgan prodded.

"They never did do anything right, those surgeons," he complained. " 'Twas your mama made this leg whole. Those Army doctors wanted to saw it off! Your mother's one fine doctor, Morgan, for all she never went to a medical college. In the field, the doctors were nothing more than butchers. I coulda done a better job, from my years butchering hogs and deer. The ground around the surgeries was piled high with arms and legs, some of them with their boots still on! I recall, they was always calling for water . . . never enough water, never enough bandages, never enough nothin'! More men died in the medical tents than on the battlefield, Morgan. You know what saved us?"

"The ladies, Pa. The ladies saved you." This was the part of the story she liked the best.

"That's true. Ordinary ladies, like you'd see walking in East Haddam, Connecticut. They came to the front and nursed us sick soldiers, washing the most horrible wounds, begging from neighbor towns and farms for bread and tea and hardtack and dried fruit, so we could eat and get better."

"Tell about the nurses, Daddy, and the lady doctors."

"There was Mother Bickerdyke, she was a nurse, and you know, they said she never needed no sleep at all. She would sing all night, they said, to help the soldiers forget their pain. And all the other women, too, who changed our bandages, and rubbed our aching heads, and wrote letters for us who never did get no schooling. Your mam got two of them letters. And some of them women," he said, leaning forward, his face lit gold with the firelight, "women like Clara Barton and Louise Gilson and Mrs. John Harris, pitched tents and lived near the field hospitals. They worked day and night as nurses, never mind the shelling and the cannon. Never mind they never were paid a cent. I did hear me some rumors there were women doctors, out in the field, but I never did see one. 'Course, it was hard to tell. So many doctors were beardless boys. Hell, I guess they coulda been girls. Wouldn't that be something, Morgan? I wonder, would a woman doctor be better than a man? I doubt not. Yessir, Morgan, it was the women saved our lives. Even at Gettysburg . . ."

Morgan knew about the journey to Gettysburg. Daddy escaped from that Southern hospital and went marching away, looking to rejoin the First Connecticut. He never found his unit, but he did join up with a dozen men lost from the Twenty-ninth Connecticut. "Darkies, Morgan, every last man, but, hell, they didn't mind me so I didn't mind them. And good fighters, too, never mind what you hear some folks say. And together, we all found our way to Gettysburg."

Gettysburg, Morgan knew as well as if she'd been there herself, was no more than a sea of mud and blood, where the dead soldiers lay so thick on the ground, you could walk dry on their backs. Pa had been shot there, too, real bad that time. He went stone-blind for many days. He was out of his head for a time and didn't even know where he was.

". . . and when I come to, not knowin' what day it is or what month or hardly what year, there's a doctor standing over me saying he's going to saw off my leg below the knee. He doesn't know I'm awake, see, he thinks I'm still in a fever. So, Morgan, when I said, in the loudest voice I could gather, 'Oh, no you don't take off no leg of mine!' well, good God Almighty, that doctor near jumped out of his skin. He was that took by surprise.

"He says to me, 'If I say your leg comes off, off it comes, and no argument.' And I says to him, 'I'll kill you first, Doctor, and I'm not a man to make a promise and not be keepin' it.' 'We'll see,' he says, and out he goes.

"But he didn't come back, Morgan. And I decided it was time for me to get out of there, before they started hacking me into little pieces. So it was back home to my wife and child for me. They told me Lee had been pushed out of the north and was in retreat, and that the war was still a-going on, with the Union winning. But I didn't have the heart for it no more."

"And so you came home. And you and Mam had me."

"Did we, now?" He was joking with her. "Well, lemme look on you. Yes, I do see my eyes in you, though the rest of you is pure Injun. Yep, we had you and here you are."

"Did you really hop all the way back home, Daddy?"

"I surely did. My leg was going rotten. Here, lemme show you . . ." To Morgan's delight, he got up and, taking a big stick to use for a pretend crutch, he began to sing one of his Army songs and to hop all over the place. He made a complete circle of the clearing and then his foot got tangled up in a tree root. He twisted around to keep himself from falling but he fell anyway. It looked so comical. Morgan laughed and clapped until, suddenly, she realized that the look on Pa's face was not jokey. He was in pain.

"Daddy, Daddy!" she cried and went running to him. "Are you all right? Can you get up?"

"Oh, sweet Jesus, I've gone and done something queer with my leg, Morgan. I heard her ripping. You know anything about a ripping sound?"

"Here, lean on me and I'll help you." He was mighty heavy, but from his grimacing and groaning, she could tell his leg hurt real bad. He couldn't put weight on it, so he had to hop on the other foot. Together, they got him settled next to the fire, and she piled up grass and dirt under his leg to hold it up in the air. That's how Mam had taught her. "It's a muscle in your leg, Daddy. You done pulled it the wrong way. But don't you worry, I know how to take care of that pain. I'll get some gum from that big old pine. Soon's you chew it, you'll feel better. We can rip up my petticoat to make a nice tight bandage. Don't you worry about a thing. We'll get you fixed up right smart."

When Todd opened his eyes, dawn was turning the sky a pale misty yellow. For a minute, he couldn't figure where he was. Then he remembered. He'd gone and twisted his leg last evening. Behavin' like a damn fool, Todd thought, prancing around showing off in front of his daughter. Served him right. Still, the leg had hurt something fierce. He tried to move it a little. Testing, like. And damned if it didn't feel a lot better. Stiff as hell, and still hurting some, but he could move it up and down without wanting to scream with the pain. That Morgan! That little girl could do some good doctoring! She gave him pine gum to chew last night, and rubbed the leg in back of the knee with some kind of gooey stuff from under the bark that she cooked up. It hadn't seemed to be helping much and he was going to tell her so, but the next thing he knew, here it was, morning. He remembered waking a couple of times in the night, trying to move the leg. But he fell right back to sleep.

"Morgan! Hey, daughter! You took good care of your Pa . . ." He looked around, but realized she wasn't there. "Morgan? Morgan!" he bellowed, trying to push himself to his feet. Damn leg wouldn't hold his weight. Well, then, he'd crawl on his hands and knees if he had to. By God, if anything had happened to that little girl—! Then he heard her call to him that she was just a-gathering herbs and would be right there. Now he recalled. She'd said when it was daylight, she'd go pick some wintergreen and crush it and make a tea that was good for killing pain. He surely hoped so because his trying to get up had set the leg to throbbing. He needed to be able to walk home.

Easing himself up, where he could put his back against a

tree, he thought about Morgan taking care of him yesterday. She never cried nor made a fuss nor acted like she was scared that her daddy was hurt. Just got all brisk and doctorly, like Annis when she was doing her healing. Damned if he didn't follow all her orders, too, like she was the mother and him the child. Morgan had good hands, searching but gentle. When she was doctoring him, she seemed different—older and sure of herself. It made him proud, damned if it didn't!

Here she came, quiet as an Indian through the trees. Well, she *was* Indian. Part Injun. Annis was half; her pa had been an Englishman with the same curling red hair as Becky, so she said. What did that make Becky and Morgan? Half of a half, that'd be a quarter. Each of them, one-quarter Pequot Indian. And you couldn't find two sisters looking more different. Becky, you'd never know there was any Injun in her at all, but Morgan, except for her light eyes, she looked like she just walked out of her wigwam. She was mighty handsome, like Annis, with that same look that seemed to see right through you . . .

The first time he had gone calling on Annis, he had walked twenty miles through the hills. He'd heard about her, and wondered just what this squaw looked like, and how she did her magic. He wasn't much for talking, he had no sweet words to give her, and anyways, she scared him half to death, being so tall and fierce. He was a tall man, well over six feet, all the Wellburns were, but her head came to his chin. So he said howdy-do and left. He couldn't get her out of his mind, though. He found her . . . not beautiful maybe, but exciting. He sneaked back to her clearing, so she wouldn't know he was there. She was loosening her long shining hair out of the thick braid. Her feet and breasts were bare, and she was heading toward the creek to wash herself. He gazed on her long legs, her tight buttocks, and her breasts, which were so large they drooped from their own weight. He felt himself to go weak in the knees and strong in the groin. He watched her splash in the water, watched her soap up that smooth tan skin, watched as she wrung her long wet hair like a piece of wash, her head bent and her body a-calling to him.

When she came walking out of the water, her naked body clean and tall and proud, he was standing before her, buck-naked and ready for her. His heart was a-pounding because he was afraid she'd scream and push him off, but he wanted her more than he'd ever wanted anything. She didn't holler. She came to him and said, "I knew you'd be back."

"Hell, *I* didn't know I'd be back."

She smiled. "I put a spell on you. You are my man now, and I am your woman. You'll never leave me." He laughed, thinking there wasn't a woman alive could tell Todd Wellburn what he would and wouldn't do. But she was right. He never left her place. He didn't want to. Not till the war. Patriotism took many a man away from his life, some of them for good and all. He'd been lucky.

"How you feeling this morning, Daddy?"

"Real fine, Morgan. You done good. It ain't all fixed, not yet, but it's better."

She had the wintergreen for tea, and she told him she'd found some turtle eggs they could fry up for breakfast. "Daddy, tell me another story. You never tell stories at home," she said while she fixed their meal.

"A story about what?"

"My mother."

Todd felt himself flush. Good thing she couldn't read his thoughts. Or, wait a minute! Annis said *she* could see into peoples' hearts and minds. Quickly, he began to talk.

"You know your mam's father, the trader, the Englishman, he went up the Connecticut River by canoe. Said he'd make the trip all the way to Vermont or bust. Well, he must've busted because he never came back home. There she was, your mother's mother, Margaret she was called, with two babies and nobody to take care of them. So she came back to her kin and they took her in. She was a great healer, your grandma, or so I've heard, but she couldn't heal her own broken heart. She died of it, and that left your mam to take care of her little brother. Tristram. I dunno if she ever told you about Tris. He got the shaking fits, he'd fall down and foam at the mouth, just like a mad dog. He'd always been that way, so she tells me. He wasn't no good for hunting or trapping, and she says it made him angry. He called himself a woman, useful to nobody and no thing. Well, one spring day, she come back from tilling their garden and found Tristram laying in the clearing all bloody. He'd shot himself in the head with their rifle."

"Was he dead?"

"Was he dead? What's wrong with you, child? Of course he was dead. Made your mother right sad. She'd tried everything she knew to keep them fits away, even belladonna. She felt like she was no damn good at healing. But we know better, don't we?"

"She healed your rotten leg when you came back from the war."

"That's right. She looked at it and felt it and smelled it and then, hist! Into the anthill with it. It hurt something fierce but when them ants was done, my leg was clean and ready to heal. And here I am, years later, still a-walking on it! Yessir, your mam is one good healing woman."

Morgan handed him his wintergreen tea, and he sipped it. In a very small voice, she said, "They call her the Squaw."

"Well, they are plumb ignorant, Morgan. Squaw! That shows you how much they know! They don't know nothing! That's why she hates going down into the town, hates being stared at. Your mama knows what they call her but you know something? She knows they need her. She says, who do they ask for, when someone has the ague . . . or has a bad burn . . . or is in long labor . . . or has a strange sickness that won't go away? They call her the Squaw, but only the Squaw has the healing spirit. And so do you, Morgan. You got that healing spirit that's in your mother's family's blood. Listen to me. You learn everything you can from your mam, you hear me? You'll be a famous healer, Morgan. They'll come from miles around to have you doctor them, just like they do with Annis."

"And will they call me Squaw, too?"

Todd pulled in breath and eyed his young'un. Her eyes were the eyes of a woman grown, not a child. "Probably, yes, they will," he said sadly.

She thought that over a minute. Then she said, "Well, then I won't pay them no mind."

* * *

It took three days before Todd could walk without his leg buckling under him. But Morgan's medicine helped. He was able to sleep. She went out to the traps and he cleaned what he'd caught, so no time was lost, really. Except school for Morgan. She pined after school. She already knew how to read and do her numbers. Far as Annis was concerned, Morgan could stop her schooling right now. But the child did love it. As for him, he was restless to get home. He wanted his wife. He was hungry for the touch of her and her woman's chatter and her good cooking. And wait till he told her that Morgan was a natural-born healer!

But he never did get the chance to tell her. The minute he and Morgan walked into the yard, it was clear something odd was going on. A dozen people were sitting or crouching in the dirt yard, one of them blind, and another in a litter. Three of the women were pregnant. What were all these people doing in front of his house?

Annis came a-running to greet them, excited as anything.

"Todd! Morgan! Oh, it's wondrous! It's like a dream come true!" she said. Todd had never seen her so fluttery and nervy.

"What's a dream come true, Annis? Calm yourself and talk slow, so's I can hear what you're trying to say."

"Becky! It's Becky! Our Becky has been touched by a healing spirit, and she talks to angels!"

Angels! He and Morgan exchanged a quick startled look. Becky—talking to angels? "Our daughter, Rebecca Wellburn, what thinks the whole world is evil and out to kill her?"

"Hush, Todd! Hush, now. All that's over! It's a miracle!"

"Annis, you ain't no Christian!"

She flushed, but her chin came up, stubborn as a mule. "No, but the pastor says it's a miracle and he *is* a Christian."

She pulled him into the yard, talking six to the dozen. A couple of days ago, it seems, one of Annis's patients came up the path on a mule. The woman was spotting and staining, and wanting so much to hold onto her baby, because she'd already missed three times. "When I examined her, I could see there was no stopping it. But, Todd, no sooner did I open my mouth to say it, when Becky came out'n the house. I vow there was a glow around her, and she told the woman an angel said she would be healed. Becky gave her water to drink and touched her. And she stopped bleeding!

"And now look! All these folks is waiting for Becky to ask her angels can they be helped. And they're bringing chickens and flour, even some sugar and molasses. We're gonna be rich!" Annis crowed, while Todd could only stare with his mouth wide open. "Our Becky's famous!"

4

Late February 1882

Annis kept her face blank—she was good at that, being half Indian—but all her senses were alert and watching, waiting for Becky to start acting up. All the signs were there. Becky's eyes were shifting around, and every once in a while she turned her head sideways. Annis knew what that was about. Becky's lips were moving as she silently spoke with her spirits. She thought if she turned her head away, nobody could see. Once she started moving her lips, it wouldn't be long before she was talking out loud. And pretty soon, she'd be yelling and cursing and carrying on something fierce. Annis was determined not to let that happen again today. A half dozen people were waiting outside on the porch. The February thaw had brought them out, and she didn't want to lose them.

The last time Becky got restless this way, she ended up screaming at the people gathered in the clearing, yelling that she knew what they were after, that she could see their evil thoughts floating in the air. Suddenly she was waving Todd's hunting knife around, and everyone skedaddled. For a while, nobody came up the hill to be cured or to find a husband or lift a curse, and when Annis went down into East Haddam, folks avoided her eyes. Some of them crossed the street so as not to be anywhere near her. Lucky the women still wanted her for birthing babies, or the family would've gone hungry during the winter of '81. She'd never forget last winter, never. It had been a nightmare.

Then, one day in the spring, Becky was wandering in the woods and came upon a little girl curled up asleep in a pile of oak leaves. She picked the child up and brought her to Annis, saying, "Here's my baby, Mama. I told you I was having a baby." 'Twas all nonsense, of course, the child looked to be three years old. In any case, she was the spittin' image of Amelia Hapgood, the greengrocer's wife, right down to the stickout ears and limp brown hair.

Annis sent Morgan down into the town to tell Mrs. Hapgood that Becky had found a child looked enough like her to be her younger self. Well, it turned out that the little girl, Elizabeth her name was, had got lost from her mama when they were out in the woods gathering berries three days before, and could nobody find her. They thought she'd been eaten by a wolf, and her mother was sick from weeping over her lost baby.

Ezra Hapwood come riding up on his roan mare, as out of breath as if he'd done the climbing instead of the horse. Never even bid Annis a good day. "I hear tell your girl Becky found—" he says. That minute the young'un come running out of the house, yelling "Papa! Papa!" And then he was all smiles. He blessed Becky over and over as he scooped his child up onto the saddle in front of him. Then he says, "I'm sorry we ever doubted, Miz Wellburn, that I am. For here's a miracle and she's sitting right here with me. I thought we'd never see this dear child again, not in this life." His voice cracked and tears slipped out of his eyes. It was sweet. But it was sweeter still when, the very next day, folks began coming back, up through the hills to the Wellburn place, to ask favors of the girl who spoke with the angels.

Amos Whitbeck from Killingworth came into the house now, handing Becky a shawl that had belonged to his daughter, disappeared these last six months. Annis watched him as he tearfully begged Becky to find his Margaret. Annis wanted to laugh. She knew where Peggy Whitbeck got lost to—and who with. She'd done run away from a penny-pinching father who smacked her if she wanted to so much as go to a church dance! Annis, who kept her ears open all the time, had heard the blacksmith's wife talking with another woman at the general store, saying how Peggy run off one rainy night with one of the Cole boys from Madison. The woman knew because her hired girl was friends with Peggy and was in on the secret. Annis wondered just how many knew that secret by this time. Amos wasn't one of them, that was for sure.

Right now, Amos was losing patience with Becky, whose eyes were roving everywhere. Annis knew that Becky's mind was a-wandering, which meant Annis would have to feed her the right words to say. She thought about it for a moment, and decided Becky ought to tell him how the picture she sees is all blurry, like through water; that maybe Peggy had gone to the water. That should keep him from finding the poor girl. What Annis had heard was that the lovers were headed up Massachusetts way on horseback, not on the river at all.

Becky was fingering Margaret Whitbeck's shawl, whispering, "Pretty, pretty, oh so pretty." Then she looked up and said, "Hark! Did you hear that?"

Before Amos could say boo, Annis put in, "I heard it. I heard the word 'water.' " Sometimes Becky would just pick up on what her mother said and go on with it. Sometimes she wouldn't. You had to watch her careful, every minute. You never knew, with Becky.

"Water," Becky repeated. "Yes, water." Annis let her breath out. "What's that? She's in the river? Oh poor thing, poor thing, in the river, in the water—"

Amos was beside himself. "You mean . . . she's drowned?"

Annis spoke right up. "Of course not, Amos. She means Peggy took a ship. Or a canoe . . ."

"A canoe . . . ," Becky repeated dreamily.

"Well, I'm a-going to find her. We have a rowboat—not a canoe, but close enough, I say. The Connecticut River, hey?"

"The Connecticut River," echoed Becky.

Annis relaxed. This one was going to go fine. With a serene smile, she accepted the bags of cornmeal and flour Amos had brought for payment. "If I find her, there'll be more, too," he promised, and off he went, telling the others waiting outside on the porch how Becky had done her good works yet again.

The fact was, everyone wanted to believe in Becky and her angel voices. She'd become famous all along the river. Folks came from as far as Wethersfield and Saybrook, even one fellow from way up in New Hampshire. Annis heard what they told each other while they waited to see Becky. It wasn't only cures they came for; they could also ask her questions about the future and she'd answer them. If they gave her a piece of clothing from someone, she'd tell all about that person. That had been Annis's idea, and she was right proud of it. She knew Becky didn't talk to anyone but her spirits—and mostly they were mean spirits, intending no good to nobody. But if folks wanted to believe in angels, and if it made them feel better, who was Annis to tell them it weren't so? She never saw a person leave this place without a pleased smile, never. Maybe Becky wasn't what folks thought, but she never did no harm. And if it made the Wellburns better off, why, who was to say no to that?

Becky had turned almost all the way around on her chair, so she faced the fireplace. Oh dear, Annis thought. It wouldn't be long before Becky began to yell at her spirits, and maybe run around the clearing, threatening folks like she sometimes did. "Just one more!" Annis called out. A disappointed murmur arose outside, but the others cleared the way for young John Hampton and his wife, Sally. Last week, they had come up to see Becky, wanting to know why their little babe, just two months old, had suddenly died in his cradle. They brought his little wrapper with them, so Becky could hold it and the angels could see it. That time, Annis didn't have to give the words to Becky.

"You find the woman has a dress made of this same material," Becky said, her eyes narrowed down to slits, "and that will be the witch that smothered your baby with a spell."

Then Becky just stopped. No matter how many times John and Sally begged her to tell them what to do to find that witch, not a word would she utter. Annis had to tell them that if they found the witch, they should dance around her house by the new moon—which would be in two nights—three different times, if necessary. "Then the witch will die," Annis told them, and Becky, like she ofttimes did, said the same words after her: "And the witch will die."

Today, they came up to thank Becky and to leave two chickens. The witch was gone after they did the dancing. Gone entirely, disappeared into thin air. The couple had decided Dorothy Granding, a little old bent crone who lived alone, dressed all in black, and never had been known to speak above a whisper—if you could coax her to talk at all—was the witch. Little Miz Granding had something amiss, and she was never quite right, but Annis knew the poor little thing was no witch. They'd probably scared her into a hidey-hole somewhere. Well, never mind.

"That's good," Annis told the young couple. "You done real good. I'm sure your little one is looking down from heaven and smiling." They loved that. The couple started on their way back down through the mountain, and the rest of the people followed. In a few minutes, the porch was empty.

Annis was glad to see their backs. And not a moment too soon. Becky jumped up, muttering, and took herself outside. Running off into the woods, she called, "You'll not find me!" as she disappeared into the trees. "And if you do, I'll cut out your heart!"

Morgan had been brewing up some remedies, staying real quiet and out of sight. Annis had almost forgot she was nearby. So when Morgan said, right at Annis's shoulder, "Don't they realize they probably scared poor Miz Granding so she had to run off in the night?" it took Annis by surprise.

"Hush your mouth, now, Morgan. What harm does it do? Look how the mother smiles because she thinks she rid herself of her baby's killer. And if Miz Granding slipped out in the night, not wanting someone to maybe decide she should go into the river, well . . ."

"But Mam, it ain't right—"

"Now you listen to me, Morgan Wellburn. You ain't but thirteen years old, not old enough to sass your mother. If I say there's no harm, well, there's no harm, and there's an end to it.

I'm dead tired and my head aches. I'd surely like some camomile tea, Morgan."

"Yes, Mam, I'll get it." Morgan turned quickly, so Mam wouldn't see how mad she was. Her back hurt; it was as hot as the fires of Hades. Too hot for brewing up medicine, but nobody in this world cared how she felt! Her mother had plenty of time to stay with Becky and help her do her cures. But when Morgan had a word to say, suddenly her mother was tired and had the headache. She never had time for Morgan, not since that day when somebody decided Becky talked to the angels. The few times Morgan complained, her mother said that Becky needed her, and that Morgan, who was bright and had the healing power, was strong enough to do for herself. "It's a relief to me, Morgan," that's what Mam said to her. "I can trust you to do what needs be done." She patted Morgan's hand, and Morgan could see that her mother's thoughts were already flying straight to Becky. *Well, I need you, too,* Morgan wanted to say, but she knew it was no use. The only good thing was that she got to doctor a lot of her mother's patients these days. And they liked the way she took care of them, too.

Of course, it was nothing like what people thought of Becky. Becky was so special, so pretty, so . . . so famous. Even Morgan's best friend, Lizzie Bushnell thought so. Morgan wondered sometimes if Lizzie wasn't eager to be her friend just because she was the sister of the girl that had angels speaking to her. But Lizzie said no, of course not, and wasn't I your friend even before Becky got famous? Lizzie was somewhat fat and puffed a lot—she had trouble breathing—but she was the daughter of the Reverend Enos Bushnell, a respected member of East Haddam society.

When the camomile tea had steeped enough, Morgan poured a cup for her mother and brought it to her.

"Oh bless you, Morgan. You're such a help to me."

Morgan, warmed by the kind words, blurted out the question that had been stuck in her brain for a long time. "Mama," she said, reverting to the baby name, "how come angels speak to Becky and not to me? I'm not bad or anything and I do good . . . *well* in school."

One time she'd asked Lizzie's pa—'cause he was the preacher, wasn't he? A man of God. She figured he ought to know. And he said, "Maybe you're not spiritual, maybe you haven't prayed hard enough. We must all strive," he said, staring deep into her eyes in a way that made her want to squirm, "to be better than we are." She didn't think that was any kind of answer. "Mam?" she insisted. "Why don't they talk to me? I tried. I got on my knees and I asked them to but they just wouldn't."

"Oh, Morgan," her mother sighed. "What can I tell you?" She fell silent for such a long time, Morgan thought she'd forgotten the question. But then, she sighed again, and said, "You was right, Morgan. Before. It's a lot of hocus-pocus. You and I know they ain't no angels that talk to Becky. It's her spirits, the same ones that's been bothering her for so long. But, like I said before, there's no harm to it, not if it makes people feel better. Come to that, a lot of healing's the same. I've had women rolling around in their beds, a-screaming with the pain of childbirth, and just as soon as I'm there and they see my face, why, that pain just calms itself down. They trust in me, Morgan, they know I'm gonna help them and that soothes them. Of course, after that, I have to give 'em the right medicine . . ."

Morgan nodded. She'd seen that happen and knew it was so. There was a power in having folks know you were a healer, just in the knowing of it.

"You have the healing spirit in you, Morgan. Same as me and my mam and hers and back to the beginning of time. It's a good thing."

Morgan wasn't so sure of that. The other young folks in town kept a safe distance from her. She didn't know if it was because she was a healing woman or because she was Indian or because she was ugly. She knew she was ugly. Becky was considered a beauty, and no two sisters ever looked more different. Besides, no boys ever looked at her or pulled her braid. She'd die of the loneliness if it weren't for Lizzie. Even though, sometimes, she thought it just wasn't worth it. Lizzie always expected to lead, to give the orders, to get the best parts when they acted in their plays. She lorded it over Morgan, and often said, "Go home now," out of the blue, if she got bored or peevish. But Morgan felt that Lizzie found her exotic because she was part Indian and already a healer and—especially, Morgan thought—because she was Becky's sister. Once, Lizzie told Morgan that the two of them were some kind of cousins, because Lizzie had been delivered by Annis. That evening, Morgan asked Mam if that made her Lizzie's cousin. Her mother laughed and said no, not at all, "though it's true, I was there to catch her when she was born. I tell you, that baby came out of the womb complaining and whining, just like she does now."

Last fall, Morgan had been invited to attend a real play with Lizzie and her parents. She would never forget that magical evening. It was at Mr. Goodspeed's Hall, built right on the river bank. A marvelous place, built only five years ago; big as a castle—six stories!—and they said the horseshoe-shaped theater up on the top of it could seat three hundred people. The night she was taken by the Bushnells, Morgan could only sit and gawk. It looked to her like the whole state of Connecticut had taken seat, waiting for Mr. William Gillette to come out and play Sherlock Holmes. So many people, so many white bosoms with sparkly jewels and gentlemen in flowing ties! One of Mr. Goodspeed's river boats had brought people up all the way from New York City. Lizzie pointed out that the New Yorkers were the ones wearing the ostrich plumes and lined capes and diamond necklaces. Diamond necklaces! Morgan had never thought to see such a thing in her entire life! It was all beautiful: the people and the theater. The huge velvet curtain parted like magic when the play started, and thousands of candles and oil lamps lighted the front of the stage. She felt a bit odd in her homespun, while Lizzie was tricked out in a silk satin dress with flounces, but as soon as the room was dark and the play began, she forgot everything except what was happening on the stage. She came out of the theater dazed, hardly knowing where she was, wishing she could go back inside and watch it all over again. She knew she would probably never get to see another play, not unless Lizzie's folks decided to take her. But it inspired her and Lizzie to put on their own little after-school theatricals, in Lizzie's room at the back of the manse. Lately, however, Morgan was needed at home—to help with the chores or to see to a patient—so there had been little time for playacting.

A sound behind Morgan made her turn. Becky was back, sitting on the good rocker out on the porch. Why? Morgan wondered. Everyone had gone. But then she saw Lizzie, puffing into the clearing, looking very red in the face, her hands to her chest. Right behind her was her pa. And look at that: Behind *him* was his great friend the Reverend Carstairs from all the way up in Wethersfield. All of them were bundled up against the cold, but they looked heated after their climb. The two preachers came panting and puffing up through the trees. When the Reverend Bushnell stopped halfway to the house, his fist on his chest, catching his breath, Morgan was struck suddenly by how much Lizzie and her pa looked alike. Oh dear. Did that mean Lizzie would grow up to have a round little potbelly and a bulbous nose?

As they came closer, the Reverend Bushnell's voice could be heard saying, "And here we are, Brother Carstairs, this is the place. That girl with the red hair on the porch, she's the blessed child who communes with the angels. You'll see . . . it's quite remarkable."

Morgan marveled. Had Becky seen the threesome making their way up? Did she know they had come to see her? And did she care? That possibility had never before occurred to Morgan. As far as she knew, Becky spoke with her spirits and Ma translated for the people waiting. But maybe, Morgan thought, her sister liked all the attention. Could be she was enjoying this—this playacting. Yes, that's what it was, like a play on the stage, *exactly* like.

The two ministers approached the porch. "Miss Becky," the Reverend Bushnell intoned, his breath making white puffs of smoke, "I've brought the Reverend Carstairs all the way from Wethersfield to speak with you."

"Wethersfield," Becky snapped back. "Evil is as evil does. I say Wethersfield will burn."

Mr. Carstairs went pale, and he held a hand out as if to halt Becky's words. "Just as I have been preaching," he marveled.

"The young folk of Wethersfield have been carrying on, making fun of the word of the Lord. Haven't I been saying that very same thing? Wethersfield will burn. Oh, angels in heaven," he said, looking up at the sky and becoming quite emotional, "how shall I change their wicked ways?"

"Strike down those who have wicked ways!" shouted Becky. "Wicked, wicked, wicked!" In a minute, Morgan knew, Becky would be coming off the porch, wanting to strike down the two parsons.

But before she or Mam could move, Mr. Carstairs had fallen to his knees in the half-frozen mud, his hands together in prayer, shouting out to the Lord to look down on His poor sinners and help them mend their wicked, wicked ways. Mr. Bushnell went on *his* knees, too, and so did Lizzie, good wool dress and all, right onto the cold dirt yard. It occurred to Morgan that Lizzie looked mighty stupid with her eyes rolling back in her head and putting what she thought was a holy look on her face.

"Poor sinners!" Becky shouted. "Burn in Hell! Get your devils away from me, away from me! No, I won't stop, I won't! And quit that everlasting noise! No, no, I won't have it!" She called out some words in the old language: Indian words. She only knew a few and they were mostly names of herbs and plants. She recited a list of them, as if she were in school. Well, Morgan thought, now the two preachers would know that Becky wasn't speaking with any angels in heaven. But Mr. Carstairs lifted his hands upward and shouted, "Hallelujah! She speaks in tongues!" And Mr. Bushnell cried, "Amen!" And so did Lizzie. All looking so religious right there in the yard, with the turkeys hanging upside down and skinned squirrels and all.

Morgan and Mam just stood and watched. Then Becky turned her chair right around and sat with her back to everyone, her arms tight across her chest, rocking furiously. After a few minutes, Mr. Bushnell noticed. He put a hand on his friend's shoulder. "Miss Becky wants us to leave," he said. And without a good day or farewell, they all left. Morgan waited for Lizzie to turn and wave to her, but her best friend just

walked away without a word. Becky spoiled everything for
Morgan.

"Why don't you go back to the woods, where you belong!"
Morgan yelled at Becky. "Take your misery and get away
from us!"

Becky got up and whirled around. "A knife in your heart!"
she shouted, and Morgan shouted back, "I dare you! Double-
dare you!" Her heart was pounding hard against her ribs.

Becky gave her a look of such hatred that Morgan recoiled.
She thought, *Now she's going to do it. She's going to kill me.*

Out of nowhere, Pa appeared, pounding across the yard,
yelling Becky's name. That stopped her. She screamed, "No,
no, you'll not do it!" And off she went, fast as the wind, into
the woods. Not a backward glance for Mam or anything else.
In a minute, she'd disappeared, and it was suddenly so quiet in
the clearing, Morgan could hear the ragged sound of her
father's breathing and of her own. She felt a bit dizzy.

"What'd you do, to set her off like that?" her mother cried,
from behind her.

"Why are you mad at *me*? I don't shout at folks that they're
evil and I'm going to cut their hearts out! So why are you
yelling at me?"

"You know better than to rile her up," Pa said. "Now she
could be gone for weeks."

"Oh, that would be terrible!" Morgan heard herself saying.
She could no more stop herself than she could stop breathing. "Then folks wouldn't come up the hill and bring us goods.
The Wellburns wouldn't be famous anymore. Well, I see what
goes on. I know that Becky waves her hands over a burnt child
and everybody shouts it's a miracle, but it's Mam who gives
a salve that cures the burn. I see how Becky says whatever
comes into her head and it's Mam who tells folks what it
means. It ain't real, none of it's real, and I'm not sorry I riled
her up. I don't care! Don't you see pretty soon everyone'll
know what I know?"

"I ought to wash your mouth out with soap," Mam said.
And Daddy said, "You don't care that you chased her off?
When we're eatin' the last of squirrel stew, you'll sing a dif-
ferent tune."

Morgan didn't answer. Pa turned on his heel and walked away from her, and when she turned, Mam had gone into the house. No comfort there. Morgan thought, *No, I won't cry. I'm thirteen, nearly fourteen. I don't care and I won't cry.*

Sounds in the night. Man voices, talking low. Coming after her. "You're a stupid girl, you deserve to die." No, different voice. Her great-great-grandmother. "You better run, or they'll push their things into you and hurt you, hurt you, hurt you."

"Hurt me, hurt me," Becky whimpers. She stands up and begins to run.

"There! Over there! I see her! See the hair?"

"Let's get her!"

"Hear she's hot as a pistol!"

Giggles. Laughter. Boots, crashing through the underbrush, after her.

"No, no, no!" Becky shouts. "No!" They laugh louder. Very close.

"You see what I told you? Evil is as evil does. You'll get what you deserve," says the spirit of great-great-grandmother.

Becky freezes. Spirit arms have got ahold of her and she knows she cannot move. She is standing there, back to a tree, arguing with great-great-grandmother, when they find her. They all do it. First one and then two and then three and then four. She counts them and then she counts when they shove their hard things into her, counts and counts not to feel what is happening. One of them slaps her, says for her to stop that crazy talk, slaps her again. She feels nothing, nothing, nothing.

"Stop that, Henry! What you want to hit her for?"

"She's talkin' crazy!"

"I ain't had my turn yet. You gonna spoil her!"

They laugh. Push, push, shove, shove. It hurts.

"Hurts, does it, magic girl? Guess you ain't never had a real man before!" Laugh and laugh.

Hurts and hurts and hurts.

"See, you stupid girl? Now you're going to have a baby," shouts great-great-grandmother. "The devil's baby. Becky will have the devil's baby!" Becky shouts back.

"Hold on, there, Brad. She's bleedin'. Bleedin' bad . . ."

"Let's get outta here!"

"Hope you had a good time! Tell them angels how good it is to fuck!" Laughing. Boots crashing in the underbrush and then nothing. Nobody.

"Get yourself home and get rid of that devil baby. They stuck their pitchforks in you and made you a devil baby. You got exactly what you deserve! You get rid of it. I know . . . you cut that baby right out'n your belly," says great-great-grandmother.

She hurts real bad. They banged her head on the hard ground. They held her too tight. She heads for home, like she was ordered. But first, she crawls around until she finds it. The hunting knife she took from where Pa keeps it. And she stabs that devil baby in her stomach, stabs it and stabs it to make sure it's dead.

Late that night, with a sickle moon high in the sky, Morgan woke all at once, alert and listening. But to what? Then she heard it: a moaning outside, in the woods. She got up and felt her way down the loft ladder, tiptoeing to where the lanterns were kept. She lit one and crept out in her bare feet and night-dress. She found Becky lying on the ground at the edge of the birch grove just behind the house, her dress hanging in tatters from her body. Her fair skin gleamed in the pale moonlight. She was clutching her belly with her hands. When Morgan stooped down to look, she began to scream. Becky was pouring blood from her stomach.

Mam came running out, yelling, "Where are you? What's happening?"

"Come quick! Bring bandages! Becky's been stabbed and she's bleeding to death!" Morgan found herself sobbing and weeping as Pa picked Becky up and carried her inside.

For weeks, Becky lay on a pallet near the fire, having soup and gruel with belladonna in it and snake oil spooned into her mouth. Pa collected cobwebs to put on the wounds, and Mam used a balm she made from the bark of slippery elm and poultices of plantain to soothe the hurts and itches. Becky was feverish, but the cuts began to heal and they looked mighty clean. Her eyes remained closed, though, and she muttered to her spirits almost all the time. They were able to piece together what must have happened from her rambling. A group of men had found Becky and had taken turns raping her. Morgan, who had seen animals mating her whole life, wondered why anyone would want to mate with Becky. She was as likely to scratch you as say good day. But it was clear that's what they done, Daddy said. There were bruises on the insides of her thighs and on her shoulders where they had held her down, and dried blood that had run down her legs. Becky, sure she was pregnant with a devil, had dragged herself home, found Pa's hunting knife, and stuck herself in the belly to kill it.

Morgan got the job of stopping folks from coming up. She told them Becky had been in an accident and would not be seeing anyone for a time. But Morgan heard what Mam said to Pa after she went upstairs to bed. "Becky ain't the same, Todd. Her spirits are telling her she has to die. The child's in torment, and I doubt she'll ever be better. If we didn't tie her down onto the bed, she'd be long gone. She keeps wanting to go. The way she's getting now, she puts me in mind of Quare Auntie. And I don't know what we'll do if she stays like this. I just don't know."

Sure enough, one night in March, when everyone was fast asleep, Becky managed to untie herself and out she went, into the night. Try as they might, and call as they did, there was no getting her back to the house. Morgan thought she saw Becky one morning behind an oak tree. Morgan didn't call out. Instead, she tiptoed over, real quiet, but as soon as she got near, she heard a whisper of a sound, and when she looked behind the tree, there was no sign of Becky—nor anyone else, either. She wondered if Becky had turned into a spirit. But Mam said maybe it was just that Morgan had wanted so bad to find Becky that she imagined she saw her. Maybe so. And maybe Becky was dead.

Folks kept coming up to ask was Becky ready to see them, and Morgan kept telling them no, not yet. She wanted to tell the truth but Mam and Pa were against that. "I'm pondering the situation, Morgan," her mother said. "And soon I'll know what we got to do."

Well, one April morning, when Morgan was getting ready

to go to school, Mam called her to the porch, saying she
wanted to have a talk. She said Morgan was to sit in the
rocking chair Becky had always favored. When Morgan asked
why, Mam got riled and snapped, "Just do as I say, young lady,
and listen with both your ears. 'Cause what I'm a-telling you
is mighty important."

"I'm going to be late for school, Mam."

"More important than school, you hear me? Now sit!"

Morgan sat where she was told and folded her hands in her
lap, but inside she was resentful. No need to talk to her in that
sharp voice, not when she'd been taking on most of her
mother's patients all fall and winter. *And* doing a lot of the
medicines and gathering the herbs. She'd hardly had a minute
to keep up with her schoolwork.

Her mother began: "Now, Morgan, no reason on earth we
should stop doing good business just because Becky's done
gone. I've been a-thinking and here's what came to me. It'll be
you will sit here in the rocker and talk to the angels and—"

Morgan couldn't believe her ears. "No, ma'am!" she said,
right in the middle of her mother's sentence. "I won't! I won't
playact and I won't lie! I've got the healing spirit, you said so
yourself. I'm a healer, a *real* healer. Aren't there women who
ask for Morgan Wellburn instead of Annis? Yes! And you
want me to sit in this rocker and pretend I'm like *Becky*?"

Annis stormed off the porch and into the house, slamming
the door behind her as hard as she could. Then Morgan heard
the bolt rasping as it slid home. Her mother had locked her
out. "I don't care!" she hollered. "I'll go down and live with
Lizzie Bushnell. See if I don't!" Her mother unlocked the door
then, saying, "You'll do as I say if I have to tie you down."

You just see if I do, Morgan thought. That day, she went
down to school, although she hardly heard a word the teacher
said, she was that busy figuring out what she had to do. And
when she got home, she snuck into the house to get her medicine bag and quickly stuffed her other dress into it. She had
been planning to go out the window come nightfall, but she
had a better idea. She told Mam she needed to hunt up some
wintergreen and off she went, across the clearing. The last
words she heard from her mother were, "Oh, and we could

use some squawweed, too, Morgan. And don't be all day at it, neither!"

Morgan called out "Yes, ma'am!" As she trudged down the trail, she was thinking how unfair her mother was, always favoring Becky, even now that Becky had disappeared deep into the woods. The more she thought on it, the more Morgan came to the conclusion that maybe there weren't any spirits at all. And that meant her mother was lying to her, too. That wasn't right, it just wasn't. She made up her mind. She went straight down the mountainside, on the familiar winding path through the woods, to the place by the river where they hid their dugout canoe. Some days Pa used it for fishing, but he'd gone up to Glastonbury, hunting rattlers for snake oil. The canoe bobbed gently at its mooring. Morgan's eyes filled. She sure would miss her daddy, and maybe Mam, too. But it just wasn't fair.

She climbed into the canoe and settled herself. For a minute or two, she hesitated, until she thought about sitting in that rocker and playing crazy. She untied the canoe and pushed off. Turning to look back, she said, "Good-bye, everyone. I don't know where I'm going, but I sure ain't staying here." The river's current took the canoe then, and she had no time to think of anything but steering past the rocks and not getting killed.

5

The Same Day

The river was a devil in the springtime. When the ice melted, tons of water came rushing down to the Sound all the way from Vermont, shattering boats and drowning unlucky sailors. You had to wait till the end of summer for the river spirits to calm down and become a little sleepy. Mam had warned her about that, from the first day she gave Morgan the paddle and taught her how to steer the canoe, when Morgan was but five or six years old. "This here river never got tamed," Mam said. "She's like a doe . . . real skittish." Mam taught her that the river spirits were female, and that the river's name, *Konektikut*, meant "on the long tidal river" in the old language. That meant it not only had its own currents, but was pushed back and forth by the tides in the Sound. "So you got to keep looking sharp, Morgan. You can't be sitting back and dreaming, not on the Connecticut River."

Morgan recalled how, when she was a little girl, her mother seemed so tall and strong, with all the wisdom of the world in her broad calm face. Picturing Mam made Morgan's eyes sting. She might never see her mother again in this life. She couldn't bear to think about leaving her father at all. She might never walk back into that clearing and go up onto that porch, not ever. All at once, she felt hollow, as if her insides had left her, and she had to fight herself not to turn the canoe into shore and make her way back home. She had left and that was that. She was not about to become another Becky. But what was she going to do? She didn't even know where she was heading, except downstream. Right now, she'd best stop thinking and watch out for sandbars. There were thirty of them in this river. Rocks, too, big ones. Not that she was scared. She knew how to handle a canoe.

She had a bag filled with medicines and a head filled with healing. She also had her mother's amulet for luck, the one handed down for hundreds of generations of her family. Surely she would need its good luck wherever she ended up. Soon as it started getting dark, she'd go ashore and walk to the nearest town and tell folks that she knew how to fix their ills and complaints. She'd tell them what she could do: She knew how to stop the pain of menstruation. She knew how to get rid of head lice, how to lance a boil, and ease an earache. She knew how to birth a baby. She knew which plants were good to eat and which were poison. She could bring a fever down and set a broken limb. She might be young, but she was a healer woman. She'd make her way, she would, and never again have to take orders from anyone. Never!

When the first cold drops of rain began to fall, the sky was still clear, just a little hazy. But she heard the rumblings of thunder in the distance and she knew that, in the springtime, the weather could change in minutes. She paddled faster, looking on both sides of the river for a good landing place. She might not be able to reach a town if the rain got heavier. Black clouds were moving quickly up from the Sound, so she pushed the canoe as fast as her arms could paddle.

It didn't do any good. Within five minutes, the sky was totally black. Thunder filled the air and jagged streaks of lightning speared through the sky. As the rain pelted down, a wild wet wind began to blow, kicking up waves that slapped at the canoe and slopped over, soaking Morgan's boots. She began to shiver. Reaching out for the medicine bag—if she lost that to the river, she'd lost everything—she pulled it back to her with her feet and held it fast.

Through the sheets of gray rain, she saw something rearing up in the middle of the river. She couldn't tell exactly what it was, but she did not want to find out by crashing into it. The dugout canoe was sturdy and strong—she and Pa and Mam had made it together—but a mean gust of wind could send it sliding sideways to crash against the rocks. Using all her skill and every bit of strength she had, she paddled herself closer to the shore. She hadn't a notion where she was, couldn't see a thing through the curtain of water that sluiced down from that angry sky, and didn't know where it might be safe to land. But land she must. Grunting with the effort, she backpaddled, sending the canoe into a spin. It was another struggle to stop it turning in tight circles. She paddled fiercely, switching from one side of the boat to the other, breathing hard and mouthing, please, please, please. She did not want to die, not before she'd done a single thing on her own.

When she felt the bump, she tried to see where she'd landed. Well, not exactly *landed*, but fetched up, caught in a tangle of river weeds and rushes. First thing, she took her medicine bag and hung it across her chest, to keep it safe. One of Pa's good hunting knives was in there, too. She got out, and wading waist-deep in the swirling water, through the muck, dragged the canoe behind her.

The boat was so heavy and she was so tired . . . and so cold her teeth chattered. If she could just make it to shore, she'd be all right. She kept telling herself that, ordering one foot and then the other forward, making herself keep pulling, even though her arms felt like they were going to fall off of her body. Just when she was sure she couldn't move another step, a pole appeared in front of her. She grabbed on to it and felt herself being pulled. Lord, it felt so good. A voice came shouting out of the rain, "I've got the canoe. I'll make it fast. Let it go. Let it go!" She could make out a figure dressed head to toe in oilskins. She asked no questions, just let go and got herself up on the bank. Never did solid ground feel so good under her. By then, she was on her hands and knees and it took a mighty effort to push herself to her feet, but she did it, so she could help her rescuer pull the canoe up on the bank where it could be tethered to a tree. They made a good team, working together without words. Once the canoe was truly fast, Morgan realized she was sobbing. Tears poured out of her eyes, but her face was so wet with the storm, it was all the same.

"Thank you, mister," she said, trying to keep her voice steady. "I don't know what brought you down here in this hard weather, but you sure saved my life."

"I saw you from the widow's walk atop my roof," the stranger said, and with a shock, Morgan realized it was a woman. "Anyhow, I thought I saw you. The wind kept blowing the rain like a big curtain, back and forth. I saw you, then I didn't, then I did. Finally, I said to myself, Get yourself down there, Gracie my girl. If it's a spook, you'll know soon enough. And if it's some poor soul caught in a storm, you're sure to go to heaven for making a rescue." Great gusts of laughter.

Morgan stared. A *woman*, a town lady, had got the nerve to slog down here with a pole, to help drag her out of the raging river. "Well, a good thing for me you did, Mrs.—"

The woman took her arm, leading her away from the river. "It's Doctor. Dr. Grace Chapman of Chester, Connecticut, at your service. And you are—?"

"Morgan Wellburn. I come from the hills above East Haddam."

"The hills above Haddam . . . wait a minute. There used to be a family of Indian healers settled up there. You know them?"

"You might say that. That's my family. We're still there."

The doctor took long strides; Morgan had to stretch her legs to keep up, especially since the rain still lashed at them. "Watch out for the big roots here. We turn right and there's a kind of path . . . never mind," the doctor said, shouting now to be heard above the howling of the storm. "I'm so sorry. You're wet clear through. Never mind directions! Hang on to my coat! We'll get there, never fear!"

Morgan did as she was bid, ducking her head against the biting rain and following without another word. Then, as suddenly as it had arrived, the wind shifted, blowing the clouds into ragged tatters, and the moon was revealed. The rain stopped.

The doctor stopped walking to peer into Morgan's face. Morgan stared back at her rescuer, and liked what she saw. Dr. Grace looked to be a bit younger than Mam, or less worn out, with thick wavy hair pulled back in a loose bunch. She was a big woman, taller even than Morgan. She looked strong and kind. Morgan thought her beautiful.

"You look all done in. Let's get you home now . . . It's not far, just across that meadow . . . And dry you off before you catch your death. How long were you fighting that river before I caught sight of you?"

"Dunno. I don't even know what time I left. I was so mad—" Her eyes and throat filled.

"Well, bless me for a fool. It must have been some quarrel. Never mind, you needn't tell me. Come on, because here we go. Just a few more steps."

It was quite dark, but Dr. Grace stepped along, very sure of her way. At last, a lighted window glowed like a beacon out of the black. "There's my house," Dr. Grace said. "Nothing fancy, but it's all mine." Against the light of the moon, the house looked huge to Morgan: a big square shape, two stories high, with a widow's walk on top surrounded by a black iron railing.

"Well, come on. You'll stay with me a day or two. It'll take that long for you to dry out. And then we'll see." Her new friend laughed again. She seemed to laugh a lot, Morgan thought. Morgan liked that.

As they headed down a path made of stones laid flat in the earth, listening to the wind, friendly now, pushing the last of the storm away, Morgan realized she was feeling something very much like happiness. A woman doctor! She'd always wished she could meet one and here one was, pulling her out of the river like a good spirit, and inviting Morgan into her home.

The doctor led her into a little room with stone walls that were lined with pegs and shelves. After she hung up her wet coat and hat, the doctor took a skirt and a thick shawl off two pegs and handed them to Morgan.

"They're probably too big, but they're warm and dry and that's all that counts right now, eh?" She grabbed a towel from another peg to wipe the rain from her face. "Here, dry yourself off. When you get out of those wet things, use that door over there. It leads to the kitchen, which is where I'll be, heating up some nice hot soup. That should take the chill off!"

Morgan was glad to shuck her wet clothes. Her medicine bag, she hung on a peg to dry out, but these soaking-wet things? She left them in a heap on the floor, ran the towel over herself, and pulled on the dry garments. As she walked into the big warm kitchen, she could smell the rich aroma of beef soup, mixed with the fainter aroma of drying herbs that hung from the ceiling beams. The doctor, swathed in a big apron, was slicing bread.

"I'll bet you're hungry."

"Starving."

"Well, take a seat at the table and I'll be pleased to serve you."

"Dr. Chapman . . ."

"Everyone calls me Dr. Grace."

"Dr. Grace, what shall I do with my wet clothes? They're making a big puddle out there."

"Why, bless you, just leave them there. There's a drain in that floor—isn't that a clever idea? Tomorrow, Mrs. Wainwright, my daily, will make them wearable again. Now just sit yourself down and get something warm into you. I want to see some color in those cheeks."

Never had anything tasted so delicious as that dark soup, thick with barley and mushrooms and greens and bits of meat. Morgan tried to be polite, but it was so good and her stomach was so empty, she couldn't seem to get it down fast enough. Somehow she knew she needn't be too careful of her manners with Dr. Grace, who was easy and pleasant, and who also ate with great gusto.

"So. You're from that family of healers above East Haddam. You a healer, too?"

"Yes."

A sudden sober look from under the curved brows. "Good thing I pulled you out of the river. Healers are hard to come by, these days. These medical men, they're so in love with their newfangled germ theory, they don't leave any room for the art of medicine. They call me an irregular, you know. An *irregular*. I'm not scientific enough to be a *real* doctor. You ever hear the like? Oh, here. Have another slice. Here's peach jam from last summer. Try it. And, if I'm not mistaken, there's half a pie in the larder . . ."

"Will you tell me more? About being a doctor. My pa, he always told me it was the ladies who saved his life, in the Great War. He heard tell of women doctors but he never did see one. Oh, he'll be ever so pleased when I tell him . . ." Her voice petered out, as she realized she had left home and would not be telling her daddy anything.

Dr. Grace reached out and put her hand over Morgan's, just for a moment. "Your pa sounds like a man of good sense. And how about his daughter, eh? What in the world were you doing out in the middle of the river in the thunderstorm?"

"I . . . I had a quarrel with my mam."

"Oh. Well, I know what that's about."

"Why? Do you have a daughter?"

Dr. Grace laughed but not like what Morgan had said was funny. "No, I don't, although I had a mother and that amounts to the same thing, eh? I'm a Civil War widow; my husband died very young and I never thought of marrying again. First, I didn't have the time, and then I was suddenly too old to have

children. And I certainly wasn't about to marry some old widower looking for someone to take care of his young'uns and
cook and clean for him. Oh no, not Grace Chapman! I'm
sorry. I am a blatherer, I admit it. And you must be mighty
tired and wanting to sleep." She made a move as if to get up
from the table.

"No, really, Dr. Grace, I love hearing you talk. And I'm sure
I couldn't sleep, not a wink. Too much to think about."

"I know that feeling, too. I often stay awake thinking,
sometimes about things I can't change." She smiled at Morgan
and said, "Your father said the nurses saved his life? I can
believe that. I often think my husband wouldn't have died if
he'd had the proper care. More men died in the hospital tents
than on the battlefield, you know that?"

"That just what Pa always said."

A snort. "Well, your pa was right. Them with their heroic
doses of calomel! Never mind if it kills the patient, and it
killed plenty in the war, let me tell you! But never mind that,
say they, the doctor has done his duty." More snorts. "You
ever hear of Sam'l Thompson?"

"No," Morgan said. "Never heard of Mr. Thompson."

"He had a system of doctoring, a lot like what your people
have been doing since the beginning of time ..." Morgan
could feel her eyes closing and she willed them open. Dr.
Grace noticed. "I'll tell you about Sam Thompson tomorrow,
how's that? It's time for you to go to bed. Doctor's orders. Tomorrow, we'll talk. Might be, I could use a healer woman in
my practice ... We'll see. But right now, up the stairs with
you."

The bed was soft and the sheets smelled of fresh air. Morgan snuggled into the eiderdown, trying to sort out her thoughts.
A woman doctor, a real one, a nice one. One who said she
might be needing a healer. The town was Chester, she'd said.
That had a nice sound to it, warm and friendly. In a town
named Chester, where a woman could be a real doctor, was
there a place for Morgan Wellburn? And then, all at once, she
was asleep.

SECTION TWO

Morgan Wellburn
Dr. Grace Chapman
Silas Grisham

6

October 1882

How grand it was, to be living in Dr. Grace's big house. How lovely to sit on the front porch in a rocker—so different from the front porch and the rockers of the little house in the clearing—and sip a cup of tea, gazing out over the property's lawns and grasses and wildflowers and heavy old trees. In a few more days, it would be All Hallows' Eve, and soon all the leaves would be gone and the wind run chill, but right now it was Indian summer, warm and golden. The grass at the front of the house, clipped by two elderly pet sheep, was still green.

Morgan was content here. True, she had bothersome dreams at night, full of running and hiding and watching for the unnamed people who were after her, and when she woke, her heart would be beating fast. But in a few minutes, the dreams faded away. As soon as she opened her eyes and looked around the neat little room that was all hers—a room with two windows, a bureau, and a narrow bed with four posters and its own blue and red quilt—she was always flooded with delight. She had not been meant to spend her whole life in a dirt clearing in the woods, else why had her parents sent her to school? She knew she'd let them down, running away like that, but they'd be fine. Wasn't Annis Wellburn famous for birthing babies, all the way up to Springfield in Massachusetts? And her father was a good hunter. And they didn't have her to feed and clothe, that was a saving, wasn't it? They'd be all right even without Becky's "miracles."

Anyway, she loved this house with its fine furniture that

smelled of wax and lemon oil, the heavy brocade draperies, the silver teapot and bowls that Mrs. Wainwright shined up every week. It was a house filled with wonders: A big looking glass in Dr. Grace's bedroom! A grandfather clock, its shining pendulum swinging back and forth, and a great key in its back for winding up! The silver spoons and the fine linen sheets and the lace curtains and the brass candlesticks!

Morgan had to laugh, thinking of how Lizzie had lorded it over her because the Bushnells had a Turkey rug on the floor of the parlor and flowered dishes that matched. Dr. Grace had three different sets of dishes, each with little plates and big plates and cups and saucers and soup bowls and berry bowls. There was just no end to Dr. Grace's china dishes. Reverend Bushnell's pokey little manse, which had once seemed so large and elegant to her eyes, was nothing compared to Dr. Grace's big white house on Liberty Street. Four acres of land behind it, enough for a small fruit orchard and a kitchen garden, flowers too, and of course, an herb garden for medicines. The herb garden was now Morgan's ... What was the word Dr. Grace had used? *Province,* that was it. The herb garden was now Morgan's province, Dr. Grace had insisted, since Morgan had been working with herb medicine her whole life. "You'll tell me what more we need, or what needs taking out. You're in charge now, Morgan."

Morgan rocked and sipped and waved at the driver of a hay wagon going by. The house sat square and solid, not far back from the road, shaded by two old white pines, one either side of the front door, and a small grove of maples. In the back stood a carriage house and behind it, an old summer cook-house and sheds for the chickens and geese. They had every-thing they needed, right here, save a cow. So they bought their milk and cheese from the Bailey farm down the road. Of course, Dr. Grace often got paid in kind, just like Annis did. Many folks didn't have cash but they might make Dr. Grace curtains for a bedroom, or give two months' worth of fresh eggs, or a pig, or shoeing for Patsy, the mare.

Since the house was on the road to the Hadlyme ferry, hardly half an hour passed without someone on a wagon or a carriage or a horse riding by. Everybody waved because everybody knew Dr. Grace. They were beginning to know Morgan Wellburn, too, so now they waved to her. That pleased her immensely. She hadn't realized how all alone the Wellburns were, up on their tiny hidden property. She hadn't realized how lonely she had been all of her life. But that was changed now, and here she was, in a whole new life.

For days, rain had been pouring out of a low dull sky that made the light coming in the windows look dirty. When patients came in to see Dr. Grace, they'd dripped and grouched and complained of rheumatism and catarrh. The waiting room at the front of the house was filled with the sound of coughing. But today, the light was clearer and brighter and the sky curved overhead as white and smooth as an egg. Morgan breathed in the midmorning air. And suddenly, breathed in the smell of something scorching. Oh, lord! She'd been boiling up some medicines on the stove, two large pots, and had completely forgot them with all her woolgathering. She ran into the house and down the long hallway to the kitchen. Sure enough, the black elderberry mixture had boiled over and the thick syrup was burning on the hot stovetop. Quickly, Morgan took the tongs and pushed the big pot to the back of the stove, checking to see how much had spilled. Not much. That was a relief.

Black elderberry syrup was very good for curing the influenza, and Dr. Grace had told her the influenza season would soon be upon them. "December to March," Dr. Grace said. "That's when it strikes. I don't know why—nobody knows why—but we do know it's true. And we'll be needing gallons of elderberry syrup, so you might as well start cooking it up now." Annis always used snake oil for the influenza, or yarrow made into tea, but if Dr. Grace said black elderberry syrup, Morgan was ready to learn. After all, Dr. Grace was a real doctor.

She was still scouring the mess on the stove top when Mrs. Wainwright came in the back door, tying on her apron and wrinkling her nose. "Now what have you done to my nice clean stove?" she grumped. "Mixing up one of your nostrums, are you? Well, it smells dreadful. Why Dr. Grace wants to use my kitchen to cook up these messes, I'm sure I don't know.

There's a perfectly good cookhouse out back where there's nothing to be harmed. But 'tis not for me to say, is it?" All of this while she moved briskly about the kitchen, pulling down bowls and spoons and peering into barrels to see if she had what she needed.

It had taken Morgan awhile to get used to Mrs. Wainwright's streams of grievances. But now she realized that they meant nothing. It was just the housekeeper's way of letting you know you were in her domain and you'd better look sharp while she was there.

"It's only the elderberries boiling over," Morgan said. "And you'll think they smell like the sweetest lavender when you get the influenza this winter."

"Not I! I keep myself well fed and healthy."

More than well fed, Morgan thought, eyeing Mrs. Wainwright's ample proportions and three chins.

"And what's *this* a-cooking?"

"Bilberry and hawthorn berry."

"Now that one I'll be needing. Come winter, my rheumatism acts up something fierce. Well, take care, Morgan. Keep a sharp eye on that pot for the sake of my stove." She began to bustle about the kitchen, loading the big iron stove with more wood to heat up the oven. It was Monday, and Monday was both laundry day and bread day. While the stove was good and hot, they'd heat the water for washing and the oven for baking. Morgan moved her pots with their herbal mixtures well to the back of the stove, where they could simmer and cook down.

"Shall I help you with the dough, Mrs. Wainwright?"

"No, dear, I'll do it. In any case, here comes the Old Leatherman, bless his soul. He'll be wanting something to eat. There's a bit of Vermont cheese in the larder and a small loaf of last week's bread and you might take him some apples, too, though the Lord knows we could use them in a pie, but there's no sense in talking to deaf ears . . ."

The housekeeper's voice followed Morgan like a spool of sound unwinding behind her. Morgan put the food into a basket. She was eager to finally see the Old Leatherman. She'd heard so many stories about him, but, until today, he'd never come around. And there he was, coming up the path to the back door, his clothing all made of leather, just like they said. He scowled and stared at her as a wild animal might, wary and ready to run.

"Well, hello there, my friend. Welcome back." Dr. Grace had come out so silently that her voice startled Morgan. The Old Leatherman said nothing, but he did hand Dr. Grace a flower he had picked from her garden. Nobody else had such large black-eyed susans. Dr. Grace thanked him as if he'd brought her a diamond. Morgan thrust the basket toward him. He reached out and grabbed the bread and the cheese, which he put into his leather pouch, and then the apples. Without even a nod of thanks, he turned and walked out the back gate.

"I wonder where does he come from?" Morgan said. "And what turned him into a wanderer?"

"We all wonder that, Morgan. Poor lost soul, the least we can do is give him food."

Morgan sighed a little. Here was another reason to love Chester, she thought, a town that would take a total stranger into its heart. She was so glad she had ended up here!

A horse came galloping around the house. It was one of the men from Otis Marshall's bit-and-auger factory, all in a lather, crying, "Dr. Grace! Come quick! Mrs. Marshall's been taken bad! She's at Bradley's down at the Cove. Garden Club meeting!"

"Is she bleeding?"

The man turned red but nodded yes.

"We'll be there directly." He galloped off, and Dr. Grace went running into the house for her doctor bag, saying, "Morgan, you hitch Patsy to the buggy. You'll be coming with me."

Morgan ran to do her bidding. She loved going into town. Into the buggy they climbed, Dr. Grace cracked the whip, and the good old mare trotted off, down the road toward Bradley's.

"No fool like an old fool," snorted Dr. Grace. "Otis Marshall should just be happy with his two little girls and stop trying for a son! This is Eleanor's third miss in as many years. But does he care? Men and their craving for an heir!" She shook her head.

Morgan knew who Otis Marshall was. He was an important man, the treasurer of the Agricultural and Mechanical Society of Chester. They'd had their yearly fair last month, September 27th and 28th, at Town Hall. Morgan had gone, saving her pennies to pay the admission fee of ten cents. It was a wonderful fair. People came from all the nearby towns to take part in it. Otis and his wife, Eleanor, had been very much present the days of the fair, all dressed up and sweeping from room to room, shaking hands and chatting with everybody. They were very rich, of course, but very nice in spite of it, Morgan thought. When Dr. Grace had first introduced her to the Marshalls—"my new colleague, Miss Morgan Wellburn"—they'd shaken her hand and said they were glad to make her acquaintance and never asked so much as a question, to find out what part of the sky she'd dropped from.

Otis was old, as old as Dr. Grace, and bald as an owl, but Eleanor was a plump good-natured young woman not yet thirty-five. She was his second wife, his first having died in child-birth after waiting ten years to become pregnant. And now his second wife was having difficulties. Morgan had heard Otis talk about the son he had to have— "otherwise, why have I worked so hard to build this business?"

Holding on hard to her seat as they rounded a corner a bit too sharply, Morgan shouted, "Why are some people so dead set on boy babies?"

"Well, Morgan, don't you know, in many places, a woman can't own her own property. She can't inherit from her father."

"But why? It seems to me—" Morgan stopped talking altogether as Dr. Grace rounded another corner, even harder. For just a moment, the buggy was tipped sideways, riding on one wheel, and then old Patsy put on some speed and it righted itself.

"Yes? It seems to you . . . ?" Dr. Grace said, just as if they hadn't nearly had an accident. Everyone in town knew to get out of the way when Dr. Grace came driving through. A few had talked to her about it, but, she'd told Morgan, "I said to them, 'Well, and shall I go slowly when I'm coming to help *your* family?' That kept their lips closed."

"It seems it's not that way with Indians. It's the women in my family who get the healing spirit, direct from Bird, and she was a woman and *moigu* . . . shaman, you know," Morgan said. "Girls couldn't be warriors but they were important." She thought about it for a moment and then added, "We have the babies, don't we? Don't you think we ought to be above men?"

Dr. Grace laughed, turning into the curved main street. They could see Bradley's big building ahead, with all the lumber piled at its side and a group of workmen talking and pointing. Daniel Bradley was redoing it, turning it from a gathering place into a tenement, not a move that was popular in town. But for now, the Garden Club was still holding meetings in the building. Dr. Grace clucked at Patsy, and the horse pulled into the front of Bradley's, where she came to a halt.

"Once upon a time, Morgan, or so I've read, folks worshipped a female god because pregnancy was a mystery and a miracle. But once they figured out that men had a part in it—!" She laughed again. "I've had a pile of trouble, being a woman and a doctor, Morgan. But it's getting better, and I'll bet you that fifty years from today, there'll be hundreds of women doctors—maybe thousands!"

And I'm going to be one of them, Morgan thought to herself, pleased at the idea.

Dr. Grace hurried into the building, saying she'd either be but a minute or she'd be back with Eleanor. "You stay here, Morgan. That way I needn't tie Patsy. It's fine if she crops at the grass by the road."

Morgan got down to stretch her legs and rub the horse's side. "Nice old girl," she said softly. "Good old girl." The horse seemed to understand. She lifted her head and nuzzled Morgan's neck and Morgan giggled. The sun was shining brightly now, not hot and moist as it had been all summer, but soft and golden. It was going to be a beautiful day, and all of Chester seemed to know it because the Cove was quickly filling with wagons and strolling townsfolk. Children were playing up and down the road, chasing a ball, a dog, or each other, their voices filled with laughter.

As she watched, the pitch of the youngsters' voices changed to a teasing chant. Morgan saw a woman—no, she was more a girl—walking down the road. Her gait was odd and oddly familiar. There was something about the way she held her

head. Of course. She reminded Morgan of Becky. When she
got closer, Morgan could see that the girl was talking to herself. Or to an invisible someone. She'd heard a few hushed
words spoken about "Crazy Mariah" but nobody seemed to
want to say what was wrong with her. "She's mental," was all
Morgan could get from Mrs. Wainwright, who generally could
not be stopped on any subject.

The children were shouting, "Crazy Mariah! House on fire!
Muck and mire! Crazy Mariah!" and following her. She seemed
not to hear them or see them, so they ran to get closer to her.
One child bent down and picked up a stone and flung it at her.
It hit her in the back, and Mariah turned, her face twisted with
anger. "Stop it!" she shouted. The children laughed and they
all began picking up stones and pelting her with them. The
girl didn't run; she stood still and wrapped her arms around
herself—as if that would protect her.

Morgan didn't think about it. She ran to Mariah and stood
in front of her, shouting at the children, "What are you doing?
How can you be so cruel to one afflicted?"

For a minute, the group was struck dumb. Then one boy
spoke up: "You her mother? You her sister?"

"Aren't we all God's children?" Morgan said, amazed at
her own words. "Get on with the lot of you. Go on, scat, and
leave this poor soul alone, you hear? She can't help the way
she is!"

They went. Morgan was astonished and pleased. Then astonished again, when Mariah turned and spat at her, shouting curses
and words Morgan had only heard once or twice before in her
life, from some drunken men. "Get away from me, Squaw!"
cried Mariah. " 'Fore I scratch out your eyes!" She turned and
ran past Morgan, kicking at her as she went.

Morgan rubbed her calf where Mariah's foot had landed,
thinking, *Just like Becky.* But Mam always said that the spirits
who had taken over Becky were led by one really angry one—
a dead relative who hadn't been buried properly, perhaps.
Morgan had believed that her family was easily possessed by
spirits, some good and some wicked. So when she'd heard the
gossip about Crazy Mariah, she had not expected to see someone almost exactly like Becky. Could a white family, an En-

glish family, be visited by Pequot spirits? She didn't think so. She was beginning to think that maybe it wasn't spirits . . . at least not entirely.

She didn't realize how far off her thoughts were, until she felt a hand on her shoulder.

"Come on," Dr. Grace said. "I've sent Eleanor home in their buggy. Perhaps if she stays in bed, quiet, she won't lose this one." They climbed aboard and clucked the mare into a trot, heading for home.

"What's on your mind, Morgan?" she said all at once. "Something's eating at you, that's plain to see."

"That girl . . . the girl they call Crazy Mariah . . ." And Morgan told Dr. Grace what had happened.

When she stopped talking, Dr. Grace made a face and said, "Some folks are just plain ignorant and don't know enough not to talk in front of the young'uns. As for Mariah . . . oh dear, it's a sad tale. When she was younger, she was as normal as you and me, Morgan. Suddenly, she began to be afraid of things, to hear things nobody else heard . . . I don't know how to describe it to you."

"You don't have to," Morgan said, slowly. Should she tell? She decided yes. "My sister . . . She's like that Mariah. But, see, people thought she heard angels. They came from miles around, to have her touch them and tell them what to do."

"I heard tales of that girl. Your sister, you say? That's very interesting, Morgan. If you don't mind, I'd like you to tell me all about her and I'll write it all down. Will you do that?"

"Of course. But . . ." Morgan hesitated. "Do *you* believe that my sister heard angel voices?"

"She might have," Dr. Grace said. "She could have heard anything. How can we know? But it does sound very much like this illness of the mind they call *dementia praecox* . . . Oh, no, it's . . . I read recently there's a new name for it. *Schizophrenia.*"

An illness of the mind. They had never thought of Becky as being sick. But suddenly, Morgan saw that it might be. If Becky heard angels, she also heard frightening things, things that made her lunge at you and call you evil, or cower in the corner and whisper. At times, she could be old Becky and talk like she used to, too. "Do you think my sister has this dementia precocks? Or that other thing?"

"I can't say without seeing her, or hearing more about it. But it might well be. I'm pretty sure that's what has ahold of poor Mariah. I saw several patients in Philadelphia when I was a girl, and in Boston hospitals, in Syracuse, too, who were a lot like Mariah, and they had *dementia praecox.*"

"I was brought up to believe that spirits come to people in my family, and that we have the power to talk to them or at least to hear them when they speak. I've been in some doubt about it, lately, but still . . . I had a great-great-great-, oh I don't know how many greats grandfather who shook and quaked from a spirit that came into his body. And his sister also talked to the spirits and finally wandered off to live with them. And then there was Quare Auntie . . ."

"Who?"

"That's what they called her but she had a real name. Her Christian name I don't know, but in the old language she was Small Sparrow. She lived in the woods and talked to the spirits. Every once in a while, she would come to our house to get food or to read the future. She was terrible ugly, scrawny and scratched, her hair all filthy and matted and full of knots. I believed Quare Auntie had great magic. Mam always said her family was full of magic and healing powers . . ." Morgan's voice faded a bit. She heard herself talking about magical powers and all of a sudden, it sounded . . . she didn't know *how* it sounded, but she was sure that Dr. Grace would never believe in it. "Are they sure about this dementia precocks thing? Sure that it's a disease?"

"As a matter of fact . . . Nobody is sure about it, and nobody can see where it comes from. But enough people have observed it . . ."

"In other words, it might be spirits."

Dr. Grace laughed. "I suppose it might just as well be spirits as anything else. Yes, you're right about that."

The doctor pulled smartly into the yard near the horse shed and told Patsy to whoa up. As they led the horse into the stable, Morgan suddenly remembered. "Was Mrs. Marshall spotting?" she asked.

Dr. Grace looked grim. "Yes. I hope it won't be another miscarriage. She did carry two to term."

"I could give her something," Morgan said. "To hold the baby in. It always works."

Urging the mare into her stall, Dr. Grace shut the gate and turned to regard Morgan. Then she said, "Why not? Yes, why not? Aren't I the one always griping that these so-called regular doctors won't give any other ideas a chance? They destroyed the hygienic movement, Morgan, sneering at our strange ideas. We said folks ought to bathe regularly, get daily exercise, go out into the sunshine, and cast off their fears of night air, damp, and drafts . . .

"They fought all those ideas, like demons they did, and then they stole them, and now they take all the credit!" She laughed. "Well, I don't want to be guilty of fighting a good idea just because it wasn't mine. But when we give your brew to Eleanor Marshall, let's just say it's a tonic. So no one can accuse us of witchcraft."

Dr. Grace said it as if it were a joke, but Morgan thought to herself, Who's to say it isn't . . . and so what if it is, if it works?

7

June 1883

Young Will Bryant, lying on Dr. Grace's examining table, was hollering blue murder—and who could blame him? He'd gone shinnying up a tree to rescue his cat, crawled out onto a limb without thinking that a branch strong enough for a twelve-pound cat might not hold his nine-year-old weight. And down they'd all come in a great crash: branch, cat, and rescuer. The cat bounded away without so much as a backward look, but poor Will had broken his leg and couldn't stand up. His older brothers had carried him in five minutes ago. Will, as white as a sheet, cried out at every step as they came through the waiting room stuffed with women and children.

Morgan came out of the examining rooms—she was in charge of admitting the patients—and saw in a glance that it was an emergency. She told the others who were waiting, "I think we'd better take Will right away."

"Don't you worry, Morgan," said Sarah Cromwell, in with her monthly cramps. "We can wait. Looks like his leg is broke, don't it?"

"Sure does." You had to wonder, sometimes, why they came in to see a doctor. Most of the women were pretty fair doctors themselves, if it wasn't anything too complicated or strange. But they did love Dr. Grace; they came to her for everything. Her patients were mostly women and their children. Pregnant women. Women who wanted to be pregnant. Women who were pregnant and didn't want to be. Children with broken bones or bad gashes in their feet from running around barefoot. Well babies. Sick babies. It was always noisy in the waiting room, full of cries and hushes and gossip.

Sarah Cromwell spoke up. "I'd wait a year to see Dr. Grace. She changed my life, that's what she did, just by telling me maybe the allopath wasn't treating me the right way for my fainting spells. 'Open those windows, Sarah,' says Dr. Grace, 'and take some beef tea. You need building up, not bleeding.' And blessed if she didn't go down to my kitchen and order me some grilled liver and fresh vegetables. And I felt better the very next day!" There was a murmur of approval; there always was, every time Sarah told her story, which was just about every time she came to see the doctor. "Anemic, that's what I was, and all that bleeding was just making it worse."

Another woman chimed in. She'd gone to a regular doctor, too, because . . . well, to tell the truth, all her friends were going. It was for her cramps, so bad some months she couldn't even get out of bed. But after one or two purges—"they do like their purges, don't they, Sarah?"—she came right back to Dr. Grace.

Old Mrs. Foster spoke up. "Ginger tea, that's the thing for cramps."

"That's all well and good as an old-fashioned way, Mrs. Foster, if you don't mind my saying it. But Miss Morgan here, she gave me her own medicine, squawweed they call it, and I was right as rain. You know what they say about Indian healers—"

At that moment, Dr. Grace called for Morgan to come hold young Will while she pulled that broken bone back into place. Morgan was glad to go. She didn't want anyone asking her too many questions about where she learned about healing, and maybe figuring out that she might know the girl who spoke to the angels. Everyone in Chester had heard of Becky, seemed like, though they didn't have her name or know exactly where she lived. Somewhere near East Haddam, that's all they knew, up above Goodspeed's Hall. Morgan didn't want anyone to think she had magic. Folks already looked at her as if she had some kind of special touch. She knew she had the healing spirit, but that wasn't magic. It was just what she had learned from her mother, and the natural ability she'd been born with. The Indian tribes had been using most of these same medicines since the beginning of time, or so Mam had always told her. All the plants and herbs she made medicine from grew everywhere around here and anyone could gather them. But not many seemed to know how to use them. They'd rather take their troubles to an expert.

Morgan had given Will something for the pain as soon as his brothers brought him in. He still wasn't exactly comfortable, but at least now his howls had turned into moans and a person could hear herself think. Morgan positioned herself by the boy's shoulders, hunkering down so she could hold him tight and talk softly into his ear. "Now, Will, this will hurt you some. Here's a piece of leather for you to bite on. Dr. Grace is real good at setting bones, you know that, so she'll be real quick. All right, then." She tightened her grip on Will, giving Dr. Grace a little nod. One of his brothers was holding the leg above the knee. "Hold it real steady, now, Sam," said Dr. Grace, "and we'll *pull*!" As she said the word, she did it. Will opened his mouth to yell with the pain, but Dr. Grace said, "There, then." And Morgan said, into Will's ear, "It's all over."

"It's over?" The boy was dumbfounded.

"That's right. Now Dr. Grace will put splints on it and tie it real tight and then you can go home."

"Morgan, you fix a bottle of your belladonna mixture for Will here to take with him."

"I have some fresh made," Morgan said, and ran back to the pantry, where they had a physick cupboard. All the plants and herbs she needed to make what Mrs. Wainwright still called "Morgan's messes" came from her garden right by the back door. She poured a measure of painkiller for Will and stoppered the bottle tightly. A few swallows of this should put the pain to sleep . . . and Will, too.

Coming out of the pantry, Morgan saw Si Grisham handing his mother down from their surrey. Poor Mrs. Grisham, who didn't look good at all, was limping. When they got closer, Morgan could see a big angry mark on the side of Mrs. Grisham's face, and that her eye was swollen shut. Morgan waited a moment to see if she could catch Silas's eye—they had become quite friendly of late—but his attention was all on his ma. He had a worried frown on his face.

As soon as the Bryant boys left, Morgan quickly said, "Dr. Grace, Mrs. Grisham has hurt herself again. Real bad, this time." Dr. Grace's lips thinned and she gave a sharp sigh. "She's always falling down the stairs and bumping into things, it seems," Morgan added. She thought there was something odd about Amelia Grisham's many accidents, and she knew Dr. Grace thought so, too. But, hint as she might, Dr. Grace said not one word about it.

"I'll see young Mary Bardwell first. She's due soon and she's healthy as a horse. It'll only take a minute. And then you bring in Mrs. Grisham." The minute she mentioned Silas's ma, her tone became grim. Morgan was more curious than ever. But she did as she was told. When she showed in Mary Bardwell, the woman gave her a big smile. Morgan had managed to stop her from miscarrying five months earlier. Back in the waiting room, Morgan said, "And Mrs. Grisham, Dr. Grace wants to see you next." Not a woman in the room turned to look at the wounded woman, though they all knew her.

Silas whispered something to his mother and followed Morgan out of the room. "Oh, God," he said in a low voice. "This time, she's hurt so bad. He—she—her leg got twisted under her. It's all swole up under her skirt. I know, because I couldn't get on one of her boots. She's wearing a bedroom slipper."

"Wait till I bring her in to Dr. Grace," Morgan said, fighting the urge to put her hand on his arm, fighting the even bigger urge to put her arms around him and comfort him. She was secretly in love with Silas Grisham, but she would die if he ever knew. They had met in the meadow, while she was checking to see which plants grew around Chester. Silas was hunting fossils that day. Once she started talking about her medicines, though, he wanted to know about healing plants, too. He just loved natural history, he told her. He was reading law with Judge Jenkins in Deep River, because his father thought he should be a lawyer, instead of working at the forge. Jered Grisham was the town blacksmith. But Si didn't really want the law, he told her, he'd far rather be doing what she was doing: finding out what plants were good for what, making little drawings of them and describing them so they could be found again. In fact, what he really wanted was to travel around the world and discover plants and animals nobody in Connecticut had ever seen. Like Charles Darwin, he told her, and she had nodded in agreement, though she hadn't a notion who Mr. Darwin was.

Morgan thought Silas was wonderful, so different from all the other young men, who spent their time flexing their muscles and showing off, with never a thought in their heads. She hoped he would be famous and discover many new plants.

She saw that Mary Bardwell was leaving. "Let's bring your ma in to Dr. Grace now, Silas. And then we can go into the kitchen. You look a mite sick. I'll give you something to build up your blood."

"You have anything to build up a man's courage, Morgan?" he asked bitterly. "Never mind, forget I said that. I'll take Ma in and meet you in the kitchen."

Mrs. Wainwright had gone home to give her husband his dinner, so they had the whole kitchen to themselves. Morgan made Silas a beef tea, which he sipped at without appetite or pleasure. Finally, he set it down on the wooden table with a thump.

"I'm seventeen, Morgan!" he announced, as if she didn't already know. "Seventeen. A man grown. I should be able to—I ought to—Why can't I—" He stopped and banged a fist on the table.

"Silas, what's the trouble? I've never seen you so bothered."

"I can't tell you. I want to, but I can't." He began to pace around the big kitchen, his hands jammed into his pants pockets. Watching him, Morgan was torn between worry and admiration. He was the handsomest boy she'd ever seen: tall and slender with a lean, interesting face, deepset eyes that crinkled at the corners when he smiled, and silky dark hair with one lock that was always flopping down over one eye. He had the habit of flinging his head a little bit, to toss the hair back, but in a minute, it was back down on his forehead. He usually wore spectacles and some teased him, calling him Four Eyes. That made Morgan mad; it reminded her of the names she'd been called her whole life. But Silas told her he didn't let it get to him. "I learned a long time ago how to keep my feelings deep inside. That way, nobody can get to them." Well, he wasn't doing that now.

"Whatever it is, Si, you know I won't tell."

"I know that. It's not—" He drew in a raggedy breath that sounded full of pain. "Oh, God, Morgan, he beats her all the time. He hits her over and over and she cowers before him, begging his *forgiveness*! It's so horrible, Morgan. This time, he picked her up and threw her, actually threw her down the cellar stairs. I went after him. But he picked me up, just as if I were a kitten—" Silas's voice broke and he turned his head away, swallowing audibly. "—and he said, 'You mind your manners, boy, or you'll be next.' Then he let me drop, Morgan. My own father let me drop like I was a piece of garbage, and he laughed at me. I'd have grabbed an andiron from the fireplace and clubbed him with it, but poor Ma was crying out that she couldn't get up. Her leg had twisted under her. I had to see to her, I *had* to!"

Morgan grabbed both his arms. "Of course you did. Of course you did!" He looked as if he might collapse right onto Mrs. Wainwright's clean kitchen floor. "You did right, Silas, and now Dr. Grace will see to her."

"What good does it do? He hits her whenever he's displeased. 'Displeased,' that's what he calls it. It can be anything that sets him off. If the meat isn't done quite right or she 'looks at him funny.' And when she's pregnant, he gets worse than ever." Si bent his head, but she saw the tears in his eyes. "I think it's his knocking her around so much that makes her miscarry. He's a brute, Morgan, and I should have killed him. Then he could never hurt her again!"

"Now, Si, you don't want to be thinking that way." Morgan was horrified but not terribly surprised, to tell the truth. Amelia Grisham had too many "accidents" by far. She always said it was her clumsiness. Nobody on this earth, Morgan thought, could be *that* clumsy. Morgan was also aware that Mrs. Grisham had miscarried several times over the years. Everybody knew that. Silas was an only child, and everyone in town had heard Jered Grisham blustering how it was a poor kind of female couldn't seem to hold on to a pregnancy. "Has he ever . . . you know . . . hit *you*?" she asked Silas.

His shoulders slumped. "Yes," he said.

"And did you hit him back?"

"Once. Once I threw a bucket at him—hit him, too—and he beat me pretty good. I was ten, and Dr. Grace came to the house to tend to me. He greeted her and shook her hand and told her how a gang of boys had jumped me for no good reason except that I wore spectacles. I remember her saying, real loud, that maybe the constable should be called and given those boys' names. Well, Pa, he bumbled around for a minute or two, until Dr. Grace stood up and faced him and said, 'Jered, listen to me good because I'm only going to tell you once. I never want to see this boy in this condition again, do you hear me? Because if I do, it may have to be taken to a judge in Hartford or Middletown. Do you understand?' And Pa said, 'You think you can talk to me that way because you're

a doctor.' And she said, 'And you know how everyone believes what a doctor tells them. Isn't that right, Jered?'

"Ever since then, he's left me alone. But I wish he'd go for
me instead of Ma all the time. She can't take much more! And
neither can I!"

"There are lots of men like that, Silas. Your pa isn't the only
one. My mam . . . she was a healer, you know . . . she had
three or four patients whose husbands threw them around. She
always told them to leave, take the kids and hide up in the
woods. Like our family."

"Your family hid in the woods, Morgan? But why?"

Oh dear. She'd always carefully avoided talking about
where she came from, and here she was, blabbing away.

"It's a long story. I'll tell you the next time."

"But—"

"But now we have to think about your ma. Why doesn't she
leave?"

"I don't know!" His hands were balled into fists. "I've
thought and thought about it and I can't figure it out. She's
always telling me *I* should leave."

"Why don't you?" Her heart began to beat hard. If he left
Chester, she would die.

He looked at her in horror. "And leave her alone with him?
I couldn't!"

"Your mother is not as helpless as you might think . . ."
Morgan said, after a moment. She told him what Dr. Grace
had told her.

Amelia Grisham used to send away for patent-medicine
abortifacients, ordering them from advertisements in the newspaper. Female Regulator. Periodical Drops. Woman's Friend.
Graves Pills for Amenorrhea. " 'Though perfectly harmless
to the most delicate, yet ladies are earnestly requested not to
mistake their condition as MISCARRIAGE WOULD CER-
TAINLY ENSUE,' " Morgan quoted. "You see, they aren't
allowed to say outright what the pills are for. Abortions aren't
supposed to be happening, that's what Dr. Grace says. This
woman who lived out in the country near Killingworth, she
used to give abortions, and everybody knew it. Then a girl died
and she was arrested and taken to Hartford and put on trial."

"Well, if God makes a baby, maybe we shouldn't interfere," Silas said.

Men were such innocents, Morgan thought. "You have no idea," she said patiently, "how many ladies quietly end their pregnancies—nor how often. Dr. Grace says she'll bet there's at least one abortion for every ten live births, just around here. Listen, Dr. Grace says your mother even ordered an abortion instrument, which she used once, but then Dr. Grace yelled at her. She could kill herself that way, you know. Do you think she threw it away? Oh no. She passed it along to another woman. Who was mighty glad to get it, I might add."

"All right, she's ended her own pregnancies. But what am I going to do about . . . *him*? What can anyone do against him?" Silas moaned and buried his head in his hands.

"Don't you worry, we'll think of something," Morgan soothed. An idea was starting to form in her mind.

At the end of office hours, around three in the afternoon, Dr. Grace put on her bonnet and her gloves and announced that she'd be taking out the buggy for a while. "I'll be back before supper," she said. Something in her face told Morgan not to ask any questions, but she was pretty sure it had something to do with Silas's mother.

It was nearly dark when Silas came back to see Morgan. He'd walked, he told her, because his father had saddled up their horse and galloped away to God knew where. Si was out of breath and even more upset than he had been earlier.

"Dr. Grace tried to talk sense to him. She went to see him at the smithy this afternoon, and I guess she must have given him holy whatfor. Because when he came home for supper, he was in a fury. He grabbed Ma and twisted her arm behind her, so hard I could hear something go *ping*. He made her promise she would never go to 'that female so-called doctor' again. I could see he'd broken her arm, so when he started to leave, I asked, 'What about this broken arm, Pa? You can't leave her with a broken arm!' 'Oh, can't I? And who's to stop me? She got exactly what she deserved, siccing that old maid quack on me!' Then he said, 'And by God, you'll go to a *regular* doctor'—excuse me, Morgan, but those were his words—

'someone in the Male Practice who knows what a man has to put up with from females!' And out he goes."

Dr. Grace always snorted if someone mentioned the Male Practice. "Since when," she liked to say, "is healing a commodity that can be charged for according to the 'amount' of healing! Nonsense, that's what it is. Either the patient improves or he doesn't." She hated the idea that the more a doctor did, the more he could charge. "That's what's called heroic medicine, Morgan, and it never did make any sense to me. They just use the most powerful remedy they can get their hands on and you know what that is? *Calomel!* During the Great War, they must've used up a hundred ton of calomel—big doses for acute problems, small doses for chronic problems. Didn't care what kind of a problem it was!" By this time, Dr. Grace would be all red in the face. "There's just one trouble with calomel," she'd say bitterly. "It kills you!" No, Dr. Grace did not think much of the Male Practice, and she liked being labeled "irregular" even less.

Well, maybe tomorrow, Jered Grisham would force his wife to a "regular" doctor, but tonight, at least, someone who cared could help her. Morgan got up from the rocker to go get her medicine bag. "I'll set your mother's arm."

"No, no, what if he comes back? I'd never forgive myself," he said, taking her hand, "if you got hurt because of me." How her heart leapt up at those words. "You tell me what I should do and I'll do it. To fix up her arm. Tomorrow, after he's gone, maybe you can come see her."

"Of course." She told him, slowly and clearly, how to set the arm and how to bind it so it wouldn't heal crooked. Then she gave him a vial of painkilling medicine. "But before you start, give her a good shot of whisky. And tell her I'll be over first thing in the morning."

The next day, Morgan was at the Grishams' back door bright and early. She knew the smith would be at his shop by daybreak, building up his fires. The farmers would start bringing in their horses for shoes and their tools for mending soon. Later on, it would be housewives, with pots and pans to mend or a hook to be made. He'd be busy till dinnertime, when she'd be long gone.

Silas's ma was scared to death; anyone could see that. She kept looking around to make sure her husband wasn't sneaking in the back door. She said to Morgan that she told her husband she'd never go to a Male Practice doctor. "Well, if you won't go to an allopath, you'll damn well dose yourself with pills from the store," he'd told her. "I know how Dr. Grace hates patent medicines," Mrs. Grisham said to Morgan. "But what can I do? If he says no more Dr. Grace, then no more Dr. Grace is how it will be." And tears began to leak out of her eyes.

All the time Amelia was talking, Morgan was checking on the arm, making sure it would mend properly. Silas had done a fine job, and she told his mother so. "Morgan, listen," Mrs. Grisham said, still crying, "please don't tell anyone about this. And don't try to call in the law. You see what happens if anyone tries to help. There *is* no help for me. I just can't seem to do things right. I don't know why. I was smart enough when I was a little girl, learned my letters faster than anyone else in the schoolroom. But now . . . I just don't know . . . I can't seem to keep my mind straight on anything."

Morgan said, "There's nothing wrong with your mind, Mrs. Grisham, nothing at all. You pay no heed to what your husband says. He's only trying to put you in doubt of your own thoughts. Now . . ." She paused. Could she trust this woman? Mrs. Grisham was bright enough, and pleasant, but faced with her husband, she became helpless and frightened. Still . . . she *was* an intelligent woman. Morgan knew she'd been a schoolteacher before Jered Grisham swept her off her feet in a whirlwind courtship. She was still pretty, though mighty peaked and pinched-looking. Well, she was Silas's mother, and Morgan would do anything to have Silas take her hand again and smile tenderly at her.

"Listen, Mrs. Grisham. In my family, there are many shamans, many witches. And I have a charm, an amulet . . ." She reached under her blouse. "It has been in my family since the beginning of time. It has magical powers. One of my many-times-great-grandmothers was a *moigu*—that's Indian for witch doctor—and she owned this amulet." She lowered her voice. "It can hunt down a person for me. I know the chants. I know how to make the offering of Indian tobacco ... It grows in these parts, you know. I could take some to a private place, burn a little of it, and wish evil on him. Your husband." Mrs. Grisham turned even paler and reached out to clutch Morgan's hand, but she didn't say a word.

"Or," Morgan confided, as Silas's ma stared into her eyes, almost not breathing, "I can go gather some grave dirt and bring it in here. Or, give me something he wears next to his skin and I will take it to the graveyard. Maybe that's easiest. A nightshirt, maybe."

Mrs. Grisham looked horrified for one moment, and then so hopeful, it was heartbreaking. Suddenly, her face closed and became a perfect blank as the sound of footsteps was heard.

"Excuse me," she whispered. Getting up from her chair, she began bustling about, preparing the noonday dinner for her husband, even though it was nowhere near dinnertime. Morgan felt so bad for her.

When the smith walked in, Morgan was struck by how large a man he was. He had bulging muscles and those same deepset eyes that Silas had, only his were mean as a snake's.

"Who might you be?" he asked, looking her up and down boldly.

"A friend of Silas from the town, Mr. Grisham."

"Pretty tall for a woman ain't you? Where's Silas, then?"

"He's with Judge Jenkins, Jered, as he always is this time of day," Mrs. Grisham said.

"So he is, so he is." Butter wouldn't melt in his mouth, Morgan thought. Maybe he thought she was going to leave. Well, she wasn't. She had a feeling that, the minute the door had closed behind her, he'd be giving Amelia the back of his big meaty hand. Morgan's hands itched to feel his thick neck between them. "Well, then, I only came by to make sure my little Amelia here was mending." He reached out and grabbed her arm, squeezing it, and she yelped with pain. "Not too good, I see," he said. "Maybe you'll listen to me and go to a real doctor next time." He turned to Morgan with his false smile. "She is the clumsiest woman in ten counties, I vow. Falls down if you say boo."

Morgan kept her face the same, but she wanted to kill him

so badly that she could taste the mixture of blood and bile rising in the back of her throat. It was frightening.

She excused herself quickly, and left. Her plan had now taken a very definite shape. On her way out, she went to the clothesline and took down a large shirt. She knew it was his, not only because of the size but because there were thousands of tiny little burns in it—probably from the forge. She rolled up the shirt and tucked it under her arm. She'd take it to the graveyard without saying anything to anyone. She was going to put a curse on Jered Grisham he'd not soon forget!

8

July 1883

Grace leaned back against the doorjamb, enjoying the heat of the afternoon sun on her face, even though ladies were never supposed to allow a freckle or a sunburn to sully their lily-white skins. She reckoned, after the life she'd led, she was no lady. But that was fine. Being a doctor meant she was exempt from a lot of the rules of polite society. In a funny way, it was like being desexed. And considering . . .

She was drifting off to sleep and that wouldn't do. Her office hours were over—the waiting room was always packed in the summertime, when children were free to roam and climb trees and swim and hurt themselves—but there was some cleaning up to do. She was sleepy; she'd been wakened by a knock on the door in the wee hours of the morning—the distraught father of a sick baby—and had got back at daybreak.

Opening her eyes, she tried to concentrate on watching Morgan pound plantain leaves, near her on the porch. "Jered

Grisham's down with a high fever," Grace told the younger woman. "Came on him real sudden, and won't let go. He's raving, so sick he doesn't know I'm attending him. Amelia won't trust anyone else. She says if he opens his eyes and seems to be himself, I'm to jump and run." She laughed briefly. "Well, she should know I'm not about to do that. I'm not afraid of Jered Grisham—especially not the way he looks now. He's weak as a newborn babe. If he weren't such a great ox of a man, I'd say he was dying."

The blood drained out of Morgan's face; she looked like death. What in tarnation was going on? The girl had been going out in the evening lately, saying she needed fresh air, needed exercise, wanted to look at the stars. Grace didn't care if Morgan was out sparking in the dark—she'd noticed how the girl looked calf-eyes at young Silas—but somehow she didn't think it was romance that kept Morgan out at night. No, it was something else. But what?

Morgan spoke at last. "Dying?" she asked in a faint voice.

"I've seen a sickness like this before, and always in summer. But it usually strikes children. Sometimes it causes paralysis. There's a girl in Essex who has to be in a wheelchair. It took her legs. I must say, I've never seen it come on so fast, or so hard." She watched Morgan's face. Yes, the girl was fussed, definitely. "Silas tell you anything about his pa being sick?"

"No. Well, he said something yesterday, but only that his pa was laid low with a fever. Not about him raving or anything . . ." Morgan was talking very fast. Grace decided she would give a good deal to be able to read that young woman's mind. "My pa used to be sickly-like," Morgan went on quickly. If she thought Grace couldn't tell when someone was changing the subject, she had another think coming. "He was strong and clever, but he'd take sick real sudden, with headaches I guess. As much as Ma and me would doctor him, we'd just have to wait for him to get better. The worst was when his right leg gave him pain. The rebs got him when he was fighting in the Great War."

" 'The Great War!' That's not what I call it! It was a civil war, Morgan, and that means brother against brother! A terrible thing. Oh yes, the young men thought it was a great adventure.

And, I must admit, so did the rest of us at first. What a sight it was, all those handsome young men, so eager to dress up in their uniforms and die for the Confederacy."

"The Confederacy! But—"

"I was living down South when the first shot was fired. I'd just been married . . ."

"Married?" The look of amazement on Morgan's face was comical.

"Yes, married. I know I seem older than God to you, but once, I was a pretty young thing, and very happily married to Jedadiah Chapman, son of the Reverend and Mrs. Curtis Chapman of Memphis, Tennessee. Jed came to visit a cousin in Philadelphia, you see, and the cousin's family were friends of ours. I was Grace Henderson then, of Philadelphia, daughter of Dr. John and Emma, sister of John Thomas, eighteen years old and full of life. Jed and I were seated next to each other at a dinner party . . ." She laughed. "Actually, the dinner was in my parents' house. My mother had decided to put us together 'to see what might transpire.' Poor Mama, she longed to see me safely married, because Papa took me with him to the hospital. I went on rounds with him, and he explained anything I wanted to know. Which was everything!" Morgan wiped off her hands, and joined her on the bench. "I didn't even quail at the sight of blood—much less faint, as a proper maiden ought to do. So you see, Morgan, it was urgent that I become engaged before I destroyed my reputation forever!

"Being a good and obedient daughter," Grace continued, with a little smile, "I obliged by falling in love with Jed Chapman. But when we said we wanted to be married by Christmas and back down to Memphis by the New Year, my mother wept. 'Mother, this is what you've always wanted for me!' I protested. 'But I never thought your husband would take you right away from us, all the way to Tennessee!' Mama said Tennessee as if it were the name of a disease.

"Nevertheless, by January of 1862, Mr. and Mrs. Jedadiah Chapman had taken up residence in Memphis, in his parents' large brick house. A place filled with beautiful things: china figurines, gilt mirrors, carved mahogany furniture from England, every kind of beautiful carpet and velvet draperies, even an ornate ebony piano that the ladies played. But few books. I noticed that right away, and no Bach for the piano, only light tunes for singing or dancing. My mother-in-law, Mary Martha, and Jed's sisters Sally and Cissie were good looking and always elegantly dressed. They were the kind of women I knew my mother would approve. They were demure and giggly and given to gossip. Once or twice when I ventured to talk about my visits with my father to the hospital, I was begged to desist, 'or, I vow, Grace, our mama will faint dead away!' Indeed, Mama Chapman would be fanning herself energetically and calling for one of the servants to bring her a glass of port for her nerves!

"It was a very different world than the one I had grown up in, Morgan. But I loved Jed so much, it seemed as if nothing else mattered. Then, suddenly, he'd signed up with Israel Fellowes' company, ready to join the battle. We couldn't have been in Memphis more than two weeks. There was such war fever, then, so much patriotic fervor. All the young men wanted to go and fight for the Confederacy and their land. Many of the wealthy plantation owners in the South formed private military companies, which they outfitted and trained. Fellowes' Followers his group called themselves, and they were all dying to go wherever the fighting was. They died, all right, and Jed was one of the first . . . But that was much later, of course.

"General Grant had been sailing up the Tennessee River and on the sixth of February 1862, he was only four miles from Fort Henry, very close to us. Of course, Jed's company rushed to join General A. S. Johnston's forces, sent to defend the fort.

"I was left at home with the women: my mother-in-law, two sisters-in-law with hardly a single brain amongst them—or so I thought—and the slaves. I was at my wits' end because I hated being idle. In his family, unlike my own, a good education and keen mind were considered something of an oddity, to be hidden from view. They all kept shushing me at dinner parties and dances, and then explained how Yankee women were so unusual, weren't they? With Jed gone, I had no one to talk to, no one to hold me tight, no one to look into my eyes

and tell me I was all the world in one person . . . no one to
make love to me, no one to love.

"There was nothing to do but visit other gossipy women, or
call in the dressmaker, or give teas. However, we all scanned
the newspaper for news of the war. So I was aware when most
of the troops were withdrawn from Fort Henry, leaving the
fort open to attack.

"During the next ten days, the rebel forces did nothing to
stop Grant's advance. In fact, they decided to abandon Fort
Donelson, too. All the higher-ups escaped by boat at night,
leaving General Buckner there with 11,500 soldiers. Buckner
asked Grant for his terms and Grant's answer—a surprise,
since the two had been friends at West Point—was no terms
except 'unconditional and immediate surrender.' To everybody's
consternation, Buckner agreed and Grant's forces got 11,500
prisoners, 40 cannon, and, most importantly, food. It was damned
hard to get supplies to the troops when they were on the move—
even a bunch of women in a mansion in Memphis knew *that*.

"You can imagine how happy and relieved I was, when at
last a letter arrived from Jed, who was in Murfreesboro. I still
know every word of it by heart. 'My darling wife,' it began, 'I
write you, wishing I had better news to give. We are with General Johnston, hoping to move in a day or two to unite with
Beauregard's forces at Corinth. We are not happy about the
surrender and abandonment of two of our forts. I wish I understood better what the generals are thinking, but such is not to
be my fate, as I have yet to meet one face to face . . .' I read
that part aloud to everyone. When I started to go on, I saw his
words of love, and I mumbled something about the rest being
of a more personal nature. Which made my sisters-in-law
giggle and my mother-in-law fan herself fiercely.

"Now that we knew where Fellowes' Followers were, we
all grabbed for the paper every day. We read aloud to each
other and traced events on a large map of Tennessee that Jed's
father had brought us. When Grant sent six divisions to Shiloh, Johnston's boys, my Jed among them, moved against the
Union forces. I marked his path with a pen and prayed for my
husband . . .

"Is all this war talk boring you, Morgan?" Grace asked.

She had forgotten how much she remembered. It was flooding back.

"No, no! Pa used to tell me stories, but his were all about the dirty rebs, of course. Oh, I'm sorry, I only meant that it's interesting, to hear the other side. What's strange is, it sounds pretty much the same," Morgan said.

"I think when you're wet and cold and hungry and fearing for your life every minute, it doesn't matter which side you're on. It *is* the same. Well. What happened is that on April seventh the Union forces went on the offensive—they had fresh troops—and by four P.M., Johnston's boys were in retreat— very bad news for us women waiting at home. On the same day, Morgan, an island in the Mississippi River was taken by Union forces. That meant, you see, that the river was open nearly to Memphis. Well, you never heard such a wailing and a weeping as there was in the Chapman household that evening . . .

"As for me, I was thoroughly fed up. I'd been reading that women up North actually left their homes—even their children, if they had them—and went to tend wounded and ill soldiers. But not in Memphis, not from *that* house! In that house, panic and hysteria reigned.

" 'Oh dear Lord, what's to become of us now, Mr. Chapman?' cried my mother-in-law. 'What *shall* become of us?' To which he gave no reply, just mumbled, 'Now, Mother, now Mother.'

"That would just set Sally and Cissie off. 'We'll be raped, that's what, Mama!' 'We'll be killed! Grant's men will bust down the door and come right in here and shoot us dead and then steal everything in the house. You know what Yankees are like. Oh, except for *you*, Grace.' " She snorted at the memory. "And then there were cries of 'My silver!' 'My jewels!' 'My trousseau linens!' That last was from Cissie who planned to marry Abel Carter when he got back from the war. *If* he got back, I thought. If any of them got back. Well, I for one was not going to sit there having the vapors and weeping.

"I had a good long talk with myself. I was a woman of the North, now wasn't I? And there I sat, knitting socks and listening to silly women become hysterical! What else could I do? And then I had it. I could take myself up to Shiloh and find Jed. Once I'd done that, I could concentrate on tending wounded soldiers. I knew almost as much as most doctors. I could be a big help.

"Once decided, I wasted no time. I left that very night, after the house was sound asleep."

"Weren't you scared?" Morgan asked. "A woman, alone, at night, during a war?"

Grace paused, an amused look coming over her face. "Well, I didn't go alone into the dark exactly as a woman, Morgan. I hacked my hair off to just below my ears so I could pass for a boy. Being tall and having a fairly husky voice I felt I could be a very young boy whose voice had not totally changed."

"That was so brave!" Morgan said, admiringly.

"I guess it was. Although, at the time, I didn't think of it that way. I just knew I had to do *something* useful and it was the only way. I dug in Jed's wardrobe and came up with riding clothes and a broad-brimmed hat. I had small breasts, so it was easy to bind them down with a length of linen. Another cloth wound round my waist and the pants fit just fine. 'Not a bad-looking young man,' I thought, and I tipped my hat to myself. 'How do you do, sir?' I said to my reflection, trying to imitate Jed's Southern drawl. I was mighty pleased with myself, let me tell you! I grinned at the man in the mirror and christened him Beau. I'd be Jed's brother Beau.

"On my way out, the steps creaked a bit, and my heart began to race, but nobody stirred. Out through the kitchen I went, out the back, glad I'd taken a cape from the hall stand. It was a bit chilly. Each step I took in the darkness made me ever more sure of myself, and by the time I got to the barn, I was all set for adventure. In fact, I felt just like a young man would, striding out to the barn, picking myself a fine steed, saddling up, and riding out, on my way to Shiloh.

"When I got there, though, I found that Johnston's army had left, marching north into Virginia. But the ground at Shiloh was covered with the wounded, the dying, and the dead. The stench was horrible; even the horse reared up, wanting to leave. I tied him to a tree and walked about, hoping I would not see that beloved face with the blue eyes dimmed by fever . . . or worse. If I heard a moan, I stopped to see if there was anything I could do. But I had nothing but the clothes on my back, not even a water bottle. I heard voices talking and I listened, eager to learn any news of Johnston's boys. One soldier, too young to have grown a beard like most of the others, lay dead, a puppy in his arms. Two of the walking wounded were trying to get the dog to leave its master. As I watched, they coaxed the animal to them, but he only whined and cried and ran back to the corpse, curling up in the lifeless arms. I wanted to cry, but I couldn't. If I gave into my feelings and wept, the game would surely be up.

"I'd noticed three huge tents that had to be the hospital wards. I walked up to the first one, took a deep breath, and walked in. The place was crowded with wounded. The smell was awful, and the air filled with moans and cries. Most of the patients had been laid on the bare ground as there were only a few cots, and those were saved for delirious and dying men. The light was dim, but after a minute or two, I could see two or three women, their heads swathed in turbans, their dresses covered by aprons stained with dirt, blood, and God only knew what else. They were moving from man to man, seeing what had to be done. Well, I reckoned, so would I. I strode about the tent, gazing at each patient. I had my hands clasped behind my back, an imitation of my dear father when he made his rounds, trying to look as if I were a doctor and belonged there.

"As I came close to one of the cots, I saw that one of the women was draping an amputated arm with a dirty blanket. I raced over to her. 'Please, ma'am,' I said, making my voice as gruff as I could, 'when there's an open wound, you must put only clean cloths on it, and clean dressings.'

"My heart was pounding in my chest, I can tell you, as I waited for her to unmask me. But she only bowed her head and said, 'I'm sorry, Doctor. But we're awfully short on water for washing up.'

"I was elated! It was going to work! So I put myself into the role with passion. 'Short on hot water? When it's there to be had in every river and stream?'

" 'We've not got the vessels to boil it in, nor the slaves to fetch it for us. And when we ask for help from the town, they spit on us. They think all women here are . . . camp followers. It's all we can do to make sure each man gets a sip of water and brandy and a spot to lie on. There's no medicine to be had, not since the federal blockade. We do what we can, but what we need are more doctors. You're a godsend.'

" 'Not yet, I'm not,' says I. 'But perhaps I can help. Which way is the nearest town?'

"She pointed out the way, and I got on my horse and rode off. I went from house to house and from store to store, begging for large pots, for old material for bandages, and galloped back only when I was so loaded, I could carry no more. The townsfolk had promised to ride out with as many cots as they could muster. As I rode, I thought. They had all taken me for a doctor . . . a doctor I would stay. And who was to say nay? I knew enough to behave properly as a doctor. I knew enough to realize that the amputation I'd seen in the tent had been very badly done. It was already infected. I made plans. I would put hot towels on it and see if I could draw out the pus, but, judging from the man's fevered condition, it was probably already too late. Seeing the filthy state of things in that place, I wouldn't have been surprised to learn that some stupid surgeon had hacked off the arm with a dirty ax. Or the sword the soldier had killed others with. It was the same ignorance my father kept fighting in his hospital. What I'd seen in that tent made my blood boil. Men were dying, not from the battle but of poor treatment or no treatment at all. And now, the stupid blockade that declared medicines to be a contraband of war! It was sinful!

"When I re-entered the tent, I was greeted with warmth and relief by the weary volunteers. Someone else was there, a volunteer surgeon, a man who introduced himself as Charles Gillis. Suddenly, I was not so sure of my disguise and I was very nervous, talking to him. He seemed to find me a perfectly acceptable male, however. He thanked me profusely for the badly needed supplies. 'We need everything we can get, although I'm not sure how much good it'll do,' he said. 'Many are suffering from exposure, or dysentery, and from mumps, diphtheria, chicken pox . . .'

" 'Children's diseases!' I cried, unable to believe my ears.

"He gave a wry smile. 'Yes. So many of our Southern boys come from the most isolated rural places you can imagine. They'd never been exposed until they left home. And now, all those childhood diseases are raging through the ranks. It means they can't fight for a while, but at least they're not dying. What's causing all the deaths, and there are far too many of them, are dirt and unsanitary conditions. Not to mention all the amputations,' he finished, with a grimace.

" 'All surgeons want to cut, that's how they're trained.' I had to bite my tongue. I'd almost said, 'My father says.' I would have to remember that *I* was the doctor.

" 'True enough,' he said. 'I'm a surgeon. But to cut only because it's fast and needs less care than an infection—! That's tantamount to murder, in my opinion. But there's nobody to give my opinion to—except you, now.' He laughed. He reminded me of Jed—not in his looks, although he too wore spectacles that softened his eyes—but in his cheery good humor. He said, 'You see, Doctor—but I don't even know your name!'

" 'Chapman. Beau Chapman.' I looked him square in the eyes, though the lying still bothered me.

" 'Dr. Chapman, you're the answer to a prayer. No, don't bother with those boys over there. They'll all recover. They all have the measles! And these have bloody feet from marching and fighting without shoes. Here's one got trampled by his own horse, frightened by the cannon. But here's the fellow I'm concerned about. He took a tolerable lot of shot in his knee and some idiot amputated, instead of digging the shot out. And now, you can see what's transpired. His leg is swollen with infection, up into the groin area—*what is it?*'

"I had made some kind of involuntary sound as I stared at the patient. The fellow with the amputated leg was my own beloved, my beautiful Jed. Not beautiful now. He was covered with lice, stank to high heaven; his eyes were open but focusing on nothing. And I could say nothing, do nothing that might give me away. I wanted to fall to my knees and gather my darling boy in my arms, and cry my grief to heaven! And I could not!

" 'My h—my brother!' I cried, glad that my poor whirling brain could still function. 'It's my brother Jed! Oh, Jed!' I felt free to weep—even the bravest man might weep for his brother—and I knelt by him, saying, 'Dr. Gillis, please, hot water and a clean towel of some kind.' I didn't know how long it took Gillis; time was standing still. Jed was trying to talk, but only a hoarse whisper would come out. 'Brandy here!' I cried. 'And quickly!' I wet his lips with the brandy and poured a little into his mouth, watching with gratitude when I saw him swallow.

"When Gillis came back with a steaming piece of wet cloth, I washed Jed's face. The tears were pouring down my cheeks, and over and over again, I prayed, 'Oh, God, please, God!'

" 'I hate this war!' I cried, holding Jed's hand, willing him to open his eyes and see that his sweetheart had come to him. But he was not in his right mind, and while I knelt by him, his breathing became more labored and, as I watched in horror, he struggled more and more for air. In the end, I watched him die, unable to do anything to help him or ease his suffering. Then I put my head back and howled with grief and no one remarked upon it or found it strange. When at last I was able to quiet my cries and slow my tears, I became aware that Dr. Gillis and another surgeon were standing beside me.

" 'I'm sorry. . . ,' the other man said.

"Then Gillis explained: 'We need to move your . . . brother outside. There are men who need to be out of the weather.' His brown eyes were soft behind the glinting spectacles.

" 'Of course,' I said. Of course. Because Jed was dead. *Dead.* And my life had changed forever.

"I don't know where I found the strength," Grace said to Morgan, who hadn't moved even an inch, she was that enthralled, her eyes wet with sympathetic tears. "I helped bury him, I know that, and I took his spectacles—I still have them—and his Bible. Someone had stolen his pocket watch and the fob, as well as his good leather boots. There was nothing else I wanted, except to leave that place and get back home. And that didn't mean Memphis, Tennessee, I can tell you that. I was determined to get back to my own mother and father, in Philadelphia, or die trying."

"Were you still pretending you were a doctor and a man?"

"Oh yes, of course. I followed Johnston's army northward, to Virginia. Someone in Shiloh had taken my horse, so I began to walk. Then I saw a horse wandering in a field, and took him. I rode along with the straggling lines of men, moving east toward Pittsburg Landing. The men were sure they would push the advancing Union troops right into the river and win the day. By then, it was the second week in April. Before long General Buell arrived with fresh troops and routed the Southerners. When they retreated to Corinth, I didn't go with them. Along the way, I'd picked up better garments—from dead men, Morgan. That was what everyone did. You had to, if you wanted to survive, and I wanted to survive. I had a buckskin jacket and leather pants and hat and could be from anywhere. So I dropped the Southern accent I'd put on for the rebs, and moved up through the Union lines, asking for my real brother, John Thomas Henderson of the Fifth Pennsylvania. I became George Henderson, surgeon, and I attached myself to the first Union troops I found.

"Virginia was beautiful, Morgan, with broad peaceful farms, and oats and wheat growing just as if there had never been a war. No more swamps and rutted impassable roads there. Instead, well used country roads in marvelous condition. The Union army picked up cattle and let the horses and cattle forage in the fields as they went. We took what fruits and vegetables were growing, of which there were plenty. Every once in a while, we'd all come to a halt to reconnoiter and find out what was happening with the rebel army. Otherwise, we just kept moving, leaving the sick and wounded behind with medicine and food. Many was the time I was tempted to stay back with them and tend to them, but I needed to get home alive. So I did the best I could while I was there and had to be content with that.

"All along the way, there were the dead and the nearly dead. Every kind of building was pressed into service as a hospital. I tended soldiers in stables, churches, warehouses, schools, courthouses. We all worked so hard to save them, but most of them died anyway. After a while, you just had to harden your heart or you felt you might die, too, of the grief.

"In July we came upon the Union field hospital at Savage's Station. McClellan had his headquarters there, so it was an important place, busy and bustling. Norfolk and Portsmouth—those are cities in Virginia, you know—had already fallen without any bloodshed, and most of Virginia was Union territory."

Grace stopped speaking for a moment, seeing the scene in her mind's eye. It had been a long, long time since she'd allowed herself to remember any of it. She'd put it all away, in the same place where she'd tucked away her love for Jed Chapman.

"Savage's Station was just one small house, that's all. The wounded and sick lay all about on the ground under the trees and in twenty large tents that had been pitched in the garden. Dr. John Swinburne was in charge of medical care. I introduced myself, as Dr. George Henderson, of course, volunteer surgeon, and offered my help.

" 'Pleased to have you, young man,' " Swinburne said, 'although we could have used you more a couple of weeks ago. It happens that we have help coming. Dr. Albert Baunot of Pittsburgh, Pennsylvania, is on his way with a corps of surgeons and nurses. But you'll be welcome among them, I'm sure. We never have enough doctors.'

"Oh, Morgan, let me tell you, my heart sank. I'd met Dr. Baunot, when he visited Father's hospital in Philadelphia. Not just one casual meeting, how-do-you-do and good-bye, but two or three times. He and Father were friends from their medical training, and Dr. Baunot had eaten with us at home, several times. Would he recognize me and send me packing? Or, worse, just see through my poor disguise and make me a laughingstock? Well, I reckoned there was no backing down now. It was a chance I had to take. So I smiled and said I'd be most pleased to meet Dr. Baunot and in the meantime, where was I needed? The answer was: everywhere.

"I worked so hard, Morgan, and not just at doctoring. We all pitched in and did whatever needed doing, from laundry to foraging to feeding the animals to surgery to reading out the funeral service. Since there was little medicine, we used folk remedies from our grandmothers' days. Dogwood bark for fever. Sweet gum bark boiled with milk for dysentery. Holly bark to chew for a cough.

"At Savage's Station, I saw the famous Mrs. John Harris at work, nursing, writing letters, and doing wonderful good deeds for the sick and dying soldiers. They loved her, Morgan, and there wasn't a soul could accuse *her* of being a camp follower!"

"But Dr. Baunot! What happened with him? Oh please, don't keep me in suspense!"

"Ah, Dr. Baunot. Well, he came charging in with his horses and his supplies and his nurses and his attendants, and had not a minute to glance in my direction. Once, I thought the jig was up. I was working on a man's shoulder—he'd taken several balls in it, I'd removed them as carefully as I could, and cleaned out the wounds. I was bandaging it when Dr. Baunot came by. He stopped to watch me, walked on, and then stopped in his tracks, and I said to myself, *Here it comes.*

"He whirled around, fixing me with his eyes. I can tell you, the sweat was trickling down my back and my heart was thumping hard. But I stared him straight in the eye. I was sure he would point a finger and reveal me as a medical imposter and, even worse, a woman trying to pass as a man. He stared at me, then shook his head as if to say, *No, no, I only imagined it.* 'Sorry,' says he. 'Carry on, Doctor, carry on. Neat work, by the way.' And away he went. Then I knew I had nothing to worry about, I was going to fool them all. There was laughter of relief all through my body but I dared not let it out. The call was a bit too close for comfort, though, and I left a couple of days later, saying I had to find my brother.

"But something important had happened to me, Morgan. I had grown up. There's nothing like a war to push you out of innocence. More important, I knew I was going to go to medical college when I got back home. I knew I had to be a doctor, a real doctor, because that's what I was born to do."

"Oh, Dr. Grace," Morgan said, her eyes shining. "Do you suppose I could be one, too?"

"Yes, of course, you could. Why not? You're real good at it—gifted, I'd say."

"I am? Really? Oh, to have you say it, Dr. Grace—! It makes all the difference! Just wait till I tell Silas!"

"I'm sure he'll be pleased to have your confidence," Grace said dryly. And, she added silently, *I hope you also tell him what you've been doing so mysteriously every night, before you get yourself into real trouble.*

Morgan had been good at keeping her secret, but it didn't take a genius to figure out that a girl who grew up with shamans and witches and spirit talkers was not out every night just taking a walk and looking at the constellations. No, she was making some kind of magic, Grace was sure of it. But *what* kind of magic? That was the question.

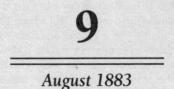

9

August 1883

"Pa's dying," Silas said.

"Dying?" Morgan's mouth went dry but she kept her voice even. "But . . . I thought . . . wasn't he just sick with a fever?"

"It just keeps getting worse. You remember how he couldn't move his legs. But now, it's . . . Sometimes you can hear his breathing stop and you think, *That's it.* Then, suddenly, he'll make this odd noise and begin to breathe again. Very scary, it is."

Morgan had put on a listening face, but she wasn't really listening. She was shriveling inside. It had worked. It had really worked. She'd done it. Only now, she didn't feel so good about it. It was one thing to say the words to put on a curse, but it was quite another thing to hear how Mr. Grisham couldn't move and almost couldn't breathe, and to know it was all your fault.

Still, she'd known even before meeting Silas this evening that things were bad. Dr. Grace went over every day, twice a day, to see what she could do for Jered Grisham. Sometimes, she took Morgan with her.

This morning, Dr. Grace had asked, "Anything in your medicine bag that'll do magic on him? Nothing I'm doing is helping at all." She'd actually said the word: *magic.* It gave Morgan the fantods. It was terrible to have such a secret, wishing she could ask Dr. Grace for help but not daring. Mam had warned her. Mam had always said, "Don't go using spells before you know what you're doing with them." *But I had to be so smart,* Morgan thought, squirming. She'd been so mad at Mr. Grisham and now look what she'd done! She didn't know how to take *off* the curse! She wished she could turn time around and go back to that day when she'd taken his shirt off the clothesline. She'd leave it right where it was!

But she couldn't go back in time, and there was an end to it. She'd have to search her memory and see if she couldn't come up with something to reverse the spell. The minute she got back home, she promised herself. In the meantime, it was a fine evening, and the sky had begun to turn dark blue around the edges. One pale star was already visible in the heavens. And she was with Silas. Being with him meant everything to her. Every minute they had together was precious. The meadow they were strolling through smelled sweet with just a hint of the dirt underneath. Every living thing was heavy with its own ripeness. It was the part of summer she liked best, before the changeable late August weather arrived with its damp heat that sat like a wet blanket over all the countryside. Silas held her hand fast, and every few seconds, he turned to give her that special smile of his. So, she knew he'd stopped thinking about his father, too.

She was on fire with wanting him. She could hardly wait. She wanted to run, run, run, to their secret place, throwing off her clothes as she went. But Silas liked to draw out the waiting. He said it drew out the pleasure. So they ambled, pausing to pet a horse, to pick a bouquet of black-eyed susans, to admire a family of cardinals feeding together. Morgan felt fever-ish with anticipation. They headed toward a grove of aspen, and right beyond the aspen, the pond. It was their own private spot, one where they were sure of privacy. The pond was small and had snapping turtles, so nobody fished there and no chil-dren wanted to use it as a swimming hole. They'd never seen another living soul, nor any sign that anyone else had ever been there. The first time, they'd made love in a forest of tall waving grasses. They had been here so often that now all the grass where they liked to lie, close to the water, was beaten down smooth. Fortunately, there was still enough tall growth, away from the banks, to hide them from anyone walking by.

Silas seemed calm and serene while walking there. But the minute they reached their special place, as soon as he was sure they were hidden from view, he changed. He grabbed her and kissed her hard, forcing her mouth open, pulling her in close to him so she could feel his excitement, pulling at her skirts, unbuttoning his pants, all in a rush of quick breathing and moans of pleasure. As her clothing came off and he could touch her bare skin, his eyes glazed with desire, and he cast his garments away so she could touch him. Clinging and kissing and fin-gering and moaning, they fell to their knees, and then he turned her onto her back, thrusting first his fingers into her and then his stiff hot cock. She cried aloud and pushed his buttocks to bring him closer, deeper. So lost was she in her own dizzying sensations, she hardly knew who it was sucking her nipples, kissing her belly, pushing that big stiff thing into her. She just knew yes yes yes, that she wanted it, she wanted it, she wanted it *now*. She had no shame, even when she heard herself cry, "Push it in harder, harder!" Even when she heard herself beg for more. She felt Silas stiffening and swelling inside her and he began to move very fast. A minute later, with a shout of "Jesus! Jesus!" he came, and collapsed over her, breathing hard and smiling.

Until Silas, not many men had been interested in her. Maybe that was a good thing. Because here she was, no marriage ring on her finger, not even a promise of one, getting hot all over the minute Silas put a hand on her, turning her head and open-ing her mouth for his kisses like a hungry bird, her mind flying off somewhere and a fever between her legs. What was there about her that made her like doing this thing, hankering after it, thinking about it all day long?

She thought she loved Silas, but what if she was just a wanton? Of course, maybe Silas didn't love her, either. From their first kiss, he had wanted her, wanted *IT*, so badly. He'd say anything, tell her anything, just to put it between her legs. She knew that. But what of her? Was she bad or not?

Today, Silas was extra sweet, kissing her throat, her lips, the tip of her nose, murmuring how sweet she was, how lovely, how wonderful. How could she think even for a minute that there was anything bad about loving him?

Morgan blurted, "I think it's time I should ask you to come calling, Silas. Nobody even knows we . . . we're friends."

"Well . . . I dunno, Morgan. Maybe we shouldn't rush things too much."

"What does *that* mean?"

His eyes shifted and he moved away from her, pretending he had a cramp and needed to stretch. "What?" Morgan insisted.

"Well, it's Pa, after me all the time to better myself and so forth. . . ."

"Nothing wrong in that," Morgan said. After a moment, she added, "There's more."

"Well . . . Dammit, Morgan, don't look at me like that! It wasn't me saying you're only a halfbreed and nobody even knows where you come from!"

Morgan felt cold as ice. "Dr. Grace knows where I come from."

"Oh, Morgan, I know it's stupid. But at the same time . . . you can't blame him, can you? He's my pa and I'm his only child. You can't blame him for thinking I should find a nice rich girl who can buy me a good law practice, where I can sit at a big mahogany desk and wear a collar and tie, and not have to bow and scrape for every Tom, Dick, and Harry who has a nickel to spend. Aw, Morgan, I'm sorry I said anything. Don't turn away from me. I'm only telling you what Pa says. That's not how *I* feel, Morgan dear."

He bent his head and gave her a tender kiss, but she was still chilled by that word: halfbreed. It stuck in her mind—stuck in her craw, to tell the truth. And what had happened to his hatred of his pa? Why was he all of sudden quoting the father who always bullied his wife and son into whatever he wanted?

"Sorry for saying halfbreed," he whispered into her ear. "That's Pa's word. I hate it." He nuzzled into her ear, pulling her close, rubbing her back and her thighs, telling her how beautiful she was, how soft her skin, how sweet her lips. She could feel him getting hard again, she could feel herself melting. It was so sweet, to forget everything but the feel of their two bodies meeting and merging.

By the time they were exhausted, she had just about forgiven him. She wondered how many folks in town thought of her as the halfbreed. Did it ever stop?

"Morgan?"

"Mmmm?"

"You do love me, don't you?"

"Of course I love you. I wouldn't be here . . . this way . . . if I didn't love you."

"Well . . . I gotta say something, Morgan, but you must never repeat it. Promise?" She nodded. They both sat up in the grass, pulling on their clothes. A serious matter required clothing. "Morgan, this is it. I ain't specially sorry that my pa is dying. I am sorry he's suffering. Dr. Grace told Ma he's suffocating slowly and that must be horrible. But, he never had a kind word for me, and you know how he treats my ma. I say it's God's will he's been struck down. And if God wants him dead, I don't have to be sorry."

She'd just been thinking about that! She was so glad he said it that her words just slipped out . . . "Not God's will, Si."

"What do you mean?"

Should she? He had made an admission to her. He trusted her; she had to trust him. That was what love was about: trust. "I did it," she blurted.

"What? What are you talking about?"

"I was there, bringing something to your ma, when he came home, sudden like. I saw how scared she was, how she had to fawn over him, and I saw how cruel he looked at her. I wouldn't look at a wolf that way, Silas. In my family, we know what to do with a man like that." He was gripping her hand, hard, his eyes wide, listening. "I took one of his shirts off of the clothesline and went to the graveyard with it. I ripped it into six pieces and buried those pieces separately. Then I burned tobacco—Indian tobacco, you know, that's the only kind that works—and said a couple of other spells, just to make sure."

She hadn't known quite what to expect—but it certainly wasn't being jerked her to her feet so roughly. "Get your clothes on. All of them. You take me there," he said, in a hard voice. "I want you to show me."

"Silas?" She didn't like the edge to his voice.

"Come on! It'll be dark in a few minutes, and I want to *see* where you did your Indian magic!"

They hurried to the old graveyard, crashing through an old stand of pines. It was nearly pitch-dark when they got there, with thick shadows everywhere. She could see that Silas was spooked. What a religion was Christianity, that made its believers afraid of their own dead relatives! Unbelievable. They had to hunker down to see the dark spots where she had burned the tobacco. She could no longer see Silas's features clearly, so she couldn't tell how he felt about any of it. But, dark or not, she knew exactly where she had buried all the pieces of shirt and she dug up the sleeve for him. "When I told your ma I could do it, you should have seen her face! It was all lit up!"

"You're a damn liar!" His face was so close to hers, she could feel his spit.

She recoiled. "I'm not! I don't lie!"

"Well, this time you are lying, and I want you to take back that curse! Take it back! Take it off!" He grabbed her by the shoulders, shaking her. "It's Godless, what you're doing! It's against the church, against Jesus—against God! It's . . . *Satanism!*"

"Satan! Satan has nothing to do with my religion."

"Religion! You call this pagan stuff a *religion*? It's evil, pure evil. Pa was right, you Injuns are nothing better than savages!"

Morgan reached out for his hand, but he shook her off. She pleaded with him for understanding, saying she knew he hated his father, and so did his mother. While she was talking, she began to cry. "Your pa beat your mother, Silas. He threw her down the cellar. He slammed her against the wall. He broke her arm and her leg. What I did for your mother was meant to help!"

"Take it off! The curse or whatever it is! You take it off and you take it off NOW!"

She could hardly think straight, she was so frightened of him. He was in a terrible rage, and she realized she never should have confided in him. Still weeping, she said, "I'm not sure I know how to take a curse off, Silas. I was only taught how to put it on. But I'll go——"

Out of the darkness came a blow across her face that sent her stumbling backward. She tripped over a rock and fell to the ground. She could feel the heat of his body as he bent over her, breathing hard with fury. She cowered, shielding her face with her arms. But another blow did not come and she heard him move back.

She got to her feet. The whole side of her head hurt, and there was a strange ringing in her ear. She still couldn't believe he had done that to her. Sweet, gentle Silas who wanted to study botany. *Just like his pa.* Morgan carefully backed away from him; now she could see where he stood, a darker shape against the deepening sky.

"I'm leaving now," she said to him, imitating her mother's sternest voice. "I'm going home and you'd better not come after me, Silas Grisham. You just remember I know spells and other magic, and you keep your distance."

So saying, she turned and picked her way out of the grave-yard. Her heart was racing. She walked softly, listening for his footsteps. Suddenly, he came running up and his arms shot around her from behind, holding her fast. She screamed, but then she realized he was trembling and that his encircling arms were not holding her back. He was hanging onto her—for comfort!—he was crying, his tears wetting the back of her neck. She turned around, into his desperate embrace.

"I'm sorry, I'm sorry. I don't know what came over me. I'm so sorry. I love you. I love you. Don't leave me. Please don't leave. I'll never do that again, never."

She was so relieved, so happy. She lifted her lips and he took them in a frenzy, sucking and biting on them, tearing at her clothes. Together, they sank to the ground again. *He loves me,* Morgan thought. *That was just a crazy thing that happened.* He loved her and that was all that mattered.

10

April 1884

She was Pequot—beautiful, tawny, and very tall, her buckskins a pure dazzling white, as was the large bird sitting on her head. She was coming after Morgan. *But why?* Morgan thought. *What have I done, that she strides toward me with such fierce concentration?* Morgan tried to walk backward, but she had forgotten how . . . that was strange. And when she went to turn around to escape, she couldn't do that either. Sweat broke out all over her body and she stood, frozen, as the woman advanced on her. Morgan could see that she was angry.

Morgan woke up with a start, her heart pounding, sweat between her shoulder blades and under her breasts. It was not the first time she'd dreamed about the Indian woman with the white bird. Morgan knew who she was: her many-greats-grandmother, Bird. It had to be. Who else could it be? Ever since Jered Grisham died, last summer, Bird had come often to her dreams. She had a message to give Morgan, and Morgan thought she knew what it was: *You have misused the magic of your ancestors, which was given to you at birth.*

Now Morgan opened her eyes. For a moment, she was completely lost. The morning sun was not shining in her bedroom window. Matter of fact, she wasn't in her room upstairs, but curled in the big Boston rocker in the front parlor, and it was dark outside. She had been alone in the house for two days. Dr. Grace was spending the better part of a week in Boston, consulting with one of her doctor friends who wanted her to see a new surgery and listen to some papers, whatever *they* were.

Morgan had been left to care for all the patients, and she was very proud to be so trusted by Dr. Grace. But it was exhausting. She'd sat in the rocker only for a minute, to rest, after the last patient in the afternoon had left. She must have fallen asleep immediately.

When the dreams first started, Morgan had promised Bird in a very loud voice that she would never use witchcraft again. Still, her ancestress kept appearing to her, and it had been almost a year now. What else did she want? Morgan was willing to do almost anything to send Bird back to the spirit world, but what could she do? She couldn't bring Jered Grisham back from the dead.

She did not like to remember how Mr. Grisham had died, horribly, unable to swallow and then unable to breathe. She'd been there, with Dr. Grace, at his bedside every day. She watched him struggle to take in air. She saw his eyes bulge out with his fear and suffering, and felt her own bowels turn liquid with terror. He deserved to be in agony, she tried to tell herself. But to have brought about such a horrible slow death, even to a wicked man like him—! No, no, she would never again try such a thing.

It didn't help that Dr. Grace thought it was perfectly natural. "It doesn't happen often, with this illness, but it does happen. There's nothing to be done about it, except pray. And I haven't seen that help much." The doctor ruminated some more, about the flurry of fevers that had hit Chester, mostly affecting children, about the same time Jered Grisham started complaining. "Was that before or after the church picnic, Morgan?" Dr. Grace had asked. Morgan knew it was after, because she remembered the church picnic at Waterhouse Pond very well indeed. She and Silas had sneaked off into the woods to find a private place, and they were almost discovered by a group of young'uns on a treasure hunt.

"After the picnic," she told Dr. Grace, and the doctor said, "Very interesting." But she never explained why.

Morgan thought Silas should be grateful to her, for setting him and his ma free from Jered Grisham's awful tyranny. Well, maybe not grateful. But instead, he had been distant and strange lately. She knew he was aggrieved. He'd had to stop reading the law and take over the smithy, so his mother would not starve. And she knew he blamed her for that, too.

Not that anything had stopped their walks out into the woods. Matter of fact, he seemed even more avid for their meetings. He often came over in the middle of the day, leaving the hired help to attend the forge, and pleaded for her to come with him. "Silas, we have patients, you can see that," she'd say. And he'd say, "We can just run across the road to the horse shed. It won't take long, I swear." Once, she actually gave in to him, pretending she had a grippe in her bowels, and went. But she was so ashamed of lying to Dr. Grace that the next time she said, "No, Si, and don't ask me again. 'Cause I won't, and that's flat. Not when there are patients here."

She tried to understand how he could always be wanting to be with her and then turn around and look hateful at her. She couldn't bring up the subject of his father at all. She wanted to make him understand. But his face would tighten and get a mean and ugly look. So she never straightened it out with him, but she thought about it all the time. And dreamed about it. She couldn't help wondering if Silas had told his ma about the curse. Amelia was polite to Morgan, but never warm like she used to be.

Morgan got pregnant once, but of course, she knew how to take care of it. Silas was very angry when she told him she was in the family way, and obviously relieved when she got rid of it. He, who always said what God gave should not be got rid of. She wished she could talk to Mam about this whole thing. Annis Wellburn would know what it was about. Her mother always did have a way of cutting right through the nonsense. But Mam wasn't here and Morgan was not going to go back to the house in the hills. She knew well enough that she didn't like Silas's behavior, not one bit. If she let herself, she'd hear herself saying, *Get rid of him. He means you no good.* She knew that. But it was so nice to feel like a regular young woman with a young man courting her. After all the years of being an outsider, she wasn't quite ready to give up the good feeling of being wanted like other girls. And, to her mortification, she did like the other part just as much as he did. The minute she saw him, she was ready. "Like you're always in heat," he'd say, laughing. "Well, I'm not going to complain, not me, not when I've found heaven right here on earth."

Oh lord, he'd be over soon, scratching at the kitchen door. He hadn't left her bed till just before dawn, and then she had to practically push him out the door. It was as if he was wanting to get caught. But if someone did see them, Morgan thought bitterly, she'd be the one reviled and shunned, not Silas Grisham. She promised herself that if he couldn't be more careful, she just wasn't going to let him in. But she knew that was brave, foolish talk. She'd never be able to refuse him.

Dr. Grace had told her, just before leaving for Boston, that she wanted Morgan to stay with her in the practice and become a partner. She said she'd send Morgan to medical college to take the courses she needed. Imagine, being Dr. Morgan Wellburn! It made her heart swell with happiness. She had planned to tell Silas the good news the minute she saw him. Once she was a doctor, she'd be rich enough to buy him a good business. He hated the smithy, hated the hard work and the heat and the dirt. He should be pleased to think he might soon be set free. But with Dr. Grace gone and the house theirs, he had only one thing on his mind and it was not conversation. So he still didn't know.

She ate the stew left by Mrs. Wainwright and was cutting herself a piece of sponge cake when she heard a loud knocking, not at all like Si's careful little scribbles and scratches. Otis Marshall stood at the door, looking very nervous. "It's time, Miss Morgan. Eleanor said I should come get you right away." Morgan ran for her medicine bag, washed her hands and face, and grabbed a woolen shawl. The buggy was waiting. So, in she went, and the horse began to trot almost immediately.

* * *

It was a hard birth. The child's head was too large for Eleanor's narrow frame and she was in terrible pain, though she tried hard not to holler out. When the poor woman began to weaken, panting for air, Morgan realized they had to try something different. She gave Eleanor a strong potion to deaden the pain, and then ordered her to get out of the bed and squat.

"Like an Indian squaw?" Eleanor asked in an insulted tone. "Oh dear, Morgan, I'm sorry. You just took me by surprise."

"Like an Indian woman. It will make the labor easier, I promise you."

Not even an hour later, screaming and shouting, half in pain and half in triumph, Eleanor Marshall pushed her child's head free, and in a moment Morgan had his whole body in her hands. The dents in his soft skull were covered with blood and slime, but he was a beautiful boy. She turned him upside down, to drain his nostrils, then gave him a spank and he began squalling loudly.

At the sound of his cry, Otis came racing in. "What in the name of almighty God are you doing on the floor, Eleanor!" he cried.

"Never mind that," said Morgan briskly. "Help her into bed. Then I'll introduce you to your son."

"A son! God be praised!"

"Otis, please. Help me up, sweet boy. I'm too weak to do it myself."

"Oh my darling Eleanor, of course. Here, my angel, here, let me tuck you in. There. And now, Miss Morgan, Otis Junior, if you please."

"But we agreed, sweet boy, on Henry . . . Oh, never mind. Otis Junior it shall be."

"Otis Henry," said the new father, grandly. "Otis Henry Marshall."

By the time she got home, everyone in Chester knew where Morgan had been all night, and that Eleanor Marshall had finally produced an heir. Morgan was so tired, her eyes kept wanting to close. The thought of her bed was like a golden promise.

In a stupor, she climbed the stairs, peeled off her garments, and fell into bed. If Silas came a-knocking, she wouldn't hear it. He would be angry with her. Well, that was too bad, she thought, and fell asleep.

When she awoke, she climbed out of bed and stretched luxuriously, feeling very pleased with herself. She had successfully brought that huge baby into the world, and saved the mother's life to boot. Otis Marshall had kissed her hand and called her a heroine, and so she was! Shivering a little in the cool morning air, she washed and dressed herself with care.

She was going to be a doctor, a real doctor. Dr. Morgan would put on her good blue skirt and white shirtwaist with the blue stock. Dr. Morgan would wear polished boots, all buttoned up neatly. And then Dr. Morgan would go down to the kitchen and fix some bacon and eggs and about a pound of toast. She was ravenous!

Later that same night, after midnight, Morgan was awakened by hysterical shouting outside the house. She opened a window and leaned out to call: "Here I am! What's the trouble?" And the frantic shout came back: "Come quick! Little Otis is dying! You gotta do something!"

Silas was in Morgan's bed, flat on his back, snoring loudly. Morgan leaped out of the bed and ran for her clothes. As she pulled them on, she shook him. "Silas! Wake up! It's in the wee hours and I've been called to the Marshalls. As soon as I'm gone, you leave. Silas, do you hear? Don't you dare fall asleep, do you hear?" He grunted and rolled over, dead to the world. Disgusted, she turned away, grabbed her medicine bag, and ran down the stairs.

She climbed onto the horse behind Otis, and hung on to his belt as he galloped off. While they rode, he shouted the news to her. One of his sisters accidentally pricked baby Otis with a pin this morning, and he bled and bled from a little tiny wound. They used spider webs, like Morgan had taught them, and finally it stopped. But now, he was failing, and nothing had happened, nothing at all. He did take a tumble out of the bed, when his mother's back was turned, but he couldn't have been hurt because he landed on a pile of pillows. "He was crying hard and suddenly, he stopped crying and began to look funny. They're all hysterical, in the house. But I told them,

Morgan has healer's hands. She'll fix him up just fine. Isn't that right, Miss Morgan?"

The truth was, she didn't know. Dr. Grace wouldn't be back until tomorrow morning. Morgan wished she were already here. But it was no use wishing for the impossible. She had to do what she could do. She might give the baby some sassafras, which was known to cool the blood—or sometimes the opposite. Nothing was certain. The medicine that worked on one person might be bad for the next: Everyone knew that. If the moon was waxing or waning, that made a difference. Vaguely, she remembered something about people who were called "bleeders." But blessed if she could recall what she had heard about them, or what to do about it.

Little Otis did not look well. His skin had a grayish cast and his little limbs were limp and motionless, swollen in places and horribly bruised. He was bruised on his chest and back; yet he had fallen softly onto a pile of feather pillows. Morgan was at a loss. Nothing her mother or Dr. Grace had ever taught her was going to help this child. He was not bleeding now, but he certainly looked as if he were. He was wasting away, minute by minute. The only cause she could think of was a curse. But who would curse this newborn child whose parents had awaited him so eagerly?

Then the thought struck her. What if she carried bad magic with her? No, it couldn't be. She wouldn't *let* it be. She put the baby into warm water and then into cold. She massaged his poor little limbs, which made him scream and cry, and all the time she watched as he faded and failed. Finally, he died. She turned, tears sliding out of her eyes, to tell the parents.

The hysterical woman who called Morgan a filthy savage and beat at her with her fists was almost unrecognizable as the amiable Eleanor Marshall. "Killing babies is all you people know! Killing innocent babies!" Otis pulled Eleanor away and held her tightly. He said nothing at all, just let her rail and shriek. Morgan was shocked and hurt, but she couldn't find the strength to stand up for herself. She slunk out of the Marshall house and walked slowly up the road, toward Dr. Grace's house. A few minutes later, Otis Marshall galloped by her, barely missing her, heading for town. By the time she reached the house, there was already a crowd, yelling and hollering. A few hurled stones at her and one rock struck her in the shoulder. "Baby killer!" she heard. "Indian witch!" "Squaw!" "Halfbreed!"

Where were all the folks she had helped since she'd been here? She'd eased rheumatism and birthed babies and set bones and cooled fevers. And now she was a squaw and a witch? Yesterday, they came to the office and waited patiently for her to see them. Today, they were ready to stone her. Nothing in her life had ever hurt as much. She let herself into the house, and sat weeping all night in the rocker in the front parlor. It was a long while before the mob got tired of yelling and broke up, heading for their own homes.

The next morning, feeling terribly sad and betrayed, Morgan hitched up the buggy and went to the landing to meet Dr. Grace. Usually, she found the busy scene at the dock fascinating: the sailors unloading, men shouting, well-dressed passengers disembarking, others saying farewell as they boarded. But today she was filled with a vague sensation of dread. She had dreamed of her ancestress again but could remember nothing about it.

Dr. Grace must have seen something in her posture because, the moment they met, she said, "What's wrong, Morgan?" Morgan opened her mouth and began to cry. Dr. Grace grasped her hand and squeezed it. "I'll drive the buggy," she said, "and you tell me the whole story."

It was such a comfort to tell the sad tale. Morgan had just got to the part where baby Otis kept failing and nothing seemed able to stop it, when they turned the big curve that led to the Cove. There, in the middle of the road, a large group had gathered outside Silas's smithy. Morgan stopped speaking. Fear gripped her.

Amelia Grisham, looking pale but determined, stepped in front of the buggy, forcing them to halt. "Dr. Grace, you're all right, we all love you. But you got to get rid of that savage before she kills us all," Mrs. Grisham announced, her face set in grim lines.

"What is this? How many babies have we all seen die soon after birth, and nobody able to say why?" Dr. Grace's voice showed no particular emotion.

"This is different. I *know*." Amelia folded her lips together.

"I can say no more. There are innocent ears here. But this young woman is a witch. Be warned."

"Oh nonsense!" snapped Dr. Grace, losing her patience. "And shame on you, Amelia Grisham, for spreading such foolishness!" She clucked to the horse and drove on. As they rode, there were shouts of "Witch" and "Squaw" and even "Daughter of Satan!"

"My advice to you, Morgan, is not to listen. They're all upset, because Amelia's got them riled. You know how New England still loves to find witches behind every bush." She spoke lightly, as if it were nothing, but Morgan was crushed. How quickly they had all changed toward her. It was frightening. And Silas . . . where had Silas been while his mother was calling her wicked names?

Morgan was excused from seeing patients. "Just for a few days, until this blathering is finished," Dr. Grace said. Morgan spent the day upstairs, trying to read, but she couldn't. She couldn't stop thoughts from tumbling about in her brain. And, truth be told, she was really looking out the window, waiting to see if Silas would come down the road. It was nearly dark before she heard him ride up. She was sitting on the front porch, wrapped in a shawl. The evening was fine and fairly warm, but she was cold down to her bones.

"Evening, Morgan," Silas said. He did not come to her, but stood on the edge of the porch, near the steps, as if ready to bolt at the first sign of . . . *what?* she wondered.

"Good evening, Silas."

"Um . . . I'm sorry . . . for what happened." He paused, perhaps waiting for her to say it was all right. It wasn't all right, and she was saying nothing until she knew what he was about. "My mother . . . she's . . . well, she knows about . . . you know."

Morgan assumed that "you know" was about the curse in the graveyard. "Your mother knew it all along, Silas. I told her exactly what I could do. She didn't say, 'Go and do it,' but she didn't call me a savage, neither."

"Aw, Morgan . . ." His voice trailed off and he shifted his position. "Look, there's no talking to people, once they make up their minds. And they've all made up their minds about you."

"And you believe them."

"No, I don't believe them . . . well, not all of it. But Morgan," he added, his voice rising, "you got powers that normal people don't have. I been pondering whether you put a spell on me, the way I'm always hungering for you." He began to whisper. "Right now, right this minute, I just want to come over there and haul you off this porch and take you into the horse shed and—"

"Yes, I know what you want to do," Morgan said coolly. "And I want it, too."

"Well, then," Silas said, in an entirely different voice, "let's go, Morgan. I'm burning for you."

"I know you are. But tell me, Silas, do you love me? Would you ever want to marry me?"

"Well . . . right now, I gotta . . . how can I tell Ma, the way she feels? Have some sense, Morgan, we gotta wait for that. Still, no reason we can't meet . . ."

"At night, in the dark?" Strange, how distant she felt from him and from everything he was saying.

"Well . . . until things calm down . . . Come here, Morgan, I'm dying of wanting you. It feels just like one of the iron rods in the smithy." His voice sounded clogged with lust.

Morgan got up from the rocker and walked to him. His arms went around her instantly, one hand on her buttocks, pulling her in close, the other hand rooting around for a breast. His open mouth came down on hers with urgency and he groaned softly. Morgan felt nothing. She pulled away from him and said, "No, Silas."

Hoarsely: "What do you mean—no?"

"I mean no. No more, Silas. No more. You've just been fooling me all along. I can see that now. You don't love me!"

"For Jesus' sake, Morgan! This is the second one you killed. What if I rile you one day? Will you put a spell on me?"

"You keep talking that way and I certainly will," Morgan said. She was not terribly surprised when he slapped her across the face. She gave him an icy smile and said, softly, "Like father, like son." A sound came from his throat. She could feel him, fighting the urge to strike her again, and she thought, *Go ahead, Silas, just you go ahead. I will make sure you suffer.* A moment later, he wheeled around and ran off the porch.

Morgan walked into the house, her cheeks burning, her heart aching. There was no place here for her. Dr. Grace was standing at the bottom of the stairs, on her way up to bed.

"Silas?" she asked, and Morgan burst into tears, saying, "You see, how little it takes to make them turn on me for a halfbreed no-good? That's what they were always thinking, underneath the sweet smiles and the thank-yous. In their hearts, they were saying, 'Of course she can do magic, she's no better than a savage. She's not really a Christian, is she? Not really one of *us*. That'll make her evil, won't it? Make her a witch!' I did everything I knew how, to save Mrs. Marshall's baby! He was born just fine. I didn't do anything to him!"

"I know that. I'm certain sure you did everything. Babies die, Morgan, beyond the help of medicine of any kind. Don't you worry yourself over it, you hear? In a week or two, this tempest in a teapot will have died down, and soon it will all be forgotten."

"Forgotten?" Morgan said. "Forgotten? Well not by me!" She turned and ran, down the hall and through the kitchen and out to the road, ignoring Dr. Grace's shouts. She needed to get away from here, away from hate, away from *him*. Away, as far as she could go!

11

April into May 1884

When she became too tired to move one more inch, Morgan left the road and sat down under the nearest tree. She had no

idea where she was and didn't care. She was so furious at all
of Chester, especially that coward Silas Grisham, she hardly
knew which direction she'd chosen, but she thought she was
probably heading for Deep River. That was fine. Anyplace but
Chester was fine. She was glad she'd had on the woolen
shawl; the night was chilly and damp. She wrapped the shawl
tightly around herself and leaned back against the rough tree
trunk. She was sure she wouldn't sleep a wink.

She was wrong. When next she opened her eyes, morning
was breaking. The sky was a brightly lit mist. She had dreamed
of Bird again, a dream full of warnings and pleadings. But, try
as she might, details kept eluding her, fading until she could
remember nothing but a smell. And she couldn't place even
that. She found a fresh brook farther back in the woods, and
there she washed her face and wet her hair to smooth it down.
Without a mirror or hairbrush, she couldn't pin it up, so she
plaited it in one thick braid down her back. Folks thought
that's how Indian squaws wore their hair. Morgan knew better,
because Annis had told her that Pequot women wore their hair
tied back so it looked like a horse's tail, or loose.

The day was cool and calm, with only a few thin clouds
moving across the sky—a good day to walk. She started through
the woods, picking mushrooms for breakfast. She'd love a cup
of tea! How she'd like to be burrowing under her quilt in her
own room. If only she could just go back to last week, when
she thought she'd become a real doctor and maybe even marry
Silas Grisham. If she could cast spells and do magic the way
they thought, then why was she here, wandering in the woods,
trying to figure out what to do with herself, while they all
stayed safe and snug in their comfortable lives?

What was she going to do? It would be so easy to turn
around, go back, and pretend that nothing had happened. Dr.
Grace was probably right: The uproar would be forgotten as
soon as the next sensation came along. She'd have Dr. Grace
for protection; nobody would dare treat her *too* badly. But was
that any way to live? Being careful, being polite and always
on edge; waiting for someone to remember and bring up the
deaths? No, Morgan decided, she could not do that. She had to
leave Chester. Tears filled her eyes at the thought of leaving

Dr. Grace, and the nice house, and Mrs. Wainwright, and everything. Dr. Grace had become a second mother to her. When she left *this* mother, there'd be no anger to help push her on her way. Just a great void, an empty place.

No sense making herself miserable, Morgan decided, sniffling back her tears. She'd do what had to be done. The first thing was to go back to Chester and tell Dr. Grace her decision. She needed to get her medicine bag, and Dr. Grace would never object to her packing up a dress or two and some possessions: her nice nightdresses, and the pewter handmirror and hairbrush set she'd got last Christmas.

She wasn't sure which of the pathways, in and out of the woods, were which, or even all of the well-traveled roads, either. She followed a road she thought she recognized, but after a while, she couldn't smell the river. So she turned east, into the sun. All of a sudden, she thought of her canoe. She'd have to check it over to make sure there were no leaks or rotten places. It hadn't even entered her thoughts; yet, what better way to get to another town?

Before long, she realized she'd gone too far, because she smelled the river but hadn't passed any of the familiar houses outside Chester. She must have turned downriver and was coming into Deep River. She could hear some kind of commotion: a lot of hollering and church bells clanging like the world was coming to an end. And then she got a whiff of . . . what? . . . roasting meat? Not exactly. It was an odor that gave her much unease—was this the smell from her dream? She hurried on. At the edge of town, she saw three girls fourteen or fifteen years old, huddled together, chattering with great excitement.

"Excuse me. What's happened?"

"Oh, Miss, it's terrible, just terrible!"

"One of the big boats—"

"Steamship, Maggie, not boat. One of the big steamships has blown up."

"Blown up? But . . . how?"

The girl who knew it was a steamship spoke up. "The boiler exploded. The ship was just coming into the pier with the passengers out on deck and all their relatives waiting on the dock, when boom! Suddenly it was all afire!"

"People are burned and they're screaming . . . oh, it's horrible! And everybody running around, yelling and crying!"

"Well, I'm going there to see can I help," Morgan said. "Over there?" And she pointed east.

"Yes, Miss, but they won't let you anywheres near. We know. We tried and they shooed us away, told us to go home to our mamas."

Morgan looked the girl straight in the eyes. She looked a bright girl, small and blond and sensible. "Were you going there just to gape and gossip? Or did you think you might help out?"

"Well, I wanted to see if I could do something. But they—"

"They wouldn't let you, yes. But I'm a . . . doctor. Dr. Wellburn. I'm sure they'll let me try. Lead me there, and I'll say you're my helper. You others . . . it's bound to be stomach-turning. You still want to come?"

They thanked her, but no, they thought not. Morgan motioned to the blond girl, and together they walked swiftly down toward the Deep River landing.

"I'm Jane Morgan," the girl said.

Morgan laughed. "And I'm Morgan Wellburn. We should make a mighty good team, sharing a name between us."

On their way, they kept meeting people who had tried to get close, and folks who had managed to get close but were sickened and had to leave. Crowds milled around, not knowing where to go or what to do. Stopping at each little group, Morgan asked questions, until she had a notion of what lay ahead.

When she heard the name of the steamship, a chill ran right up her backbone. *Water Bird*, sister ship to *Water Witch* and *Water Queen*, sailing out of Hartford to Brooklyn and New York. That must have been the message in the dream she'd forgotten so fast this morning. She was meant to find the damaged *Water Bird*. Was it not her own name in the old language? A feeling like bubbles rose in her chest. Somehow her future was bound up in her being here and nowhere else today.

She learned that at least four sailors had been badly burned, and several passengers too. "The doctor says it's hopeless," one out-of-breath man told her. "He keeps putting on butter and lard and they're just getting worse, screaming to let them die. It's dreadful, dreadful!"

As they neared the harbor, the smell became stronger. Now, of course, Morgan knew what it was: burned human flesh. She shivered. Suddenly, she got a flash from last night's dream . . . smoldering fires . . . a glimpse of water . . . And that smell. So. The spirits *did* speak to her, just in a different way. She thought, *I'll have to tell Dr. Grace about that*. And then remembered that she was planning to leave Dr. Grace, and she felt very lonesome, suddenly.

She and Jane Morgan pushed their way down to the crowd. The patients had been laid out on the dock, and a harried-looking man with a short beard was kneeling by one, shouting for more grease and quick! Morgan knew very well that burns should be treated first with vinegar or, failing that, cold water. Mud made a good poultice until something better could be got. The doctor didn't seem to realize that he had all the healing agent he needed, right there under his knee. Shouting, "I'm a doctor, a doctor" and "Doctor coming" got Morgan and her helper onto the dock. Morgan asked where she could find the captain of the ship, and someone pointed to a tall blond man with curly hair. "Captain Walter Prentiss," she was told.

Grabbing Jane's hand, Morgan headed straight for him.

"I'm a healer woman," she said, when she got his attention, "I practice with Dr. Grace Chapman over in Chester. Morgan Wellburn is my name and I know what to do about bad burns."

"Thank the Lord," Captain Prentiss said fervently. "Since Dr. Bolton says he's done all he can. What do you need, Miss Wellburn?"

"Plantain leaves, lots of them, and the bark of the slippery elm. And vinegar. And soft material, very light, for bandages."

"You shall have all you need," the captain said. He turned to a small knot of sailors. "You . . ." he barked. "This lady is a doctor. You get what she tells you."

"Aye, sir." She gave her orders and off they went.

Morgan was suddenly totally calm. She moved among the poor suffering souls lying there on the dock, making mental notes about their burns. She'd never seen the like, not on a living person. She rolled up her sleeves, and knelt down to examine them. Bad burns, scalds, in some places almost no skin left. She got right down to business, asked for warm water, into which she put some of the inner bark of the slippery elm—that and the plantain leaves had appeared, as if by magic. The mixture quickly became a gummy mucilage, with which she would dress the worst burns. Lighter burns would be washed off with cold water and then vinegar. She made poultices of plantain leaves. Jane stayed with her, following Morgan's instructions. Moans and cries filled the air, but Morgan hardly heard. She had work to do and everything around her disappeared, save what she had to do.

One fellow, writhing and moaning piteously, had had half his face charred off. She could barely force herself to look at it, but once she did, she knew he was a goner. She needed some strong painkiller. "Jane, you go ask the captain for strong spirits, the strongest he has." The girl ran and returned with a bottle. Murmuring soothing words to him, Morgan poured the whisky down the patient's throat, then more, and yet more. After a few minutes, his moans became a bit softer and she moved on. There was nothing more she could do for him. Jane, still by her side, had gone quite pale at the sight of him. It occurred to Morgan that the girl might faint, if she didn't get out of here.

"Jane Morgan, you've been a great help, but I want you to go home now. You need to rest."

"If you're sure you don't need me."

"You're a good girl, Jane, and you've helped more than you can know. You go on, now."

After that, Morgan was completely involved in the patients she needed to help. She knelt by them, moving from one to the other by walking on her knees. "Vinegar," she ordered, and a jug appeared in her hand. "Cloth." All the burns were anointed with the vinegar, causing the victims to twitch and shout in pain. But she knew it would help them heal.

"Bring me a bucket of cold water. Take it right out of the harbor." Suddenly, she thought about how Dr. Grace insisted on cleanliness if you were working with open wounds. There weren't many injuries more open than bad burns. Would harbor

water be clean enough? Oh, how she wished Dr. Grace
were here.

"Cold water? Whatever for?" The voice that came from
somewhere just above and behind her was male and caustic. It
was the doctor, looking down at her like she was an apparition.

"The burns, sir."

"Oh, for— That's not the proper treatment for burns,
Miss . . ."

"Doctor," she said, with such force that he drew back a
little.

"Pardon me, Miss—er, Doctor. But surely you know that
burns—"

"Respond very well to cold water or vinegar and *not* to
butter or any other kind of grease. Grease just makes them
cook."

"And where did you learn *that*?"

Might as well be hung for a sheep as for a lamb. "In Geneva
Medical College," she lied, her eyes wide and earnest. That's
where Dr. Grace had gone to school.

"Now, with all due respect to Geneva Medical College,
that's absolutely stu—"

Captain Prentiss stepped in, "Doc, you said you'd done all
you could. This young woman seems to know a thing or two. I
say let her have a try. Better than letting them all die."

The doctor grumped a bit and stomped away, muttering.

"Not a jolly soul," the captain remarked. "But you needn't
pay him any mind. You're doing a fine job. I never saw a
young lady so tireless. Here, let me help you move that big
fellow . . ." And he stayed with her, doing the most menial
tasks, running everywhere and yelling for help from his crew.
He told his men they'd do better keeping busy than standing
around thinking about what had happened. He held the
mucilage on a flat piece of wood so she could scoop it off and
cover the worst burns. He carried the water and the vinegar.
And he took the plantain poultices, holding them out for
Morgan to take as needed. Finally, it was done—at least for
the moment. Morgan got up off her knees and paced up and
down to take the tingling out of her legs. The captain walked
with her.

"You're very quick with your hands," he said in an admiring tone. "My daughter was, too. Verity, her name was."

"Where is she?" Morgan asked.

"With the angels. She died some years ago of measles. She'd have been twenty this year . . . about your own age, I warrant."

She almost blurted out that she was only sixteen. Then she realized that she could never have gone to medical college and have finished it, not at sixteen. So she said nothing, just made a noise that might be understood as agreement.

It came as a shock to her when she turned in her walk and looked eastward, toward the Sound, and saw that the sky had darkened. The evening star, all by its lonesome, was already bright in the sky. The captain called for lanterns. His crewmen lit them and laid them out by the victims, one at the head, one at the feet. A few poultices had to be reapplied, and one of the passengers, an elderly man who the captain said had tried to rescue the weak and the aged from the sudden inferno, had given up the ghost.

"He'll have a swift ascent to heaven," he said, removing his hat and bowing his head briefly. "You see, Morgan, these burns are worse than most because when a boiler blows, it's not just flames but steam. To tell the truth, I do believe the steam does more damage."

The captain said Morgan should go into town and find a bed to sleep in, but she would not leave her patients. She did accept a tot of brandy from a narrow leather flask he carried, and some bread and cheese. Then she curled up against a post on the dock. The night was filled with the sounds of suffering, but many of the victims were able to sleep, however restlessly. Remembering Pa's stories of the war, and Dr. Grace's tales, too, she began to sing. She sang "Greensleeves" and "Barbry Allen" and "Black Is the Color" and then "Greensleeves" again. Those sailors nearby who knew the tunes sang along. At some point, between one word and the next, she fell asleep and knew nothing until the sun rose the next morning. She dreamed of Dr. Grace, bending over her and covering her with a blanket.

She awoke suddenly to a new day, a misty one. In fact, there was a blanket over her. She'd just put it into her dream. She wondered why she'd awakened, and then she heard the sound of labored breathing. On her feet in an instant, she swept her eyes over the twelve patients left. The noise came from the young man who'd lost so much of his face. As she made her way to him, he stopped breathing. Just like that. When she examined him, she saw that his nose and probably his throat, too, had closed up trying to heal the burns. He had choked to death, poor fellow. Morgan took both his poor scorched hands in hers and wept for him. He was somebody's son, maybe somebody's brother or sweetheart, and he couldn't have been more than seventeen, by the looks of him.

Someone knelt beside her and put a light hand on her shoulder. When she turned her head and saw it was Dr. Grace, she cried harder. Pulling Morgan close, Dr. Grace let her weep until she was so tired all she could do was whimper.

"How ever did you find me?" Morgan asked, scrubbing her wet eyes with her sleeve.

"We had half the town out looking for you, Morgan, but nobody could figure where you'd headed. They went every which of a way, as they used to say in Memphis. I was worried half out of my mind. But when I heard about this boat disaster, I had to come help. And here I find you, doing what you do so well."

For over a week, Dr. Grace stayed with Morgan in Deep River. They took a room at an inn where they could get their meals as well. First, they had to move the casualties from the open dock. It was almost May and all the trees were budding, but it still got cold at night and often rained. The victims had to be bedded down and protected. "Morgan Wellburn has saved all but two of the worst burned men," Dr. Grace told the captain. "We don't want the survivors dying of exposure. You go see if there's a hall—even a barn will do—where there's room to set up a field hospital."

He found an old stable, which was starting to fall down, but still had four walls and a roof. The good citizens of Deep River all brought linens and blankets and shawls and vessels of various kinds. Many of the women offered to do nursing, among them young Jane Morgan. Soon there was a little infirmary, busy and active and filled with the sounds of female voices. The captain came often, checking to see if they needed anything, or carrying in a huge basket with sandwiches and pickles and such. Captain Prentiss was a resourceful man with a quick mind, and Morgan couldn't help notice that Dr. Grace liked him a lot. But all his smiles and attentions seemed to be for Morgan, who was young enough to be his daughter. Younger. She guessed he missed his dead child.

Time passed in a busy blur, and before they knew it, the patients were well enough to go to their homes safely. The crew members who had been burned, four of them in all, wanted to sail off with the captain as soon as the boiler was repaired, but he refused. "Next trip, lads. I'll save your places for you. Right now, you go home and get healed."

New crewmen were found, a new cargo was loaded aboard, and one bright afternoon, the captain came to the now empty infirmary, where Morgan and Jane and Dr. Grace were doing the last bit of clearing out. "We'll be setting sail tomorrow," he said to Morgan. "You've made a miracle here, Dr. Morgan. Whatever you want, that I'll give to you."

She didn't hesitate, not for a second. "Wherever you're going, give me passage."

A great smile split his weathered face. "I'm heading down to the Brooklyn harbor, and I'll take you along, with pleasure."

Morgan turned to Dr. Grace, who looked as if she'd been slapped. "Oh, Dr. Grace, it's not that I don't love you. You know I do. I'm truly sorry. But I've been doing a lot of thinking. Let's get back to the house and I'll tell you all about it. I think, once I've told you what I've figured out, you'll agree that leaving is what I must do."

Dr. Grace turned her head away, but not before Morgan saw the tears in her eyes. It was very hard to hurt Dr. Grace, who had done so much for her. "And if you don't agree, then I'll stay on for a little while longer," Morgan added.

"My dear Morgan, of course I'll listen to you. And, knowing you as I do, I'm sure I'll understand why you feel you must go."

Even if you don't understand, you'll never say a word, will you? Morgan thought. *You'll never say anything to keep me if*

moving on is what I want. In the same moment, she realized
that the big white house in Chester was really her home now,
and that—if she ever wanted to—she could return. That helped
her to feel she could leave more easily.

Morgan hugged Dr. Grace hard. "Thank you," she whispered. Then, she turned to the captain. "I'm going home now,"
she said. "But tomorrow morning, bright and early, you can
expect me here, ready to go."

And go she would, chin up, heading straight for Long Island
Sound and Brooklyn harbor, and who knew where after that.

12

May 1884

The trip to Brooklyn harbor usually took a bit less than a day
and a night—"Twenty-three hours," Captain Prentiss told her,
in that exact way he had. If you asked him the hour, he also
told you the minute and the second. In any case, he wanted her
to know they were going a bit slow this trip, and it might take
longer than twenty-three hours. "I'm a tad cautious right now,"
he said. "You have a boiler up and explode on you, Morgan
m'girl, and you don't ever sail out without wondering will it
happen again."

"But accidents are always happening, Captain," she argued.
"If we pay attention to every one of them, we won't be able to
go forth or back. We'll always be saying maybe it'll happen
again."

"It's true, Morgan, that life does make a man careful. But
that's the kind of man you want at the helm of your ship, isn't
it? I'm sure the repairs will hold and, whatever happens to

Water Bird, I can always hoist sail and get her in to shore safely. But the passengers, now, you can understand how they might be a mite jittery. So I'll be going slower than usual— we're 'way behind schedule, anyway. A few hours more won't make a difference. I'm just grateful I wasn't carrying any perishables, like pineapples, say, or they'd be rotted by now."

"Pineapples!" Morgan repeated, very impressed.

"To be sure," said the captain proudly. "We sometimes go to the Caribbean Sea to pick up pineapples and oranges and sugar cane. The port of Brooklyn, Morgan, is the very heart of the fruit trade. When we get there, you'll see. There's everything, from all over the world. Lemons. Grapes. Bananas. Figs and dates. All sorts of nuts . . . ah, and oranges. Delicious!"

Morgan had never eaten an orange. She was sorry they weren't part of the present cargo, because she was sure that, if she said she'd love to have one, she would get it. The captain was very fond of her, though he hadn't said so. But, she could tell. He had that same look about him that Silas had always got when he was in a hurry to get her down on the grass by the pond. A man his age! Morgan could hardly believe it, but she knew it was so.

"All we have this trip is timber and slates from Vermont and a load of brownstone from our own Connecticut . . ."

Morgan made a little movement and the captain's hand dropped from her shoulder. He was a nice-looking old man with his curly hair and neat little beard. She found his yellow hair beautiful, but he was too old. His daughter who had died would have been twenty—four years older than Morgan was this very minute. Maybe she should say something to him about her true age.

"It's a heavy load we're hauling and I want to ease my passengers' minds. So we'll be going just a bit slower than usual." He'd made the same point three times. That would drive her crazy, if she had to put up with it for long.

So, it was going to be a day and a half on the water before they got to Brooklyn harbor. Morgan was of two minds about the length of time. On the one hand, she was eager to see what Brooklyn might be like—she knew it was bigger than Deep River or East Haddam, and dozens of ships put in at East

Haddam. Four or five at the same time, sometimes! So she figured she'd see at least ten ships at once in the Brooklyn harbor.
She could barely contain her impatience. Imagine, ten big
steamboats like this one, all in the same place. Captain Prentiss had told her that Brooklyn was a very large and beautiful
city with many houses six stories tall. That she would have to
see to believe! That was taller than the tallest barn.

On the other hand, eager as she was to get to their destina-
tion, she was enjoying life on a big river steamship. It was
luxurious, and fancy beyond anything she'd ever seen in her
life—except maybe the Goodspeed Hall. Her room—the captain called it a stateroom—was far grander than anything in
Chester or Deep River or even Middletown or Hartford, she
was sure. It was surely richer than anything in Dr. Grace's
house. Morgan remembered how impressed she'd been with
the doctor's "wealth" when she first got there. She thought that
house was the end-all and be-all for elegance. Truly, it was a
wonderful house, a beautiful house—and she would never say
a bad word about Dr. Grace's things, they were lovely. But, oh
my, the staterooms on *Water Bird* were splendid! There were
thirty-one, all different sizes, with some opening up into the
one next to it—so a whole family, including grandmother,
could travel together. Captain Prentiss told her that each stateroom had furnishings of a different color. Hers was done in old
rose. It was fitted with a thick Brussels carpet, and velvet
tapestry, and satin brocatelle curtains. There were rosewood
chairs, a built-in bed with fringed curtains, tables of rosewood
with marble tops—all polished and shined and brushed every
single day. She felt beautiful herself, in her stateroom. She felt
like a princess.

The captain suggested that she walk about with him whenever he was free. "I'll give you the first-class tour, Morgan."
Of course, she said yes. She'd never been on a steamship
before and wasn't likely to be on another any time soon. She
wanted to see everything there was to see.

He loved to brag about *Water Bird*, telling Morgan how the
ship's frame was constructed of the best white oak, chestnut,
locust, and cedar and her keelsons, planking, and ceiling were
of the first quality of white oak, yellow and white pine. None

of this meant much to Morgan, but she ahhed and oohed because it really did all sound wonderful.

"She's fastened with only the best—copper, galvanized iron spikes and bolts—and she is the fastest boat on this run," he said. "Here, look at this hardware, you see how nicely it's been wrought?" When his hand curled around her elbow, she had to turn her head so he wouldn't see her amusement. By suppertime, Morgan knew that *Water Bird* was 272 feet long, her beam 27 feet, her hold 8 feet deep and that she could carry 865 tons.

Before the boiler blew, Captain Prentiss told her, they had stopped at all the big hotels along the river: the Griswold Inn at Essex and of course the Gelston House at Goodspeed's Landing. The only place that Morgan saw, however, was the last one on the Connecticut River, Fenwick Hall at Saybrook Point, where they picked up eight passengers.

"Now that we no longer have to let passengers off at Greenwich to catch the New York coach, I'll be taking you all the way into Brooklyn harbor. And there," he said, smiling, "you'll see a sight you won't soon forget."

"What's that, Captain?"

"Don't you think, considering what close friends we've become, Morgan, that you might call me Walter? That's the name my mother and father gave me the day I was born, and I'd be mighty pleased to hear it come from your own lips."

"Of course, Walter, if it pleases you." She waited to see if he'd answer her question, and when he didn't, asked, "What's the sight I'm to see that will be unforgettable?"

"Sight? Oh, in the harbor at Brooklyn. They call it the Eighth Wonder of the World . . . you know the other seven wonders, of course . . ." Well, no, she didn't. She'd have to get out an encyclopedia next chance she had, and look it up. Dr. Grace had always encouraged her to do that, saying, "I could tell you, but nothing sticks like the thing you learn yourself." She doubted the captain had a big encyclopedia on board, so she just looked as wise as she could and nodded. She tried to guess what "the wonder" could be, but the captain said he wasn't going to tell her because it would spoil the surprise.

A fancy supper was served in the saloon, consisting of a

cold roast of beef and fresh fish and baked potato and a condiment she'd never tasted before. Pickled crabapples, they were, spicy and rich. She liked them and kept asking for more, until she felt all eyes turned to her. The others were probably wondering just how many pickled crabapples one young woman could stuff into her mouth. Her cheeks burning, Morgan pretended to examine the one on her plate and then said sweetly, "I'm in a quandary. I've been trying to guess what spices are used in making these." In a moment, the entire table was busy arguing over what was used besides cloves and ginger and allspice. Nobody was paying her any mind, to her great relief, and she cleaned her plate.

If she was going to go out on her own, she thought, she had to fit in, watch her manners, and not draw too much attention to herself. It appeared that society folk frowned upon any behavior that looked too eager and enthusiastic. Apparently, the thing was to seem rather bored with everything, as if you had already seen and done and tasted everything there was to see, do, and eat. She could do that. All she had to do was look across the table at a fashionable young woman called Molly, though Mary was her real name. Molly was pale and slender, and she pushed her food around her plate but ate nary a bite. She said "Oh, really?" or "Is that so?" to everything that was said. Perhaps young women were not supposed to have opinions; well, she'd see about *that*, Morgan decided. It would be very hard for her to keep her opinions to herself.

After dinner, when she and the captain were standing on deck, chatting, enjoying the gentle breeze, watching the white foam waves break on either side of the bow as it cleaved the water, she asked him. "Captain Prentiss, everyone was gawking at me, at supper. I suppose it was because I seemed greedy for those crabapples. But they were so tasty and I didn't know it was bad manners."

"Not at all, dear Morgan. Bad manners? It was a compliment to the person who put them up. And I thought," he added, leaning closer to her, "that you were to call me Walter."

"I'm sorry—Walter. But that girl, that Molly—she didn't eat more than a nibble and she's from New York."

He snorted. "Fashionable girls may think starvation is stylish: I do not. Do you want my advice, Morgan?"

"I would much appreciate it."

"Be your own adorable self."

Morgan was stunned. She could find no words. Worse, she felt herself blushing fiercely. Perhaps he couldn't see, in the dark.

"I'm sorry, I have offended you," he said, after a moment.

"No, no. Not offended. But . . ."

"But you do not wish my attentions. I understand. I've been widowed these past six years, Morgan. It's been mighty lonesome. I did enjoy married life so much and it has been hard since my dear wife—" He broke off and Morgan, feeling a surge of sympathy, turned and put a hand on his arm, saying, "I'm so sorry for your troubles."

In an instant, he had scooped her into a muscular embrace and his mouth was on hers. At first startled, Morgan found herself responding to his ardent kiss, allowing her body to bend into his, allowing her lips to open. It felt good, the closeness, the ardor. She was all alone in the world and heading off into the unknown. It would be so easy, to say yes to the captain, to become a wife, cherished and loved.

And confined. Caged. Expected to behave a particular way. Housebound. In a panic, she pulled back from him, pushing him away.

"My dear Morgan, I humbly beg your pardon. But surely you have noticed . . . you have seen how much I admire you. You have such spirit . . ." He backed away from her, holding his hands, palms up, as if to say, *See, I keep my distance.* "Forgive me, but I have found myself becoming fonder and fonder of you. I would never take advantage . . . You looked so lovely, standing here, so tall and dark and strong, like a ship's figurehead . . . I was carried away. Say we are still friends?"

"Of course," Morgan said. "But friends only. I am too young yet for marriage and—"

"And?"

"Nothing," she said, thinking briefly of Silas. It made such a pain in her heart that she pushed the thought away. "I am not ready to think about such things as marriage, that's all."

"I hope you will write to me when you are settled. I would like to come visit you on one of my trips to New York or Brooklyn. Would that be acceptable to you? I wish to be sure you are all right, after all, a young woman on her own . . ."

"Don't you worry about me, Captain Prentiss. I'm a physician and midwife, I'll have no trouble getting along, I promise you."

He turned his head away from her. She had hurt his feelings. Again. She had to learn to be more tactful, and she wondered if she ever could. After a moment, he said it was time to get some sleep, "because I intend to wake you in the morning, in time to see the Eighth Wonder of the World." She was happy to hear that he sounded as calm as usual.

As he'd promised, Walter Prentiss knocked at her stateroom door just after daybreak, calling out, "We're coming into the harbor, Morgan. Hurry."

She was already washed and dressed, having awakened before sunrise, filled with excitement and wondering what was ahead of her. She just knew it was going to be good because she had seen Bird in her dreams. Her ancestress had nodded to her, and the bird had flapped its wings, although it did not leave the top of Bird's head. Surely that meant she was doing the right thing.

Morgan hurried up on deck and then gasped. For it was an astonishment: two great gray stone towers with huge gothic arches, rising to heaven, looking for all the world like two enormous churches floating in the air. Between them she could see a roadway with horses and carriages and wagons moving across it. Traveling in the middle of the air! It was breathtaking.

Behind her, Walter Prentiss chuckled. "Well, my dear Morgan, that is the Great New York and Brooklyn Bridge. Is it not a marvel to behold?"

Morgan could not answer. For the Great New York and Brooklyn Bridge was not the only marvel. There was so much to see, on either side of the ship. Tall buildings—so many of them, so crowded together!—pressing in on the shores. It seemed as if the buildings might topple over into the water at any moment. A hundred smokestacks sent their black plumes into the air. The river itself was jammed with boats of every description. Her head kept turning as she tried to take in everything. Small boats, puffing smoke and tooting, pulled barges behind them. Sailing ships, their great sails furled, prepared to put in. Steamboats like *Water Bird*, some smaller and some even larger, moved back and forth. The sidewheel steamers, the captain said, were ferries that would take you from New York to Brooklyn and back for a fare of two cents. He pointed out other boats to her: California clippers and Indiamen and, on the New York side, barges that had come all the way down from the Erie Canal. Scurrying around like bugs on the forest floor, moving deftly between all the great ships, were the small craft—rowboats and flat-bottomed boats and sculls. Why they didn't all bump into each other and crash, she could not imagine.

The Brooklyn Bridge! It was above them, darkening the sky! As the ship sailed serenely under it, Morgan craned and gaped and went running from one side of the deck to the other, crying, "Look at this!" and "Look at that!"

When they were past the bridge, she turned to look back at it, and saw that there were people walking on it. *I'm going to walk across the river on the New York and Brooklyn Bridge as soon as we land,* she promised herself. Marvelous wasn't the word for it!

"I see you like Brooklyn harbor," Captain Prentiss said. He gazed fondly down at her. He was amused because she found the sights so exciting. Well, let him be. She didn't give a fig. She loved this place! She loved the river and the bridge and the towering buildings and the thousands of people thronging the streets that led to the piers, going this way and that.

"A bit different from Deep River, hey? And out there, Morgan, on Bedloe's Island, the French are going to erect a mighty statue, a lady so I hear, who will symbolize liberty. And see, over there? See all the guns? That's Staten Island, ready to defend New York and Brooklyn should an enemy try to attack."

"Who would want to attack New York and Brooklyn?" Morgan wondered.

The captain laughed heartily. "My question, too, Morgan. But we must always be prepared for the worst, hey?"

Slowly, *Water Bird* began her turn, into Pier 1, the first of the huge docks, and Morgan could see the men with their hooks crowding up to the side of the ship. "Longshoremen," the captain explained. "Looking for work, unloading."

"We're in Brooklyn?" She had to be sure. It was hard to tell which was Brooklyn and which New York, they looked so much the same to her.

"Yes, indeed. This neighborhood above the harbor, up on the clifftop, is known as Brooklyn Heights. It is quite a pleasant area, I believe, and I've been told there are many boarding houses there for young working men and women. If you're willing to wait an hour or so, I'll be happy to escort you—"

An hour? Impossible to wait that long. Her feet were fairly dancing in their eagerness to be off the ship and into the streets of Brooklyn Heights.

"No. No. Thank you for everything, Captain, I'm eager to be on my way!"

The day was so clear, bright, and sparkling, she felt as if she could float right off the ship and into the street. So much life! So many ships! So many people! She loved it here! *Loved it!* She had finally found the place where she belonged. She was sure of it. And here, she promised herself, she would stay.

13

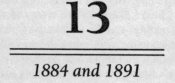

1884 and 1891

Gawking and staring and tripping over her own feet, Morgan made her way through the crowd at the foot of Fulton Street. It was a wonder she wasn't run over by one of the dozens of loaded wagons, or a messenger boy running to the ferry. Everyone was in such a hurry! She was pushed and shoved and bumped from every direction. Obviously, this was not the time to look at the sights. These Brooklyn people spoke a strange English, and many didn't speak English at all. How in the world would she ever find her way around such a frenetic, crowded place? She said, "Excuse me," hoping to ask the way to State Street, where Captain Prentiss had told her she'd find lodging, but people rushed along so fast, they didn't hear her. Or they didn't care. Nobody paused and nobody stopped. Finally, she planted herself in front of a boy pulling a loaded wagon, and said, "Please," very loudly.

"Yes, Miss?" He stopped, but was poised to bolt as soon as he could.

"Please, where is State Street?"

" 'Way down the other end. Follow Fulton and head south . . . *that* way," pointing with his thumb. "You'll see it soon enough." And he was off again.

Filled with pedestrians and noise, the slope looked like a giant anthill. But that was the way to State Street so up the hill she walked, not minding it a bit. She was accustomed to hills and, anyway, there was so much to see. Finally, the street curved around and flattened, and she figured, since she was at the top, she must be in Brooklyn Heights. The street was lined with shops and businesses and bore a great deal of traffic—goods wagons, carriages, cabs. All sorts of vehicles moved rapidly in both directions. She stopped to ask an elderly gentleman who looked kindly if State Street was down that way and was told, "Yes, indeed, just a block or two past City Hall." The grand white building with a golden dome looming over everything must be City Hall. She was going the right way.

Brooklyn Heights was a pretty place, with many trees, but the houses were different than any she had ever seen before. They were square boxes, three or four stories tall; all in a row, in twos and threes, and all alike. Most had a long flight of stairs leading up to the front door. Why in the world, she wondered, wouldn't they put the entrance down at street level, like normal folks? And every house was decorated with ornate black iron railings and fences. But no gardens.

When she passed a nursemaid pushing a baby in a kind of bed on wheels, she asked again if she was going the right way to get to State Street.

"Right as rain. It's but two blocks more." The nursemaid eyed her satchel and medicine bag. "Is it a rooming house you're looking for, then?"

"That's right," Morgan said. "I'm just arrived in Brooklyn." The nursemaid smiled and said, "Aye, and that's no surprise. Mind, when you get to State, turn to the right and head for the water. Look for the store at number twelve. The landlady's a friend of mine, Catherine Enright. You tell her Maureen sent you." Her kindness warmed Morgan, who had been starting to feel rather small and lost. The city was so vast and so strange, it made her dizzy. At the same time, she was fascinated. It was so different from East Haddam or Chester. The roads were made of fitted stones and the streets just went on and on— house after house after house and no end to them. So many wagons and carriages and riders whizzing by, the horses' hooves striking sparks from the roadway.

Turning onto State Street, she started the downward trek toward the harbor. She could see the forest of masts at the foot of the hill. *Here I go,* she said to herself and, shifting the satchel from her right hand to her left, she started to look for number twelve. To her chagrin, house numbers were often missing, or, if there was one, it didn't always make sense. In one block, she'd seen two houses marked "58," one on either side of the road. Then the next number was 43.

Row houses with their long flights of steps and cast-iron railings were quite the fashion around here, she could see that. She liked them. In between the houses, there were various businesses. She glanced into an office of some kind, and saw men sitting at writing tables, dim behind a dust-covered window. A boarding house and a cabinetmaker's shop were next. She was hesitant to ask if they knew Catherine Enright; she didn't want to be taken for a hayseed. Down near the bottom of the hill the only businesses were saloons—so many of them! Several vehicles had passed her on the roadway, and she had to move into the gutters, which ran with dirty water. She walked by a smithy, averting her eyes because it made her think of Silas and all she'd left behind. She did not want to be reminded; she was going to begin a whole new life. She'd make something of herself, and there'd be no mooning over some boy.

Her satchel had grown quite heavy. She felt as if she'd been walking a long time with still no sign of 12 State Street, and was beginning to wonder if she'd somehow gone the wrong way. Then, almost at the end, she found a grocery store with a big window. Looking in, she saw, behind the counter, a plump young woman with dark hair piled atop her head in a kind of twist. Could that be Catherine Enright? Oh, how she hoped so. A sign on the door said OPEN, but still she hesitated, feeling a bit shy. The woman looked up and motioned for her to come inside. With relief, Morgan opened the door, asking: "Is this number twelve?"

"Yes, ma'am. Catherine Enright at yer service. You're new here, are you not?" She had the same accent as the nursemaid.

"Very new," Morgan said, laughing a little. "I just got off the steamship from Deep River, Connecticut. A woman, a nursemaid, was kind enough to give me your address . . . Maureen, she said."

"Well, good on her. Put down your burdens, Miss, and tell me how I might be of service."

"I need a room. To live in."

"Do you now? As it turns out, I've a room upstairs. Vacated this very morning by Lizzie Coyle the dressmaker who moved across the river to Manhattan, to be closer to her work. Would Miss—uh . . ."

"Wellburn. Morgan Wellburn."

"Morgan, is it? Like in the story of King Arthur."

"Yes." Morgan smiled, very pleased. "Exactly. I was supposed to be a boy and when I wasn't, my father said let's name her Morgan anyway."

"Imagine that! And a pretty name it is. But . . . wasn't Morgan le Fay a witch?" Catherine Enright's eyes were mischievous. "I don't know about renting to a witch, Miss Morgan."

"Morgan le Fay was a white witch . . . and good witches run in my family."

"You don't say so!" Mrs. Enright looked more awed than scared, although she crossed herself.

"I'm part American Indian," said Morgan. "And my mother

told me she's directly descended from two *moigu* . . . medicine
men."

"And you, Miss Morgan? Are you tellin' me you're a wad-
dayacallit, moygoo, too?"

Morgan laughed. "Not really. I've trained for two years
with a doctor."

"A doctor, now! Can you do birthing?"

"Of course."

"Praise be. We haven't had a midwife in these parts since
Maggie Malone died of the consumption. And little Annie Carrigan, she's due about now. She lives right around the corner on
Furman Street, above the saloon. So we can put you right to
work, I'm thinking. Yes, you'll do nicely. Come along." She
turned the sign on the shop door around, so it said BACK SOON,
and took off her apron. Opening a door into the back of the
building, she motioned for Morgan to follow her.

As they climbed the three flights of stairs, Catherine Enright
talked. "I'm a widow woman, you know, though I'm but eight
and twenty. I lost me husband to the mumps, of all the damned
things. Could yer believe it, girl? And him a big strong fellow
never sick a day in his life. He was gittin' better, you know,
when his heart gave out, sudden like. And the sudden grief
caused me to miscarry. So I haven't even a babe to keep me
company."

They'd reached the top floor and Morgan was just a little
out of breath, but not Catherine Enright. Flinging open the
door to a small room under the eaves, she continued with her
story. "Plenty of fellows court me, you know—don't I have a
business, and some money put by. But I haven't met the one
I'm meant for, not yet. So I'm biding me time. And how do
you like it? 'Tis a wee bit small, but see, there are two windows and that's a new coverlet on the bed and this trunk will
hold what you've got quite nicely, don't you think?"

Morgan liked her, liked her a lot. "Well, Mrs. Enright . . ."

"Cat. That's what I'm called. Cat Enright and I'll be pleased
if you'll do the same."

"Yes'm. I like the room, Cat. I'll take it."

"And I'm that glad for it. Come back down, why don't you,
and I'll make us a cuppa. While we're having our tea, you can

tell me how you came to Brooklyn Heights from all the way up there in Connecticut."

But the kettle had barely gone on the stove when a small girl came running into the store, saying "Cat, Cat, Mum's having it, right *now*!"

"Is she now? Look here, Mary Clare, this lady is new to our neighborhood and what do you know, she's a midwife! Isn't that grand!"

Morgan found herself being whisked away to Furman Street, to the Carrigan family's three small rooms. She delivered the baby that very night, a fine big girl. There were four or five women standing around the bed, commenting on everything. They were amazed at how often Morgan washed her hands, something Dr. Grace had taught her. And she explained to them how childbirth fever could be caused by dirty hands and instruments. They clucked and nodded but said, "Well now, that was hard to believe." They had to admit, though, that she had the touch. She had good hands and knew how to talk a babe right out of its mother's womb. When the child, who was to be called Maeve, was at her mother's breast, there was supper waiting at the next-door neighbor's kitchen table. Morgan met many new people that evening, for the word spread quickly that the Carrigan baby had been delivered by a new midwife living in Cat Enright's house. She didn't get to bed until nearly midnight that night. And she was so exhausted, she slept through until the next afternoon.

Morgan soon knew everyone on the block—especially the other tenants who rented rooms at 12 State Street. Anne Cushing, widow; Bridgit McNulty, a seventeen-year-old orphan who worked days in a big house on Orange Street; and Timothy Mahon, the lame printer. She walked around to become familiar with the immediate neighborhood. On the corner of Furman and State there was a saloon, as there was on the corner of Columbia and State. Farther along on Furman Street, there were two more saloons. A great deal of drinking went on everywhere in the neighborhood, a lot of drunkenness, a lot of noisy fighting. When some of the men got drunk, they went home and hit their wives and children. Morgan knew because she quickly became physician to the women and children who lived nearby. Her patients told their friends, and soon she was known to the working people of Brooklyn Heights, Cobble Hill, and most particularly, Irishtown, hard by the Brooklyn Navy Yard, where the little frame houses were crammed into mean rutted streets that ran with sewage.

She charged these poor people very little, sometimes nothing, and she often took her pay in loaves of home-baked bread or a hand-sewn apron, or maybe just a promise. Her patients thought her wonderful; they thought she performed marvels and miracles, but that was only because she knew healing techniques most of them had never heard of. Still, nobody minded that her ways were strange. They only knew that what Morgan Wellburn did for them worked and that, besides her healing ways, she had something even more important—a good heart.

The first time Morgan saw Della Blessing was on the corner near Cat's house. The child leaned on a makeshift crutch, holding her free hand out, saying, "A penny for a little crippled girl." She had large liquid dark eyes fringed with thick curling lashes. The rest of her face was hidden behind layers of grime. As for the color of her hair, who could tell? It was filthy and matted and crawling with head lice.

Morgan, of course, dug into her pocket and gave the child three cents. She was rewarded with a dazzling smile. "Oh, thank you, lady. Thank you."

"How old are you, child?" She was a tiny little thing, but starvation often stunted growth. Still, when she answered, "Three," it was a shock. Why, she was nothing but a babe. Who would let such a little thing out to beg all alone?

During supper that evening at Cat Enright's table, Morgan asked about her. "I don't remember seeing her before."

There was a small silence. Then, Cat said, " 'Tis Della Blessing. The Blessings used to live on Columbia Place and then, one day, they were gone. And now, like the bad penny, they've turned up again."

"The little girl has so many bruises and scabs," Morgan remarked. "She must fall down a great deal."

Glances were exchanged, and Cat snorted and said, "Fall down, is it? Not likely! It'll be her brothers and sisters knocking her about. 'Tis a shame, but what's to be done?"

"Why don't her parents do something?"

"Ah, Morgan, you know how it is. Her da's on the docks, and many's the time there's no work at all. And her mother does piecework, all day and half the night. Most of the time, don't you know, they're too exhausted to see anything. She has that clubfoot, poor little mite, and the other children, they do nothing but make fun of her and cuff her and push her down."

Bridgit McNulty, a little mousy creature who normally had barely a word to say for herself, burst out with "And who's to help her? That's what I want to know! This was supposed to be the Golden Land, where everyone was rich! A pack of lies, that's what we were told! And there she is, but three years old, half-starved, with never anyone to give even a wash to her face, while she stands on her one good leg, begging for pennies!" Then she blushed scarlet and looked fiercely down at her plate.

Morgan said gently, "I'll see to her cuts and bruises, and maybe I can manage to wash her off while I'm about it. Would you be willing to bring her bread and cheese and a morsel of meat from someone's plate, Bridgie?"

The girl's face became even redder, but she nodded. "That I will." After that everyone at the table pitched in and said they'd like to do something, too. Would a penny help? Or an old shirt with a few mends in it? People could be good, Morgan thought. It was a shame they had to be pushed and prodded, though.

The Blessings lived on Furman Street, not far from 12 State Street. Furman was a typical crowded working-class street with too many people living in too little room. There wasn't enough work on the docks, and far too many saloons beckoning. Morgan had a lot of patients there. Since she was called upon as physician, healer, nurse, and midwife, she saw everything that went on in those meager households. She saw how hard everyone worked—children, too—and even so, there never seemed enough to eat, never any free time. The young-sters were all so pale and thin, and the women seemed always pregnant or nursing.

Morgan knew that a woman could limit the number of her children. Annis had told her, in the ancient days, women of her tribe never had more than two or three. "And if you think it's by chance that there's only you and Becky," she had added, "you can just think again." But when Morgan suggested to her most worn-out patients that having fewer babies might make life a bit easier, they either laughed at her for being so naive or said that what God gave them, they would accept. The sad truth was that since only one out of four seemed to survive, some wondered what difference it made how many they had.

For the next three years, Morgan and her fellow lodgers made sure that little Della had enough to eat—when her brothers and sisters didn't steal it away from her. Tim Mahon, the printer, who was a dab hand at carpentry, made Della a crutch that was padded where it went into her armpit, so she wasn't always sore and bleeding. Della's mother, Rose, came over once to thank them. You could see right away that the child looked just like her mother, down to the pallor of her skin. But there was something vacant about Rose. Morgan would give her medicine and she would forget to take it. She never seemed to know where any of her children might be. Cat Enright said it was drink—"tipples in secret, that one. I'd wager my life on it." But Morgan thought it was the lack of food; the woman was as thin as a shadow.

Drunk or not, poor Rose Blessing was dogged by bad luck. She became pregnant several times and miscarried with heavy bleeding. She was often so sick, she could not finish her home work. Her husband, Conor, was killed in a brawl on the docks. Diphtheria took the three older children. Then one day Della came hobbling to the grocery store, tears streaming down her face, asking for "Doctor Morgan." One of the women on the street sent her son to fetch Morgan—she was seeing a patient with a festering sore—and she came running to see what was the trouble.

"We have to go across the river and live under the Great Bridge where there's piecework to be had," Della said. "And, oh, I don't want to go. I'll never see you or Tim or Bridgie again, never! What will I do? They'll push me down and laugh and call me Gimp!" And she burst into fresh tears.

Morgan did not like it, either, and here was Rose, pregnant again. "Conor's farewell gift to me," she had said, in a rare attempt at humor. She had not been well with it and was too thin by half. But what could anyone do? At least she was going to live with her friend Joan, another widow with two little ones. Times were desperate. Together, two women and their children might be able to make their way. So off they went.

Word came to Morgan, a month before the due date, that Rose, bleeding and feverish, was calling for Mrs. Wellburn. Morgan knew Rose did not live in a nice place, but nothing could have prepared her for what she found. The big building was directly under the stone battlements of the bridge. She entered into a dreadful stench-filled darkness. Except for a few minutes around noon, no natural light ever penetrated into the building. She had to yell for someone to show her the way, and shortly, a child came running with a torch. He explained as he led the way that their only light was the electric light that went on for the Great Bridge and the streets at night. She felt like a mole, groping her way through pitch-black, narrow hallways. But, after a few minutes, her eyes adjusted and she was able to see some details. When the child lit a candle stump from his torch, she saw that she was in a tiny room with a small stove and a sewing machine under one window, a table and a rickety chair, and an old mattress on a dry-goods box, set in one corner. On the mattress lay Rose Blessing. She gave Morgan a wan smile. Suddenly, something grabbed Morgan around her legs. She nearly fell over. The creature was Della, little Della, who looked to be starving, her cheeks all caved in and her eyes sunken in her head.

It took an effort of will not to cry out at the horror of the place. But Morgan controlled her feelings and her voice. Squatting next to Rose, she told Della, "Now don't you worry, I'll take good care of your ma."

Rose did not have a high fever: however, she was weak with hunger and still bleeding heavily from her miscarriage. Morgan went to boil some water but there was no coal to heat it. "It's five dollars for the rent and coal costs twelve cents a scuttle," Della informed her. "In a good month, if she works very hard, Ma can make nineteen dollars."

"If I did fine sewing," Rose whispered, "I could earn more. But I'm always sick, and it's hard, when you've nothing to eat for days."

While she cleaned up Rose and did her best to make her comfortable, Morgan heard more details, and with every word, she became angrier. Everyone who lived in this terrible place slept by day and did piecework by night, using the bridge lights. It saved the price of candles. They sewed overalls at a dollar a dozen: "it's heavy, hard work, and it takes sewing fourteen hours straight to finish a dozen a day. Joan does it, but she's strong." It was a rare day that Rose was able to make a whole dollar. Most of the time, she contracted out for sixty-six cents a day.

Morgan sent the little boy—one of Joan's, she discovered— out to buy food and beer. "See if you can find some apples," she ordered. "Bread. Cheese. Potatoes. Tea. Coal. Get coal. And hurry, please." She gave him two dollars, hoping he wouldn't run away with it. But he did no such thing. She felt so guilty at having thought it that when he returned, laden down with his purchases, she gave him an apple all for himself.

Tears trickled out of Rose's eyes as Morgan spooned tea into her, then bread soaked in beer. Rose had lost most of her teeth and her gums were raw and sore. "The river's the best place, I'm thinking, for them that wants ease," she said in a weak voice. "Such life as this isn't living."

"I'm going to help you, Rose," Morgan said. "You can't give up. You've little Della to think of."

"You take her. I'm done for."

"Ma, don't say that!" Della cried. "Don't say that!" But Rose's head had flopped to one side and she fainted.

"You're not done for, not yet," Morgan said grimly. Giving Rose a shake, she half dragged, half carried her outside and down the street, with Della hobbling quicker than you might have imagined, right behind. Morgan headed straight for the Hester Street Free Dispensary.

It was Saturday, "the Hebrew holiday," which meant the

dispensary was mobbed. In fact, there was a line all the way down the stairs and into the street. At first Morgan thought they would wait their turn. But Rose, who had rallied and walked some of the way, was beginning to crumple again and her eyes looked horribly glassy. There was no time to wait.

"Follow me, Della," Morgan said, and, holding Rose firmly around the waist, began to force their way past the patient line, yelling, "I'm a doctor! Please let me through! This woman is dying." By a miracle, all three of them managed to gain the top of the stairs without anyone tripping and tumbling back down.

In spite of the large crowd waiting on benches, it was peaceful in the waiting room. The large space had benches painted different colors. At the far end of the room in a railed-off corner—the distributing bureau—sat the physician in charge, holding a pad of tickets the same colors as the benches. Morgan had been here before, so she knew that red meant surgical; blue, medical; yellow, eye and ear; gray, diseases of women and children; green, dental. All tickets were numbered; when your number was called, you could go in. A fee of ten cents was charged for those who could pay; those who could not were treated free.

Morgan, still holding Rose, who was as limp as a rag doll, was second in line. The man in front of her was asked for ten cents. "It's the government ought to pay to keep us alive, and that's a fact!" he bellowed. "God knows they suck the very life out of us!" A ripple of laughter rose from the benches, but he fished in a pocket and came up with the money, spoke with the doctor, and was given a green ticket.

Morgan had to ask Della to dig out two nickles from her purse, and they were issued a gray ticket. She dragged Rose to the gray benches, and sat gratefully. As thin and frail as she was, Rose Blessing was a dead weight, and Morgan wasn't sure how long she could have kept holding the sick woman upright. Fifteen minutes later, Morgan and her charges were allowed into the medical room.

The sparsely furnished room held a table with the doctor sitting behind it, two or three wooden chairs, and various instruments near the washstand. A nurse, in her crisp white cap with the frill and her starched white apron, stood nearby. Wisps of the nurse's fair hair had escaped the cap, her clothing was wrinkled, and Morgan noticed that the pocket on her apron was torn. But her eyes were intelligent and thoughtful as she looked over the odd trio. The physician also looked them over, but with an unmistakable irritation. Morgan could guess what he was thinking. What had taken her so long to bring him this woman, so obviously at death's door? He picked up a pen, motioned the three of them to take seats, and was preparing to take a medical history, when another nurse poked her head around the door to plead: "Doctor, would you mind? Emergency. It looks like a cut artery. Work accident."

"Nurse Apple will take the patient's history," the doctor said, and left.

"If *this* isn't an emergency," said Nurse Apple, astringently, "I don't know one. And I do. However . . . name?"

Morgan told her Rose's name, her age, and her nationality, which Della said was English. "I wouldn't know where she was born. Do you, Della?"

"I heard her talk about Liverpool."

"That's good enough. What's really important is what she's suffering from."

"Malnutrition," Morgan said. "Too many pregnancies. Too much work and too little hope. You should see the horrible place they are forced to live in. No, you shouldn't see it. It shouldn't exist."

Nurse Apple smiled. "I agree, absolutely. But we have to write down what ails her."

"And you can't say 'too little hope.' I know."

Della, who had been silent, but attentive to their conversation, suddenly spoke up. "Ma's been drinking again. She tries not to, but she says it kills the pain."

"I don't think your mother is in this condition from genever, child," the nurse said, kindly enough. She turned back to Morgan.

"She recently miscarried," Morgan answered the unspoken question. "It's not the first time . . . and I think she lost a lot of blood." Morgan told her the whole story: how she knew Rose Blessing and how Della had sent word to her. "I came as quickly as I could, but I found Rose as you see her. Della's a good child. She's been starving, too, and you see she has some trouble walking. By the time I got there, today . . ."

Nurse Apple gave a brisk nod. "Not your fault, of course not. It's the usual blind disregard by the authorities. How the city of New York can allow their citizens to starve and die, and do nothing—!" Nurse Apple's face reddened with her outrage. "One day, the downtrodden of this earth, all those who are invisible and unheard, will rise up and overrun those who choose not to see them." She stopped suddenly, looking stricken, and said, "Oh dear. Excuse me. Working in this dispensary is a lesson in forgotten people. And . . . I tend to get rather . . . inflamed about certain injustices. But I do beg your pardon."

"No, no," Morgan said, "I quite agree with you. I'm physician and midwife to poor immigrants mostly. I've wondered, myself, why there must be all the unnecessary suffering I see."

"What I hate the most," said the nurse, as she deftly examined Rose, jotting down notes on a pad, "is my lack of power to help. Oh, I can nurse, I can alleviate some of the physical pain. But if I want to change lives, I must go to college and become a social worker."

"To college!"

"At my age? Yes. Four and twenty is not so terribly old."

Morgan, who was twenty-three and knew she was considered an old maid, smiled. "Not a bit old. I am simply in awe of a woman who makes time to go to school. And it is interesting to meet someone who sees what I see. My patients say either that it's the will of God or that they have no luck. And they shrug and accept that what is must always be. As for the rich folk in the neighborhood, *they* say the poor have always been among us. And they shrug and turn away."

Nurse Apple gave a smile, her first since Morgan had come into the room. It revealed two unexpected dimples and made her almost pretty. "You should come to my neighborhood. It's full of people with unusual ideas. There's always a meeting *somewhere* about redressing an injustice. I myself belong to a group trying to stop white slavery." To Morgan's surprised look, she nodded. "Oh yes. Young immigrant girls come to find a new life, and the jackals sweet-talk them into indenture . . . and worse. And what else can a girl do to make enough to live on? We're lucky, you and I. We have skills and we get a certain amount of respect. But look at this poor woman here, reduced to starvation because she wanted to stay decent." She said directly to Della, who was all ears, "Now don't you worry, we're going to do our best to make your mama better." Then, to Morgan: "The group I belong to was started by a woman who's a social worker and a Socialist. That's the sort of person who lives in my neighborhood."

Morgan had no notion what a Socialist might be and was ashamed to ask. She was very impressed with Nurse Apple's sophistication and knowledge. And she was but one year older than Morgan. *I have a lot to learn,* Morgan thought.

"What neighborhood is that?"

"Greenwich Village. Have you ever been there?"

Morgan flushed. "I hardly know Brooklyn."

"Tomorrow, come take lunch with me. I'll give you directions. Better yet, I'll meet you at the Manhattan terminus of the trolley and we'll walk or take a cab. We'll go to the Brevoort. The food is plentiful and cheap. And I'll show you the sights. Some of them will turn your stomach, I should warn you. There are brothels and vulgar dance halls and rowdy bars and drunken men crowd the streets, even in the daytime. But there are whole clans from Italy and France and Spain moving in." Her voice was so animated, even as her hands kept working, swabbing cuts and cleaning sores on Della's legs and back. "Poor child, you must fall a great deal. Yes," she continued to Morgan, "everything is changing, in the Village. Artists are beginning to move in. And we'll never be bothered with heavy traffic because there are so many skewed streets and little alleys and sudden dead ends. And all the Minettas—Minetta Lane, Minetta Court, Minetta—oh, but never mind that now. Here he comes, finally. The doctor. Oh, by the way, I'm Adelaide, Adelaide Apple."

"Morgan Wellburn."

"Pleased to make your acquaintance, Morgan Wellburn. Well . . . would you like to see Greenwich Village and meet my friends?"

"Indeed I would! I'm . . . I came here from a little hamlet in Connecticut and . . . I look forward to meeting you in the Village and learning something new."

"I think you'll find it interesting," Adelaide Apple said. "And, what's more, I think we'll be great friends, you and I."

14

1891, Greenwich Village

The weather had turned fine and Adelaide was delighted. When she'd awakened this morning to the sodden sound of rain, she had jumped out of bed to look out the window. It would clear; it *must* clear. She wanted the day to be perfect. By the time she got to the trolley terminal at 11:00, sure enough, the sun was shining brightly, and all the puddles were giving off steam as they dried and shrank. Morgan was already there, waiting for her. A new friend. Addie's heart lifted.

"What would you like to see?" she asked as soon as they had greeted each other. Morgan said, "Whatever you think would interest me. Everything!"

"Oh, there's so much to see! Come on then. Mind where you walk."

"I have heard," Morgan said, as they set off, walking west, "that Greenwich Village is becoming a haven for artists, writers, and other freethinkers. Will we see some today?"

"Probably not where we're going," Adelaide said. "Unless you really want to. I can take you wherever you like, though."

"No, no. It's your neighborhood. I just wondered how one recognizes them?"

"Well . . . many grow their hair long, very long. And they're queerly dressed. Any old garment worn any old way. But we probably won't see many Bohemians . . . that's what they're called, I really can't say why. They tend to keep to certain streets . . . even in certain buildings. There's one known as the House of Genius, because every man who has rooms there is some sort of artist or writer."

"House of Genius? And who named it that?" Morgan looked amused.

"Why . . . I don't know. I believe they did, themselves."

"Of course," Morgan said dryly, and they both laughed. "We should take rooms in a house," Morgan commented, "and call it the House of Medicine!"

At that moment, Adelaide asked herself, *Why not?* "Where do you live now?" she said aloud.

"In Cat Enright's boarding house on State Street in Brooklyn Heights," Morgan told her. "But I must admit, I am beginning to feel cramped in my little room. I'm very fond of Cat, I like the other boarders, and it's very convenient. Still . . . one small room for great big giant me."

"The Amazons were tall," Adelaide said. "And they ruled their world."

"Oh, thank you for those kind words. I hope I didn't sound self-pitying. My patients are always tipping their heads back to look up at me and saying, 'My but you're a big 'un, aren't you?' I don't mind, really. In fact, it's useful, as they don't dare disobey the big 'un."

"Oh, but I'm sure you wouldn't—oh, I see. That was meant to be ironic. I'm afraid I haven't a good ear for that."

"You have a fine ear, Adelaide. You hear very well what your patients need."

Adelaide felt herself blushing; it was her curse. "I'm in cramped quarters, too," she said, changing the subject. "And I've been thinking lately . . . about buying a house."

"A whole house? Isn't that very costly?"

"I have money, pots of it. Oh dear, I hope you don't think I'm putting on airs. My grandmother left me a great deal of money in her will."

"A house—! What a dream! My grandmother left me only a magic amulet."

Addie didn't want to ask exactly what Morgan meant by that. It might be another jest; she didn't know. "If two people bought a house together and split the cost . . ." she began, and then scolded herself. Just because she liked Morgan Wellburn so much did not mean Morgan was inclined the same way.

Once again, Adelaide changed the subject. "A few years ago, these were quiet streets. It really was like a village, small and peaceful. But now—" But now the streets were crowded with swarms of newcomers, immigrants—Germans and Irish, Italians and Spaniards—who brought with them their large noisy families, the strong smells of unfamiliar food, and a polyglot mixture of languages. Once-elegant private houses had become tenement slums, with ragged washing hanging from every window and women leaning out, their elbows resting on the sills, gazing down at the teeming streets filled with pushcarts, peddlers, and hordes of children.

"This was once a respectable neighborhood," Addie said, raising her voice to be heard, as they pushed their way through the crowd on the northern edge of Washington Square. "Wellto-do families exchanged calling cards and behaved in a proper manner." She laughed. "And now, we have noisy foreigners. We have . . ." She flung her arms wide. "We have lodging houses, studios for starving artists, beer gardens! There are those who deplore the fall of Greenwich Village, but I see new ideas coming in and, down here, all the usual rules have disappeared!" She smiled broadly. "Is that not wonderful?"

Morgan, who had been quite silent, looking from one scene to another, burst out laughing. "Adelaide, you had me quite fooled. I thought you were going to be one of those who deplore the ruination of this place. And here you are, applauding it! I do like that. Tell me more, please!"

Completely warmed by this response, Addie reached out for Morgan's hand and squeezed it, then just as quickly pulled her hand back. She had once had a very close friendship with a girl at boarding school, and it had ended badly. She had been careful ever since.

By the time she was fourteen, Adelaide Apple knew enough not to look into mirrors. She was not pretty. Her mama often gazed at her, shaking her head sadly, sighing what a pity that Addie had taken after the Apples and not the Bernsteins. "But never mind, my darling, you have your inheritance—and intelligence, of course. You will do well, never fear." But Addie knew that beauty was everything, and she was sure she would never do well.

What a miracle, when Bonnie Metzger chose her—plain chubby Addie Apple—to be her special friend. Bonnie was petite and lively. They were both new girls in the tenth grade at the Goodman School for Young Ladies, a boarding school in Westchester County. They sat next to each other in the first assembly, and Bonnie whispered comments to her all through the many speeches: The headmistress resembled a bulldog. When would they ever have fun with all the work they were supposed to do? Did Addie suppose Latin had killed the Latin professor, considering it was a dead language? Didn't Addie think Mr. Goodman was terribly handsome?

Never had anyone sought out her opinions before; never had another girl whispered and giggled with her. What a lovely warm feeling it was. Adelaide was smitten. From that first meeting, she was devoted to Bonnie Metzger.

For a month or two, they were inseparable. At meals, the girls were assigned to tables of eight. Addie and Bonnie always sat next to each other. "I depend on you, Addie," Bonnie told her. "You know how to get things done." She often sent Addie to the head table to ask for more dessert or extra napkins, "because they listen to you, Addie." It wasn't only mealtimes, either. Bonnie always sent Adelaide to the headmistress to ask special favors. Adelaide gladly went, in a glow of happiness.

They did their schoolwork together in the library and then went upstairs together, usually to Bonnie's room, where they talked and talked. Where Bonnie talked and talked, actually. Adelaide was content to sit and listen, while she brushed Bonnie's long, thick, dark curly hair. She loved the crisp feel of it as it curled around her finger, loved the smile of pleasure on Bonnie Metzger's face. Bonnie insisted, "Nobody knows how to get the tangles out without hurting me, nobody but you, Addie."

Addie told Bonnie how disappointed her mama was in the

way she looked. She told Bonnie that her father found a child in the house a nuisance, and that was why she was at the Goodman School. One night, she admitted to Bonnie that she'd never had a close girlfriend before. And, in her enthusiasm, she told Bonnie Metzer, "I love you, Bonnie, I love you more even than my parents!" And she put her arms around Bonnie and kissed her.

Suddenly, Bonnie wasn't sitting next to her at table. Bonnie wasn't asking her for help with her geometry or Latin. She wasn't wheedling Adelaide to "just start my composition, I never have ideas like you do!" She ignored Adelaide, and she wouldn't answer any of Addie's notes, asking what she had done. Bonnie began to walk hand in hand with Emma Diamond, who was stupid and stuck-up but gorgeous. The two of them whispered together and giggled. Often, they looked over at Addie and giggled louder. Adelaide, drowning in her unhappiness, was always on the verge of tears. She lost her appetite and picked at her food.

One day climbing the stairs, her head down, she bumped into somebody. "Oh dear," she said. "I'm so sorry—" When she looked up, it was Emma Diamond, grinning at her, not moving aside.

"You're so clumsy, Adelaide Apple. No wonder your mother can't stand the sight of you! No wonder your father wants you out of the house! No wonder Bonnie didn't want you *kissing* her!" Emma kept her voice low, so that nobody else could hear. Then she moved to the side, and laughing, ran down the stairs, pushing by Addie deliberately. Someone else laughed, too. It was Bonnie, close behind Emma. The sounds of their laughter floated up the stairs.

Something seized ahold of Addie then; she felt it like a wave of first hot and then icy cold. Bonnie Metzger had told someone else all of Addie's secrets! She had told about the kiss, the token of Addie's love! Bonnie had found it awful and amusing! It was too much, too terrible, too humiliating! Adelaide began to shake and then she began to scream. A storm of weeping overtook her, which she was unable to stop. Oh, the betrayal . . . the hilarity . . . it was unbearable.

"You!" she shrieked. "Both of you! You, Bonnie, and you, Emma! You are hateful! You are horrible!" Two heads far below her swiveled in unison, two blurry faces turned up to her.

Weeping loudly, Addie ran the rest of the way up the stairs and into her room, slamming the door behind her. Oh, horrible, horrible! She flung herself onto her bed, pounding her fists soundlessly into the comforter in frustration. After a time, someone knocked on her door, and she heard voices. Bonnie's voice, too. She would not answer. She did not hear the door open. She felt a hand on her head and she turned. Bonnie was bending over her, saying, "Addie, please. Mrs. Goodman says you will make yourself ill. Please calm yourself."

Through her swollen lids, Addie looked up at her tormentor, once her beloved friend. Bonnie's tight curls and full dark lips no longer seemed beautiful, but evil and ugly. Addie rose up and grabbed a handful of Bonnie Metzger's hair and pulled as hard as she could, shaking Bonnie's head back and forth. "You hateful girl! You traitor!" Addie shrieked. Bonnie, she was dimly aware, was screaming, too.

Someone pried her hands away from Bonnie's head. The headmistress called the local doctor, who came to the school in times of emergency. His name was Dr. Hurd and he pronounced Adelaide to be suffering from hysteria—"typical of females who have overtaxed their brains," he declared. Addie knew she was not hysterical. Her brain had not been overtaxed by thought, as Dr. Hurd believed. But she was sent home anyway. She was told she would be allowed to return the following term, if she could promise Mr. and Mrs. Goodman that she would behave like a proper young lady and control her tendency to hysterics.

Of course, she had refused to go back to that terrible place. How could she return, when she had been publicly humiliated? Her dear mama did not understand at all—"The thing to do, my poor child, is lift your head high and *dare* them to think badly of you!"—but Papa said, "We'll hire a tutor and there's an end to it. Best not to force her, when she's got no talent for getting along in society."

Adelaide knew she was prone to have crushes on women, and that it sometimes made them back off. She realized she must be very careful not to scare Morgan Wellburn away. She was really taken with Morgan, so tall and commanding, so exotic looking, so levelheaded. If only *she* could be that way; then she would be a leader instead of always just following along.

"Come, let me show you Bleecker Street. Bleecker Street," she added, "really is a terrible shame. Just a generation ago, it was a proud and fashionable roadway, you know, with beautiful homes. And now . . . but come. You'll see."

Bleecker Street was truly dreadful, even in broad daylight: dirty, crowded, raucous. At the corner of Bleecker and Thompson, they could hardly move through the dozens of pushcarts and their customers who pushed and shoved to get to the front of the pack. Everybody shouted at the top of their lungs. Morgan was amazed, saying there was nothing like it in Brooklyn Heights. "You can buy anything here," she marveled, staring at the scene. "Food . . . clothing . . . bedding . . . pots . . . anything and everything."

"Further along the street, there are other—um—goods for sale, not so savory," Addie said. "Come along, you'll see." Morgan gaped as they passed one dance hall after another, and brothels, too, where heavily rouged and powdered girls lounged against walls and lampposts, smoking small cigars, wearing as little as possible and giving bold looks to every man who passed. Every second building held a dime museum with signs promising "spicy French sensations" or "secrets of the seraglio." In the alleyway between two saloons, a man with a filthy face and ragged clothes—a boy, really, in his teens—was pushing a needle into his arm. Morgan was puzzled by the sight, and Addie had to explain. "Probably a morphine addict," she said. "There are many, I'm afraid." As they walked along, various sellers accosted them, men, women, little boys and girls, wanting them to buy shoelaces or oranges or flowers or toothpicks. Morgan stopped and gave a penny to a little girl for some matches.

"It's appalling," she remarked. "That human beings should have to live this way. We were poor, but I went to school. These children, I'm afraid . . ."

"Are lost to decent society? Oh yes. But, you know, most of

them are dead by nineteen or twenty. Yes, it is dreadful," Adelaide agreed, seeing the look on Morgan's face. "Be careful," she added, in a very different tone. "See those boys on the corner? Probably pickpockets. Hold your purse close to you . . . ah. There."

A sudden commotion at the corner made them hurry to see what was happening. An old woman lay on the street, moaning, while a boy of nine or ten, holding a bicycle, yelled at her for walking right in front of him and causing damage to his machine.

"I've seen this before," Addie said. "While everyone is standing around staring, his little friends are picking pockets . . . *Hoy! You over there with the green cap! I see what you're doing!*" The boy with the green cap made a mad dash for the next street. The rotund gentleman he'd been standing behind turned, patted his pockets, and called loudly for the police. Everyone nearby had turned to look at them, and Addie could feel the color climbing in her face. She blushed so easily, she hated it—especially in front of a new friend. Whatever had come over her, to shout out like that?

"Good for you!" Morgan cried. "I guess he got away with the gentleman's purse, but you frightened him into running off. Now he won't rob anyone else. Quick thinking, Adelaide!"

Addie was saved further embarrassment by the cries of the woman lying in the street. "And what about me, hey? Everyone busy looking to see what's what, but nobody to help an old woman what's been knocked over by a scalawag!"

Morgan slid Addie an amused look, and together they ran over and lifted the woman to her feet. "Now, mother, calm yourself," Morgan said in a firm voice. "I'm a doctor and my friend here is a nurse. You're in good hands." Morgan quickly looked at the woman's slight bruises and, in a moment, pronounced her quite fit. Addie dusted her off with a clean handkerchief. Addie could hear the crowd's murmurs of "woman doctor . . . imagine . . . ever see the like?" She looked straight at them, proud to be in the company of such a competent person.

They continued on, much more companionable than before. "We make a good team, Adelaide," Morgan said. "It's really pleasant to be with another woman who doesn't feel the need to squeal and scream at the sight of blood or even dirt." Pleased, Addie said, "I was afraid I'd made a terrible mistake, bringing you down here to see the underside of life."

"Not at all. It's quite new to me. But, you know, I doctor mostly poor people and so many of them have such mean lives, too. That woman I brought to the dispensary, Rose Blessing, for instance, and her little girl. I wonder how long they'll be able to survive. I fear for them, and I know there are hundreds more . . ."

"Thousands," Addie corrected.

"But you're so quick to help," Morgan said. "I admired the way you shouted at that young thief. I was sure you'd go running after him and tackle him to the ground."

They smiled at each other, but Addie was bemused. Morgan saw her as strong and brave, much as she saw Morgan. She'd never thought of herself that way. Yet, when a social issue or a matter of fair treatment arose, it was true, she would quickly lose her shyness. *Well, what do you know?* she said to herself. *And to think I never saw that myself.*

"I'd like to go to a meeting with you," Morgan said. "The group that's fighting white slavery . . ."

"The Society for the Protection of Young Women."

"Yes. Would you take me? Do you think I could join?"

Addie clasped both of Morgan's hands in hers, and this time she didn't care, she was going to hang on. "Would I? I'd be delighted. We can use every new member we can get." Her heart was singing. They *were* a good team, they were. Morgan had said so. Maybe they could stay friends. Maybe she needn't be all alone in the world anymore!

SECTION THREE

═══════════════

Morgan Wellburn
Alexander Becker, M.D.
Birdie Grace Becker
Adelaide Apple

15

July 1904, New York City

Morgan had left the house so quickly, she just hoped she had everything. As she passed one of the stores on Fulton Street, she gave a sideways look at her reflection in the window. She looked fine, she decided. In fact, she looked completely up to date. The Gibson girl look was very popular, and who was Morgan Wellburn to fight the latest rage. She was wearing a shirtwaist, and a long skirt with a wide belt around her waist. Her hair was swept up in the popular pompadour and, of course, she wore hat and gloves. Her old leather medicine bag looked a bit strange, but she wouldn't be without it. She still wore the shell amulet her mother gave her, tucked away between her breasts. It was supposed to be lucky; she hoped so. In any case, it was an antique.

She was pleased with the way she looked, but . . . she wasn't getting any younger, was she? Thirty-six this year, an advanced age for an unmarried woman. She'd long ago made up her mind she didn't care. Her experience with Silas, so long ago, had taught her a lesson. She would never again put herself in the position of being secretly despised. She knew that she was too tall, too dark, too strong looking, with a bold nose and a direct look that many men found disconcerting. She just plain frightened a lot of her suitors. Well, and so be it. She was a respected physician, especially in the poorer communities, even though they listed her as a nurse in the *Brooklyn Eagle Directory*. She really should go to medical school, like Dr. Grace was always telling her to do. But there was no time; she

167

was always so busy. Anyway, what difference would it make for her to go to school? Her patients didn't ask to see her graduation certificate.

She took the trolley across the bridge, enjoying the breeze that blew through the open car. The view over the harbor, even after all these years, still thrilled her. Vainly, she tried to smooth out her wrinkled clothes. The high collar on her shirt-waist was starting to wilt from the heat, and she could feel the long strands of hair on her neck that had come loose from the combs. What did it matter? she asked herself, as she pulled out two combs and attempted to restore her once-neat hairdo. She was going to attend a birth, not a fancy-dress ball. A message from Addie, saying there was a problem birth at 45 Ludlow Street and *hurry*, had brought her out into the midday heat.

Getting off the trolley on the Manhattan side, she all but ran down Ludlow Street. The place was a tenement, and she took the stairs two at a time, as she usually did. Why did all the emergencies have to be on the fifth floor? When she got to the landing, she was damp all over inside her clothes and just a bit out of breath. She looked down the dingy hall. Someone had cracked a door open a little and she could hear a familiar voice: Adelaide's. She went down the hall, leaned inside the open door and called, "Addie?"

Her friend came running out from the back room. There were only two rooms, and both were dark and—judging by the swarms of bugs in the front room—filthy.

"Morgan. At last. Am I happy to see you. The poor girl, she's trying very hard but this baby just doesn't want to be born. Breech, I think. I've felt her belly and I can't be sure, but I think it's also facing the wrong way." Now Morgan could hear the low-pitched whimpering from the next room. "She's been in labor for nearly twenty-four hours." Morgan could hear the sounds of weak coughing. "She's worn out, poor thing," Addie said. "And the baby's tired, too, I think. When I listened a moment ago, the heartbeat seemed fainter to me."

"I don't like the sound of her cough, either. She might be consumptive."

"My thought exactly, Morgan. She's not strong at all and I'm afraid . . ."

Morgan put a hand on her friend's shoulder. As if Addie hadn't enough to do at her regular job, she came down to the Lower East Side every Saturday to volunteer at the Hester Street Free Dispensary, where the poorest immigrants always came. The dispensary must have sent her to the woman's home—if such a word could be used to describe the dreadful hovel.

"Together, we'll make sure she survives. Haven't we always?"

Thirteen years after their first meeting, they still worked together when necessary, were the closest of friends, and the proud owners of a beautiful house on the Heights.

"Why don't we just go on in and see what you think." Addie blew strands of hair away from her eyes, but they flopped right back down. Her hair was always coming loose from her pompadour, buttons were forever falling off her blouse, and hems on her skirts loosened themselves and drooped. She was very fair, so blond that her eyes looked lashless. A round, plump, short woman, she looked to many people as if she couldn't keep a thought straight in her head. They were wrong, as Morgan knew very well. Adelaide Apple was extremely intelligent and competent, and always ready to right a social wrong. If she lacked anything, it was humor. She was not a woman with a playful turn of mind, and Morgan sometimes missed that. But Addie was kindness itself. Morgan had never been sorry about their decision to buy a house and live in it together. Surely, neither of them would ever marry.

When she walked into the bedroom, Morgan was taken aback. A man, very blond, very elegant, was sitting by the bedside, holding the woman's hand and trying to reassure her. Anger boiled up in Morgan's chest. So! The father of the child! They had no shame, no shame at all! She belonged to the Society for the Protection of Young Women, and she had seen too many scenes like this. A rich man, probably married, fathering a child on a poor immigrant girl he had seduced. Well, she wanted him out of here, and said so, briskly. "You're not needed, sir. I'm the doctor and I'll see to her."

At that, Adelaide, who was moistening a towel to put on the woman's forehead, began to laugh. "Morgan, let me introduce

you to Dr. Becker. Dr. Alexander Becker. Alex, this is my
friend, Morgan Wellburn, I've told you about."

Morgan was, for a change, speechless. A doctor! Quickly,
she rearranged her thoughts and her assumptions. A doctor—
well, that was different. She prepared herself to apologize, but
when he turned his head to acknowledge the introduction, she
found herself gazing into the brightest, bluest eyes she had
ever seen. Her heart began to beat a little faster, and she told
herself to stop being so stupid. She begged his pardon, stam-
mering a little, and busied herself with preparations, asking
questions about the pregnancy. Inside, she was bubbling. At
last it had happened. After all the suitors and lovers and heartache and, yes, sometimes despair, it had finally happened. The
man she was meant for was here. She could not look at him
again, although she was longing to. They were meant for each
other, she knew it. But how would she ever make him see it?

Alex Becker had always thought of himself as a man in control of his mind and his emotions. Yet he had just been thrown
into a state of utter stupefaction. All because of a tall woman
with jet black hair, eyes as deep and unfathomable as the
ocean, and a gaze that had pierced him.

He needed to know her—in every sense of the word. He
needed to hold her—to learn what was behind that cool and
piercing gaze—to know her mind and her heart—to . . . to . . .
By God, he was thinking like a smitten schoolboy! He was
thirty-four, a rich man who would be even richer when his parents were gone, a respected physician. He was not the sort of
man to fall in love at first sight. He was not the man to fall in
love at all. It was ridiculous, and in another moment, he was
sure, he would feel normal once more.

"Of course, yes," he mumbled. "Adelaide's friend. Morgan."
His mouth went dry, his voice came out in a croak.

"Morgan Wellburn. Midwife," she said.

Wellburn. An English name. But she did not look English.
She looked . . . he did not know what she looked like. He had
never seen another woman like her. She was tall and broad-
shouldered, her hair the color and sheen of jet. She might be
part Chinese, or from Araby or Persia, with those high cheek-

bones and proud nose. He thought her the most beautiful creature he had ever seen. *Morgan Wellburn. Midwife.*

He said something more, something about how Adelaide had praised her, anything to keep her looking into his eyes. She colored then, and became all midwife, asking him details about poor Margaret. The patient lay exhausted on the narrow bed as her uterus contracted over and over to no avail. The babe was turned totally around. He explained that he had tried the forceps, had tried some manipulation, as had Adelaide. Nothing helped. One of them would die, mother or infant, maybe both, unless she could do something. He got up from the chair next to the bed, and bowed Morgan Wellburn toward his seat. Standing close behind her, he said, "Please. Do what you can. We have accomplished very little, I'm sorry to say."

Alex watched the midwife as she rolled up her sleeves and took over—no fuss about her, no posturing. From the look of her, she had forgotten his presence. She was vigorous and sure, and she had good hands, strong and deft—the hands of a surgeon, he thought. Of course, no woman would ever be allowed to be a surgeon. He stared in admiration, watching her examine mother and fetus. She was extremely competent.

He had been struggling for a long time with this difficult upside-down breech birth . . . and then in she came, ordering *him* out of the room. That had surprised and startled him. Adelaide had laughed, probably at the look on his face: He was accustomed to *giving* the orders. When he turned and met her eyes, he had felt such a jolt that he nearly grunted aloud. He thought, *Here is a real woman. A woman I could love.* Without a word being spoken, he felt something happening between them. He would bet on it.

Spoken like a true son of Max Becker, Alex thought with some bitterness. Maximilian Becker, scion of the Becker shipping business, well-known rake, bon vivant, man about town. His father was gambling and whoring away the family's fortune. It was common knowledge that Max Becker couldn't keep his hands in his pocket or his pecker in his pants. Alex's mother chose to blind herself to what everyone in town knew: that Max had had a succession of mistresses, and was often seen squiring music hall singers, actresses, and other women of the demimonde.

Alex looked like his father and was uncomfortably aware of it. He and Max were handsome men. But Papa had finished too many bottles of port over the years and, at fifty-five, looked somewhat dissolute, with bloodshot eyes, a rapidly developing paunch and double chin. Rather than exercise or go on a slimming diet, his father had his clothes tailored to hide his growing belly. Ostensibly, he was president of Becker Trading Company, Imports and Exports. In reality, he was rarely in the company's offices. Alex had been expected to take over for Papa; but he knew little and cared less about the business. He had fought fiercely to go to medical school. Luckily, he'd had Mama on his side, for once in his life.

Morgan Wellburn had calmed the patient. She was gently rubbing the girl's belly and speaking in a low soothing voice. Gradually Margaret's eyes began to close. "That's right," the midwife said. "I want you to rest for a short time, and then we will try something else. But right now, you're too weary. So rest—ease yourself—sleep . . . That's right, that's good."

He would not have believed it possible, but in minutes, Margaret was sleeping, her eyes moving rapidly back and forth behind her eyelids.

Morgan turned on the stool and stretched her back. "Labor has stopped. The body knows when to cease its efforts. But we don't listen to our bodies enough." Then she turned her gaze on him again. "You are an obstetrician?" she asked.

"Generalist," he told her. "Although, when I come to the Lower East Side, I usually serve as gynecologist and obstetrician."

"Alex is an angel, Morgan. He comes every week to the Hester Street Dispensary and gives abortions to women who do not want another child," Addie offered. "He charges nothing for his services."

Alex sent her a pleading look. Addie knew better than to heap too much praise upon his head. It made him uncomfortable. "So many of their husbands have deserted them," he said to Morgan. "How can a man do that to a woman he loved enough to marry? Just leave her and their children? We all know what happens then. The children go to an orphanage, and the wife—?" He spread his hands. "I find such behavior unforgivable."

"Yes, it's very sad. The trouble is that the men emigrate first, and live alone for so many years while they earn the wife's passage money," Morgan Wellburn said. "They fall in love with someone else," she added, and blushed. He wondered if the blush meant that she had one of those unfortunate emigrés as a lover? The thought made him—what? Angry? No. Jealous. *Jealous*. He could hardly believe his own absurdity.

"I do not believe in that sort of love," he snapped, and then flushed himself. "Well, perhaps they do fall in love," he muttered. "No matter. Those men don't think of the consequences. Mrs. Wellburn, you would not believe the numbers of women left to fend for themselves. The *Forward*, the Jewish newspaper, prints pictures of men who have forsaken their families. They cover the entire front page of the paper. So I do what I can."

"I'm sure your patients are very grateful to you."

"They love him," Adelaide said. "His private patients, too. And, Morgan, Alex attends at Bellevue, not Mount Sinai, as you might expect. Even though he's from a wealthy family, he prefers to minister to the poor of this city. Is that not splendid?"

"Adelaide, I must ask that you cease and desist," Alex protested, laughing a little. To Morgan, he said, "Adelaide likes to make much of me. You mustn't pay attention."

"Oh, but I always pay attention." Her tone was cryptic, but she was smiling. "You attend at Bellevue? A wonderful hospital, always trying new things, I understand."

"He works day and night, Morgan. And night and day. We all wonder how he survives." Adelaide again, but never mind Adelaide. His eyes kept returning to Morgan Wellburn's face. Those light eyes, so surprising in the tawny skin. She was so exotic looking, like a Persian princess. *Oh, for God's sake,* he told himself impatiently, *stop this nonsense. Remember you are a physician, here with a patient.* He had to get his mind off this woman.

So he talked of Bellevue—how a doctor saw every medical problem in the world there. It was the perfect place for a new doctor to train; the ideal hospital for a doctor to set his hand to just about anything. He was enthusiastic, and he did enjoy his profession and find it endlessly fascinating. But that was not the real reason he worked such long hours, answering every cry for help. He wanted no time to brood, having pushed every emotion—love, lust, even friendship—out of his life.

Part of his need to work was to get away from his mother. Hester Wollheim Becker, Hettie to her friends and *Maman*— pronounced as it was in France and in upper-class Christian society—to her son. They were always at odds, he and his mother. She wanted her son to marry, to comport himself as he ought. She wanted him to produce a son to be his heir and a daughter-in-law for her to bully. She wouldn't leave him alone about it. In fact, Hettie Becker's great flaw was that she couldn't leave *anything* alone. Once she had an idea fixed in her head, she'd go over and over it, reworking her arguments until she drove her opponent out of the room. Alex's survival method was to go even further: out of the house, volunteering his services, and burying himself in his practice.

The Beckers lived in twelve rooms on the entire sixth floor of a new, large, luxurious building on Riverside Drive near 100th Street. It boasted a lobby so vast and filled with marble statuary that Alex thought it might rival the Parthenon. He despised the overblown look of it, handsome as it might be. Alex had loved their old house on lower Fifth Avenue, but apartments were the latest thing for the well-to-do. So, naturally, his *maman* had to have one. She loved whatever was the newest social fad, and she was always on the lookout for what others in her circle were doing, in order to outdo them.

Why did he remain with his annoying parents, as if he were a dutiful and loving son? Inertia, he thought. At his parents' home, all his needs were taken care of. There was always a clean shirt, fresh sheets, plenty of food, good books, servants to fetch and carry. He didn't have to think about any of it. He had come to hate thinking about any of his needs. When sex became an urgency, there were plenty of high-class houses in New York for any man too fastidious for the downtown whore-houses. He had no need for a more tender arrangement. He had put all his emotions away, packed into the attic of his mind where, he assumed, they were gathering cobwebs.

Margaret stirred and moaned. Morgan Wellburn took charge.

"I'll need both of you," she said. "We're going to put Margaret on her feet. Margaret, you'll be fine, I promise you. Here . . ." She urged the woman to stand. "That's good. Now. Dr. Becker and Nurse Apple will support you, one on each side. Do not think about anything but your child, who will soon be born. Do not worry. We will hold you firmly."

They did as Morgan bid, while she continued with a stream of reassuring words. "And now we will help you sway from side to side, Margaret. Have no fear. This will help your baby turn himself around in your belly."

Alex had never heard of such a thing. He thought it arrant nonsense, but he held his tongue. She seemed so sure of herself. He and Adelaide moved Margaret gently from side to side, and in a moment, Margaret was helping them. He was astonished. She had seemed at the end of her strength, but she had even stopped whimpering. Her eyes were closed as she swayed and he could hear her deep, heavy breathing. And all the while Morgan was on her knees, gently manipulating the fetus, talking to it, encouraging it to turn, turn, that's the way, that's right, that's good.

He was so engrossed in studying the scene, he was startled when the midwife said, "There! I do believe he is in position now." At almost the same moment, Margaret cried out, and began to grunt loudly as her belly contracted. The final stage of labor had begun, by God. With her strange techniques, the midwife had managed to get the baby into position for birth. He had never seen the like.

"Quickly! Get her on the bed!" They obeyed without question, he and Addie. Margaret yelled as the child's head crowned. Then, in a rush, the newborn emerged, sliding out so quickly, so slippery, it took both Alex and Morgan to hold him.

"He's an eager little fellow, isn't he?" Morgan cleaned the child's mouth, sucked out his nostrils, and held him upside down. In seconds, he started to squall. "My baby," Margaret said. Tears poured from her eyes, but a smile lit her face. "Let me hold him."

"He's a bit bruised, Margaret, because of his arduous journey. But he's fine. Just listen to him yell for his mother," Morgan said.

Margaret kept weeping her thanks. "I was sure we would both die. Bless you, midwife. Bless you."

"Yes, well, I was happy to help. You save your blessings for your son. Now please listen to me. I will be sending you a char who will clean this place. But you must keep it clean, if your child is to live to see his first birthday. Do you understand me?"

"Yes, ma'am."

"Boil your water," Morgan told her, "for everything. Wash your hands whenever they are the least bit soiled. And be sure to drink plenty of beer. It will help bring in your milk."

Adelaide was bustling about, peering into cupboards and searching shelves. "There's nothing to eat here," she announced. "I'll run out to get something." When Alex handed her money, she took it without comment. They had done this often.

With Addie gone, there was such a profound silence, Alex felt he must speak. "Mrs. Wellburn . . ."

"Please. Call me Morgan."

"Morgan. I've never seen this—your technique. It was quite miraculous. Wherever did you learn it?"

"From my mother" was the cryptic answer. She smiled at him.

"Please. Don't play with me. I would like to learn how to do that. So many infants are lost—"

"I'll be glad to teach you. And I did learn it from my mother, who learned it from hers, and so on—back to the beginning of time, she used to say. My mother is part Indian and this is how they do it."

"Indian. You mean American Indian."

"Yes, Pequot. Once, they ruled most of Connecticut, where I'm from. Now, of course . . ." She shrugged and threw out her hands.

He stared at her. It had turned into the most bewildering day. Morgan was a bit disheveled and her inky hair had come loose from the carefully rolled pompadour, but to him, she was beautiful. American Indian. Of course. That's what she looked like. And she knew ancient birthing techniques that were far more advanced than anything he'd been taught in medical school. He wanted to see her again. No, he *must* see her again.

"Will you teach me what you know of birthing? And perhaps . . . other things as well?" They looked at each other for a long minute, and then he extended his hand. She took it, and he felt something . . . electric between them. He could hardly bear to let her hand go. He hadn't felt like this in—had he *ever* felt like this?

"You must tell me a time that is convenient, and I will teach you what my mother taught me. She delivered me herself, under a tree, squatting. Squatting is much the best way. Unless, like today, the mother has become too exhausted."

"You are a most unusual woman," Alex said.

"I believe you mean that as a compliment and I thank you. But, Dr. Becker . . ."

"Yes?"

"Perhaps you would give me back my hand? I should like to hear about your own background, too." He relinquished his grip, feeling the heat rise in his face. He was behaving foolishly, and yet he seemed powerless to stop it. He mumbled an apology, as she smoothly changed the subject. "You have children?"

"No children," he said shortly, stepping back involuntarily. "I am not married."

"Oh. I—I'm sorry. I didn't mean to pry."

"You didn't pry. It's—it's a subject I don't like to discuss. I was married once—years ago. It—it ended badly, that's all . . ." He turned his head, willing the memory away. But of course, it came anyway.

He was only eighteen, a boy, really, all gonads and no brains. She was a beautiful blond girl with soft curls and soft eyes and soft luscious breasts. He wanted her so desperately, he thought he would burst with it. Her name was Daisy Belmont, and his parents were eager for the match, since her father was a distant relative of the August Belmonts and therefore accepted in the best society. Daisy was seventeen, a year younger than he, and not terribly smart. She imagined herself in love; it made her friends jealous and he was very handsome. And very persuasive.

"I love you," he had told her, "I adore you. I worship you. When we're married, I'll hire a dozen maids so you need never lift a finger. You'll lie in bed all day and wait for me to come home to you." That made Daisy giggle. Everything he said to her made her giggle. She was determinedly empty-headed, but very willing to open her legs for him. Once he had taken her maidenhead, she was all eagerness. He had only to tell her how much he loved her. So, he lied and lied, and they made love every chance they got. Then, quite unexpectedly, she was pregnant.

He thought his *maman* would die of mortification. "Why are men so nasty?" she said, wrinkling her nose in distaste. "Even you, Alex. And I thought I raised you to be a gentleman." Alex bent his head to receive her tirades; he couldn't look her in the eye. He was already aware of his father's constant phi-landering, and it embarrassed him to see his mother pretend that none of it was happening. Well, at least she didn't say, "You're just like your father!"

The wedding was hurriedly planned, and they were married before the bride could begin to show her shame. Six months after the ceremony, Daisy Belmont Becker died of childbirth complications, along with the baby, a little boy. Alex blamed himself for her death. He had seduced her for his own plea-sure. He had told her flattering lies just to get between her legs. He was just like his father, a rakehell and a scoundrel, with no feelings for the weaker sex. For his own gratification, he had sent an innocent girl to her grave. And his child, too, his son. He vowed that never again would he allow his baser instincts to get the better of him. Never again would he act like his father. He would stay away from decent women, and as for marriage—*never!*

Maman, who had not been able to forgive him for "ruining" Daisy, now could not forgive him for refusing to marry again. "You should be ashamed, a man your age, still a bachelor. And you so good-looking, any woman would want you. You should make a life for yourself! Marry, have a wife, have children for your father and me. I want a grandchild before I die." Since she was but fifty-nine, still youthful, with not a bit of gray in her hair—well, maybe just a bit—this cry of approaching death always made Alex laugh. But without humor. He did not find his mother humorous.

His life had been changed forever with those deaths. Medicine became everything. He had become accustomed to feeling nothing. So, today, to turn around, to look into this strange woman's eyes and feel her intensity like a blow to the solar plexus—that rocked him.

She was speaking to him. "I asked how you and Adelaide met."

"We've worked together for years. She never mentioned me to you?"

"Yes, of course she did. The angel doctor?" She gave him an amused look. "The wonderful man who gave of his time every Saturday to help her poor unfortunates? I heard a great deal about him." She sat down and motioned for him to do the same. "But not by name."

"And yet," Alex said, "she has mentioned you every single Saturday since she and I began to help immigrant women get abortions. By your full name."

She looked quizzical. "I wonder why she never spoke your name?"

He thought he knew why. He liked Adelaide; he approved of everything she stood for. She was solid, hardworking, intelligent, and had a well-developed social conscience. There was nothing fuzzy-minded about her; he liked that. They were of one mind about many things . . . and they were alike in that they both kept themselves emotionally aloof from others. Of course, even though he had sworn never to allow himself sexual feelings again, he had not been able to cut himself off from his own nature. He had sometimes found himself yearning briefly for one woman or another, over the years. But never for Addie, not even for one fleeting moment. He had never felt anything even remotely sexual emanating from her. And her manner toward him, while friendly, you might even say intimate, had not a bit of flirtation in it.

He had no doubt that she was a Sapphist. And now that he

had seen the two of them together, he was convinced that Adelaide was in love with Morgan Wellburn. A thought chilled his backbone: What if Morgan—! But, no, it couldn't be. He would know.

Adelaide came bustling in at that moment, carrying a large basket with bread and cheese and other viands in it. "The boy will be up with a pitcher of beer shortly."

"Addie, Morgan and I were wondering why you never mentioned the name of the wonderful doctor who gives abortions for free?" He smiled to take the sting out.

"The won—? Oh. You, you mean. Why? I—I think I must have said your name. Maybe I thought it wasn't necessary. I don't know. I don't remember. How silly of me . . . why, I can't say . . ."

Addie was so flustered, Alex thought it would be a cruelty to pursue the point. He glanced at Morgan and found her looking at him. He would bet his life she was thinking precisely the same thing. It was time for him to go. He was working on an important paper for one of the medical journals. But first . . .

"Mrs. Wellburn, I know that I should wait for you to invite me, but I am unwilling to wait. I would be honored," he continued, making a small bow in front of her, "if you would allow me to call on you."

She flushed and smiled into his eyes. He could not hide his delighted grin, knowing her answer already.

"Call! Whatever for? Morgan has no time!" When both of them turned to give Addie an astonished look, she realized what she had said, and turned scarlet. She began a flurry of activity, setting down the bread here, moving it, putting it back. She didn't look at either of them.

In his most calming, casual voice, Alex said, "I am hoping Morgan will make a few hours for me, so that I may come to pay my respects to you both one evening."

Morgan said, in a tone that matched his, "Of course. We should both be happy to see you. Shouldn't we, Addie?"

"Oh, of course. Of course."

"Why don't you plan to come for supper on Wednesday? It won't be anything fancy, but we are both passable cooks. And perhaps Adelaide will prepare her famous blanc mange in your honor," Morgan said. Their eyes had locked.

"Of course, of course, silly of me. I don't know what—" Adelaide fussed, moving about the tiny room, her fair skin still blotchy with her agitation. Alex tore his eyes from Morgan's, trying to think what to say to Adelaide that might calm her. Finally she stopped her bustling and, turning, accidentally met his gaze. Her eyes were bleak with pain. "You are most welcome, Alex," she said. "Of course."

"Thank you both for a delicious supper," Alex said, taking his napkin from his lap and putting it on the table. That should signal the end of the meal, he thought.

But Addie was sweetly adamant. "A bit more dessert, Alex? I know you liked it. No? Then some hot tea. I'll put on a fresh pot."

"Addie, it's really much too hot for tea, don't you think?" Morgan's voice was gentle; nevertheless, Adelaide flushed as if she had been scolded.

"Of course. I'm—I'm insisting too much. It's a great flaw of mine, or so my mother always told me. I'm so sorry, Alex. I—"

"Perhaps," Alex interrupted her, "we could take a stroll down by the harbor, where there might be a stray breeze."

"I'd love a walk," Morgan said. "I'm quite . . . overheated."

She fanned herself with a large Japanese paper fan. She told him it had been given to her years ago by a ship's captain who was a friend of hers. "He brought me here, to Brooklyn Heights."

"Then I am eternally grateful to him. Were you with your family?"

"No, no, quite alone. I lived in a boarding house not far from here until I met Addie. It was her idea that we buy a house together and, as usual, she was right."

"It's a very fine house." Three Clinton Street was four stories, brick, with brownstone steps up to the parlor floor and a heavy black iron railing. Nice, neat, not fancy, but with a very pretty front door, a double glass door with an arched window above. To the left of the broad brownstone stairs, there was another entrance that led to the garden floor where, in the front rooms, Morgan saw patients. Behind her medical office were the kitchen and dining room. In a tiny backyard garden, Morgan and Addie grew flowers, and she planted her medicinal herbs.

"When we first talked about buying, we looked in Manhattan and then near Prospect Park. But I soon realized I needed to stay close to my patients. Besides . . ." Morgan gave him a brief smile, fiddling with her teaspoon. "I had become accustomed to the quiet backwater of Brooklyn Heights."

"So we looked on Clinton Street, because everyone knows it as Doctors' Row," Addie put in. She was trying hard to put off the inevitable moment, Alex thought, when he and Morgan would be alone. "Morgan really liked the idea that, one hundred years ago, doctors already had their offices here—"

"Until we discovered that the popular name was Murderers' Row because of all the women who had died at the hands of doctors there." Her eyes slid to meet his.

"Nevertheless, here you are . . ."

"Nevertheless . . ." The silence drew out, and Alex tried to think of a new topic of general conversation. They had already discussed Addie's real job as a social service worker on Ellis Island; they had argued amiably about her causes. Morgan had gently teased her friend, saying, "I don't know where you find the time to do everything." And Adelaide had answered by saying, "Better a career than a husband." That had been an awkward moment.

Alex rose, pushing his chair back under the table with care. "What do you say, ladies? A stroll by the water?" Their eyes kept meeting and holding. But he must be patient and gentlemanly and not hurt Adelaide Apple. "Addie? Will you come?"

"No, thank you. There's the cleaning-up to do. Oh dear, I didn't mean . . . No, I'd really rather stay here and tidy up." Addie had become quite pink in the face. "Really. You two . . ." Her voice cracked a bit. "You two go ahead."

At last, they were outside, in the heavy heat of dusk, alone. Together. Alex was as nervous as a boy calling on his first sweetheart. He wanted to plunge ahead, take her in his arms, declare his feelings, and dare her to deny her own. But if he did that, Morgan might very well scream and run. He ached to kiss her. Before the evening was over, he *would* kiss her and be damned to the consequences.

"Poor Addie," he said. If Morgan asked him what he meant, then maybe he wouldn't kiss her.

"Yes. Poor Addie. But I don't quite understand why she's so upset."

Disappointed, he said, "You don't?" They began to walk. He had no idea where they were heading, and he cared not a whit, so long as she was by his side.

"Oh, I didn't mean—" Morgan pulled in a breath. "Yes, I know why she's upset—she senses . . . something happening. But why *so* agitated? Other men have called on me."

"She knows this is different," Alex said.

Her face was a glimmer in the dimming light. She did not answer for a moment, and he found he was holding his breath. "I suppose that's it," she said finally. "This is different."

Enough, Alex said to himself. He stopped walking and so did she. For moments, they stood facing each other, trying to look into each other's eyes. But it had become too dark. He reached for her and pulled her close to him, resting his cheek on hers. A soft involuntary groan came from his throat and he held her tighter.

Morgan twisted her head and searched out his mouth with hers. Morgan put her arms around his neck and pulled his head down to make the kiss deeper. She pulled away for a moment, and then, with a tiny cry, lifted her mouth to his again, hungrily. They kissed and kissed, moving their bodies to fit, ever closer. They made sounds, said half words, spoke each other's names. He wanted her—so urgently, he even thought of lying in the soft grass somewhere, anywhere, and *now*.

My God, they had not spoken a coherent word to each other since she said "This is different." He lifted his head, gasping for air, and said breathlessly, "We must talk about this."

Morgan laughed, a delighted gurgle. He was sorry he could barely see her, in the velvety darkness. "Dear Alex," she said, "I don't think we need to talk. This is . . . exactly what it is."

"I think I'm in love with you," he said. "Can you believe that?"

"Yes, oh yes. I believe that."

"And you love me." Suddenly, he was sure.

"Yes."

"You know this is impossible, don't you? You know this doesn't happen, this *can't* happen." He still held her waist with his hands.

Her voice came calmly out of the night. "I know. But it has."

"Come with me. I have a private office in Manhattan. I want . . . I need . . ." He stopped. He could not believe the words coming from his mouth. He could hardly believe their ardent embraces. But pure joy was bubbling in his veins like champagne. "I'm in love," he said, happily.

"Yes. In love," she agreed. "I want to make love to you, Alex. Take me home with you." She stepped up to him, as close as she could get, so close they could have made love right then and there, had they not been clothed. Her scent was dizzying. Her mouth was satin. "I'll let down your hair and wrap myself in it," he said. "And then—"

"Take me home, Alex. Take me home with you, make beautiful love to me."

He did and they did. They took a cab, sitting decorously beside each other, not speaking. Alex felt he was barely breathing, and he was sure Morgan felt the same way. He felt he knew everything about her and every thought she was having. He imagined they were attached in some strange, otherworldly way. And it did no good to tell himself, *Stop thinking this way! This is nonsense! You and this woman—this beautiful, mysterious, familiar woman—hardly know each other.* There was something between them . . . electrical . . . magnetic . . . He did not know what it was, but it existed.

As he took her elbow to lead her up the steps of his building, he could feel his arm trembling with anticipation. He hoped she was not aware of it. Still behaving properly, he gestured her into the hallway, unlocked the door of his office suite, and stood aside to let her go in first. Then he kicked the door closed and reached for her. But she was already close to him, her lips lifted to his. As he kissed her, he began to undress her, fumbling with the unfamiliar fastenings. Morgan removed his hands and, swiftly, surely, began to drop garments, while he stood watching her. She never took her eyes from his and she didn't pause until she was naked.

With a groan, Alex held her close, kissing her eyes, her nose, her hair, her shoulders, her breasts—her beautiful breasts—her belly. He fell to his knees, worshipping her. She said, softly, "Alex, please. Take off your clothes and let me love you."

They made love on the thick Turkish carpet, too quickly because it had been so long for him. Eventually, they moved to the soft leather couch, which he covered with a sheet, and made love again, slowly, sweetly. She was delicious, all softness, silken, velvety, every part of her, and he was in a delirium of love and lust, tenderness and appetite. There was no pretense in her, no fakery; she met his every thrust eagerly, answered his words of love, responded to every move and every change. For a long time, they stayed joined but unmoving, looking into each other's eyes, softly kissing. They were like two mindless bodies, urgent for release. He had never known a woman like her. And he knew, as certainly as he had ever known anything, that he would never know another woman, not as long as he lived.

16

September 1905

"Listen, Clara," Adelaide said, for the tenth time. "And look. Watch my mouth." She pointed to her lips and carefully and slowly, pushing her lips out, said, "Wa-ter. Would you like a glass of water?"

Clara screwed up her face, concentrating as hard as she

could, and said, "Vater. Vould you like gless vater." She smiled, pleased with herself.

Addie sighed. The girl had no knack for language. In fact, she had no knack for learning American customs, either. She still wanted to put all the cooking pots on the table, instead of using serving dishes. When Mrs. Mulligan, their new and much beloved daily, took the pots back and showed her the proper way to serve, Clara still thought everyone at table was free to dig in with a spoon. She tossed the silverware in a mound on the table, for them to grab. No matter how many times Agnes Mulligan showed her the correct way to do place settings, it all just flew out of Clara's pretty head.

"I am talkink good?" Clara said, dimpling. "I am gattink better?"

She was a charming child, anxious to please. Addie smiled back at her and decided not to give Clara another lesson in pronouncing "ing." "You are getting better," she agreed. "Now, let us discuss . . . talk about what will happen when our guests arrive."

"Gasts," Clara said. "Mister Backer and Missus Backer and Doctor Backer."

"That's right. Dr. Becker and his parents." Addie allowed herself a moment to ponder why Becker became *Backer*, when at the same time, Apple became *Epple*. If Clara could make both sounds equally well, why not make them in the right places? Adelaide was glad she hadn't chosen to become a teacher; it would surely drive her mad.

"Gasts is wery important," Clara ventured.

"Our guests are very important, yes," Adelaide agreed, emphasizing the sounds she wished Clara could hear. But she knew better. Clara couldn't hear the difference. As Addie regarded Clara, she wondered why in the world she had taken pity on this girl and none other. She saw so many, at Ellis Island, who were lost and frightened and at the mercy of every evil person. She had never brought anyone else to live with them. Was it because the girl was so pretty and eager to please? Addie didn't like to think it might be . . . that other thing. Her own horrid longings. But no. She had never so

much as taken the girl's hand to show her how to do something; she left that to Mulligan.

Clara had been with them for three weeks, and, Adelaide
had to admit it, she seemed very limited. Morgan thought it
was the language problem. Clara had so little English and
Morgan had no Russian at all. But even Addie, who spoke
Russian fluently, had trouble getting Clara to understand.

Addie had come across Clara at Ellis Island, when she was
called in to translate for the girl. Translating was one of the
things Women's Immigrant Aid paid her to do. Addie was
their representative at Ellis Island, handling the many difficulties and problems that bedeviled the new immigrants. She was
one of some two dozen men and women who represented one
social service organization or another. They translated, took
those who needed it for medical treatment, explained what
was happening and what was going to happen next. They sent
telegrams, held hands, soothed, calmed—whatever was needed,
they tried to provide.

The inspector who had sent for Adelaide to deal with Clara
Optakeroff was completely out of patience. The girl's husband-
to-be had apparently come to meet her, and instead of smiling
and being happy, as was expected of her, Clara was distraught.
"Ranting and raving," the inspector said, peevishly. "She insists
that this man is not her intended." Everyone was ready to label
the young woman a hysteric, and either hand her over to the
bearded young man who kept saying, "She is beink my vife,"
or to send her back home to Russia. But when the girl clung to
Addie's hands, speaking rapidly in Russian, saying *I don't lie,
my mother taught me never to lie, this man is not the man in
the picture, I swear it, lady, please, don't let him take me* . . .
Addie was certain she was telling the truth.

"I'll straighten this out," she promised, and sat the young
woman down with a glass of tea. Patting her hand, Addie said,
"Calm yourself and tell me. I will listen. Show me the picture
of your intended."

The girl burst into fresh tears. She had lost the photo—the
brown picture, she called it—but she remembered well what
he looked like. He was very fair with ears that stuck out. She
pushed her own small ears out with her hands to show Addie

what she meant. "Light eyes," she kept repeating. "Lady, please believe me, I don't know who this man is who wishes to take me away. But I will not go with him, and if you send me back to Ekatrinislav, my father will beat me. He has too many daughters." And she burst into tears.

Addie studied the fellow who was waiting outside the fence. He was dark and bearded, fierce looking. Clara said that he scared her. *Well,* Adelaide thought, *he scares* me. But why would he claim a complete stranger? The matron said he'd come all the way from a chicken farm somewhere in western New Jersey. That was a good distance to come to pick up an unknown.

She could have gone to the inspector and said she believed Clara was telling the truth. The man would be sent away, the girl be put on the next boat back to Europe, and the case would be settled. But Addie's curiosity was piqued. The girl was so lovely, so alone, so frightened. She got another glass of tea for Clara, put in a lump of sugar, and told her not to move. "I'll come back in just a minute or two."

Through the fence, she beckoned to the bearded man. "What is your name?" she asked in Russian.

He looked startled. "Kiril," he said, then clamped his lips tight shut. No last name? Addie wondered. And why not?

"Look," she said to him, "I know you're not the man Clara was expecting to see. If you don't want to tell me what this is about, that's fine. But you will not walk away from this island with Clara . . . What's her last name? Do you even know?"

He had to consult a piece of paper. "Optakeroff."

"You are going to marry her and you don't remember her name? You look much more intelligent than that. Come on, now, let us have the truth, and quickly. I am a busy woman."

He flushed, glowered at her, turned to walk away, but changed his mind and came back. "All right," he said, still in Russian. "I am not the man she expected. His name is Oleg Savchuck. We work together, on the farm. When Oleg saw her photo, he did not like what he saw."

"Is your friend Oleg perhaps blind? She is a very pretty girl."

"Yes, I think so, too. But Oleg, he likes them fat and fair.

Like his mama. And she is very small and dark, no? Oleg, he threw the photograph on the floor. I picked it up and told him, 'You don't want her? I'll take her.' But he said no, a bargain is a bargain."

"So where is he?"

"Oleg, you understand, is a bit of a miser. He did not want to miss a day's pay."

Addie gazed at the young man, who no longer struck her as so fierce looking. Under that heavy beard, he was quite good-looking. And *his* ears didn't stick out. Perhaps she should talk to Clara about accepting a substitution. Why should a young girl, all alone in a strange country, go to a man who didn't like her looks, and was a penny-pincher besides? She was about to say something to Kiril, when he went on.

"I liked the photograph and now that I see her, I like her even better," he said. "She has dimples. I—Oleg favors dimples. And, although small, she is not skinny, she is soft. We—he—we like soft women." He flushed. "I will take her to him and he will like her."

What was all this I—he—we talk, Adelaide wondered. Aloud, she speculated why a hardworking man such as Kiril was willing to give up a day's pay? Out of friendship? She thought perhaps there was something else going on. Would Kiril like to say what this was?

"Lady, why not? Do not friends do favors for each other?" He had turned really red and was frowning in a most ferocious manner. "Why should you distrust what I say? Why should I lie to you?"

"That is precisely what I am wondering, Kiril . . . Mr. uh—"

"Horoshevsky. Kiril Horoshevsky." He stared into her eyes, not blinking. But he did not fool her. Something was going on and she was not going to let Clara Optakeroff leave Ellis Island with this man until she knew what it was.

Walking away from the barrier, he paced back and forth, his hands clasped behind his back. He muttered to himself; he argued with himself. After a few minutes, he came back, clearing his throat.

"I—he—we—" There it was again, Addie thought, the I and he and we. "She was promised to Oleg. He does not wish

to give her to me outright. So. We will both take care of her."
He looked belligerently into Addie's eyes.

"Yes," she prodded. "So you will both take care of her,
and you will both—?" She thought now she knew what their
plan was.

"We will both be her husband," he blurted after a moment.

Adelaide gave him a level look. "This is done in Russia?"
she asked innocently.

"Well—no, not exactly. But sometimes, high on the steppes
or deep in the woods . . . sometimes, yes. I have heard stories.
Lady, there are no Russian women in Barnes, New Jersey, you
understand? None. In New Jersey are only chickens. We will
take very good care of her!"

"I see," Adelaide said, her tone even. "You will share her.
One night she will sleep in your bed, and the next night she
will sleep in Oleg's bed. Is that your plan?"

He mumbled something, and took a step backward to put
space between them, as if she could reach him through the
fence. "I find her very pretty," he said. "I will make sure . . ."

"I see. There are other Russians working at this farm, other
young men?" He nodded. "I see," Adelaide said, not letting her
voice rise. "And soon, I suppose, you and Oleg will be selling
nights with her to all your friends."

"Lady, no!"

Adelaide put her face very close to the fence. "Kiril Horoshevsky," she said, her voice low but biting, "Clara will not go
with you. I will not allow it. Never. And if you come looking
for her, I will call the police, do you understand?"

"But, lady—"

"Now you listen to me, young man," Adelaide said, stam-
mering and mispronouncing her words in Russian because she
was quite angry. "This is a sixteen-year-old girl, not a cow or a
piece of machinery, to be handed back and forth, or traded for
a bowl of borscht! Get out of here and don't let me see your
face, ever again!"

He fled. Men!

Later, she told Morgan that she didn't know what got into
her. "Sometimes I surprise even myself."

Having sent him on his way, Addie had wheeled around and

marched back to where Clara Optakeroff was sipping her tea. "Come with me, Clara," she said, feeling very light-headed with her fury. Holding Clara by the hand, she went to the inspector and said, "It was the wrong man entirely. I sent him packing."

When the inspector started to say that Clara would have to go back on the next ship, Addie cut him off. "I have decided to give this woman a job."

"You, Miss Apple?"

"I, Mr. McLaren. She's a pretty little thing. She'll make a good parlor maid." Later, when she brought the girl home and was explaining the whole thing to Morgan, she began to giggle. "Parlor maid!" she said. "The last thing in the world we need!"

And parlor maid was just about the last thing Clara was able to be, Addie thought. She and Clara were sitting at the dining room table, Clara with her hands clasped in her lap. The girl with her heart-shaped face, delicate features, and dark hair plaited around her head, was very charming indeed. Her full red lips fairly invited kisses . . . never mind that. How much longer was it going to take to teach her how to offer a cup of tea to their "gasts"?

Morgan had been standing just outside the dining room watching Addie try to teach the unteachable. She was not sure why her usually rational friend had appeared one evening several weeks ago with this beautiful little creature in tow. Addie had said something about parlor maid, but that was ridiculous. They did just fine, the two of them and Mulligan. And they had gone over the budget several times to make sure they could afford Mulligan. They didn't need a parlor maid. Still, Morgan thought, now that she was here, it would be wonderful if Clara could actually learn enough to help. Today, Morgan felt she needed all the help she could get. She was not quite sure why she had invited Alex's parents to come for tea— unless it was sheer perversity.

They did not like her. If, indeed, they gave even one moment of thought to her. The one time she had met them, at the opera, between Act 1 and Act 2 of *La Bohème*, they had been aloof, hardly acknowledging Alex's introduction. Then they had turned back to face Alex and chat with him. Morgan had been left out of the conversation entirely. She had to stand there, next to Alex, trying to keep a pleasant and interested expression on her face, while his mother and father ignored her.

She could see that he was embarrassed. But once he began to explain, she realized why he was so uncomfortable. "They don't know about me." Her whole body turned cold as if all the blood had suddenly drained out of it. "You've never told them about me. You've never even mentioned my name."

He did not answer her immediately. They were pacing sedately in the lobby, sipping champagne, carefully not looking at each other. Finally, he said, "Morgan, you don't understand about old-line Jewish families like mine—"

The remark was instantly familiar and instantly hurtful. She interrupted him. "No, Alex, it is *you* who does not understand. You don't understand about halfbreeds like me." She lowered her voice and leaned close to him. "We don't sleep with men who are ashamed of us."

Then, stooping to scoop up her skirts, she ran down the carpeted stairs. He ran after her, of course, followed her outside, where it was snowing. He swore his love for her, insisting he was not ashamed of her. He said it was his parents he was ashamed of. They were both shivering in the cold. His mustache gleamed with droplets of melted snow. She was crying, which surprised her. She thought she had finished with tears for such an ordinary insult. He pulled her into his arms, murmuring into her damp hair, kissing her throat, just under the ear. In the end, they had hurried back inside to collect their coats and hats. Then, they had piled into a cab, falling into an embrace immediately, kissing avidly. At his office on 23rd Street, they had made frantic love on his bumpy leather couch. It had been very exciting, very passionate. Even now, whenever she recalled that evening, she shuddered with remembered delight.

Going into the dining room, she said to Addie, "How are we doing?"

"Just fine," Addie said bravely. Morgan studied her friend. Adelaide had taken such pains with her hair and her costume today, but already, she looked as if she were beginning to come apart. Of course, trying to make Clara understand could do that to you.

"I suggest we forget the lessons for today and have Agnes serve," Morgan said.

"Not at all," Adelaide said firmly. "Clara will do just fine. Won't you, Clara?"

"Yes, lady." Clara dimpled prettily. "Now I go to chicken?"

The puzzled look on Addie's face was comical. "Where? Oh. The kitchen. No, Clara. Today, I would like you to answer the door."

"Pardon?"

"Answer the door. Oh dear." Addie switched into Russian and spoke rapidly. In English, she said, obviously coaching, "Good afternoon. Please come inside." Clara repeated it. "Good efternoon, pliss comink inside."

"Very good."

At that moment, they all heard the door knocker and turned to look in the direction of the front door. Nobody moved, until Morgan said, "Clara. Our guests are here."

It took a moment, but Clara finally understood what was wanted and went scurrying away. They heard the door open; they heard Alex's voice and then—nothing.

"Morgan, look at yourself," Adelaide said. "You're wringing your hands."

She was. She stopped and said, "How I am dreading this afternoon."

"My poor darling. You should not have invited them."

"I know. But they made me so angry . . . Never mind, I think we'd better rescue Clara." Both of them ran out, to find Clara standing there bobbing a curtsey over and over, having forgotten what to say. Morgan rushed to Clara's aid, saying brightly, "Good afternoon. Welcome. Won't you come in."

"Pliss comink inside," Clara said, suddenly remembering her lines. She smiled at the Beckers, very pleased with herself. Hester Becker smiled coldly as one eyebrow shot up. *How terribly low class!* the arched brow seemed to say. Morgan also noted the way Hettie's eyes took in everything as they moved down the hall to the front parlor, and that her lip curled in disdain. Damn the woman for a snob.

Morgan couldn't bring herself to look at Alex, although she felt his gaze on her. She was unable to take her eyes off his mother. The woman was so pretty, so exquisitely dainty, and so very small. She was several inches shorter than Morgan, with a tiny cinched-in waist and little hands. The feather on her hat curled around and under her small chin. When they were all finally in the parlor—it felt like a journey of several miles—she turned to Morgan and said, "We meet again, Miss— uh. And do you know, I had forgotten how very large you are." She let off a trill of silvery laughter. "Alex, she makes me feel so terribly tiny. And you are—?" she turned abruptly to Addie.

"Adelaide Apple. Morgan and I share this house."

"I see."

Hastily, Alex said, "Mama, please sit on this chair here."

"Only if you sit by my side, dearest son."

"Of course, if you wish." He shot a look at Morgan that begged for understanding, but her blood was beginning to boil. It was going to be even worse than she had imagined.

Alex's father, Max, bowed courteously enough to both Morgan and Addie, and Morgan noticed that his eyes lingered on the Russian girl. Clara, who noticed too, simpered happily. Oh dear. Morgan sent Clara to the kitchen to fetch the tea. Happily, Addie knew enough to go with her, to make sure it was tea she brought out and not the pickled crabapples. A conversation, of a desultory sort, began, all of it emanating from Hettie Becker.

"Morgan. Isn't that usually a surname, rather than a given?"

"My father's family name. My father gave it to me."

"And you are from—?"

"Connecticut, *Maman*," Alex said, an edge to his voice. "I've told you that, several times."

"Well, we don't know anyone in Connecticut, darling Alex, although there's quite a wonderful tailor in Middletown. He served the Wollheims, you remember, Max." She didn't wait for her husband to respond, which was a good thing, since he was leaning back with his eyes closed. "We have old friends who visit their family there . . ." Hettie said. "Middletown—

the town where Wesleyan University is situated," she explained
to Morgan. Morgan's "I know" was ignored.

"What *is* his name?" Hettie went on. "Max, you'll remember, a good German name."

His eyes opened. Bright blue, just like Alex's, but without
the warmth. "Why in hell should I remember the name of a
dressmaker, for God's sake, Hettie?"

She ignored that, too. "Wrubel," she said. "That's it. Miss
uh . . . do you know Mr. Wrubel the tailor? Only the best
people go to him. He's quite wonderful, I hear. No? Well, of
course not." More of the tinkly laughter. "I mean, I don't even
know if you've ever been to Middletown." She gave Morgan
a sharp look and suddenly Morgan knew that she was not
dressed to Mrs. Becker's satisfaction. She was wearing one
of the new, shorter skirts, what they called a health skirt. It
showed her ankles and, apparently, Alex's mother did not
approve.

Hettie switched smoothly to their journey from Manhattan.
"This is my first visit to Brooklyn, you know. We have no
reason to come here, in the ordinary way. So many unpaved
streets! We are not so primitive, in New York. When we got
off the ferry, I could not believe my eyes. Atlantic Avenue is
a rutted dirt road! Fortunately, there were several horse cabs
waiting there, so I didn't have to worry about dust. However
do you manage?"

Morgan hoped she was smiling. Her face felt stiff. "I usually take the trolley across the Great Bridge."

"Ah . . ." Hettie said. "The trolley." From her tone, it was
clear that "trolley" was also déclassé. "I understand that Brooklyn has a greater population than New York. Very interesting.
But you have no great buildings, as we do. You've heard of
them, I suppose? Apartment houses, they're called. We live in
one on Riverside Drive. They are the very latest thing, you
know."

Hettie looked around the room, which up until that moment
Morgan had thought was terribly elegant with its Turkey rug
and matching couches facing each other in front of the fireplace. Suddenly, she worried that maybe it looked . . . bare.
Neither she nor Adelaide had wanted an overstuffed house

with fringes on everything and Oriental rugs overlapping and pictures hanging, ceiling to floor. They knew that was the popular decor, but they did not like it. There were no velvet draperies with bullion fringe in the front parlor, just the original shutters. Two couches and two chairs with plum upholstery. Two or three paintings they had picked up at auction. Looking at it through Hettie's eyes, though, Morgan wondered . . . and then Hettie said, "Yes, well this is a dear little house, quite nice details. It will be most splendid when you finish the decorations."

Clara came in then, biting her lower lip and concentrating very hard on carrying the tea tray. At her reappearance, Max Becker, who had been slumped in his chair staring out the window, came back to life. Sitting up, he smoothed his blond mustaches and straightened his ascot. When Clara poured a cup of tea and handed it to him, her hand was shaking so hard that the tea slopped into the saucer. He reached out to put his hand over hers and helped her put it down on the tea table in front of him. "There, my dear child, that's right," he said. Morgan thought he was much too close to the girl and that he left his hand on hers too long to be accidental. But at that moment, Hettie Becker asked her another of her annoying questions and she had to turn her attention away.

Teatime was awkward. Though Morgan tried to be polite, the visit was becoming more and more difficult. She wished Alex would say something to change the subject, but he obviously preferred to pander to his mother, murmuring, "Quite so" and "Hmmm," and leaving Morgan to handle the woman all alone. As for Adelaide, she did not exist. Hettie didn't address a single sentence to Addie. She was the most aggravating, insulting woman!

Furthermore, Alex's father was really rather disgusting. The man was openly flirting with little Clara, paying her compliments about her command of English, asking her to come with him to the window and show him "the sights." There were no "sights" on Clinton Street, just houses. What was the man up to?

"Clara, please pour us some more tea," Morgan said, more sharply than she had intended. When the two of them turned from the window, the girl's cheeks were glowing pink with pleasure. Lounging in his chair again, thrusting his long booted legs out in front of him so that they were almost touching Clara, Max Becker smoothed his thick wavy hair with his hands. He looked at the child from under his lashes.

"Clara has recently come to our country, Mr. Becker," Morgan said in her sweetest voice. "She understands only a little English, and even that she is likely to misinterpret."

"Indeed," murmured Max Becker, looking even more interested.

"She's a pretty little thing," Hettie said. "But you have to watch them every minute, you know, these foreign maids . . . especially the Orientals." She gave one of her silvery laughs. "They tend to become—ah—in the family way, if you take my meaning." Morgan gave the woman a hard look, to no avail. "And when that occurs," Hettie continued, just as if Clara were not standing there, listening to every word, "of course the girl has to be turned out at once."

"Absolutely not," Morgan took pleasure in telling her. "Should such a thing happen, I would simply give the girl squawroot, and she'd soon be rid of it."

The color drained from Hettie's face. She picked up a napkin and began madly fanning herself with it. "Oh, dear, oh dear. Rid? Rid of it? How might this happen?" She looked as if she really did not want to be told. Morgan didn't care.

"You see, Mrs. Becker, an infusion of squawroot brings on the menses."

She thought the woman would faint. Even her uncaring husband half rose from his chair, saying, "Hettie, my dear, are you quite well?"

Recovering herself, Hettie said, "Might I inquire, Miss uh, how you know so much about unnatural medical practices?"

"Not unnatural, Mrs. uh," Morgan said deliberately. "As it happens, I am descended from an Algonkian witch." She smiled. "In my family, we know quite a bit about how to help a woman become pregnant, and how to stop a pregnancy, which is ever so much more efficient than having a doctor do abortions—"

She felt eyes boring into her and when she turned, both

Addie and Alex were staring at her. *No, no, stop, please,* their stares begged. Alex was shaking his head very slightly and rolling his eyes heavenward. She was about to mention how she had met him when, suddenly, as if she could read his mind, she knew that he had never mentioned to his parents that he gave free care at the dispensary. *He's afraid to tell them!* Morgan thought, and she looked away from him, feeling contempt and sadness.

Alex hurriedly broke in to tell *Maman*—how Morgan hated that affectation—about Adelaide's job as a social service worker. Hettie, happy to change the subject, turned to Adelaide and pretended interest. "Do tell us what you do, Miss Apple. I know no social service workers, so I am totally ignorant."

Addie looked nervously at Morgan, and launched into the story of poor little Clara at Ellis Island. "She became so excited that the inspectors assumed there was something wrong with her," Addie said. "You have no idea how little thought they give to the strangeness of coming into a country where you cannot speak the language. If someone can't understand, the inspectors immediately assume they must be mentally defective. They gave Clara the test, which she did not pass, of course . . ."

"Did not pass? And yet, here she is." Hettie looked at Clara as if she had turned into some kind of bug.

"Yes, but Mrs. Becker, the test is stupid," Addie said. "I defied the inspectors to do as well as Clara had. One of them took me up on my offer and guess what?"

"I cannot imagine," murmured Hettie.

Addie laughed merrily. "He didn't pass, either."

Hettie Becker did not find the story amusing. "No wonder they're letting in all that riffraff!" she said. "Oriental peoples from Russia and Poland and Lithuania! Really! Low-class, all of them! Furthermore," she said, turning to Morgan, "I do *not* approve of irregular doctors. I'm very sorry, but I must say it. Give me a proper European-trained medical doctor who has the proper background in science. Midwives are fine in their place, I suppose, but really—! A household that condones sin and shame—!"

She stood up, ignoring Alex's remonstrances and announced, "It is time for us to leave, Alexander. Maximilian. *Maximilian.*"

"Yes, dear," said Max, rising languidly from his seat.

When his wife and son were outside on the doorstep, Max lingered, pulling Morgan aside and muttering about, er, um, ending pregnancies. Did she do this often and might he—that is, would she—?

Finally, exasperated, Morgan asked, "What is it you want to know, Mr. Becker?" She was thoroughly sick of all of them.

"You understand, I don't wish to shout this. Yes. Well, in fact . . . Should a . . . lady friend find herself in an—um— embarrassing situation, might I send her to you?"

Ah, now she understood perfectly. "You needn't bother sending them all the way across the river to me," she said with some asperity. "Your own son can do the honors. He's at the Hester Street Dispensary every Saturday! Doing that very thing!" And closing the door behind them, she burst into tears.

Adelaide wanted to comfort her, but Morgan pulled away. "We are more different than I had imagined!" she said. "Did you see how Alex bent the knee to her? To that stupid snobby woman!"

Gently, Addie said, "It's his mother, Morgan."

"Yes, she's my mother and there are times I'm ashamed to admit it." Alex, having handed his parents into a cab, had returned. "God, what a relief to see them gone! I'm sure you'll agree, Mor—" He stopped, staring at her. "Morgan? What's the matter? Did my father say something outrageous to you? If he did, I'll—"

"No, no, no. He just wanted to know if I'd give his lady friends squawroot if needed."

"Oh, the cad. He has no control and no taste. I humbly apologize for him."

"Not necessary," Morgan said. She felt drained of emotion. Alex apparently saw nothing untoward in the behavior of his parents this afternoon—his mother's insults, his father's open lust. To him, it was nothing. Well, it was something to *her*. She was filled with a cold anger.

"Alex, your mother . . ." Her eyes filled with tears. She stopped speaking until she could collect herself. "Your mother,

Alex, insulted Clara. More than once. She then insulted her people, the country of her birth. She ignored one of her hostesses utterly . . ."

"Oh, Morgan, that's all right. They were here to meet you," Addie put in.

"No, Addie! I won't have you making excuses for a silly, stupid, ignorant, snobbish, condescending woman. Her behavior to you—and to me and to poor little Clara, too—was . . . indefensible, unforgivable, and inexcusable."

Lightly, Alex said, "All true, my darling, but redundant."

"Oh! You find my outrage amusing! And why not? I'm so much worse than an Oriental from Russia, aren't I? I'm part squaw, the lowest of the low!"

"MORGAN!" Two shocked voices, shouting together.

"It's stupid for us to be together, Alex," she said, as tears welled up. "We're from different worlds. You can never understand mine, and God knows I shall never, *never* understand yours!"

"Morgan, please, calm yourself." Alex took her hand in his. "I am in complete agreement with you and—"

"Are you? Are you truly? Do you hate your parents? Because I do, I simply hate them! Did you see how she treated us, your *maman*? Hear how she condescended? She is a horrible woman! And your father was licking his lips over Clara! How stupid I have been, to ever think we could . . . Nothing will ever come of it! I have learned my lesson, at last. I shall never see you again!"

Alex turned pale and released her hand. "You don't mean that, Morgan. You cannot mean it."

"Oh, but I do!"

"Please, dear Morgan, you're overwrought. I know they were perfectly awful, but it's meaningless, because I l—"

"Meaningless to you, perhaps, Alex. But not to me. Now, please, leave."

"I will speak to you tomorrow eve—"

"No! You will not. I do not wish to speak to you."

"Morgan, please."

She had stoked her anger to a fine blaze now. If everything else burned up with it, so be it!

"I mean it, Alex. We are finished. Please do not try to see or speak to me." When Addie made an involuntary cry, she whirled to glare at her friend and Addie shrank back. Then Morgan turned to face him. She felt indominable and fierce, like a warrior woman. "Good-bye, Alex!"

She did not know what she expected, but it was not his leaving without another word. Nevertheless, that is what happened. One moment, he was standing in her entryway, looking pleadingly at her; the next, he had turned and was gone, slamming the door behind him.

17

December 1906

"How long has it been," Dr. Grace asked, "since you last took the boat up to Chester and paid me a visit? A long time," she answered herself. "Too long by far." She put her teacup down with a thump.

Morgan gazed fondly at the older woman. It hadn't been a whole year, she thought, but Dr. Grace was getting on and, to her, doubtless every missed moment was important. In fact, Dr. Grace suddenly looked *old*. Her hair was nearly white, and the porcelain skin was starting to wrinkle. She looked the same, but . . . sunken, smaller. How old *was* she? If she'd been a girl of seventeen in 1861 . . . Morgan tried doing the arithmetic in her head and then gave up, using her fingers hidden under the kitchen table in her lap. Grace Chapman was sixtytwo. Not such a great age; surely she had many years ahead of her.

"And how long has it been," Morgan countered, "since you

last were here, in Brooklyn? It was still a separate city then, wasn't it? That's seven—no, eight—no, seven years ago. I'll wager you haven't been down here since 1896."

"It can't be *that* long. We saw *Uncle Tom's Cabin* at the Brooklyn Academy of Music on . . . what's the name of that business street?"

"Montague."

"Yes, Montague, exactly. And I remember your City Hall had lost its cupola not long before, along with its bell and its clock. There had been a fire."

"Well, Dr. Grace, that fire was in 1895. And it's Borough Hall now, since we've become a part of Greater New York," Morgan said. "So it's over ten years! Shame on you!" She laughed.

"I know, I know. I always mean to come. But every time I'm ready to start the journey, something happens to one of my patients." She looked around the kitchen. "You've done a great deal to this house, I see. It's the very latest word, I'm sure."

Morgan nodded, recalling the big old-fashioned kitchen in Chester, which had been exactly the same the last time she visited as the first time she'd laid eyes on it. And probably still was.

"Mrs. Mulligan complained about the range, so we decided to replace it. And once we started with the range . . ." She laughed. "Then Timothy, the foreman of the work crew, began to get ideas. He'd sidle up to me and say, 'Now, Miss, while we're about it, what do you think about bigger windows? Wouldn't that bring in the bright sunshine, now?' She imitated his Irish brogue. 'And wouldn't it be grand, to put the range right into the old fireplace and keep that foine old brick . . . or what would you say to some new cabinets with doors that close, instead of these open shelves, loike? Oh, and a lovely copper hood . . . and a fine long worktable covered with marble for rolling out the pastries, now.' Timothy was quite the talker. He painted such beautiful pictures of the modern kitchen. And we kept saying, 'Oh, Tim, what a good idea!' In the end, we reckoned that as long as all these men had already made a mess and they were already here and we were comfortable with them, why not? So now we have a fine coal range and next to it, three ovens, including a warming oven. We've even got a big hot-water tank, which you cannot see because Tim cleverly hid it in a closet. But the rest of the house . . ."

"The rest of the house is lovely. You have electric, I see. How nice, not to have to trim or light lamps. And here am I, still using kerosene in Chester." Dr. Grace held up her hands and looked at them woefully, as if they were covered in black soot. "It's beautifully warm here in the kitchen. No more crouching in front of the fire, getting scorched in front while your back freezes!" She laughed and added, "All of Brooklyn looks changed. I was surprised to see a new bridge. What do they call it?"

"The Manhattan Bridge," Addie said.

"And so many new houses! Soon, Brooklyn will be all filled up."

Adelaide laughed. "I don't think so. Not far from here, Brooklyn is still open farmland. Would you like to take a ride and see?"

"See farmland? Heavens no, I can see plenty of that where I just came from! I'd like to see the big city sights, if you don't mind." She sipped at her tea and took one of the sugared roll-up cookies on a plate in the middle of the table. "My, but these are delicious little tea cakes. I doubt you baked them, Morgan. Adelaide?"

Addie laughed. "Not I, Dr. Chapman. Neither Morgan nor I have much time for the kitchen anymore. These are Russian cookies, made by Clara, who is a wizard with the oven."

The three women turned to look at the girl, who sat apart from them in a hard chair by the kitchen window, staring out. She'd been so quiet, Morgan had quite forgotten she was still in the room. Clara turned at the sound of her name, and smiled wanly. She had been that way for over a week, morose and withdrawn. Morgan was beginning to find it tiresome. She hated pouting, couldn't put up with it. Addie, being big-hearted, said, "Oh, the poor child, think of her, all alone in a strange land. We should be like sisters to her." And she would comfort and cosset the girl, even brushing Clara's hair at night. No wonder Clara didn't act like hired help! She was treated more like an honored guest.

"You must have double the dose of maternal feelings, Addie, the way you fuss over Clara and take care of me," Morgan had remarked the other evening.

Addie had given a brief unamused laugh, and slid Morgan a look of such deep sadness that Morgan was instantly sorry she had said anything. Did Addie feel sad because she had no children? She always had said she was not at all interested in men or love or romance or marriage, only in her work. Still . . . Before Morgan could say anything, the look was gone and Adelaide was her usual sensible self, saying, "That's not maternal, my dear Morgan, that's social worker."

"Now, the last time I was here," Dr. Grace said, "Adelaide was trying very hard to get you to go to medical college, Morgan. Why did you never go?"

"I always wanted to. But, as you said of yourself earlier, each time I prepared myself to go, a patient needed me. One day, I really will go. As soon as I have time. In the meantime . . . well, my patients think I'm as good as a real doctor. After all, didn't I train under the best doctor in the world?"

Dr. Grace inclined her head. "You're very busy, then?"

"I am too busy, trying to save these poor women and their children, who are left by an unfeeling city to die of starvation and deprivation. Do you remember me telling you about the little crippled girl, Della, and her mother? I kept my eye on them, went to see them once each month. And each time, no matter how much food I brought, they were thinner and weaker. Then one Sunday, I found them dead, both of them, the child curled up in her mother's arms. Frozen. Not enough money for coal, I assume. The truth is, there was little I could do from the very beginning. It is much the same for many of my patients. Why is it that evil things befall the poor and helpless?" Her voice had been rising with every sentence and when she stopped, she breathed in deeply. "I beg your pardon. I get upset that I am powerless."

"And real power you'll never have. Not until you have your medical degree."

"Many of my ancestors were renowned as doctors and none

of them had a medical degree," said Morgan. "My very own mother—"

"Have you ever gone back to see her?"

"I'm not even sure she's still alive," Morgan answered. "Once, I put clothes into my traveling bag, determined to go . . ." A dream had started her packing, of course, a dream of the Indian woman, Bird, wringing her hands and slowly dissolving into mist as Morgan tried desperately to grab ahold of her. And when she awakened, she realized that Bird had worn the face of her mother. Surely, it was a message. So, she had planned to make the trip that very day. But by the time she had dressed and gone downstairs and was chatting companionably with Addie at breakfast, the dream had faded, and she could not recapture the feeling of urgency. "I thought I would go, to see. And then . . . I don't know. My life just carried me along and so I never went. I should, I know. I should at least see if she's alive still. I should say good-bye. I never said good-bye, but I was so angry with her. I never said good-bye to my father . . ." To her astonishment, her eyes were filling with tears.

The back doorbell rang and Clara sprang up from her chair to open the door, all signs of apathy gone. Of course. She had been moping about, waiting for a message from *him*. At the door, a boy held out a folded note, and when he said, "Miss Optak—Opakt—" Clara's whole aspect brightened.

"Is me!" she said, snatching the note from him and holding it to her bosom.

The boy stood for a moment, waiting for her to give him a coin for his trouble; but Clara just shut the door in his face, and ran out of the kitchen. They all heard her scampering up the stairs to her little room under the eaves.

"A man," the three women said in unison, and laughed.

"I wonder which one?" Addie said.

She meant which one of the many young men—the delivery boys, the construction workers, the carpenters, the grocery clerks, the two brothers who lived next door—who, upon seeing Clara, were instantly smitten. She was a lovely little thing to look at and, because her English was still so poor, she said little. That, Morgan couldn't help noticing, was no deterrent.

In fact, her blushing silences and the little glances from under her thick dark eyelashes only seemed to fan the flames.

Morgan knew that Clara was enamored of someone she was carefully keeping secret. It was clear to anyone with eyes to see that none of these boys, no matter how handsome or persuasive and courtly, made an impression upon Clara. She had been courted by one young man after the other, and not one of them had so much as been invited into the kitchen for a cup of tea. But there was *someone*. Morgan recognized all the signs. Clara pined, she moped, she went into black moods and walked about looking like a thundercloud. Then a message would be delivered to the back door—just as today—and what a miraculous transformation. Suddenly she would be all sunshine and music.

Lately, Morgan had become convinced that she knew who this mystery man was and it made her very angry. Circumstances made it extremely difficult for her to do anything about it, which made her even angrier.

"Morgan told me weeks ago that Clara was in love," Addie was telling Dr. Grace. "And Morgan should know."

"What do you mean?" Morgan demanded, feeling her cheeks begin to burn.

"You know what I mean. Morgan is in love herself, Dr. Grace. But she won't admit it."

"I am not in love," Morgan said firmly. She knew her face must be scarlet.

"You see what I am talking about, Dr. Grace."

"Is he so terrible?" Dr. Grace teased. "So unsuitable?"

Morgan swallowed hard. It was amazing, how much it could still hurt after all these months. "Adelaide is referring to Dr. Alexander Becker."

"A physician! Then not unsuitable. But terrible? Ugly? Drunken?"

Morgan gave Addie a hard look but got back only a bland stare. She knew Addie did not understand why she still refused to see Alex. To tell the truth, she didn't know herself. Sheer stubbornness, it must be, and stiff-necked pride. Every time she thought of her harsh words that day, she wanted to weep. Oh, she had been in a fine high dudgeon, very self-righteous and ridiculous. The things she had said! Yes, his *maman* was a nasty baggage who loved feeling superior, but was that Alex's fault? She had not forgotten him, although she kept herself very busy, so as not to think about him.

She had to offer some sort of story to Dr. Grace. "He comes from a very wealthy family, German Jews who disdain even other Jews who come from Russia and Poland—Orientals, they call them. So you can imagine what they thought of half-breed Morgan Wellburn." She tried for a smile. "I could see that such a match would never work. So I ended it."

"She sent him away, Dr. Grace, though he begged for her understanding."

"Did you, Morgan? Did you refuse to hear his pleas for understanding? Did you stand on your high ground until at last, when the waters had receded, you saw that you were stranded and alone?" The doctor's voice was kind enough, with a wry edge to it. Could it be, Morgan wondered, that Dr. Grace had once been in the same position?

"Yes, Dr. Grace, to all your questions. Yes, I refused and I ended up alone and wondering how I got there."

"Oh, Morgan," Addie put in eagerly. "You can still make it up with him, if you want." She turned to Dr. Grace. "He writes to her. He comes by the house. And, always, she refuses to see him."

"Morgan, dear girl, will you take a bit of advice from an old woman? Get down off your high horse and listen to what the man has to say."

Flushing, Morgan said, "I don't know why you're so mad for me to see Alex, Addie. You didn't like it at all when we began to walk out."

"Well, I'm sorry if that's how it seemed," Addie retorted stoutly. "Since I knew him long before you did. And of course, I've always counted him a friend, a good and thoughtful person. Perhaps—perhaps I didn't like to see any changes in our life. But, just because I once behaved badly is no reason for you to do the same!"

"Well said, Adelaide!" said Dr. Grace, picking up another tea cake. "But I must admit, that's very like Morgan. Morgan, you see, runs away when things become difficult. Runs off and starts anew." Dr. Grace patted Morgan's hand, to take some of the sting away from the words. "It's an old habit, Adelaide. I'm not certain she is able to change."

"In any case," Morgan said in tones that brooked no further discussion, "whether or not I am in love or anything remotely like it, I do not behave like Clara. Who is on her way back down, I hear, and I'll warrant, on her way out."

Sure enough, Clara came dancing into the kitchen, singing something in Russian. She had changed into a new dress, the same color of blue as her eyes—which sparkled with anticipation. Her face had been washed and her hair newly brushed. Morgan thought she smelled the carnation toilet water she had given the girl for her seventeenth birthday.

"I go out now," she said. "I take walk." As she spoke, she wrapped herself in the blue woolen cloak that had been a gift from Addie, and out she floated. They heard the front door slam.

"It's love all right," Dr. Grace laughed. "At least I hope so. Because that young woman is pregnant, or I've really become old and senile."

Pregnant! Morgan sat very still, ashamed of herself. How could she have missed it? Perhaps it wasn't so? No, if Dr. Grace thought Clara was pregnant, she *was*.

"Oh, that rotten lowlife!" Morgan burst out. "I thought I saw him, several times when I got off the train. And always, after I saw him, I would see Clara. Never together. He's far too clever for that!" Her fists clenched. "I have confronted her with it, each time, but she always denies it. She pretends she doesn't understand what I'm saying or begins to cry. Addie, you know it's impossible to talk to her if she's weeping. But now I am sure of it. Of course it is him. He is truly a cad!"

"Who, Morgan? For God's sake, say his name!"

"It's Max, of course. Maximilian Becker!"

"Alex's . . . *father*?" Addie turned white.

"Oh, Addie, you are so terribly naive sometimes. Yes, Max, Alex's father. Remember how openly he flirted with her during their visit?"

"But that was over a year ago . . . You mean it's been going on ever since then?"

"That's what I mean."

"But Morgan, what are we to *do*?"

"Do? I don't know. Or perhaps I do know. Where is my cloak?"

"Morgan! We have company! Where are you going?"

"To Max Becker's house, to give him a piece of my mind!" Out into the hall she whirled. Then she stopped, her hand already on the doorknob. All very well to talk of going to his house, but of course he would not be there. He would be meeting that stupid child, taking her to rented rooms, murmuring sweet lies into her ears while he hungrily peeled her clothes from her body. It was disgusting! The man was old enough to be Clara's grandfather! Did he know she was pregnant? Good grief, did *she*? What did she think was going to happen?

Morgan went back into the kitchen and hung her cloak on the hat tree. "What am I saying? They are together somewhere, of course. I can't do anything." She sat down heavily in the kitchen chair she had just vacated. "It will have to wait. Oh, I just pray she isn't thinking of having this—this love child, hoping that will force Max to *marry* her!" She turned to Dr. Grace and began to recount the whole tale.

The December air was sharp, nipping at her nose and sending great puffs of white steam out with every agitated breath. Thoughts whirled around in Morgan's head. Why was she out in the freezing cold, instead of sitting by the kitchen fire with Addie and Dr. Grace, drinking coffee and deciding which play they would see this evening? She knew why. Dr. Grace's comment yesterday, that Morgan always ran away from difficulties, had stung. Is that what she did? Well, she wouldn't do it this time. She would tell Alex what his father had done and enlist his help. No matter how he felt about her, he couldn't refuse that. Could he? Surely not. It had been several weeks since he had written her, and she thought he had finally given up on her. What if he stared at her coldly and said, "But, Miss Wellburn, I was under the impression that you wished never to speak to me again." But she had to do something; she couldn't keep running away from things. Right now she had to move before her feet froze to Clinton Street.

After a moment's indecision, she began to walk quickly toward the bridge. Riding the train across the East River, she gazed out of the window at the port, busy and active even in the dead of winter, and over at the monumental Statue of Liberty that raised its torch high above Bedloe's Island. She stared, but saw nothing, her mind was so full of turmoil. At the New York terminal, she took a trolley uptown and walked across 23rd Street to the house where Alex Becker had his private practice.

Once across the street from his building, though, she found herself unable to move. Looking up at a lighted window, she actually saw his fair head bent over papers or a book. She knew his office rooms so well. He was sitting at his desk, an enormous oak rolltop with dozens of drawers and cubbyholes. He loved that desk. Hettie, of course, sneered at it; it was old-fashioned and not good enough for her son the physician. But he cared nothing for what his mother thought. They both found Hettie—

Morgan made herself stop. There was no "they." She had sent him away; they were finished. Why had she come here? To tell him that his father had seduced an innocent girl and made her pregnant.

She knew that wasn't why. She had come here because she missed Alex. She still loved him. She was so filled with longing, she could hardly stand up straight. The anger against Max had drained away in a rush of desire. She advanced to the front steps, slowly climbed them to the door. Would Alex welcome her? He had sent messages, for months, begging her to see him, to just talk with him. He could not have changed so quickly. Could he?

And then, she imagined that another woman lounged on the buttonback leather couch, her knees covered by Alex's old quilt, perhaps leafing through one of his medical journals or gazing at him as he worked, thinking that in a moment, she would quietly get up and take off her clothes, all of them, while softly calling his name. And when he turned, saying, "Yes?" how fire would flare in his eyes, and how he would leap to his feet, knocking the chair over in his eagerness to get to her.

No! Morgan thought. She couldn't bear it if he had found another to take her place. Her heart pounding, she ran down the flight of stone steps and away from the house and away from Alex, as if the hounds of hell were after her. So she did not see his face at the window and did not know that he came racing downstairs in his shirtsleeves, too late to see which way she had gone.

18

March 1907

Adelaide stopped trying to compose the report she was working on. She put down the pen, sighed, and pushed back from her desk. Now that she was a matron, God knows she had more than enough to do every day, without having to worry about Clara Optakeroff. She and Morgan had tried talking to the girl. Morgan let Clara know that she needn't have this baby. They said they would take care of the problem and take care of her, too. Clara refused. The silly girl believed the blandishments of that disgusting old man. Why, she wasn't even his only paramour. Far from it—the old reprobate was probably bedding three or four pretty young things who also believed his flowery compliments. What was the matter with women, Adelaide wondered, turning into wantons—and worse—if a good-looking man kissed their hand and told them they were beautiful! And when they gave in, what did they get? A hairy brute who stuck a monstrous ugly thing into them, over and over, and made them cry out in pain and laughed at them for it.

She'd seen it once, when she was just a child. She'd gone looking for her nursemaid, Hilda, and when she opened the door to Hilda's bedroom, that's what was going on. Hilda and her swain, Hans, on the bed, he on his knees, her legs up on his shoulders. He was pushing something big and dark into her, laughing, and she was crying out. Addie couldn't remember if she had whimpered, but she must have. Because Hilda turned an ugly face to her and shouted, "Get out of here! Get out, you terrible child!" Hilda, who had always said she loved her little Adelaide!

Of course, Addie knew now that Hilda had been enjoying the pushing and shoving, but it had never appealed to *her*. How much sweeter, to curl into the warmth and softness of a woman's body, to curve your hand around a satin-skinned breast with its crisp alert nipple.

She made herself stop the thoughts, and immediately begged God for forgiveness. It was wrong, she knew that. It was against nature, what she wanted. Every night, she fell on her knees and prayed fiercely for God to release her from her unnatural thoughts and desires. But God never listened to her; perhaps He did not want to hear the prayers of such a sinner. Only once had she given in, when she was still living on Grove Street, before she met Morgan Wellburn.

Theodora was much older than Adelaide, a tall lanky dancer, who wore trousers and smoked little cigars. She was an exciting person to be around. She didn't give a damn what anyone thought, she claimed, and cared only for pleasure. She was good to Adelaide, sweet and loving, praising Addie's round hips and large breasts and milky skin. It had felt so good, to finally have the heat between her legs quenched, to find bliss and release. She had thought she was in love and that Teddy loved her. Then one evening, Adelaide came home from work—those were the years she was at Bellevue—to find a new young woman in Teddy's flat. Teddy invited Addie to do a threesome, explaining that she would be the man first and then they could all take turns. Teddy brought out some devices, made of leather, stuffed hard, like sausages, with straps. Adelaide stared at the leather things with distaste, and asked if that thing was going to be shoved into her. Teddy laughed and said,

"Of course, silly girl." Adelaide turned and walked out of the flat and never went back, not even to get her things. She never did find out the name of the new girl.

That was the only time she had given in, and she had learned her lesson. She knew she had to fight those feelings. Not long after that, she had met Morgan and fallen in love. She had hoped that maybe Morgan would love her, too. Morgan was tall, like Teddy, and very much in charge. But she soon discovered that Morgan liked men. After Morgan gave up Alex Becker, Addie hoped that maybe . . . but, of course, that was stupid. Morgan could no more change her nature than Adelaide could change hers. She would never dream of doing anything about her passion for Morgan. She imagined that Morgan would find it disgusting. So she kept her secret affliction hidden from the world.

A head poked into the doorway. "Matron! You're needed in the Detention Division, please."

"Coming." Addie got up, trying to smooth out her skirts. She wore a long black apron that marked her as Matron, a person of authority, responsible for all women and children immigrants and everything that happened to them. Some of the matrons were stiff and starched and always neat. Addie was her same old self, rather messy, dropping hairpins as she went. She loved her job. She'd waited seven long years to finally become matron. Once she'd got her degree in social work in 1900, she immediately went to work for Women's Immigrant Aid Society. The new arrivals she kept seeing at the dispensary every Saturday had touched her heart, and she had wanted to work for the Immigration Service at Ellis Island, where five thousand to seven thousand poor, bewildered immigrants poured through every single day including Sunday.

There were twenty-two social service workers, and because of Adelaide's background as a nurse and her keen interest in mental illness, she soon became the one the others asked about mental defectives and the mentally ill. She was often called upon to examine such immigrants. They were given simple tests, usually in picture form, which as far as she was concerned were almost useless. Look how they had misdiagnosed Clara when she first came in. Well, Clara was not too terribly intelligent, but she was neither insane nor defective, just frightened and ignorant.

In any case, Miss Apple was soon well known to all the inspectors on Ellis Island, as well as the doctors, and she found her work interesting and fulfilling. But she could see, early on, that matrons were badly needed. Three years ago, hordes of unprepared, non–English speakers began to jam the halls. They were mostly women and children, following their husbands to the Golden Land, and single girls, hoping to find a husband, or widows, hoping for the same. It became imperative to keep a sharp eye out for white slavers—slick fellows who waited near the docks in Manhattan for the boats to empty—looking for the girl or woman alone and seeming lost.

Adelaide had gone to the Immigration and Naturalization Service office and asked for a job as matron. Imagine her amazement when they said there was no such position. Miss Apple could not very well apply for a job that did not exist, now, could she? But the immigrant throngs kept growing, and this year, at last, there were openings for matron. Adelaide was one of the first to apply. According to the description, she was required "to give such aid and assistance as may be necessary to women and children detained," and that meant, she soon discovered, everything. Every day, she heard another sad story, fought another battle for someone, calmed and soothed unhappy relatives. Her starting salary was $720 a year, and if she proved herself, she could get a raise the second or third year to $840. The hours were sunup to sundown, and the island, of course, was open seven days a week. Everyone did get a day off and Adelaide's was Saturday, so she could go to the Hester Street Dispensary and keep her nursing skills honed.

She hurried to the Detention Division. Anytime she was fetched, she knew there was a serious problem. All women and children stayed in detention for at least a day or two; there was no way to prevent it. So many ships were coming into New York harbor from Europe that often they had to line up and wait for several days until there was room on Ellis Island for their passengers. Steerage people waited to be pushed onto a barge or a ferry and then they stood and waited some more, without food or water, sometimes in the rain, or the wind, or hot sun. Once they landed on the island, they were lined up in front of the main door, to stand under the enormous metal canopy, and wait.

Even when they were admitted into the waiting room, there was yet another wait for their number to be called. After so many days at sea in terrible conditions, after so much hope and so little sleep, it was too much for many. Matrons were often called to deal with hysterics, or worse.

So what was it today? She marched briskly into the Detention Division, a bright sunny room with a white tile floor and big Palladian windows. The room was crowded of course. Right across the hall was the Discharging Division, so those in Detention could gaze longingly at those who walked free. Who in the world had planned *that*, she often wondered. She found it cruel beyond belief. But she was not an architect— as she had been told, every time she remarked upon the arrangement.

One quick look around and she knew where she was wanted. A trio of women—one no more than a girl of nine or ten, she reckoned—huddled together at a table. They were from Russia or the Ukraine, she could tell by the babushkas and shawls they wore. An inspector was standing near them, looking impatient. As soon as he saw Adelaide, he called out, "Ah, there you are at last, Matron!" as if she'd been dawdling. What caught her attention was the way the older woman in the group turned to the sound of his voice—not with her eyes, but with her whole head. She was blind, then. Hadn't anyone told this family that the blind old lady would be spotted and marked and probably sent back?

When Addie got closer, she could see that the "old lady" was no more than forty. And her black shawl had the chalk mark—a big white "E"—that showed the officials at the top of the stairway had seen right away what was what. Newcomers didn't realize that one of the men standing by the stairs was a doctor who watched carefully for anything unusual. Addie imagined the woman had come up the stairs with a daughter

on either side to guide her—that would arouse suspicion—and
had turned in that blind way to a sound, and been spotted
immediately. The entire family, Mama, daughter of twenty or
so, and the girl who sat trembling, her eyes wide with fright,
looked at her expectantly.

The inspector, glad to be relieved of the group, handed
Addie a card with the information printed on it. Anya Holub,
aged forty-one; her daughter Malka, aged twenty-one, and her
daughter Tanya, aged ten, from Kiev, in the Ukraine. They had
been detained for two days, waiting for a hearing. The hearing
would be held half an hour from now and they needed an
interpreter. Addie, aware of how many times the inspectors,
overworked and harried, made mistakes about the mental
abilities of immigrants, said to herself, *We'll see.*

"Hello," she said, pleasantly, in English, looking at the older
daughter who, she thought, must be in charge. The young
woman stared at her belligerently but without comprehension.
But who knew exactly *what* this girl understood? Addie remembered only too well the day when a young man arrived at
the end of his inspection, ready to leave. He presented his
papers. He had sailed from Germany. The inspector asked
him, in German, how much money he had with him, and the
young man did not understand. The inspector tried Italian, then
Yiddish. Nothing. Then he called on Addie, who was known
to speak many languages. She tried Russian, Polish, and a few
words in Czech. Finally the young man, frustrated and in
despair, burst out with, "Does nobody speak English here?"

So she knew enough to persevere. "I am Matron Apple, here
to help you." The three faces focused on her, but nobody
responded.

"Have you no English at all?" she went on. Nothing. "So,"
she said in Russian, "not even one syllable in the language of
this country? Let me teach you your first English word. *Hello.*
This is what you say in greeting. Do you understand?"

Now the older sister, Malka, spoke up, in Russian. "How
long are they going to keep us prisoners here? This is why we
left our home, our nice brick house? Why we ran to escape the
tsar and the damn Cossacks? For this?!"

What a temper! Addie thought, annoyed. But then she reminded herself that these women, all alone and one of them blind, had come a long way, first by train and then crowded into the reeking airless space of steerage, and who knew how long they had been waiting for their hearing.

"I'm sorry you've been detained. Did no one warn you that the doctors look for blindness and other defects?" She gentled her voice. "Those who come to the United States and cannot work are sent back."

Angrily, Malka said, "Look at us. We are a family. We are not going to leave our mother in the street to die. We are going to take care of her. I am twenty-one years old and can keep books. I have two sisters already in America, twenty-four and twenty-seven. One is a secretary, the other a bookkeeper. My father is here. He works as a furrier. He has a nice apartment in the Bronx, with room for us all. Why should my mother have to work?"

"If there are three family members already in this country, all earning, why have you come through Ellis Island? Why have you come in steerage? If you had come second class," Adelaide explained, "you would have disembarked at Castle Garden, and you would already be in America with the rest of your family."

The young woman made a gesture of disgust. "Don't ask," she said, her voice grating. "We went by train to Paris and then by boat to England. In England, my mother—always a penny-pincher—said, 'Why should we waste good money on second class when we can just as well come in steerage? It's not a long trip and you girls are strong. And we can always use the money.'

"We didn't *need* that money," Malka continued, making her little sister weep. "Oh do be quiet, Tanya!" she snapped. "Mama knows what she does, what she always does, if it means saving a ruble!" She stopped, breathless with her outrage. "But no, she has to get everything as cheaply as possible—! Money means everything to her, everything!" Then she smiled a strange little smile and added, "Maybe we should let them send her back to Kiev, that would teach her a lesson!"

The little girl dissolved into frantic weeping, clutching her mother's arm tightly. The mother shook her off with annoyance and turned her head toward Malka. "Money means nothing to you . . . just so long as it's someone else's money. Your papa will be happy I saved him so much on the tickets . . ."

Malka snorted with derision. "Papa will not be happy when they don't let you into the Golden Land, Mama."

As they argued, the young one became more and more frenzied, pleading with them both to stop, please stop.

Finally, Adelaide said loudly, in Russian, "Enough! What's done is done," she said to the women. "No use crying over it! Meanwhile, let us go into the hearing and I will explain the whole thing. You will all be allowed into the Golden Land, I promise you. Give me your father's address, and I will send him a telegram to come get you."

The hearing went well, and soon Adelaide was bustling back to her office to see where else she was needed. She skirted the perimeter of the great hall where, all day long, through an intricate series of metal pens, an endless procession of people filed, step by step, bearing bundles, trunks, boxes . . . past first one examiner and then another, past the alert medical officers, the tallymen and the clerks. It was a daily caravan that could stretch over three miles. The inspector stood above the throng, behind a wooden lectern. He asked your name, tried to spell it, asked you how you spelled it. If he spelled it wrong, you were stuck with the wrong name or even a brand new name for your new life.

All day long, this slow parade waited, jerked forward, halted again. There was no end, Adelaide thought, to human hope. Because it had to be hope that brought them here with their meager possessions and their layers of clothing, the look of them announcing they were *greenehs*, greenhorns. An inspector had told her that during one day this year, twenty-one thousand immigrants had arrived in the port of New York. It was incredible. If that kept up, New York City would soon be bursting at the seams.

Adelaide headed down the corridor toward her office. Before she was halfway there, she heard the voice, calling, "Matron! You are needed at the fence." With a sigh, she marched back to where immigrants ended their voyage; the metal fence where husband, brother, or other relatives would be waiting. When she got closer, she could hear that the hubbub was in Yiddish. A young woman—pretty, but wearing an ugly *sheitl*, the wig Orthodox Jewish women wore to keep strange men from looking at them with desire—was yelling at a handsome young man on the other side of the fence. He was tall, neatly dressed, his dark wavy hair carefully brushed and his face still glowing from the barber.

The woman, who held tightly on to her two young ones, a boy and a girl, perhaps four and five years of age, perhaps twins, both with golden red hair, was shouting, "Never, do you hear me, Moishe! Never! I'll go back first!"

"You are my wife. I slept on the cutting table at the tailor shop for a year and a half to save money so I could send for you! Stop being crazy and come out! We have a nice place, two rooms!"

"God forgive you for turning into a *goy*!" the woman cried. "Children, don't look at that man. That can't be your father, your father is a Jew with a proper beard! This ... this is a Yenkee, a *goy*! So don't look on him!"

"If your children want to look on something, they should only look on you, Blume! A peasant woman in her peasant clothes and ugly wig! In this country, Blume, women don't cut their hair off. They *wear* it, right out in the street!"

The young woman burst into tears and ran from him, bumping into Adelaide. Addie began talking to her in Yiddish, telling the woman to take it easy. "It's hard, I know it's hard. I see this happen every day," she said. "Your husband likes America and America is very different from your *shtetl* ..."

At those words, Blume began to cry. "My *shtetl*," she mourned. "My mother, my father, my sisters! I've left them all behind forever and for what? That man is a stranger to me!" She looked at Adelaide and burst into fresh tears. "What shall I do? I don't want to stay here with him! I want my mother!"

"Every day this happens," Adelaide lied. "Every single day. It's a big change. But you will see, he is no different underneath. He loves you. He worked hard to send for you and your beautiful children." Blume beamed at those words, though the tears still flowed from her eyes. "It is so difficult to leave everything behind and come to a new country," Adelaide went on, "but you will see that it is very good here. No pogroms. No Cossacks. Your children can go to school and it costs nothing. The police do not beat you. They help you."

"Truly?"

"I, too, am a Jew and my mother and father came as immigrants to this country," Adelaide said blithely, not bothering to add that this journey had taken place several generations ago. But she *was* a Jew and her parents *had* been immigrants, just with more education and more money. "Look, your children want to see their *tateh*. They want to see their new home. You should at least give him a chance."

The young man had not moved from his place by the fence. He was staring at his wife, rather longingly, Addie thought. And Blume, in spite of herself, kept casting glances in his direction.

"Go, why don't you? Go tell him you will try this new life, for the sake of the children and the love you have for each other."

Finally, Blume went to the fence. Through the opening, their hands touched. After they spoke, Blume turned to say, "Thank you, lady. I will try and we will see." But now she was smiling.

Adelaide was smiling, too, as she turned to go back. She really enjoyed her job. She never knew what was going to happen from one minute to the next. When she finally got home to Clinton Street, she was usually so tired, she could hardly eat a bite of supper or keep her eyes open to read. But that was good, for then she would fall asleep the minute her head met the pillow, and would not be tormented with thoughts of her wicked desires.

19

That Evening

They ate in the kitchen, sitting in the soft glow of the electric chandelier. The air outside was warm for March, and they had opened the back door to let in some fresh air. Mulligan's meat pie was as delicious as usual. Mulligan suffered from rheumatism, in spite of the infusions Morgan gave her. She was beginning to slack a bit on the scrubbing and cleaning on account of her poor sore knees, but they had agreed that she should stay on until she no longer wished to. They did not want to give up Mulligan's cooking.

"An interesting day on the island, Addie?" Morgan asked, taking a mouthful of meat, carrots, potatoes, and crust.

"As always. I had to help bring a madwoman back, to be sent home to Sicily, I think it was. Her husband had ordered her from a brother-in-law—ordered her, Morgan, like a side of beef!—on the strength of a photo. Well, she is a remarkably beautiful girl, but quite mad. She bites people."

"Oh dear. Did she bite you?"

"No, she did not. But I seem to be able to calm the mental defectives that come through." She paused, finishing a large bite of pie, and then continued, "Of course, some of the inspectors are quite without imagination and cannot understand that a look of complete stupidity might come from ignorance of the English language." She laughed. "You'd be surprised, how many people simply talk louder and slower to the poor immigrants, as if they were deaf and not simply in an alien land."

"This girl . . . what was she like? I mean, her behavior, her general demeanor?"

"Nervous. Jumpy, I would say. And then, suddenly, quite unaware of her surroundings, muttering to herself. It was strange . . . on the ferry going back to the island, she often acted as if she were carrying on a conversation, with different facial expressions and gestures. Yet, there was no one near her save me and I know she wasn't talking to me."

"Yes . . . ," Morgan said, fork halfway to her mouth, forgotten. "She wasn't. She was talking to her voices."

"Her voices?"

"Or spirits. Some say spirits, some say voices." Suddenly, Morgan became aware of the growing interest on her friend's face. She had never told Adelaide about Becky, nor about Quare Auntie either, nor any of the other ancestors who heard things no normal person could hear. She had never told anyone.

"There was a girl. In Chester," she said. "They called her Crazy Mariah. She behaved like that, and Dr. Grace told me it was a disease called *dementia praecox*. It had another name, too, that a French doctor called it—" She stopped talking, aware that she was gibbering. "It doesn't matter. The poor girl, she has to go back to Europe?"

"That's the rule. I suppose it's fair." Addie got up to cut into a fresh loaf of bread, bringing the brown slices back to the table. "How was your day, Morgan?"

"Exhausting! I was gone all day, from just before noon, as Elizabeth Murray was brought to bed with her fifth child. I thought it would be quick—all her others have popped out as if greased—but this one did not want to leave the womb. Her labor stopped after three fruitless hours. By that time, we were both quite tired, and I began to pack up, telling Elizabeth it might be false labor. Then, quite suddenly, labor began again, and it was terribly painful. When I felt her belly, I could not tell which way the babe was facing. I even thought it might be twins. I was sure I had felt two heads. There was a lot of excitement at that thought, I can tell you. It gave Elizabeth a new dose of strength and she pushed with all her might."

Morgan paused, putting her bread and butter down on the table and taking up her glass of ale. "When it was born, at last, it nearly tore the poor woman in two. And it did not live long enough to give the first cry," Morgan said. "Just as well. It was . . . well, there was half of another child joined to it, the top half only. They were facing each other, arms tightly wound around each other, nose to nose and unable to breathe."

Adelaide went pale, her hand to her heart.

"Now, Addie, it isn't unheard of, you know. There are many stories of joined twins. There was a pair in East Haddam once, or so the story went, connected by a short membrane from hip to hip. This was when I was a child. The mother begged the midwife to cut the membrane, but when she did, both babies died. It seems they shared at least one organ. I've heard other stories about monsters born of quite normal parents. Most folks tended to disbelieve such tales, although Dr. Grace told me she once delivered a child with two heads . . ."

"Two heads—! Brrr!"

"She said it would be a sin against God and nature to kill the poor little thing. But she did not give it the slap of life, and laid it face down, so that it never started to breathe. At any rate . . . you can imagine how tired I was at the end of this day. Poor Elizabeth was quite distraught, thinking surely she had been punished for some sin. Then, when I got home, there was no fire in the grate, no lights, our supper sitting, still cold, in the pantry—no Clara, in short. I called her name, and heard a faint kind of moan. So I ran up to her room, and found her fast asleep in her bed. I decided to let her sleep." Morgan sipped her ale and stretched her back, yawning. At that moment, there came such a shriek from upstairs that she dropped her glass, spilling it all across the floor. Neither she nor Addie said a word to each other. They both ignored the spill and headed for the stairs at a run.

Sweating and twisting from side to side in her agony, Clara sobbed and cried for her mother. The tiny room under the attic was sweltering, even though its one window stood open. Addie at once went for a bowl of water and a clean cloth, which Morgan dipped into the water, wrung out, and laid across Clara's brow.

"I know, I know, you are in terrible pain. You must tell me what's happening."

The girl only wailed more loudly. "Mama! Save me! Help me! Oh, why has God done this to me?"

"God did not do this, I think," Morgan remarked.

"Quite right," Addie said, bending to pick up something from the carpet. "Look at this." *This* was an empty package of Dr. Belcher's Female Cure.

"Aha," Morgan said. "You bought these periodical drops, Clara?"

"No! I never buy them! Max—Max tell me to take them and all will be fixed."

"He did, eh? When was this, Clara?" Morgan had to raise her voice to be heard above the girl's moans and whimpers. "When did Max give you this package?"

"Today."

"Today! And you swallowed the whole damned thing?"

"I take all of it. Max tell me . . ."

"Damn the man!" Morgan said between gritted teeth. "Doesn't he know how dangerous these things are?"

"Perhaps he didn't care what happened to her," Addie suggested.

Morgan closed her eyes briefly, sighing, and said, "I'll tell you what I know when we're back downstairs. Meanwhile, God only knows what damage the stupid girl has done to herself!" Both of them were familiar with all the "periodical drops," "female regulators," and other abortives available to anyone through the mails. The pills were probably made principally of aloes or black hellebore. Black hellebore, taken in carefully measured doses, often did bring on the menses, but to take a whole bottle—!

"We'll have to give her an emetic," Morgan said. "If she vomits enough, perhaps she will survive this."

"Poor Clara," said Adelaide, to which Morgan snorted. "Clara, do try to lie still," Morgan said. "You're making the bleeding worse."

Addie changed the blood-soaked towels under Clara for clean ones, asking, "Silly child, why didn't you come to us? We would have helped you, just as we did before." Clara had been pregnant last fall, and Morgan had given her squawroot, blue cohosh . . . but in carefully measured doses. Once it was ground into a powder, she had explained, it was very powerful. She had made an infusion, and it had worked—without all this blood and pain.

"I am ashamed," Clara sobbed. As well she might be! She wouldn't hear a word against "my Mex" as she called him. She claimed Max was the love of her life, she would never love another. Just so, and here was what came of her so-called love. A pregnancy and a badly bungled attempt to abort the child.

An hour later, they finally had the bleeding under control, and Clara sank into a fitful sleep. The two women went back downstairs. "There's a pudding," Morgan said, "and I won't be cheated out of it."

Seated once more at the table, Morgan told Addie what she knew. Months ago, Max had taken a room in a hotel in lower Manhattan, at the Broadway Central—"So that's where they were meeting!" Addie murmured. They went there to make love whenever they could. When Clara found herself pregnant for the second time, she told Max she wanted to keep this one.

"And he—?" Addie prompted.

Morgan gave a laugh. "What do you think, knowing Max Becker? He left some money on the bureau and made himself scarce. Not even a note to bid her farewell! She took the whole package to punish him, can you imagine? Oh, the ability of people to lie to themselves!"

"Poor child!" Addie sighed. "Unrequited love is the worst . . . or so I've heard . . . *Morgan?*" she added, in a certain tone of voice. Morgan sat up straight, alert.

"Yes?"

"I think we should call Alex Becker. Now, wait a minute, don't start shaking your head until you hear me out. He's a doctor and he'll feel obliged to help. After all, this would have been his . . . oh my God, his brother or sister!"

"*Half* brother or sister," Morgan said through stiff lips. "And the answer is no. I shall doctor Clara myself. Once she's better, then *we* can decide what's to be done about her." And, without looking at Addie at all, she left the kitchen.

* * *

It was a lovely day, some three weeks later—a bit of spring in the middle of days of cold gray rain. Morgan let herself out of the house with a feeling of relief. The sky was lined in wispy clouds, and the crocuses were poking up their heads in every front garden in Brooklyn Heights. The trees were misty with not-quite-opened leaves of spring green, and the sweet smell of new grass filled the air. Clara was really recovered, at last, except for her lovesickness. Morgan often wondered if the girl would ever get over it. It was so pathetic, to see her longing after a man who had gone to Chicago to escape her. Her eyes were forever filling with tears, and she tended to mope. But, when Morgan left, Clara was in the pantry polishing silver under Mulligan's watchful eye. It was the first real work she'd done in weeks.

It was so good to be moving, Morgan thought, to stretch her legs and smell the sweet fresh air. Just the day for a walk across the Brooklyn Bridge. Clara's frantic love for that horrible man seemed to eat up all the air in the house. Morgan took her time on the crowded walkway, looking out over the busy sparkling harbor, thinking how it had changed since her first view of it from the deck of the *Water Bird*. The forest of tall masts was thinning out every year, as steamboats took over the shipping business.

A few years ago, probably just before the turn of the century, one of the magazines had printed a wonderful drawing in which the artist had imagined New York one hundred years hence, in 1999. No more masts, just huge oceangoing vessels, their smokestacks belching and, in the sky, great long airships with two decks of sails. Tall fanciful buildings, looking like so many chess pieces lined the island, and at least a dozen great bridges spanned the rivers. Their own Brooklyn Bridge, much larger than the others, stood in the forefront of the picture. She wondered if it would ever come to pass, a New York filled with airships and skyscrapers.

She didn't intend it, but somehow, magically, after walking and walking, she found herself in front of the building on 23rd Street where Alex had his practice and wrote his papers. *And made love to his lady friends,* said a nasty little voice in her head. She ignored the thought. She assumed he was still an attending physician at Bellevue, where they had the very latest in every kind of medicine and modern advance. Often people were not even charged for their care. For doctors, the most wonderful thing about it was that Bellevue was the one hospital willing to accept patients who were chronically ill. Alex was always a doctor with a conscience and a heart; she remembered that—among other things. He was always ready to help the poor, the immigrant, the uneducated, the superstitious and frightened. All of them received the same kindnesses. He was truly an unusual man, and she missed him so much that her heart literally ached in her chest.

Here she was, standing across the street from his building, for the second time. So close and, yet, so far. She wanted so much to climb the stairs and ring the bell but dared not do it. And she thought Clara was pathetic! *Just look at yourself,* she scolded silently, *mooning in front of Alex's rooms and afraid to go ring his bell.* She ought to leave. He probably didn't even want to see her; he probably hated her.

Then she reminded herself what his reprobate father had done to an innocent girl, ruining her forever. Filled with fine and righteous anger, she mounted the stairs, and rang his bell. When Alex himself, in shirtsleeves, his hair rumpled and his eyes bleary with sleep, answered the door, Morgan, to her horror, suddenly burst into tears.

He wasted not a minute, but pulled her inside, kicking the door shut, and took her in his arms. He held her close, kissing away her tears and then kissing her throat and her nose and then, at last, at last, covering her mouth with his. She clung to him like a drowning woman, and perhaps she was. Her head was spinning and she could not breathe. She hardly knew where she was except that she was home. She was where she belonged at last. She felt his growing excitement and pressed herself closer to him, moaning a little in her throat, putting her arms around his neck.

Finally, they drew apart, both of them breathing hard, and looked into each other's eyes. "You haven't changed," Alex murmured. "Thank God. You haven't changed."

"Nor have you."

"God, but it is good to see you, to hold you. I'm afraid to let you go, afraid you will disappear in a puff of smoke. But I must know . . . why have you come? Why today, this morning, when I dreamed of you only last night? Dreamed of loving you . . ." His eyes grew smoky and Morgan's breath caught in her throat. "Which I will do, yes . . ." He drew a line down her cheek and chin and throat with his finger, and where his finger traced, a chill followed. She wanted him so badly, she could scarcely contain herself.

"But let's get out of the hallway, where we might create a spectacle," he said, and taking her hand, pulled her into his rooms. He stood, still holding her hand, gazing at her. He had been so ardent, a moment ago. Why was he waiting? "Why have you come, Morgan?"

"It's a long story." She lifted her lips to his, supplicating.

"Tell me the story. I want no more surprises, Morgan Wellburn. We will sit upon my couch, like a lady and a gentleman, and you will tell me all. And then . . ." His voice became husky. "And then, I will take you to bed and worship your beauty with everything I have." She gave him a look that made him laugh with delight.

And so they sat down, a proper distance apart, the heat between them almost palpable, and she told him about Max and Clara Optakeroff. "I am sorry, Alex, to have to tell you this sordid story."

"Agh! If you knew how I despise that man. My mother chooses to ignore his peccadillos. She would much rather pretend that none of it is happening. He is dear Max and he is always busy 'at the office.' But everyone knows that his 'office' is whatever bed he can lure a young woman into. He generally has five or six at a time."

"Together?"

"No, no. But wait. For all I know, he might well entertain them all at once. He is capable of anything. So, you say he set up a room at the Broadway Central and has been seeing Clara quite often . . . it makes one wonder what special talents she possesses. Sorry, Morgan. I don't want to sound like—but he disgusts me. I am ashamed to admit he is my father. Quite honestly, I hate him."

"Then why do you stay in his house?" Morgan asked.

"I don't. I live here. In my rooms. As a matter of fact, I have just found out that this house is for sale, and I am thinking of buying it."

"To live in?"

"Perhaps." He gave her a thoughtful look. "But not unless— Never mind that now. We have plenty of time to plan for the future. I've been made chief of service in the department of medicine at Bellevue, you know."

Her heart lifted with pride. "Have you? That is truly wonderful. And you deserve it. They are to be congratulated for their superior taste. Oh, Alex, I am so happy for you! That's exactly what you wanted!"

He smiled broadly. "Indeed it is. I could not be more pleased. No, wait. I *could* be more pleased. My happiness lacked only you. And now I have you back at last. Together, we will decide what to do with little Clara, to take her out of harm's way. Is there anything else, my sweet Morgan?"

"Only . . . only that I have missed you so, and if you do not take me to your bed immediately, I am going to leave again."

"Don't worry," he said, getting up and holding out his hand to her. "I don't intend to waste a single moment!"

Later, lying in each other's arms, exhausted and happy, he said, "Marry me, Morgan. The years are passing too quickly, and we have no time to waste. We have both been alone too long."

"But your parents would never allow it."

"My parents! To hell with my parents! What my parents think of you doesn't matter."

"Truly?"

"Truly." He kissed the top of her head. "I must have you or die!"

Happier than she had ever dreamed she could be, she kissed his chin and said, "Now, considering that the women in my family have been healers since the very beginning of time, how could I let you die?"

20

June 1910

Bird was standing very still, staring at Morgan, weeping silently, fat tears sliding down her cheeks. The white bird sat on her head, unmoving. Morgan noticed that Bird wore the shell amulet that had been handed down for so many generations, and she had a leather medicine bag slung over her shoulder. Bird beckoned to Morgan, but Morgan was frozen, unable to move. She, too, began to weep.

Morgan awakened with a start, to find her cheeks wet with tears. Alex was bending over her solicitously, cradling a small blanket-wrapped bundle in his arms. "What is it, darling? Are you in pain?"

"No. It's nothing," Morgan said. "A dream. I've already forgotten it," she lied. The dream clung to her, even as she held out her arms to take her miracle—her very own infant daughter, the three-month-old Birdie Marlene Becker. The baby began immediately to root around, her little pink mouth wide open. Morgan and Alex both laughed.

"All right, little one, don't you worry. Mama will feed you," Morgan cooed. She could not believe how desperately and completely she loved this child. Birdie was small, pink and white, with big round smoke-colored eyes. Alex said they might stay that color or simply change to brown. She had a tiny nose and a tiny chin and silky red-gold hair. Morgan's first thought upon seeing her newborn child was, *She looks just like Becky.* But she made herself put that thought away. Looking like Becky didn't mean—and then she made herself put that thought away, too.

Morgan had given the baby her first name and Alex her other two. Birdie's middle name, Marlene, was after Alex's paternal grandmother. Her given name was in honor of that long-ago Indian witch, her ancestress who, Morgan was convinced, came to her in dreams to give her important messages. Hettie thought Birdie had been named in honor of *her* mother, Bertha. They let her think it, since Alex had said, she wouldn't understand any of the Indian lore anyway.

After a few minutes, Alex bent to kiss her, saying he would be late for rounds if he kept gazing at his two girls. Morgan kissed him back, but the dream was still haunting her. Even as the infant suckled greedily, the little fingers kneading at her breast, she pondered its meaning. The tears, the beckoning gesture . . . it must be a sign that Annis was dying. Bird had come to tell her to make a trip home before it was too late. Morgan was supposed to get as much rest as possible, since she was an elderly primapara, but she knew with a certainty what she had to do. She must take her daughter and travel up to the clearing above East Haddam where she had been born, to say good-bye to her mother. Sudden tears stung Morgan's eyes. It had been so many years, too many years. Annis didn't even know that she had a grandchild!

Alex was totally against the idea. They were sitting at the table in the dining room, eating their supper, and he had listened to her carefully. But Morgan saw the *No* coming when she was barely halfway through. "You're not strong enough," he argued. "And how are you going to get all the way up into those hills with a babe in arms?"

"I'll walk," she told him smartly. "As I always did. Oh, Alex, please don't look like that. I really *am* strong enough. And I must go. My mother is dying. I know it, I feel it in my bones and in my heart."

"I don't understand this at all. I thought you didn't care about your family."

"I—I've tried to forget them, Alex. When I came to Brooklyn, it was to start a whole new life, with nothing clinging to me from the past. But I have found that the past clings to one, whether you will have it or no."

"But, you're suddenly so sure your mother is dying. There's been no word for you from Connecticut. Or has there?"

"You must remember," Addie put in with a little smile, "that your wife is descended from witches. She has ways of knowing things."

Alex laughed, as if Adelaide had just told a joke. He stopped abruptly when he saw that both women were utterly serious.

"Alex. Darling. I swear to you that I know what I'm doing. I never told you the whole story . . ."

"It seems that you have never told me *any* of the story, my dear."

She drew in a deep breath. "After I've seen my mother, I will. I'll tell you everything." *Almost everything,* she added silently. "You know that I . . . well, I ran away from home. I had good reason at the time, but I see now that it was cruel. Perhaps it was even unnecessary. But back then, I felt it was the only thing I could do."

"They weren't cruel to you, were they?"

"No, no, no. It's a long and complicated story. After I've seen my mother . . ."

Alex gave her a wry smile. "Yes, I know, you'll tell me everything. Very well. I suppose if you must go, you must go. But send a telegram, please, to let me know you've arrived safely."

She and the baby traveled on what appeared to be the last of the great Connecticut River steamers, the *Hartford*. It was still making the trip from New York to Hartford, only not as often as previously. The ship was far from filled, and Morgan was able to converse with the captain, who told her sadly, "Oh, I don't think we'll be in business that much longer, not for passengers. The railroads are going everywhere, you know, Mrs. Becker. And the public does like the newest wrinkle." He gave a great sigh. "We've been plagued with accidents, too. The *Connecticut*, done in by a boiler explosion . . . *City of Lawrence*, lost off Block Island . . . *Victory*, lost . . . *Silver Star*,

burned. Far as big ships like this one, there's but two making
the run, *Hartford* and *Middletown*." Another gusty sigh. "You
may well be making one of the last trips up the Connecticut by
steamer, Mrs. Becker."

"Well, then, I'll mark it well, Captain. In fact, I'll write
everything down, to tell my daughter when she's older."

When they landed at East Haddam, Morgan was pleased to
see that Goodspeed Hall still stood, and the Gelston Hotel, too.
The young man at the general store didn't know the Wellburn
place when she inquired. He asked some others, but nobody
could recall precisely where it was ... Nobody had been up
there for ages, she was told. As a matter of fact, they were
pretty sure everyone in that family was dead and gone.

"Well, you're wrong. They're not!" snapped Morgan. Then
she begged the man's pardon. He was young, younger than
she, so how could he know he was speaking to Morgan Wellburn who had left before she was fifteen? Tying Birdie into a
sling made from her shawl, she walked out of the town, trying
to remember the old pathway as she went. Sure enough, when
she got to the field where the foothills began, she headed for
an elm tree, and there was the trail she'd always taken up
through the woods. Climbing wasn't as easy as it had been
when she was a child—in fact, she became quite winded—but
she was delighted to discover she hadn't forgotten a single
turning in the all-but-invisible path. Suddenly, she came upon
the tree where she and fat Lizzie had carved their initials years
ago. *Not long now,* she thought. But it was longer than she
remembered.

She stopped in a small clearing, where someone had been
cutting trees for firewood, and sat down. She nursed the baby,
then leaned against a tree trunk, remembering the old days.
When she was finished, she changed the baby, and took off her
high button shoes and stockings. Making a neat bundle, she
slid them and her hat into a space beneath one of the tree roots.
She'd retrieve them on her way back. She shook her hair loose
from the pins, tying it back with one of her stockings. There.
She felt much better—and freer, for clambering over logs and
rocks. As she continued the climb, the hill became quite steep
and she grew short of breath. It wasn't far, but she was so

warm, she knew if she didn't get rid of her city clothes, she'd faint dead away before she got there. So, she began to discard articles of clothing until she was down to her camisole and pantaloons. They were quite cool, being made of lawn, and really rather pretty, too, with blue satin ribbons threaded through the eyelet lace. She rolled her blouse and skirt into a small bundle and tucked it under one arm. Birdie was strangely content and quiet, looking about her with her large smoky solemn eyes.

When she finally reached the clearing, Morgan saw that it was a dead place. All the bushes were overgrown and grass had encroached upon the dusty yard where once so many feet had worn away all growth. No animal pelts were being tanned, no kettle was on the boil, no clothes hanging on the bushes to dry. There was no sound of humanity here, no smell of humanity. Where was her mother? Morgan climbed the three steps onto the front porch, and nearly fell through a rotted board. She twisted her ankle, which was a bad omen, she thought. Her heart was beginning to pound with nervous anticipation.

"Mama?" she called out, surprised at how her voice quavered. "Mam? You there?"

Tiptoeing, she walked into the cabin. And stood stock still, her breath caught in her throat. Her mother was there all right, but long dead—a corpse on her narrow pallet. Actually, a skeleton, with some leathery skin still clinging to her outstretched legs. Her arms had been crossed neatly over the rib cage. All bones.

Morgan stood over her mother's skeleton, rocking her daughter, and let the tears roll down her cheeks. Who, she wondered, had arranged the body so neatly—and then she knew. She turned her head, feeling that she was being watched. Becky. Of course Becky. Her sister must still be somewhere nearby; perhaps out in the woods, perhaps closer . . .

Morgan walked out onto the porch and called Becky's name, but there was no answer. Annis, long dead. And her Daddy, too, without doubt. The tears would not stop. She had waited too long. Was that what her dream had been trying to tell her?

She paced back and forth in front of the house, weeping for everything that had been lost forever. There was nobody alive who could say, "I remember when you were a baby, Morgan. I remember when you learned how to skin a rabbit. I remember telling you stories." Her whole childhood was gone now, all of it, disappeared. She was truly alone.

She walked around the clearing, hoping to find a sign of her father's grave, but she didn't see anything. She had willfully cut herself off from her family, and now there was no going back to make it right; no apologizing to Annis, no nothing. Just a mad sister, hiding somewhere. Nearby, she was certain. Peeping out through the vine-choked trees, studying her and her baby. She felt a crawling sensation up her backbone that told her so.

Then she heard a scrabbling and crunching of underbrush, and out of the trees came a scrawny filthy hag minus half her teeth, who danced around her, chanting that the house was ha'nted and that only witches could live there. "But the old witch is dead, although she still speaks to Becky. Oh yes, Becky knows. Becky glows," she cried, and cackled with laughter. It was amazing, how much she looked and sounded—and even laughed—like Quare Auntie. "You'd be best on your way, Missy. It's dangerous in these parts. There are many ghosts, many many ghosts." Her voice was suddenly sad and—almost—sane.

"What happened to Mam, Becky? What happened to the old witch?"

"Dead, dead, dead. Becky takes care of her."

"Yes, I can see that. But . . . how did she die? Was she sick? And when did she die? A long long time ago?" No use. Becky answered nothing, just began to step backward, away from Morgan and her questions.

"I'm not going into that ha'nted house, no more. Becky don't go in the ha'nted house . . . too many ghosts, no." She held her arms up in a rough cross, "to ward off the witch spirits. They come, you know, they talk to Becky," she ranted.

Morgan felt so sad that this poor mad creature was all there was left of her family. Suddenly, Birdie, who had been sleeping peacefully in her sling, awoke and began to cry, and Morgan realized she was wrong. Birdie was her family now. Birdie and dear Alex, and Adelaide Apple, too. At the sound of the baby's cry, Becky pulled back in alarm and then, to Morgan's astonishment, she smiled.

"A baby. You've had a baby, Morgan," she said.

Morgan was so surprised, she couldn't think of what to say or do. While she stood there, mute, Becky came closer and peered down at the rosy little face. Birdie gazed up at this apparition and stopped wailing. Morgan hardly dared breathe, but she was alert and ready to move quickly, if Becky should take it into her head that this wasn't a baby after all, but something evil to be smashed. For the first time, Becky looked straight into Morgan's eyes.

"What's the baby's name?" she asked, sounding for all the world like an ordinary person.

"Birdie."

"Birdie. Ma used to say our grandma's name was some kind of bird . . . Mine, too . . ." Becky's voice trailed away into silence. Touched and hopeful, Morgan reached out and put a hand on Becky's shoulder.

Becky's response was instantaneous. She pulled away, shouting and swearing and threatening to kill them both. "Becky has a knife, a sharp knife. Oh yes she has. She's cut folks before. She'll cut you both. See if I don't. I'll carve out your heart and I'll eat it, witch!" she snarled. A knife had, indeed, appeared—from where in the rags Becky wore, Morgan couldn't imagine.

"Keep your distance, keep your distance!" Shouting, waving the knife, Becky retreated from the clearing and disappeared into the woods.

Morgan sat down under a tree. Her legs were trembling. She put Birdie to her breast and, gradually, her heart rate came back down to normal. Poor Becky, poor demented creature. To think how people had believed she was touched by angels . . . Becky was insane, pure and simple. She had *dementia praecox*. Her sister was mad as had her aunt been. That made two in the family, that Morgan knew of . . . but who knew how many others? She shuddered and held her daughter closer to her body. What if this dreadful curse should strike her own innocent Birdie!

"Don't you worry, little one," she said to the tiny face. "I won't let you become mad. Surely, by the time you're grown, science will have found a cure for these dreadful mental problems. I won't let it happen to you, Birdie, I promise," she said fervently, her eyes filling.

They left the clearing a few minutes later. Morgan said a silent farewell to her mother. And to Pa. To her sister, too. She knew that she'd never see Becky again, or ever return to this place.

"We never realize," she said to the baby, starting the trek downhill, back to the river, "that when we leave places and people, it might be forever. We always think there'll be another chance, just yonder. But often, we're just fooling ourselves."

Making her way down through the woods, she retrieved her hat, gloves, and shoes as she went. When she could glimpse the roofs of East Haddam through the trees, she stopped to change the baby and put all her clothes back on. Shaking the dust and leaves out of them, she pulled on her shoes. Her hair, she could do nothing about, so she tucked it up under her hat and hoped nobody would notice.

She found she could get supper at the Gelston House, where she ate with a huge appetite. She was famished, and chicken had never tasted so good to her. She finished the entire basket of bread, too, and had two beakers of ale. The girl who brought her food answered her enquiry about cabs, saying there were several for hire right across the river. Any one of them would take her wherever she needed to go.

"Birdie," Morgan said, "Guess what? We're going to go visit Dr. Grace. She's probably more a mother to me than my own mother was, you know. You're going to love her."

The ferry took only a few minutes to get to the other bank, where Morgan asked directions to the livery stable. The cabman seemed unsurprised that she was willing to spend so much money to get to Dr. Grace Chapman's place in Chester. When they got close to the house, he said, "I hope you find all well." She didn't want to ask him what he meant. Besides, once the cab pulled up into the drive, she could see that all the curtains were drawn. Something was going on. Her heart began to hammer with dread.

A pretty young girl answered the door. She wasn't a servant, Morgan could see that by the way she was dressed. The girl stared at her, and Morgan could just about imagine how dusty and travelworn she must look. "May I help you, ma'am?"

"I'm Morgan Well—Morgan Becker. A friend of Dr. Grace, from Brooklyn in New York City. I—she isn't expecting me, but I was nearby, visiting my family, and—"

"Please come in, Mrs. Becker. She's been hoping to see you. Would you like to give me the baby? Then you can go out back and freshen up a bit, if you like."

"No, thank you, I'm fine. But who are you?" Morgan asked.

The girl curtsied. "I'm Margaret Grisham. Everyone calls me Peggy. We're all taking turns staying in the house with Dr. Grace." Her voice dropped to a whisper. "She's very ill, you know. Dying."

"Dying! But she can't be!"

"The doctor says it's no use ... Dr. Walker, from up the road. Dr. Grace has a wasting disease. But she'll be glad to see you, I'm sure."

Dr. Grace was gaunt, her body barely a bump under the thin sheet. Tears began to pour from Morgan's eyes. She thought she made no sound, but Dr. Grace's eyes opened and she slowly turned her head and slowly smiled.

"Morgan," she said in a voice as thin as tissue. "I was hoping you would come, and here you are. What's that you're holding? Your babe, your daughter? Let me see her." She reached out a wasted hand to touch the baby's head. "Red hair. Must be from your husband's side." A whisper of a laugh.

Morgan had to smile. "Not necessarily. I ... had a sister with red hair."

"Oh, yes, I remember now. Well, little girl, you are a beauty and you are lucky in your choice of parents." Looking up and seeing Morgan's tears, she said softly, "I'm sorry, Morgan. I didn't intend to make you cry. Please don't be sad."

"I can't help it. In a minute, I'm going to go downstairs and make you an infusion to help you hold on to your food. You need to put on some fat. And then I'll make you an eggnog and—"

"It's nothing we can fix, Morgan. I know."

"There's nothing we can't fix," Morgan insisted, crying even harder.

"Sorry to say, Morgan dear, but when the good Lord calls you, you go. And I'm being called in a very loud voice." Again, that paper-thin laughter. "What did you think of Silas's girl?"

"Silas's—oh. Oh dear, somehow it never occurred to me. She's lovely."

"He has three, you know. Three girls. His wife's pregnant again, though she shouldn't be. But he wants to try for a boy. Men."

They smiled at each other.

Dr. Grace closed her eyes, and Morgan thought she might have fallen asleep, but a moment later, she said, "Desk drawer, Morgan. My will. Get it. Running out of steam."

Morgan found the will, and pulled the rocker up next to the bed. Birdie was sleeping soundly so she settled her into a corner of an easy chair by the window. The will couldn't have been simpler. Dr. Grace left her house and everything in it, including the medical practice, to Mrs. Morgan Wellburn Becker, midwife, of Brooklyn, New York.

"Oh, Dr. Grace! Everything! That's too much!" She hadn't thought there could be any more tears in her this day, but here they came again, streams of them.

". . . and I hope you'll take it. You're such a good doctor. This town could use you."

"I wish I could, Dr. Grace. But I can't leave Alex, and he's attending at Bellevue, head of the department of medicine . . ."

"No, of course. Well, sell everything." Dr. Grace paused, catching her breath. "Go to medical college. Be a proper doctor."

"Oh, what a dream!" Morgan breathed. "But how can I leave Alex and Birdie to go to school?"

"Just do it, Morgan. Just do it." Suddenly, Dr. Grace's voice was stronger and her eyes blazed at Morgan. "It's only two years. God knows you've done your apprenticeship. You've done dozens of 'em. They'll take you. Promise me. Come now, Morgan, make a promise to a dying woman."

"That's unfair and you know it." Morgan saw the smile quirking at Dr. Grace's mouth.

"Damn right I know it. Not dead yet. So . . . promise?"

"Promise. I'll become a doctor. Yes, I promise."

"Good," said the doctor. She closed her eyes and instantly fell asleep.

Morgan stayed the night, sitting in Dr. Grace's room, holding her friend's hand. It was so thin and so light, like a withered leaf. At last she understood what Bird had been trying to tell her, in the dream.

During the night, Morgan fed and changed Birdie, tiptoeing around the room, which was lit only by one candle in the corner. Then she curled up in the easy chair, the baby a lovely warm weight against her. When the morning's first light came slanting through the shutters, she opened her eyes, thinking about Bird. But, try as she might, she could recapture no part of any dream. It occurred to her that Bird always came to tell her something, and she hurried to the bed. Bending low over Dr. Grace, she looked for movement.

"Sleep well?" Soft and thin as the doctor's voice was, it startled Morgan, and she pulled back with a little cry.

"Yes, I did. And you?"

"Everything now . . . a waking dream . . ."

The tears came and Morgan let them.

"Morgan . . ."

Her voice was clogged with tears, she forced it out. "Yes?"

"I love you. Like . . . my child."

Morgan began to sob. Why was she behaving this way? She had so much she wanted to say to Dr. Grace, so many important things, and all she could do was weep! "Me . . ." she finally managed to choke out, "too. I love you . . . oh! Don't go, Dr. Grace. Don't go!"

The doctor was having a hard time breathing. "Must," she whispered. "No . . . regrets . . . good life . . . especially . . ." There was such a long pause, Morgan was sure Dr. Grace had stopped breathing. Then she said, "You. *You.*"

Morgan's weeping was uncontrollable. "Dr. Grace, wait. Wait. I want you to know. I'm giving Birdie your name. Birdie Grace Becker."

There was no answer from the bed, just the faintest of smiles. Then the beloved face went slack and Morgan knew that the spirit had left Grace Chapman. *How splendid,* Morgan thought, *that the last thing Dr. Grace did in her life was smile.* She began to weep in great gulping sobs.

Some time later, another young woman came to the door. She was surprised to find a strange woman sitting on the edge of Dr. Grace's bed, crying.

"Oh, dear. Is Dr. Grace—?" Her eyes filled and overflowed.

Morgan turned a wet face to the girl and nodded. "A few minutes ago," she said. "She went peacefully and smiling. I'm Morgan Wellburn, an old friend."

"Morgan. Oh, yes, she talked about you a lot. You're a doctor, too."

"Soon," Morgan said, not entirely to the young woman. "Very soon."

21

1913–1914

August 25th, 1913

  Dear Miss Apple.

  Please, dear Miss Apple, I am prisoner here with Mrs. Smith. I am not like working on farm. Is very not nice. Very hot. Pigs and cows and mud. Dear Miss Apple, I beg you to bring me home. I behave nicely I promise to you. I forget Max Becker I promise to you. I work hard for you. Please dear Miss Apple.

  With love from Clara Optakeroff

Shaking her head a little, Addie passed the letter to Morgan. "Clara," she explained. "She's not happy at all with the Smiths and begs me to bring her back. I must say, her handwriting has improved quite a bit, although her grammar still leaves much to be desired."

"We already knew she wasn't happy, from Mrs. Smith's letters."

Alex spoke up. "Mrs. Smith didn't sound any too happy, either."

"Are you all thinking what I'm thinking?" Morgan said.

"The perfect nursemaid!" Addie cried. "It will solve all our problems, won't it?"

"I'm not so sure that Clara is the perfect nursemaid," Alex said. "Still a bit boy crazy, isn't she?" He did not mention Clara's history with his father. It was not a topic any of them ever brought up.

"Oh, I think she's learned her lesson," Addie said. "And she promises to behave. I believe her," she finished firmly.

Morgan and Alex exchanged glances. It was clear to both of them that Addie was dying to bring Clara "back home." Morgan, on the other hand, was not so sure. No matter what Clara promised, she knew from her own experience that it was not so easy to forget a man you had fallen in love with—not even after two years. Had Clara really changed? She doubted it. Morgan was thoroughly sick of thinking about Clara, about Max . . . about the whole disgusting situation.

They had sent Clara away, rather than fire her—which is what Alex wanted to do—mostly for the sake of Adelaide, who, in spite of everything, still felt responsible for the girl. Addie suggested they might find her a position at some nice farm in the country, out of the way of "temptation"—meaning Max, of course. Maybe she would forget him. Maybe she'd meet a nice young man to marry. So, Alex mentioned Abner and Sadie Smith, distant relatives of *maman*, who owned a prosperous dairy farm near Albany. They were solid citizens with twin sons of thirteen. The farmhouse itself, Alex said, was sprawling and comfortable. When Sadie Smith was contacted, she vowed she would love to have a fulltime housemaid, and promised to teach Clara all the household skills. It had all sounded so safe and sane and simple.

Alas, here was Clara, begging to come back. The trouble was, they happened to need her just now.

"I'm tempted," Morgan said, picking up Clara's letter again. "We do need a nursemaid while I'm in Geneva." Even as she said it, she still had to pinch herself to believe it. She had been accepted to Geneva Medical College and would start on October 6th, thanks to Dr. Grace. One year of study and she would be Morgan Wellburn Becker, M.D. *M.D.!*

After they had buried Dr. Grace—with just about the entire town of Chester at the graveyard—Morgan, Alex, and Adelaide went back to the house for the reading of the will. The house and the practice and all furnishings had been left to Morgan, just as Dr. Grace had said. The doctor's brother, John, had been killed in the Civil War, and there was no other close family. Morgan chose a few favorite pieces for the house on Clinton Street: a small bronze bust, a lady chair upholstered in wine velvet, and a painting of Philadelphia in a gilded frame. Then, with great regret and sadness, she put the house up for sale. She was actually pleased when Silas Grisham, now a substantial businessman and landowner in Chester, purchased it. He even paid her asking price without haggling, which—the lawyer told her—was a minor miracle.

"You must know a family secret," the lawyer joked. "I've known Si Grisham for years and I've never before seen him accept an asking price for anything." Morgan had said only, "We're old friends, Mr. Pritchett. That must be it."

She thought about Silas, corpulent and red-faced. If he wasn't careful of his diet, she feared he'd be dead of a stroke before he was fifty. He was unable to meet her eyes, even after all these years. But his money was paying her fees at Geneva. That was some sort of poetic justice, wasn't it?

Adelaide was still sorting through their post. "Look at this," she said. "A letter from Sadie Smith, to you. Hers and Clara's must have been posted the same time." She handed it to Morgan.

Morgan broke the seal and unfolded the single sheet of paper. "Oh, dear," she said, beginning to laugh. "Our decision has been made for us, it seems." She held out the letter for the others to read.

Sunday, August 24th, 1913.

My dear Mrs. Becker,

I regret having to say this, but I'm afraid Clara is no longer useful to us. She really should be married, which she refuses to do although I am at a loss to understand why. Some of our finest young bachelors have paid court to her. And, you know, my boys are older now and she has become a distraction and a temptation. I'm afraid she does not understand how impetuous young men can be. I will give her her wages, minus the fare, and send her to you on the boat from Albany on the first of September.

Yours truly, Sadie Smith.

Alex hadn't told his *maman* a thing, so how had she found out? She had received a letter, too, he guessed. In any case, the Sunday after their receipt of Sadie Smith's letter, his mother was at the house on Clinton Street, sitting in the front parlor, fanning herself furiously and declaring she was about to faint from the strain on her nerves.

Ever the dutiful son, Alex sent for a glass of cold lemonade and took his mother's pulse. Personally, he thought she looked in the pink of health. Certainly she had taken great care in the arrangement of her hair and the choosing of her dress, which was white, intricately tucked and gathered, and very narrow. He noticed how she had to mince along in the tight skirt, and wondered once again at women's willingness to squeeze their bodies into whatever was deemed the latest fashion, no matter how uncomfortable.

But, as always, he had very little time to ponder anything. His *maman* had plenty to say and she wasted no time in starting.

"I must object most strenuously to your choice of that Oriental hussy as a nursemaid for my own granddaughter who, I will remind you, is named after my own mother!" She dabbed at an imaginary tear.

"Not my choice alone, *Maman*. We've all agreed that, at the moment, this is the best possible arrangement . . ."

"Well, you're all wrong, Alexander. Remember that the

harlot cares for nobody but her own selfish desires. Sadie had the most shocking stories . . . but never mind that. I must insist, Alex, that you listen to me. Do not have that Jezebel in your house or you will regret it!"

There was another half hour of the same sort of thing. Alex only half listened. He was bored and he was irritated. Morgan would do better at dealing with this. Where was his wife when he needed her? But he knew full well where she was. With her patients, letting them all know that she would be back in a year and, in the meantime, they would be attended by Elizabeth McGuire, a very fine midwife in the neighborhood.

So he let his mother go on and on, without really hearing her. Then she paused and sat back, a look on her face that said, "There. I have told you all you need to know."

Alex pulled out his pocket watch. "I would love to chat, *Maman*, but I am due at the hospital in fifteen minutes. Why don't you come with me in the cab?" And without waiting for an answer, he rose and held his hand out to her.

She gave him a look that could curdle milk, but stood, saying, "You have not heard the last of this, Alexander."

He thought, but did not say, *Of that I am absolutely certain, Maman.*

September 15th, 1913

> *My dear Alex,*
>
> *Since you will not speak with me on the telephone, and my nerves will not allow travel to Brooklyn, I find myself forced to take pen in hand. I should like you to reconsider your former objections and send Birdie to me, to live, whilst her mother is far away attending classes. Attending classes, as if she were young and unmarried, not your wife and Birdie's mother and a bit long in the tooth at that, if you will forgive me for saying so. The child would do well to be with her grandparents, which is where she belongs under the circumstances, and you may be assured that I will teach her proper behavior and good manners.*
>
> *I will not take no for an answer, Alex, not this time.*
>
> *I remain, your loving and concerned,*
> *Mama.*

Nursemaid, they called her. *Not for long,* Clara thought, not if she had her way. And she would have her way. The old witch, Hettie, hated her; she knew that. The old witch wanted her gone, did not want her taking care of the adored Birdie. Ha! Clara Optakeroff was not a fool. Hettie Becker cared nothing for Birdie; she was not even nice to the child. She pushed and pulled at Birdie the way a child would play with a doll. And if Birdie cried or became angry, the old witch would glare at her most awfully. If Alex could see the way his mama treated his little daughter, he would send her home.

But she was good for something, Baba Hettie, because she brought Max with her. Max had not been told that Clara was back in the house on Clinton Street. The first time he came for a visit, and he saw her, his eyes popped right out. His hands trembled, she saw it. But she, she was so ladylike and aloof.

"Good afternoon, Mr. Becker. Here is your granddaughter, come to greet you. Say hello to Grandfather, Birdie," Clara had said in her best proper voice. She knew how to speak properly. Her English soon would be perfect.

Max wasn't able to keep his eyes from her. She bent over near him, pretending she saw something on the carpet, and she heard him pull in breath as he peeked down the front of her dress. When she straightened, she looked squarely at him, pulling her shoulders back just the tiniest bit to show off the swelling of her breasts. Something else was swelling, too, she could see it. She wanted to laugh out loud, but she was too smart for that. Pretending she didn't notice, she gave him a look from under her lashes, a look that used to drive him crazy, and swept from the room. Then she had to go right back, because she had forgotten Birdie. But she had got what she wanted. Max looked dazed. He was licking his lips and smoothing his mustache with one finger, the way he always did when he wanted her. He would be easy, she could see that. Soon he would come for her and they would run off together.

She had been here for three months now, and he had not sent for her. He was very polite, maybe keeping hold of her hand longer than necessary, maybe holding her gaze a moment too long. But nothing else. She wanted to scream. She did not have forever to wait! Between her legs was a volcano. She was quickly becoming an old maid, and Adelaide was beginning to say that she should look for a husband. She did not want a husband. She wanted her Max, with his endless love-making and his endless money.

Clara had become clever. She would make Max jealous. She had an admirer, a young man with thick black hair and a quick tongue. She had met him, shopping on 14th Street in New York on her day off. His name was Harold Green and he was a song plugger. But he was working on a musical show of his own, a show to go on the stage. He was crazy about Clara, he told her that all the time. She invited him to call on her, and that made Miss Apple so very happy. Clara always asked Harold to come see her when she knew Max would be visiting his little granddaughter with the old witch. Once, she introduced them, and, oh, how she wanted to laugh! It was so comical, the look on Max's face. It was a look to kill. So he still cared for her, still loved her! She would have him for her own, yes, she would; now she knew it for sure!

December 28th, 1913,

   My dearest Morgan,

   We all miss you terribly. It does not seem fair that you could not leave your classes to come home for Christmas. I know that it is important for you to earn your degree but, let us be honest, you already know much of what they teach you at Geneva Medical College—and perhaps a great deal that you could, if you would, teach them. Sixteen weeks! It seems so long. At least, you will be home with us from February until April. And then, in July, you will be a real doctor, needing no apologies for anything. We shall have you at home with us once more, and I will have you in my arms each night. Until then, my darling, think always of your lovelorn and loving

   Alex.

It was too quiet. Adelaide sensed that the moment she unlocked the front door. The house felt . . . empty. But it couldn't be, not on a Saturday afternoon. Mrs. Mulligan, she knew, was home with her sick husband today.

"Clara!" she called. "Birdie! Where are you?" Not a sound in answer. Strange. She was home early from the dispensary. They had probably gone for a walk; the weather was fine. She headed upstairs, to leave her satchel and change her shoes, and then went up the second flight to look for Clara. Clara's door was open and a body lay sprawled across the bed. Addie gave a little shriek, then a gasp. It was Max Becker, stark naked, his eyes wide open and staring, pupils fixed and dilated. It didn't take a nurse, Addie thought, to see that he was dead.

For a minute or two, she was eerily calm and unmoved. And then suddenly, she realized that both Birdie and Clara were gone. What should she do? Call the police? Call Alex at the hospital? Call Hettie Becker? No, no, and no. She had to find Birdie, Birdie and Clara. She had to think, to figure out where they might have gone.

While she was dithering, the doorbell rang. Heart racing, she galloped down the two flights of stairs, flinging the front door open. It was Mrs. Scott, the cook from Number Five Clinton and, thank God, she was holding Birdie.

Birdie began talking at once. "Addie, why were you gone? I wanted you. Clara ran away." She held her arms out and, gratefully, Addie took her.

"That girl of yours, that Clara, she left the child with me. She said for five minutes, but that was an hour ago. Is anything wrong?"

"No, no," Addie lied. "I didn't know where Birdie was. But now I do, so all is well. Thank you, Mrs. Scott. Where did Clara go, did she say?"

Mrs. Scott sniffed and said, "Not she! Always has put on airs, that one. She might have gone to meet her musical friend, the one that calls on her. Our Ginny, what's got eyes all over her head, says she saw Clara with a piece of luggage, running out the back. I wouldn't know. I've got my work to do."

"Well, thank you again for watching over Birdie. I have her now and you can get back to your work, Mrs. Scott." Addie shut the door without further ado. Mrs. Scott had been trying to peer around and behind Addie, avid to know what was happening.

Heading down to the kitchen, Addie promised milk and

cookies to Birdie, thinking she'd better call Alex at the hospital. She never did get to it, because Alex also came home earlier than usual. Addie hurried out of the living room, where Birdie had curled up on the rug in front of the fireplace and was fast asleep. "Thank God, Alex," she whispered. "Birdie's sleeping."

"Where in hell is Clara?" Alex asked.

"Shhhh. Just come with me. There's been . . . an accident."

He must have heard something in her voice, because he said nothing more, just followed her up the two flights of steps. When he saw his father lying like a rag doll on the bed, he blanched and then reddened. "There's no fool like an old fool, Addie!" he growled, his voice tight and thick. He knelt to examine the body.

"But . . . what do you suppose happened?"

"The same as you're supposing, Adelaide. That my father came here to dally with young Clara, that they came upstairs to her room, and that he had a heart attack from overexertion. Oh, my God! My father died in Clara's arms!" Alex looked up at Addie. "But Birdie! My little girl was right here, in the house!"

"No, she wasn't, for a blessing. Clara brought her next door. Birdie didn't even know he was here. She saw nothing."

Alex buried his face in his hands for a brief moment, then stood up, pulling himself together. "I warned him. I told him he had to watch his diet and his drinking. His face was quite red, you remember, Addie? He hadn't looked well for a year. I told him to be careful. But would he listen? No, he had to play sex games with women young enough to be his daughters! Oh, Christ! Never mind. We must get him dressed and downstairs . . . in the back parlor, I think . . . on a sofa, where he went—uh—to take a nap. And you found him, Addie. You went to wake him and you found him. And I," he finished, his voice sephulchral, "will inform *Maman*."

He moved quickly. Adelaide watched in admiration. Men seemed able to separate their feelings into different boxes, and to just open and shut those boxes at will. It was quite marvelous.

Together, they did it all. When they were finished, Max

looked pretty much like a man who'd taken a nap on the sofa and died quietly in his sleep.

"No word from her?" Alex said and Adelaide knew that "her" was Clara. "No idea where she might be?"

"None. Although Ginny next door seems to think she went off to find her beau, the piano player." She paused and then added, "I don't think she'll be back."

"Probably not. Although God knows *she* didn't kill him, no matter how guilty she feels. He was always bent on his own destruction." Alex sighed and headed downstairs to telephone his mother.

JANUARY 7, 1914. MRS. ALEXANDER BECKER, 22 WILSON STREET, GENEVA, NY. MAX DIED LAST NIGHT STOP HEART ATTACK STOP FUNERAL TODAY STOP YOU NEED NOT BE THERE STOP DO NOT WORRY JUST KEEP STUDYING STOP ALL WELL HERE STOP YOUR OWN ALEX

April 6th, 1914

   Dear Morgan,

   You've been back at school only a week, but it feels like a year. We became quite spoiled, having you here for nearly three months—even though you spent most of your time in the medical library. Birdie asks for you all the time, of course, but she accepts our telling her that Mama is at doctor school. She listens avidly to all your letters and loves it whenever you mention her or send your love. And you will be so pleased how she has taken to Brenda McMurphy, who is a jolly girl with the patience of a saint. They all seem to be good-natured, those Mulligans. Brenda is the daughter of Mulligan's sister, Joan, so she comes by her even temper quite naturally. As for Birdie, she is ever a delight, mischievous and lively. And you should hear her imitate Mulligan's Irish brogue! I should not laugh, but cannot help myself.

   I do not know how you find the time to write a letter every day but we are all grateful for them. Birdie is "writing" you one right now.

   Hettie, of course, still grumbles always that you should be home with your husband and child instead of "galli-

vanting about in the wilds of New York playing at being a doctor." Alex and I are ever your champions and we think it wonderful that you are doing as Dr. Grace wanted. What you wanted and, in fact, what we who love you all want for you.

Take care of yourself. And remember that I am, as always,

Your devoted friend, Adelaide

Morgan put down her copy of *Principles and Practice of Surgery* and yawned. The class was examining the various forms of hernia and syphillis ... ugh! In any case, the May evening was soft and the hour late, so the words were beginning to blur into each other. Would she ever want to be a surgeon? She didn't think so. Once she finished this spring course, she would, with any luck at all, be a medical doctor. That was enough. Morgan W. Becker, M.D. It had such a satisfying look to it. When she grew bored in lectures, which was more often than she would ever admit to any of her professors, she often found herself writing it, over and over. While Professor Van Anden went on and on about *materia medica*, she'd covered an entire page. She could hardly bear to listen to him, he was such a fuddy-duddy. She knew more ways to alleviate pain and cure disease than he did!

Materia medica was supposed to teach the class the very latest drugs and potions for the alleviation of pain and disease. Nowhere was there any mention of the remedies she'd been using for years. Herbal medicine was looked down upon as "folk medicine," good enough for farm wives and such, but not to be considered by a medical doctor. She had tried to offer her own experiences and was politely asked to desist. The professor smiled pleasantly enough, but he suggested that Mrs. Becker was, of course, at Geneva Medical College in order to learn better, was she not? He'd been so insulting! But she hid her anger. He taught only the one course, which ran both semesters. She was very nearly finished. And, she had to admit, for the most part there was much to learn and much that was interesting.

Of all the courses offered—chemistry, surgery, anatomy,

physiology and pathology, medicine and *materia medica*, and obstetrics—she preferred chemistry. At least she was learning something new. She especially enjoyed the lectures on analyzing poisons, wines, and medicines. Professor McDermott had had a great deal of experience in criminal investigations—imagine! A doctor who spent most of his time with the police—looking at grisly murders and mysterious corpses. It was almost like listening to Sherlock Holmes himself—so fascinating.

She had thought she might write her dissertation on forensic medicine. But when Alex got her letter announcing her intentions, he wrote to her immediately, saying, "It is a most fascinating topic, my darling, but remember, you must write and present your own dissertation. Then, and I cannot stress this too strongly, *you must defend it to the Board of Curators*. Why not choose a topic with which you are thoroughly familiar? Might I suggest you discuss different techniques of childbirth? You know more on that subject, I dare say, than most of the professors."

She had taken his advice, with gratitude. In fact, they had spent many hours together when she was home in the spring, putting her paper into shape. She was quite proud of it. She could hardly wait to present it and answer all their arguments. She and Alex had both laughed, thinking of how many of these elderly conservative doctors would react to her description of women squatting to give birth! But she had science—the laws of gravity, in fact—to back her up. They would have to give her her degree. Besides, it couldn't be very long before every hospital in New York was using the technique! Or so she believed. Alex had raised an eyebrow and said, "Doctors are not revolutionaries, my darling. But you should try to teach it. Of course you must!" And so she would. She had never been one to give up just because something was difficult.

First of July, 1914.
  My darling Alex,
  Hurrah! I have done it! I have passed all my examinations and have successfully defended my dissertation, which took several hours. I will receive my Medical Doctor degree at the Annual Commencement at the Literary College on

July tenth. You are all most cordially invited. I can hardly believe this is really happening! Now I can see any patient I like, now I can be on a hospital staff, and now I will be listed as "physician" instead of "nurse." Oh how I wish Dr. Grace were still alive. Perhaps she is looking down from Heaven and smiling upon me. Somehow I feel that she is.

Now that all classes are over, I shall take the train down day after tomorrow to New York and then we can all come back up for the commencement exercises.

Oh, my dearest Alex, I cannot wait to put my arms around you, to kiss your sweet mouth and hold your sweet body. It has been too long. I do love you so very much. You are everything to me. But I will see you very soon. Kiss Birdie and Addie for me.

With all my love, forever, your own
Morgan Wellburn Becker, M.D.

22

October 1918

Never in his life, Alex thought, had he been so tired, so completely worn out. He straightened up from the patient in the bed and tried to stretch his aching back. His vision had begun to blur some time ago. His eyes felt dry and swollen; they probably were, in fact. He had not slept for over twenty-four hours. Usually, he started at seven, made rounds and tended to patients until six in the evening, then took a catnap for an hour or two, and then began again. Last night, he had been one of the few medical people on duty, so he kept checking through the wards, and the nap had never happened. How he kept going, he did not know. If he did not get rest soon, though, he was afraid he would make some dreadful mistake, overlook something, or neglect someone who might be saved. Would *anyone* be left alive at the end of this nightmare? God alone knew.

He bent over the next bed: a young woman, pregnant, feverishly shaking her head from side to side, moaning, her lips cracked and bleeding. Morgan had looked like that the night he had been certain he would lose her. He would never forget it. She had been ill for two days, her fever climbing all the time, in spite of the alcohol rubs. She seemed to shrink before his eyes. He had come home for a few hours' rest, and found her in their bed, shaking with fever. So he had stayed at home, to care for her, even though he knew he was desperately needed at the hospital. People were dying as you looked at them. But how could he leave his wife, his beloved? He sat on the edge of the bed, his eyes filling with tears of terror, holding her hand, her hot dry hand that burned him, praying silently to a God he hardly believed in. What kind of God would allow hundreds upon thousands of innocent people to die of influenza like this? And every medical expert completely helpless in the face of the epidemic.

As he watched, Morgan's fever had climbed to 104 degrees, and she no longer responded to his voice. He felt the chill wind of death blowing. He fell to his knees beside the bed and prayed to God to spare her. How could he live without her? She was everything to him. He had waited so long for her. They were a perfect match, still ardently in love, still eager to talk to each other about everything. And they had a wonderful child, intelligent, lively, and curious, just like her mother. A beauty, too, with her copper hair and sea-green eyes. At the thought of Birdie left without her mother, new tears flowed from his eyes. It was not fair for a child to grow up without the love of her mother. It was not right! He pressed Morgan's limp hand to his lips, willing her to get better.

The next thing he knew, it was morning. He had fallen asleep, on his knees, his head on the bed. When he awoke, he was still in that position, still holding her hand. But her hand was no longer burning hot. His heart stopped beating for an instant. Had she—? No, thank God. She was breathing evenly;

she was sleeping. Morgan had recovered! That was two weeks ago. And already she was back with her practice, as busy as before the flu struck. No, busier, because her patients were all so nervous about this dreadful epidemic, they crowded into her waiting room even if they weren't sick. Alex thought they came just to hear Morgan tell them that she was better, that she had survived. He had noticed a long time ago that Morgan often did little more than talk to her patients. When he mentioned it, she had gently corrected him. "No, darling, often I do little more than *listen*. Sometimes, that is all that's needed." Indeed, he was beginning to see the truth of that for himself. So many deaths and yet, his family had all been spared, so far. *So far.*

With a start, he realized that he was still looking down at his patient, his mind wandering. He had forgotten what he was going to do for this poor young woman. What could he do? There had never been an epidemic like this one, never. They were calling it the Spanish Influenza but it was killing people all over the world. The real horror was that nothing stopped it. *Nothing.*

If only he could lie down, close his eyes for just a few minutes, maybe his head would clear and he would be able to think without confusion. But rest, he could not. There were too many dying people and too few doctors. The fear was always there, that if you let down for even a moment, allowed your vigilance to relax even a little bit, you yourself would be stricken. If all the doctors died, who would take care of the others?

Three doctors at Bellevue, all of them his friends, had already been taken. Dozens of nurses. Today, following him quietly, waiting for his orders, was one of the many volunteers who had come to the hospital to do whatever they could. A week ago, Mrs. Mabel Crandall, the famous—or infamous— madam, had showed up with six of her girls, offering to help. Once they might have been scorned, but not now. As it happened, Alex had met Mrs. Crandall several times when he was still living with his parents. A million years ago, it seemed. Yet, he had never forgotten. There would come the discreet knock on the door in the wee hours and a boy would give him a folded note asking him to please come to collect Mr. Becker. Max loved to frolic with two or three of Mrs. Crandall's girls at once, drinking the best champagne. Often, he would be overcome—by the wine or the women, Alex never knew— and pass out. A silent nod to the messenger, who would have brought a cab, and Alex would ride to the bawdy house and collect his errant father.

So his nurse today was a courtesan named Molly. Her flaming red hair was tucked under a scarf, and her curvaceous body had been stuffed into an ugly dress covered by a voluminous apron. "Doctor," she said, as he began to move on to the next bed. "She's gone."

He turned. "So quickly," he murmured. "So quietly. Poor woman. Poor unborn babe. I wonder if her husband can be found." He might be in another bed in this hospital. He might very well be dead, too. There was no keeping track of them.

From the other end of the ward came a hoarse cry: "Nurse! Nurse!"

"You go, Molly. See if there's anything you can do to help the poor devil." She hurried off and Alex continued his rounds. The stops were many, the space between cots and beds, nonexistent. The wards were jammed. Dozens of rabbis and priests and chaplains milled about, trying to reach the dying to comfort them before it was too late.

Down the line of beds, Mabel Crandall herself, her hair neatly tied in a knot atop her head, her dress a subdued gray, her apron spotlessly clean, her cotton face mask firmly in place, was pulling the sheet up over the head of a patient who had expired.

"Another one gone, Doctor," she said, looking up to see him. "What a shame. A young girl, barely sixteen, I'd guess. So fresh and pretty and now . . . her life cut off, just like that!"

Alex liked Mabel Crandall. She never got hysterical, and she was willing to clean up the worst messes without complaint. He found her, somewhat to his surprise, an intelligent and interesting woman who learned everything the first time you told her.

Alex balled his fists. "Dammit, I thought I might get used to it—the dying. But I can't get used to it. So much useless death and nothing that anyone knows to do. So much for the almighty power of medical science! This should chasten us!"

"Now, Dr. Becker, don't be so hard on yourself. You don't need chastening. You're always very caring. I've noticed that. You have a gentle hand and a gentle way with you. So at least the last words the poor wretches hear are pleasant."

For some reason, that made Alex feel better, and he thanked her, hoping, as he went into the next ward, that he wouldn't come back later tonight to find her dead. It had happened, so many times. What an atrocity, this illness!

He walked down the hall, looking for anything unusual. The muscles in his neck and back were tensed so tightly, they hurt. He really needed to get some respite. If he dropped of exhaustion, he'd be no use as a physician. What Bellevue did not need at this time was one more patient. He moved slowly through the hallway because it too was lined with cots. Patients who died were taken into empty labs so their families could identify them and take them away for burial. Two male volunteers in shirtsleeves were carrying one just ahead of him.

As he moved into the next ward, Alex stood aside to let two women, their arms laden with clean sheets and towels, pass him. All the laundresses had panicked and, as the *World* had put it, "abandoned their tubs." For a hospital not to have clean linens was horrible, and in the midst of an epidemic? Unthinkable!

Everyone had an opinion on how to check the spread of the disease: open the windows; close the windows; warmth; cold; go naked; bundle up. Everyone in New York was supposed to be wearing a face mask. Alex never bothered. He was sure the masks were doing no more good than Billy Sunday's prayers. The preacher was brave, you had to give that to him. He'd been holding tent meetings uptown, in spite of a city ordinance against public meetings, saying he would pray the scourge down. People came to him by the hundreds, and by the hundreds, they dropped dead. Right there in the tent, in the sight of Billy Sunday and the Lord! So prayer, too, seemed useless.

But clean linens, now, that you *knew* you had to have. When sick people were vomiting and sweating and dying in the hospital sheets, those sheets had to be taken away and

washed in the hottest possible water. And bless Miss Lillian
Wald and her people at the Henry Street Settlement House.
When she read about the mass defection of the laundresses,
Miss Lillian came in and staffed the Bellevue laundry with do-
mestic science teachers and students from Columbia Teacher's
College. Miss Lillian's people were everywhere you looked,
working tirelessly. Alex found it astonishing, that so many
were willing to risk death, and for no recompense whatsoever.

That thought led him to say a silent thank-you of gratitude,
that he himself was still alive. So far, he added silently. Hubris
had killed many a hero; he should not allow himself to feel
special.

As he resumed his slow march through the ward, he saw an
elderly doctor he knew, Fritz Hartmann, hobbling from bed to
bed. Many retired doctors—the halt, the lame, the nearly
blind—had come back to help.

Then a volunteer came in the door behind him, announcing
"One thousand eight hundred thirty-two new cases today. Two
thousand six hundred fifty-one yesterday. But in Newark,
they've reopened all the movie theaters! What do you think of
that?"

Alex turned and said, "I think they'll go to the movies and
die there."

"Well," answered the man, "they're showing Chaplin in
Shoulder Arms. So maybe at least they'll die laughing."

Alex did not find the sally amusing. He remembered all the
Army recruits, marching to their ships and dying on the way.
Late last month, the Assistant Secretary of the Navy had
landed in New York harbor, after a trip abroad to check on the
war, and had had to be carried from the transport Leviathan to
his mother's house on East 65th Street. Alex wondered now if
young Mr. Roosevelt had survived. The seamen from the
Brooklyn Navy Yard had not. Thirty of them were admitted to
Bellevue all at once, a week ago, most of them cyanotic, blue
from lung congestion, and every man jack in the last throes.
Was it a week ago? Maybe longer. That was in September, he
thought. And what month were they in now?

He turned to the volunteer and asked, "What is the date?"

"Why, the twenty-third of October." The man looked at him in some surprise.

"Oh dear," Alex said. "I've really lost track."

A nurse bustling toward him stopped and put a hand on his arm. "You look all in, Doctor. Perhaps you should lie down for a minute."

"Yes, yes, perhaps I should. Thank you, thank you."

"Shall I walk with you?"

"No. Thank you." He watched her as she walked on. She was obviously a woman of good education and breeding. Yet here she was in the midst of pestilence. Someone had told him that beautifully dressed society ladies stood every day in front of Lord and Taylor's or Tiffany's on Fifth Avenue, passing out handbills asking for volunteers. Others had offered to act as nurses in the hospitals. And, to his utter amazement, he knew one of them quite well. Hester Becker, yes, his own selfish *maman*, had actually volunteered! He was very proud of her, and when this dreadful epidemic was finally over, he would tell her so.

A voice from the left called out weakly, "Nurse! Please!" Everyone in the ward was already busy, so Alex hurried over, but by the time he got to the patient's bed, the man was dead. He bowed his head for a moment, trying to tune out the groans and cries all about him, to mourn for this poor soul for just a moment. But there was a tug on his arm and another volunteer, looking sad, said, "Dr. Becker? I have a telegram for you." His heart rate speeded up. Home? Someone stricken? After he'd just been congratulating himself!

He took the yellow paper, unable to look at it for a moment. Then, holding his breath, he unfolded it and read the message. His mother had died of the flu while acting as nurse at Mt. Sinai. The sender, a Dr. Aronson, was so sorry. Again, Alex bent his head in a kind of wordless prayer. Jewish law said she should be buried tomorrow, but he knew the dead bodies were piling up everywhere. There wasn't an undertaker of any religious affiliation who wasn't backed up for weeks. Sooner or later, he would have to do something about his mother, who at the end at least had been doing for others.

He really must call Morgan and tell her about *Maman*. He

telephoned home at least once each day, to allay any fears. But he hadn't seen his family in days, and Birdie, who was only eight years old, needed reassurance. She was terribly frightened, and who could blame her? She'd already been through her mother's illness. Her school was closed, and she was not allowed to visit any of her friends. She had bad dreams every night, Morgan had told him, awakening from them with screams and tears. Since Morgan had been ill, the child would not allow her mother out of her sight. "And she asks about you every ten minutes," Morgan had reported. " 'Where is Fa? Why doesn't he come home any more? Is he sick, too?' I try to reassure her, of course, but from the look in her eyes, I think she only half believes me." The one evening he had managed to get home to see his daughter, he had taken Birdie onto his lap to read her her favorite book, but he had fallen fast asleep from exhaustion. When she could not rouse him, the poor little girl had thought her father dead.

Going to a wall phone near the emergency room, he cranked it, but no bright voice came on to ask, "Number puh-leeze." Well, of course not. Hadn't he heard that thousands of telephone operators, a quarter of the force, were out sick? He replaced the earpiece in its cradle and stood there, leaning on the telephone, falling asleep on his feet.

Forcing his eyes open, he wobbled back toward the ward, just in time to see Dr. Hartmann collapse a few feet away. Poor old man, he didn't deserve such an end. Tears smarted at the backs of Alex's eyes. In the name of God, would there never be an end to this? Or would the blight just keep battering them, murdering left and right, on and on and on, until they were all dead?

Finally, he admitted to himself that he had to go home and get some sleep. In all these weeks of endless labor, had he saved one single person? The answer was an appalling no. So why did he insist upon staying here, slowly losing his mind? He stumbled out of the hospital and tried to hail a cab. An empty one went flying by him. Was the driver frightened because he saw the white coat and knew that Alex had been inside the hospital, in the thick of the plague? There were no other cabs to be seen. He had just about decided to go back in to curl up on a cot and sleep, when an ambulance from Bellevue stopped. The driver asked if he might offer Dr. Becker a ride somewhere.

"Uptown or downtown?" Alex asked. He would not take an ambulance out of its way.

"Downtown and then over the Great Bridge to Brooklyn. Ten new cases, very bad, in Brooklyn Heights."

"Yes. Take me. I live there." *And, please,* Alex thought, his heart thudding with fear, *don't be picking up anyone at my house on Clinton Street. Please. Please.*

When he opened his eyes, he was not sitting next to the driver in the ambulance. He was not in the street outside their house. For a moment, he felt sheer panic. He did not know where he was, and he did not know how he got there. Then the feeling passed. He was in his bed upstairs at home. It was daytime; he could tell that, although the shutters were tightly shut. He was propped on many soft pillows and he felt . . . how did he feel? Weak. Empty. Very tired.

He should be at the hospital, tending to all the sick people. He should get out of this bed this minute. But when he tried to throw off the quilt covering him, he discovered he hadn't the strength to do it. He attempted to sit up, which made him dizzy, so he lay back down. How long had he been here? Had he been ill? What day was it?

The door opened and Morgan, her face tight and wary, came in, carrying a loaded tray. When she met his eyes, she smiled so broadly and brilliantly, it warmed his heart completely.

"You're awake! At last! I was so worried!" She set the tray down on a table and came to sit on the side of the bed, leaning to kiss his forehead, then his nose, and finally his lips. "I was so afraid I had lost you," she breathed. She beamed down at him. "But I had a dream last night, and when I woke up this morning, I knew you would be all right."

"What sort of dream?"

"I'll tell you all about it when you're completely recovered. Are you hungry, darling?"

"I think I'm ravenous."

She laughed a little. "Small wonder. You've been here for

three days without a bite to eat. We did offer you water and
you took some."

"I slept for three days?"

"So it would seem. Exhaustion. At first, I was sure you were
sick with influenza, but you didn't have a fever or any other
symptom. You looked awful, though." She got up and went to
where she'd left the tray. "Coffee," she explained. "As well as
some sweet rolls. You see how I knew you would be better? I
brought two cups."

She held the cup for him to sip from and then tore off bits of
sweet roll and fed him. "Just like a baby bird," she remarked,
her voice so tender that it brought tears to his eyes. To cover
his weakness, he said, "The epidemic . . . what news is there?"

"I only know what I read in the papers but it seems to be
slowing down."

"Thank God! Well, it had to. But for a while, I wondered—"

Morgan took his hand and kissed it softly. "I'm so sorry
about Hettie, Alex. Although I must admit, she died in a glo-
rious cause. And I'm so grateful that our little family . . ."

"Hush," Alex said. "Don't let the *ayin hora* hear you congratulating yourself."

"The *ayin hora*?"

"Yiddish for the evil eye."

"Oho! So the scientific Dr. Becker and his scientific family
believed in the evil eye! And to think how your *maman* looked
down on me and my uncivilized Indian ways!" She was smiling in that wry way she had, to show him she was only fooling.

Oh, God, he was such a lucky man. He was alive; his wife
and child and their dear friend Adelaide had all escaped!

"As soon as I'm up and about, Morgan dear, I'm thinking
we should go on a vacation trip—perhaps to Europe," he said.

"A vacation? A trip? You cannot mean it, Alex. There is
always something keeping you from taking a rest."

"Not this time. But . . ." He had a sudden thought. "What if
you can't get away? Your practice has changed since you got
your degree. What about all the consults you're called in on?
What about your duties in the obstetrics department of Brooklyn Caledonia Hospital? As you know, you can't tell a baby to
wait patiently until you've come back from vacation."

"Who said 'Physician, heal thyself'?" She patted his hand. "I will somehow manage to get away if it means you will get some rest. Let me make this promise, my darling. If you will take the time for a trip—and I think you certainly need one—I shall, too."

"What day is this?" Alex asked.

"Twenty-sixth of October, 1918."

"Well, you have my promise that the Beckers will be on vacation by January 1919."

"We'll see, my love," she said, and bent to kiss him. "We shall see."

SECTION FOUR

Morgan Becker, M.D.
Adelaide Apple
Birdie Grace Becker

23

January 1921

Even if you looked out of the train window at the villages and farms and snowy fields, even if you tried to draw a picture of it, it all got boring after a while, Birdie decided. When Mama and Fa first told her they would be taking a trip on the train— all the way to Montreal, Canada!—she'd been so excited, she could hardly wait to get on board. They'd never taken a trip together. Mama had said it was years overdue, and then she twisted her mouth and raised one eyebrow. That's how you knew she was making a joke. Mama didn't often laugh out loud like Fa did.

On the way to Canada from Grand Central Terminal, it had been thrilling, sitting in her own plush seat right next to the window, with her own little table that folded down and could be put away any time she wanted. She liked looking out, watching the snowy landscape go whizzing by. They passed small towns so fast the houses turned into a blur. Once, way out in the country, where not a house was in view, just a distant plume of smoke rising straight in the air, she saw three children, all wrapped up in coats and mufflers against the cold. They stood by the tracks waving at everyone in the train. Birdie waved back.

Wherever they passed, or whenever they stopped at a station, you could see all the decorations for Christmas, trees hung with ornaments, candles, wreaths with huge red bows. Even the cars on the train were hung with tinsel and pictures of St. Nick with his bag full of toys.

Everything seemed new and wonderful on the way up to Montreal. Traveling back home, though, the scenery all looked the same. How many bare trees could you look at? She wanted a friend to talk to. Fa had played cards with her for a while, but then he said he was tired and really needed to have a little snooze. Mama said Fa was exhausted and needed more than a little snooze—"A month in Italy would be more to the point," she said. He only said, "Be grateful Ed Cordier was able to take over for me at the hospital, so we could do this." Mama, occupied with her medical magazine, had told Birdie to read her own book, a Nancy Drew mystery. But Birdie was tired of Nancy Drew, too. What was the use of taking a trip to a hotel that looked like a castle—a chateau, Fa kept telling her, a French chateau—if there were no other girls her age there? She wished they were home in New York. But it would take another whole day.

At least, it was almost time to go to their favorite table in the dining car, for dinner. She loved the dining car. Fa did, too. Whenever they went to a restaurant, Fa always sat next to her with Mama across the table, facing them both. So that's how they did it in the dining car. She loved Fa. He was wonderful and handsome and the best father in the whole world, and she was determined to be just like him. Well, she could never grow a mustache, of course. "At least I *hope* not!" Fa said, pretending that it could happen. But, she wanted to grow up and be the way he was, which was funny and ready to play. Lately, Fa was tired a lot. Sometimes, he would drop off to sleep in the middle of a game of cribbage. But she loved him the same, exactly the same.

Fa took his gold watch out of his vest pocket and said, "Well, look at that. It's Birdie's favorite time of day. Dinner time." Fa was always joking with her.

They all got up and went to the dining car. The head waiter bowed to them, and said, "Good evening, Dr. Becker . . . and Dr. Becker . . . and Miss Becker." Birdie loved that, being announced. He led them to their favorite table on the river side of the train.

The waiter handed each of them one of the heavy menus with the beautiful printing. "Train food is not as lavish as at the Fond du Lac, but really quite good, don't you agree, Birdie?" Fa always treated her as if she were, well, not exactly grown up, but as good as a grown-up. Mama and Addie loved her but they thought she was still a child. She was almost eleven, a young lady, Birdie thought. Fa thought so, too, she could tell.

"I actually prefer Mulligan's cooking," Birdie said, imitating his tone, so that both her parents laughed. "It's so good for me." Mulligan was always heaping Birdie's plate with things she felt were "good for the child"—horrible things, sometimes, like liver, ugh.

"Actually," Fa said, imitating her a little bit, "what did you think of Hotel Fond du Lac, Birdie? Did you have fun?"

"It's very hard to have fun, Fa, if there are no other people my age."

"Birdie, how ungrateful. Didn't you ice-skate and go on sleigh rides and accompany us to all the tea dances?" Mama gave her a look. "If you frown all the time like that, it could freeze on your face and then you'd look like that forever. You wouldn't like *that*."

"Oh, Mama! Only babies believe that."

Fa yawned, and excused himself saying, "Oh, how we do feel our advancing years. Here, at last, comes dinner," he added. The Negro waiter came swaying toward them. Birdie enjoyed watching him; it was a wonder to her, how the waiters never spilled or dropped anything, in spite of the fact that the train seemed always to be jerking a little to one side or the other. With a flourish, he set a dish covered with a silver dome in front of Birdie. After he served Mama and Fa, he whisked the domes off and there was the food, steaming hot. They were all having beef Wellington and a bottle of red wine, but Birdie was only allowed one sip of the wine, in a glass of water.

"Shall I cut your meat for you, my pet?" Fa said, and she nodded. She watched him neatly cutting the beef and its crust into pieces—he always joked that his surgical experience came in handy at the dinner table. He was so handsome, much better looking than the fathers of her school friends. So what if he was much older? Didn't he explain to her how men and women, like good wine, only improved with age? She knew how old he was and it *was* very old. Forty-nine. That was almost fifty, and fifty was half a century. But his hair and mustache were not gray, they were pale blond, and he wasn't the least bit bald, like her friend Jeanette's father. He was slender and he looked so elegant in his tweed suit, she thought. Mama was good-looking, too; "a fine figure of a woman," Birdie heard Jeanette's father call her. Her face wasn't wrinkled or anything, and she had just the one white streak in her black hair. "It's the skunk in me," she joked. Birdie hated that joke.

Mama had just had her hair bobbed so it looked very modern. Today, she was wearing her red dress with the belt around her hips. The dress had one of the new short skirts, and Mama said it was about time women were free of petticoats and long skirts and corsets that kept them from walking fast. She also had on a matching cloche hat and the diamond ear bobs Fa had given her. She really looked beautiful; Birdie could tell by the way other passengers turned to stare at her. The other girls at school said Mama looked like a vamp, but Birdie told them right away that her mother was not a vamp, she was a doctor.

Fa handed back her plate, and Birdie said, "Oh, Fa, it's cut perfectly."

"Does your Fa do anything in this world that isn't perfect?" Mama teased.

"No, he doesn't!"

"And your Fa loves that you are Daddy's little girl, my pet," he said. "You know your mother kept me waiting so long before she would marry me, I never in this world expected to be a father." He hugged and squeezed her and she snuggled into him, just loving it.

Mama cut herself a piece of beef. "I much preferred going out with *my* father, trapping or fishing, than staying at home with my mam. I went everywhere with him, whenever I could. And yet, here you see me, a doctor—a healer and a midwife, just as my own mother was. So I guess you're doomed, Birdie, doomed to a medical future."

"That's all right, Mama. Because Fa is a doctor." Her mother laughed, but Birdie thought that perhaps she had hurt her mother's feelings. "And so are you," she added. "Just like all the women in your family, since the beginning of time. Tell about how your mother taught you healing." She loved those stories of the olden days, and it wasn't often that she could get her mother to tell them.

"Oh, Birdie, you've heard all those stories. But wait—" She dug into her purse, red with a glittering clip to close it, and pulled out something, which she held out on the palm of her hand. It was a pale purple bead, a long one, like a tube. "This is my amulet. It's never far from me. I used to wear it on a cord around my neck. It symbolizes the healing power so many women in my family are born with. It's a piece of wampum, Indian money, which was cut and shaped by hand from a seashell, probably a clam shell. See? It's not flat at all; it's a cylinder. Someone scratched a magical symbol into it, so it was never used as money.

"My mother gave this amulet to me when I turned twelve and had become a young woman." Mama stared off into the distance. "I remember walking naked around the garden the night of the vernal equinox. The naked female body, my mother told me, symbolized the fertility of all nature and assured us of a good harvest."

"Oh, Mama!" Birdie looked around, hoping nobody in the dining car had heard her mother talk about being naked. Mama was likely to say anything in front of anyone. Sometimes it was terribly embarrassing.

Her mother knew what was bothering her and she laughed. "When I was a girl, it was considered quite natural to be naked for certain ceremonies. Naked is how we come into the world, after all." Mama looked at the bead in her hand and said, "My mother told me that this amulet had belonged to Bird, my great-great-great-many-times-great-grandma."

"Bird. That's like *my* name." She was pleased that somebody from so far back in time had the same name.

"I gave you her name for luck. Don't you remember my telling you that? Well, you were just a tiny thing. The first Bird was a doctor, a healer. A great healer, a *moigu*." The word sounded so silly, Birdie giggled. Her mother put on her doctor look, rather stern. "That's an Algonkian word, an American

Indian word, Birdie." Now Mama smiled, and her eyes did, too. "It means witch," she said in a loud whisper.

"Ooooh, a witch, how exciting. Was she, Mama? A witch? Really?"

"Morgan, really," Fa said. "You know Birdie's imagination. She wasn't really a witch, my pet, more a medicine woman," he said to Birdie. "She healed people."

Mama let her hold the amulet for a minute and then asked for it back. "I held it in my hand all the time I was sick with influenza. When I got better and was in my right mind, I immediately put it into your bed, under your pillow, Birdie. To keep the bad spirits away."

"You mean, this little bead kept me safe from the influenza?" Birdie couldn't help checking with Fa, and she could see by the look on his face that he didn't really believe that. Well, then, she didn't believe it, either. "Oh, Mama, this old thing couldn't be magic. Besides, there isn't *really* any magic, it's just stories."

"Really? And what if I told you I put it under Fa's pillow when he slept for three days and nights and scared us all? What kept Fa safe, then?"

"Science!" Birdie said, sure that it was a very good answer.

"Well, you really are your Daddy's girl," Mama said, but she smiled. "I know they teach you in school, in your history classes, that Indians were savages and deserved to be wiped from the face of the earth. But they're wrong. The Indian people were very clean and healthy and knew how to doctor people. The English settlers were the sickly ones. Why, they didn't even know enough to bathe! They came to the Indians and asked how to be healthy like the Indians were."

Mama looked off into the distance for a minute. She looked sad, sort of. "Birdie, people sometimes use the word squaw like an insult. But in my grandmother's tribe, women were the equals of men and could become respected medicine men. Not like it is today, when we're supposed to be so modern and forward-looking—and yet I'm having so much trouble being allowed to practice in a hospital." Her face had flushed pink.

"Why, Mama?" Birdie had been vaguely aware that Mama was fighting with some doctors and that they were winning.

"Because men do not want to believe that a woman can be as good a doctor as a man. Many men—I of course do not include Fa—think women cannot be as smart as men. Or aren't worth as much as men. Until a few months ago, I was not even allowed to vote for the President of the United States. For all the years since this country was founded, while its women worked and struggled right alongside their men—yes, and starved and died, too!—they were considered too inferior to have the vote. Even now a woman can't—"

"Morgan, dear," murmured Fa, "perhaps this is neither the time nor the place for political polemic." He was trying to hide a smile.

"Don't you dare find me amusing, Alex Becker," Mama said. Fa reached across the table to take her hand. Oh ugh, Birdie thought with horror, there they go again with all that lovey-dovey stuff.

"May I be excused to go back to my seat and play?"

When Birdie got back to their seats, she saw another little girl, right across the aisle, sitting with her mother, looking cross. "Are you bored, too?" she said, and the other little girl looked up and grinned. "You bet!" she said. "Do you have a doll with you?" Of course, Birdie did—although she was really becoming too old to play with dolls, she had decided—and they agreed to play hospital.

The other girl, Ida, was from Schenectady, which was a funny name for a city. Ida had heard of New York City, but had been told she would not be taken there until she was sixteen because of all the wickedness.

"Well," Birdie said, "I live there . . . in Brooklyn, but it's practically the same thing . . . and I never saw any wickedness."

When they asked, Ida's mother agreed that she could play with Birdie. "And where are your mother and father?"

"In the dining car, with dessert and wine."

"I do hope they will be back quite soon."

Birdie said the thing that always made everyone more agreeable: "Both my mother and my father are doctors."

"Doctors! Both! How very unusual." Birdie could see that

Ida's mother now thought she was fine for her daughter to play with. So they took their dolls—they each had a girl doll with flaxen braids and large blue eyes—and settled down on the seat to pretend it was the middle of the influenza epidemic. The dolls were very sick ladies, and it was the girls' job to save them.

When Fa and Mama came back, they sat down and watched the play for a few minutes. Then they asked to be introduced to Ida and leaned over to say hello to Ida's mother.

"Tell me, girls," Mama said then, her eyebrow lifted. "You're both *nurses*?"

"Yes, Mama, of course we are."

"Doctors are *men*," Ida explained.

"I'm a woman and I'm a doctor."

Both Birdie and Ida stared at her. "I know that, Mama. But doctors are men and women are nurses."

"If you insist." Birdie saw her parents exchange a look. But she and Ida were deep into the epidemic, patients were dying right and left, and they had no time for idle chat. Birdie remembered all about influenza, though it had been a long time ago, when she was only eight. Four children in her class at Packer Collegiate Institute had died from it. Several of her friends had had a parent or a grandparent die from it. Ida had lost her grandmother, too. They played for quite a while, their heads together, and then Ida said she was thirsty. So, they went to get a drink of water from the fountain. It was one of the things that made traveling by train fun, pushing the button and holding the little pointed cup under the stream of water, although it was sort of hard to drink without spilling, since the train rocked back and forth. Birdie filled a paper cup and took a sip, then handed it to Ida. They passed it back and forth, giggling. It was a good game and they didn't spill a single drop.

On their way back from the water fountain, Ida, swearing Birdie to secrecy, told her that she was not feeling too well. She had a stiff neck and felt quite hot.

"You do look flushed," Birdie pronounced. "Maybe you have a fever. Maybe you should tell your mama."

"Oh, no, please don't say anything. I'm going to lie down, I feel very sleepy. But I don't want my mother to know. She's always so frightened about sickness, and I don't want to worry her."

"All right, I won't say anything, not even to my parents."

"Anyway, we're close to Schenectady now. I recognize the houses. It was fun playing with you. So long, Birdie."

"Bye bye, Ida. I hope—" Her voice dropped to a whisper. "—you feel better." And they parted, both giggling.

Birdie broke out with red spots about a week later, and had to stay home from school. She had the measles. Everyone else in her class had already had them, so she was quite happy.

"I'm not so sure I should take care of you, Birdie. Indians didn't have these diseases, you know, they'd never even heard of measles or the pox or diphtheria," Mama teased. Then she said that even though she was really part Indian, she'd gone to school in Connecticut with children who got measles and whooping cough and chicken pox and she'd had all of them. "I'll always take care of you, my pumpkin." Birdie loved when Mama called her pumpkin—because of her red hair. Mama said red hair ran in her family.

A few days after that, Fa came down with a terrible fever. He had caught the measles, too. "My God," he said, "how embarrassing, a man my age with a child's disease. I cannot believe I went through my entire childhood without catching them. My mother probably did not approve of measles, so they dared not come to our house." He laughed, but said it made his head hurt, and his eyes, too.

Fa had to be in bed with all the shades pulled down because Mama feared he would go blind. He had a very high fever. Mama was terribly worried and took her meals in their room, sitting with him. Birdie was supposed to be a good girl, to stay in her room and play quietly and do her schoolwork. But she listened to every conversation. She heard Mama say to Addie that Fa had been so easily fatigued lately. "But when I said he should give himself cod liver oil and eat plenty of liver to build up his blood, he just laughed at me. And now he has pneumonia."

"He hasn't been the same since the epidemic. It really wore him down," Addie agreed.

That kind of talk scared Birdie. She didn't like hearing it, and she went into Fa's room, tiptoeing to the side of the bed. He seemed to be sleeping, but as soon as she got there, he opened his eyes and gave her a little smile. "Hello, sweet-heart," he said in a very thin voice, and that scared her, too.

"Fa, you're going to get better, aren't you?"

"Of course, my pet. Of course. But right now . . . sleep . . ." And his eyes closed again. Birdie blinked back hot tears and ran from the room, her heart beating very fast.

The very next night, he died. She heard Mama crying and she went running. Fa looked like he was asleep, but Mama said, "He's gone, Birdie, he's gone!" She held Birdie very tightly, but Birdie pulled away and ran down the hall to her room. They couldn't mean Fa. Fa was a doctor. Doctors didn't die. Doctors made people well. She waited until the doctor from Bellevue left. As he was walking down the stairs, talk-ing in a low murmur to her mother, she ran to Fa's room, just to make sure. The door was locked. And then she knew it was real.

She ran down the stairs, not caring that she was supposed to be asleep, not caring that she shouldn't be running around in her nightdress. "Why is Fa's door locked? Why did you lock his door? He can't be dead! He's a doctor!" She was crying so hard, she could hardly speak. Running into the front parlor, she saw her mother standing, her head bent, crying, with Addie's arm around her shoulder. Birdie didn't mean to shout, but she must have been shouting because they both jumped and stared at her like she was a ghost.

Mama held out her arms. "Oh, Birdie, oh my darling child, come to Mama." It couldn't be true, but it was. Fa was dead, no more Fa, never, never again, not ever! No! She did not run to her mother. She stood in the middle of the front parlor, her hands balled into fists, and screamed and screamed and screamed.

Birdie sat in the back of the black carriage between Addie and her mother. She clung to Addie's hand. She was very angry with her mother, although she couldn't have said why. She did not want her mother touching her. She could not stop crying, and, later, she could remember nothing of the service except the biting cold at the cemetery, and the awful sound of clods of earth being thrown onto the coffin. Thunk. Thunk. Thunk. It was a sound she would never forget.

On the way back home, lulled by the clip-clop of the horses' slow hooves, she closed her eyes. Then, Addie and Mama talked in low hushed voices.

"The measles! How could such a stupid disease take my Alex from me!"

"Morgan, Morgan, calm yourself. You know the measles didn't kill him. You said yourself that he hadn't been the same since 1918. And it's true. It aged him, and he got tired so easily."

"A child's disease!"

"No, Morgan. His system was weakened, he couldn't fight off anything."

"The measles! It killed my people, decimated them. And now it has killed my husband!" Her mother began to sob, great wrenching horrible sounds like throwing up.

Birdie sank deeper back into the cushions of the seat, wanting to disappear, to fall asleep and wake up to find this was all a bad dream. *She* gave a disease to Fa, a disease that killed him. It was all her fault. She'd caught the measles from Ida on the train, and Fa had caught them from her. She gave him the measles and he died. It was all her fault, all her fault.

Addie could say that's not what he died of, but Birdie knew better. To the end of her days, she would have to live with knowing that she gave her father the measles, and the measles killed him. She had killed her own father.

24

November 1921

Morgan looked into the mirror over her dressing table. She usually glanced at the hall mirror when she was ready to go out—supposedly to check her hair, her dress—but most of the time, she saw nothing in the glass. Since Alex's death, she had really been looking inward, at her grief. Tonight, quite suddenly, she noticed her face, and saw there were shadows under her eyes, tight lines bracketing her mouth. What she saw reflected was her mother. She had become an old woman! Well, perhaps not old, not yet. But well on her way. And look at the sagging flesh under her jaw! To her surprise, she did not like it. She began rummaging around in the drawer of the dressing table looking for . . . what? Rouge? Lipstick? Yes, in fact. She was looking for something to fix herself up. She didn't want to look like a crone, finished with life at fifty-three.

Eyeing herself in the glass, she thought, *so, once again you care what you look like.* That was good, probably. She wondered for the first time in a very long time if she would be considered a good-looking woman by any passing stranger. The trouble was, there was no one to give her the answer.

Birdie came into her room—without knocking, as usual; there were some niceties you simply could not teach that girl—and instantly began to complain.

"Mother, you're going out *again*?" The girl cast herself into Morgan's boudoir chair and sighed deeply.

Morgan fought a smile. What a little ham her daughter was. Where in the world did she get it? Maybe from Max, who certainly put on an act every day of his married life. He was Birdie's grandfather, after all. Morgan only hoped the child hadn't inherited his libido. Libido: what a fancy way of describing an old reprobate. She very carefully did not think of Becky, who had also been very good at histrionics. Morgan tried never to think of Becky, because Birdie looked so much like her it was frightening. She was delicately built, with porcelain skin, green eyes, and that gorgeous copper-colored hair, thick and curly. Just like Becky. Except, she was *not* just like Becky. She could not be. It would be a punishment far beyond anything they deserved. Morgan stopped and caught herself: Punishment? Punishment for what? She was beginning to think like a Christian. Or a Jew.

"I am going out, as I mentioned yesterday, because the open meeting on birth control, which was stopped last Sunday, will be held tonight. I am determined to hear Margaret Sanger speak. You know your Aunt Addie and me. We are not going to be stopped by *any* number of dumb policemen." She dug around in a drawer, and finally came up with a lipstick, which she applied. The bright scarlet on her lips actually startled her. "I hope we get in. Last time, we even had seats."

Last Sunday, Morgan and Addie had pushed their way through the mob, yelling, "Pardon me" and "Excuse me" as they elbowed other women aside. They could barely move through the thousands of would-be listeners milling about in the street outside Town Hall. Once they made it inside, she and Addie found what looked like the last two seats in the last row, and sat down, a bit out of breath and expectant. Although it was late, nobody had appeared on the stage yet. In fact, as they looked around, they saw that the perimeters of the hall were filled with policemen. What was going on? Nobody seemed to know.

This mass meeting, a discussion of the question "Birth Control: Is It Moral?," was to be the proud culmination of the first American Birth Control League Conference. Where was Mrs. Sanger? They waited and waited, but Margaret Sanger did not appear. And the policemen were walking around telling people there wouldn't be a meeting at all this evening. What was going on here?

A woman, out of breath, came in, and asked Addie, "Can I squeeze in here? Oh, I can't believe what's happening." The woman, disgusted and yet exhilarated, filled them in.

When Margaret Sanger arrived at the theater, she had found the door blockaded by two burly policemen. "There's to be no meeting tonight," they informed her.

"By whose order?" Mrs. Sanger asked. "We're the speakers! Mr. Harold Cox has come all the way from England and you know Mary Shaw, the famous Broadway actress. And I am Margaret Sanger."

"Yes, ma'am, we know who you are."

"Well, who gave you these orders?"

"Couldn't say, ma'am."

"So she marched across the street and phoned police head-quarters," their new friend told them, "only to be told that HQ hadn't given any such order, and sorry, but there was no way to reach the commissioner.

"Well, she was at her wits' end, I can tell you that. But she's a sharp one, Mrs. Sanger. I could see her looking around for a way to get inside. I myself managed to scoot by when a policeman turned, and I came in through the—ah, here she is! What did I tell you? They can't get the best of *her*!"

And there she was, diminutive and trim, yet so strong looking, her back so straight and her head held high, squeezing her way through the crowd to the foot of the stage. Such an attractive woman with her heart-shaped face and cloud of auburn hair! A roar of greeting went up from the throng. When she got to the stage, a policeman folded his arms across his chest and stood like a human wall in front of the steps, blocking her way. Suddenly, a man in the audience ran up, seized Mrs. Sanger, and lifted her onto the stage. It happened so fast the policeman could do nothing. Then the man leapt up beside her and shouted at the top of his voice, "Here she is! Here's Mrs. Sanger!"

Many in the crowd, bored with waiting, had not seen what was happening and had started to push their way out. At the sound of her name, though, they turned, and Mrs. Sanger called out, "Wait! Don't leave! We're going to hold this meeting!"

Well, *then* the applause sounded like a thunderstorm. Morgan found herself on her feet, Addie right beside her, clapping and shouting at the top of their lungs. People began to move back, hoping to regain their seats, joined by whoever could push their way into the hall from the street. It was mayhem, but a happy excited mayhem. Addie looked as if she had just got a glimpse of heaven. She did worship Mrs. Sanger.

Up on the stage, Mrs. Sanger tried to continue speaking. "Ladies and gentlemen. You have all seen—" As she began, two officers in blue jumped up on the stage, one on either side of her, and ordered her to stop. The audience hissed and booed, and the cry went up from different parts of the hall: "Where's your warrant? What's the charge?"

At that point Harold Cox, a former member of Parliament in England and a great supporter of birth control, who was scheduled to speak, came to the front of the stage, motioning with his hands that the audience should try to be quiet. Then he said, "I have come from across the Atlantic—" Suddenly, he was pulled back to his seat on the stage by a policeman. Many of the scheduled speakers in their chairs on the stage, stood up and tried to speak. They were all halted mid-word by interruptions from the police, while the audience roared and shouted in protest.

A second squad of policemen entered through the back, and the captain ordered the police on the stage to arrest Margaret Sanger. Anyone who protested was also arrested. It was unbelievable. Here, in the United States of America! Morgan, Addie, and the third woman all gaped at one another and asked each other, "But what's the crime? No law has been broken."

The audience went berserk, and someone started to sing "My country 'tis of thee." They all joined in, singing loudly as the police herded Mrs. Sanger and the rest of the speakers outside. Everyone followed, still singing, and crowded around the patrol wagon. Mrs. Sanger refused to go into the wagon, saying she would walk to the station.

They all followed her . . . thousands of the crowd, singing, booing, hissing, calling out insults to the police.

* * *

"Oh, that was a sight!" Morgan said, "that march to the police station. And do you know, the magistrate had to let her go. They couldn't arrest her, because she'd done nothing illegal. In this country, Birdie, we have the right to speak our minds."

"Then why were all the police there? Who sent them?"

"The Catholic Church. No, I'm wrong. It's not the entire church. It's one man, Archbishop Patrick J. Hayes." Her voice was loaded with venom. "He doesn't want the women in his archdiocese to find out about birth control. Well, perhaps he has a right to that, as their religious leader. But to stop all the rest of us from hearing what Mrs. Sanger has to say—that's not right!!"

Morgan studied her reflection. Not bad. Telling Birdie the story had put pink in her cheeks. "Why don't you come with us tonight, sweetheart? We'll be going to the Park Hotel on Columbus Circle. You can hear history being made. Wouldn't you like to be there?"

"Ugh!" Birdie said. "Lectures? Politics? Boring!"

Morgan had expected nothing else. She knew Birdie's two major interests right now were her reflection in any mirror and the drama club at Packer Collegiate Institute. Why she would want to waste her time posturing on a stage, Morgan couldn't imagine, not when she could be finding out about the important issues of the day. But, after all, she was not even twelve years old. Give her time, Morgan told herself, giving her image another long look in the glass.

The powder and rouge had its intended effect. What she saw made her smile. She thought, "I'm rather handsome, aren't I?" With a bit of surprise, she realized she was looking forward to being out of the house and into life once more. When Alex died so suddenly, she was certain she would never enjoy anything again, never smile again. Time did heal, after all. There was still a great empty space in her life, and her eyes often filled with tears for no apparent reason. But, save for the occasional memory that ripped through her, his loss was beginning to hurt less.

Morgan and Addie left the house early. There was sure to be an enormous crowd for the repeat meeting. The newspapers had covered it from all angles. In a way, they both agreed, it might have been the best thing that ever happened to the birth control movement. Just about every paper in the city had blasted the Catholic church and the police in their editorials. The fact that the archbishop had ignored the Bill of Rights in his religious fervor had brought the cause favorable editorials even in the ultraconservative papers. It had become a free speech issue instead of a women's rights issue or a birth control issue. Very shrewd of Sanger, Morgan thought.

They took the subway to Columbus Circle, changing twice to get there. On their way, they shared an evening newspaper and discussed whatever caught their attention. The Sacco-Vanzetti guilty verdict, they agreed, was a damned shame. The Ku Klux Klan should be outlawed—or, Morgan said, "lynched, one by one. Let them get a taste of their own medicine." Several people in their car turned to glare at her. She just outstared them. It was a free country, wasn't it? Adelaide had been reading *Scaramouche*, by Rafael Sabatini, and couldn't say enough good things about it. They decided they should get tickets for the new Sigmund Romberg show, the name of which neither could remember, until the young woman seated on Adelaide's other side supplied it: *Blossom Time*.

It turned out that the woman on the train, Edna, was also heading for Columbus Circle and the lecture. So they talked about Margaret Sanger and her mission the rest of the ride. Addie was a total convert and she admitted it. "I'm ready to dedicate my life to this cause," she declared. "Not only is Mrs. Sanger dead right, but she has the experience to back up her ideas. You know she was a nurse," she said to the other woman, who had not known. "Well, she was and she worked for many years on the Lower East Side. She *saw* how having too many children wore women out and made it impossible for the family to live decently."

"I understand that. I lived it," Edna agreed. "My mother was one of those women. In the end, she died giving birth to my youngest brother. I've taken care of all of them ever since, and lost my chance at an education."

"You poor thing, that's terrible. But how good of you to join the cause and fight for other women," Addie said. "I'm sure we'll be able to change all that."

"Come now, Addie, you know the power of the Roman Catholic church is considerable in New York City and State. Indeed, all over the country. Though, I must say, it isn't only the Catholics. This country is moving ever more to the right, toward conservatism. If it keeps up, and I fear that it will, we'll *never* get the right to birth control!"

Adelaide said, "I think that's true, Morgan. You'd be surprised at the amount of right-wing talk on Ellis Island these days. There are terrible negative feelings toward anarchists, not wanting to let them in, detaining them . . . and for what? For their political beliefs! Wasn't this country founded in order to give folks the freedom to believe what they want? I tell you, ladies, I get a very funny feeling sometimes about what's going to happen to immigration in this country. I think they're going to stop it."

"Stop it? They can't stop it! This country is nothing *but* immigrants!" Edna cried.

"Except for my forebears," said Morgan proudly. "I'm part Indian."

"You don't say! And your friend works on Ellis Island. What interesting neighbors I've picked to ride with tonight."

They were right in anticipating a crowd. So many women showed up to hear Mrs. Sanger in person that the whole of Columbus Circle, and surrounding streets, were clogged with people. It was difficult to move at all, and within the first five minutes of their arrival, the young woman, Edna, got lost in the mob. The word filtered back to them that there was no more room inside. The dark blue uniforms began to appear, just as they had the last time. One policeman approached them and said, "All right then, ladies, there are no more seats. Let's move on. No use standing here, blocking traffic."

"Come on, Addie," Morgan said. "He's right, you know. The newspapers will report this crowd—there must be thousands of women here tonight—and I saw the photographers' flashes before. They've already taken pictures. We might just as well read about it in the papers tomorrow afternoon. We'll never get in."

Reluctantly, Addie agreed, although she kept turning to cast wistful looks back at the throng still milling about in the street.

At 59th Street, away from the thick of it, they stopped and turned to take a last look at the spectacle.

"Oh, Morgan," Addie breathed. "Look at us. Just look at all of us! They can't withstand all of us forever. We're going to win! I'm certain we're going to win in the end!"

25

May 1923

Morgan was walking down the hall from her room to the stairway, when she heard Birdie's voice. That was odd. Mulligan had told her that Birdie was home from school and upstairs, but not that she had brought a friend with her. On and on Birdie went, her voice rising with each sentence. Morgan stopped at her daughter's door, her heart racing as she strained to hear what was being said. It was only Birdie's voice. *There was no one in there with her.* Birdie's voice kept getting louder and more agitated. Morgan was almost not breathing.

Was today the day she had always dreaded? The day the family curse captured her beautiful daughter? *No. Please, no; Not Becky's madness.*

Morgan flung open the door without knocking, crying, "Birdie? Birdie, are you all right?" Her daughter, seated in front of her dressing table, leaning close to the mirror, was startled into sudden silence. She stared blankly at her mother's reflection in the glass for an instant, then recovered, looking very irritated.

"Am I all right? You can see that I'm okay! And now you've broken my concentration. Honestly, Mother—!"

"Your concentration?" Morgan's heart was still hammering with fear.

"The play, Mother, the *play*. Remember? The Drama Club is doing Ibsen's *A Doll's House* and I'm Nora! I have the lead!" Preening, Birdie recited some lines—which Morgan could not hear through the buzzing in her ears. When she managed to calm herself down and watch, Morgan could see that Birdie seemed quite accomplished and at ease.

Was it possible the girl had a real talent? It was clear Birdie was stagestruck. She bought standing room at all the matinees, wrote letters to her idols, and was always quoting from some play or another. Of course, she was only thirteen, for pity's sake! Sometimes it was trying, having Shakespeare with the roast at dinner, or sometimes amusing. This was the first time it had turned out to be terrifying, although the possibility of the madness taking over had been much on Morgan's mind the past several years. Birdie had grown to look so much like Becky that, at times, Morgan could hardly bear to look at her, fearing the worst.

Birdie was a real beauty, with her dark copper hair, thick and wavy, her sea-colored eyes with their coppery dark eyelashes, and her small curvaceous body. Morgan towered over her delicate daughter. She was pleased and proud that her child was so lovely—and intelligent, too—but often she felt that Birdie was a changeling. She didn't know quite how to handle her, so dramatic, so temperamental. Birdie insisted that she was not going to be a doctor, but would go on the stage and become a famous actress. She constantly experimented with Morgan's cosmetics, and was always going through her mother's closet, looking for something to dress up in.

She was always falling in love, too. Not with boys—that would be too normal—but with actresses and actors. Hadn't she come back from the matinee of *The Green Hat*, announcing that she was in love with the character Michael Arlen had played? In love with a fictional character! To her mother, Birdie was a mystery wrapped in a puzzle. But the girl truly loved the theater, there was no doubt of that. She had said this morning at breakfast that she was desperate to see Marc Connelly and George S. Kaufman's *Beggar on Horseback*. And dying to see Margaret Kennedy in *The Constant Nymph*. Which had caused Addie to look up from the *Times*, to comment, "Desperate and dying—and all before you've finished your bacon and eggs! I shall hate to see what you suffer when you're in Upper School!"

"You can make fun of me all you want, Addie. When I'm world-famous, even more famous than Sarah Bernhardt ever was, with kings and queens at my feet, I won't even send you a ticket, so there! But, Addie, didn't you think Paul Robeson was divine in *All God's Chillun Got Wings*? I did, and he's so handsome."

"What do you plan to see this Saturday?" Morgan asked.

"Well, everyone says Will Rogers is as funny as a crutch—although I can't understand how a crutch is funny—but I'd really rather see *The Constant Nymph*. Susan and Jeanette want to see it, too. So we'll take our lunches with us, and line up for standing room."

Addie folded her paper and got up, preparing to leave for work. "Leave it to the young to line up, stand through a play for three hours, and come home without even a bunion."

Morgan knew that Birdie's dramatic bent was just that. But she couldn't help watching for the signs of madness—and being scared to death each time she thought she spotted something. If Birdie was still all right when she had graduated from college, Morgan told herself, then she would stop worrying. She couldn't really remember how it had happened with Becky. She thought Becky had been sixteen or seventeen when the first signs appeared, but Morgan had been so little when it all began. By the time she was conscious of Becky's oddities, they were a part of everyday life. She'd studied schizophrenia in medical books, so at least she knew what to look for. Maybe, she thought, she'd been looking too hard. Maybe she should just stop.

"I'm sorry I interrupted you, darling. My mind must have been on my patients still. But it sounded very . . . dramatic. Would you like to do the whole speech for me? I'd love to hear it."

"Right now?" There was no missing the pleasure on Birdie's face.

"Sure, now. I'll just sit here on the side of your bed, and you go right ahead."

"Well . . . actually, I'm at the end of the third act—that's the best part of the play. It's not just a speech, you know, Mother. It's a conversation . . . or an argument between this man Torvald and his wife, Nora, that's me. He loves her, but he always treats her as if she's a baby or a cretin or something. He's really wet! So . . . let me see . . . here we go.

" 'Didn't you say so yourself a little while ago—that you dare not trust me to bring up the children?' " Then Birdie's voice deepened as she became the husband. " 'In a moment of anger! Why do you pay heed to that?' 'Indeed . . .' " She had become Nora again. " 'You were perfectly right. I am not fit for the task . . . da dee da dee . . .

" 'I must educate myself. And that is why I am going to leave you now. I must stand quite alone, if I am to understand myself and everything about me . . .' da dee da dee . . . Torvald: 'You are out of your mind! I won't allow it! I forbid you!' Nora: 'It is no use forbidding me anything any longer. I will take with me what belongs to myself. I will take nothing from you, either now or later!' " Birdie's voice fairly rang; it was quite thrilling.

Morgan understood why she had thought she heard rage in Birdie's voice earlier. The character Nora was furious. She listened with interest, thinking how things were the same the world over—wasn't the playwright a Scandinavian? Too often, women were considered no more than pretty toys, and men were too thickheaded to realize that, sooner or later, their ladies were going to rebel against it. And rebel against them, as well. Strange, that Birdie could act the part of an angry, ill-treated woman, but seemed to have no interest at all in the trials and tribulations of angry women in real life.

Birdie stopped speaking, and Morgan realized, to her shame, that she had stopped listening several minutes before. She applauded loudly, saying, "Bravo, Birdie." But, in fact, she wished that Birdie hadn't become so interested in the world of make-believe. It seemed childish, somehow. The theater was fine, she always enjoyed a good play, but there were so many things happening in the real world, momentous things. Well, Birdie would outgrow it, she was sure.

As Morgan got up to leave, she was shocked to catch a glimpse of Birdie's face in the glass, dark with disappointment. But why? Morgan was sure she had kept an interested look on her face, and certainly she had clapped with great enthusiasm. There was no pleasing the child sometimes.

Morgan headed down the stairs, just as Adelaide came in, banging the front door closed behind her. "I can't believe it! The cruelty! Oh, I just can't believe it!"

"What? What? Come to the kitchen with me, have a cup of tea, and tell me what's happened." Addie was so upset, she couldn't sit, just paced back and forth between the sink and the range.

"Can you believe it? One thousand, eight hundred and ninety-six would-be immigrants—excuse me, we now call them 'aliens'—were sent back where they came from because the ships they were traveling on passed the imaginary line between Fort Wadsworth and Fort Hamilton a few minutes before midnight on the thirty-first of August. A few minutes, Morgan! But that didn't matter! They were included in the monthly quota of immigrants for August, which was just about filled. The immigration authorities kept talking about 'the law' as if it were the revealed word of God. Who was it said the law is an ass? I agree! I thoroughly agree! All those poor people, full of hopes and dreams, all sent back, all! And over a piddling minute or two! Oh, I cannot bear this, I think I shall leave the country and go live in Eskimoland!"

"Addie, please, come sit down and have a nice cup of tea. It's done and there's nothing you can do by pacing up and down in our kitchen."

"But it's so unfair!"

"Yes, it is. But who said life is fair?"

"Well, at least every reporter in the city of New York and Brooklyn and Long Island was there. It should make the front page of the *New York Times*. If it doesn't, Morgan, I will never have that newspaper in this house again!"

"Addie. Please calm yourself. I don't blame you for being upset but to banish the *Times*? Surely you don't mean that."

She smiled to show she was making a gentle joke. To her relief, Addie smiled back and then sat herself down in front of the steaming tea.

"Our new president, the ever silent Calvin Coolidge, probably won't do a darn thing about it. And I thought nobody could be worse than Warren Harding!"

They both laughed. Morgan took advantage of the change of mood, suggesting that maybe they should all take a vacation. "There's a new all-Pullman train to Chicago. Why shouldn't we go and take rooms at the Palmer House for a few days? It would make a nice change. No? Then how about tickets for the new Ziegfeld Follies. Birdie would love that."

Adelaide was not having any. "I'm going to have to leave Ellis Island. I can't work there if the authorities are going to be so inhumane. And just as all the immigrant aid societies finally got together to get some good things done! Oh, it doesn't bear thinking of!"

"Then let's not think about it for now," Morgan suggested hopefully.

"Never mind a vacation. I know what I want to do," Addie said passionately. "I want to work with Mrs. Sanger and make birth control legal in this state. God knows I've seen enough women die of bad abortions or too many babies. And so have you, Morgan. Of course, none of *your* patients."

"Oh, Addie, out of the frying pan and into the fire, is that it? What makes you think anyone will ever be able to make birth control legal? You'll just be going from one unchangeable, cruel situation into another. Remember what happened when Mrs. Sanger tried to get legislation passed up in Albany."

Addie's shoulders slumped. "I know, I know. And she had so much political backing, too. Even Norman Thomas, remember? Well, the Catholic mayor of Catholic Albany took care of *that*! Revoking the permit for the hotel meeting room where she would speak! Her appearance cancelled and moved to a private home! And that was the end of the Rosenman Bill!"

"So, I ask you again, why in the world would you want to throw yourself into such a self-defeating line of work? Why ask for more disappointment? Surely, you've had enough, at Ellis Island."

"Because of all the women who can't get help in this most modern country of ours. And let us not forget poor Clara . . ."

"Ah yes, poor Clara." An envelope with a postal mark so faint it could not be read had arrived in the mail last week. It contained two brief items. The first was a hastily scrawled note saying, "I was a frend of hers and she says if anythin happen to her, let you know." No signature. The second item was a newspaper clipping, which said that Mrs. Clara Optakeroff of the Standish Hotel had died in childbirth. "I wonder," Morgan said, "if it was childbirth or a botched abor—"

At that moment, Birdie wandered in, and began picking at the platter of meat left by Mulligan on the wooden table. "What about Clara?" she asked.

"Nothing, really. She's died, poor thing. You couldn't possibly remember Clara. You were so little when it all happened."

"Yes, I do. She was pretty and she smelled good," said Birdie. "And lots of men came to see her. One of them brought me candy. Not the one she ran away with, though."

The two women exchanged looks.

"Birdie, I'm sure you don't remember much of anything, you were far too young."

"That's not true. I remember a lot of things. What's so awful about knowing that Clara ran away with a piano player? I even saw them, a couple of times, rolling around on Clara's bed, huffing and puffing . . ."

"Birdie!" Two shocked voices in unison.

"Oh, honestly! I'm thirteen years old, I'm not stupid, you know!"

"Birdie, dear, stop picking at the roast. That's our supper. If you're hungry, take a slice of bread." Anything to change the subject, Morgan thought.

Apparently, Addie was of the same mind. She began to go on and on about the brand-new American Birth Control League and how she hoped to organize a march for it in Brooklyn . . . "What do you think, Birdie?"

"I think it's all applesauce! Who cares if women have six kids? If they want them, why not? You're so busy, going out and marching and screaming bloody murder at everything and what good does it do? Huh? The two of you are a couple of flat tires! Honestly!"

Morgan thought she ought to feel insulted, at the very least. But she was glad that the subject of Clara's sex life had been dropped. Although . . . Birdie *watched* Clara make love? She had known about it all these years and never said a word? What *else*, Morgan wondered, did her child know that she knew nothing of? The thought chilled her; her daughter was becoming a stranger.

26

June 1924

The office was buzzing with excitement. Mrs. Sanger was in town and would be dropping by. She would come after regular hours, since she was so busy giving interviews and speeches. She had given a talk at Yale University that had been covered by the *New York Times*. Now the fashionable new magazine, *The New Yorker*, wanted a profile of her. Everyone in the American Birth Control League building was floating on air.

Addie had been waiting all afternoon in a state of high excitement. Morgan, however, was simply curious. Since Morgan only came in to help answer the piles of mail once or twice a month, she was not as emotionally attached to either Margaret Sanger or the League as the others. She cared only that she did some good for the women of this country. Addie, of course, was devoted. She was actually on the payroll, as a nurse. Then, she often stayed late to help answer the tons of mail that came pouring in every day.

"They said she might answer some of the letters herself," Addie announced, her eyes checking the doorway for a sight of the woman many called Saint Margaret. Ten thousand letters flooded the office each month, all of them addressed to Mrs. Sanger. They were all answered, but the replies were generally penned by volunteers such as Morgan or Addie.

The two young women sitting at a table just in front of them were also going through the mail. Morgan couldn't help but overhear their gossiping.

"I've heard that Sanger and H. G. Wells are lovers."

"That's common knowledge. Or common gossip, who's to say? But I've heard . . . there's *another* man."

"I thought she was married to Noah Somebody, who is terribly rich."

"Marriage has never stopped Margaret Sanger from indulging in romance." The two giggled at that point. "I read that she's carrying on, not only with H. G. Wells and Hugh de Selincourt, but also with Harold Child and Havelock Ellis."

Such talk about her idol upset Adelaide. "Lovers or no lovers," she said, sticking up for her heroine, "she is always working for the cause . . . Oh! Here she is!"

Margaret Sanger appeared in the doorway, like an apparition, Morgan thought. Having seen so many drawings and photographs of the woman, it was odd to see her close-up in the flesh. There was no mistaking the heart-shaped face and the large expressive eyes, though. Mrs. Sanger's titian-blond hair was swathed neatly around her head, its pale shade matching almost exactly the beige of her coat. She was smaller than Morgan had expected.

"Good afternoon, friends," she said in a pleasant voice. "You cannot imagine how it heartens me to see everyone working so hard to make our dream come true!"

Adelaide, usually the shyest of women in social situations, rose from her place at the worktable and said, "Oh, Mrs. Sanger, it is such a pleasure to meet you in person! I do hope it is true, that you plan to answer a letter or two yourself!"

The cortège of women behind Mrs. Sanger set up a buzz of suggestions and counterproposals. Morgan caught only

snatches: ". . . No time . . ." ". . . waiting for you . . ." "Wishes
to speak with you . . ."

Margaret Sanger turned to her attendants and said, in a controlled voice, even but brooking no argument, "I am still
capable of thinking for myself." Then she turned to Addie and
said, "Have you an interesting letter for me, Mrs.—?"

"Apple. Adelaide Apple. Miss Adelaide Apple."

The wide-set eyes never left Addie's face. "Well?" she said.
"The letter?"

"Oh, of course. Yes, I have one here."

Morgan knew the letter. Adelaide had read parts of it aloud
earlier in the day. The writer was an eighteen-year-old girl
from the South, who had been made pregnant by a man she
barely knew. He had arranged an abortion for her and then left.

" 'I have to have advice and I know you will tell me the
right thing.' " Addie read. " 'I have a new friend who has
asked me to marry him. Should I tell all? I have been taught it
is a sin to lie . . .' "

"Take this down," Mrs. Sanger said, walking toward Addie.
She took the letter in her hand to see it for herself. Pacing back
and forth, she dictated: " 'You must not think of your relations
with the first boy, whom you loved, in the wrong light. If you
loved him and he loved you, God will forgive you . . .' "
Pausing a moment, she remarked in a different tone, "God will
forgive you, but perhaps not the man who wants to marry you.
Don't write that down . . . continue the answer this way: 'If
you believe such knowledge will upset your new beau, my
advice is, say nothing. Keep your head high and your heart
light.' There. How's that? Will that do?"

"Beautifully," Addie said, in awed tones.

"Margaret!" A voice from the doorway. "Mrs. Hale has
been waiting half an hour."

Again the light voice tightened ever so little. "I'm sure that
Mrs. Hale will not mind waiting one more minute, then." The
woman in the doorway made herself scarce.

Margaret Sanger looked about the room, bestowing her
smile upon one and all. "It seems that the writer Ruth Hale is
waiting to interview me, so I must run. It has been so nice

meeting you all. I am grateful for your help. We all are." And turning, she disappeared out the door.

There was absolute silence for a minute or two after she left. Addie's face was pink with pleasure. "Oh, that young woman will be *thrilled* when she receives this." And she bent to the task of writing it out.

"Wait until I tell my husband I actually met her!" one volunteer gushed. "Wait until I tell him she's *pretty*. He's always saying that the only women interested in birth control and having the vote are ugly old crones."

Addie blotted her letter, looked up, and said, "I shall never forget this day. Never. Now I know why they cannot stop us. It's because of her, the force of her personality. Didn't you find her wonderful, Morgan?"

Morgan had not much liked what she saw of Margaret Sanger. Not that she knew the woman at all, but there was something cold and distant about her. And Morgan had not missed how Mrs. Sanger, while gracious to strangers, tended to snap at underlings. But why say so? It would only make Addie unhappy.

"She looks even better than the photos, don't you think?" Morgan said, avoiding Addie's question entirely. "Aren't you ready to leave now, Addie? I'm tired."

It was seven o'clock by the time they left. Addie and Morgan took the train across the Brooklyn Bridge. The weather was fine, so they walked the rest of the way home, enjoying the clear night air. Morgan's back hurt her, as usual. She was always bending over, in her work. "I really look forward to my drink," she remarked. "And yet, I've never been a big drinker. I wonder if it seems so good because it's forbidden."

"Prohibition!" Addie said in disgust. "It seems to me that people are drinking twice as much since Prohibition started."

Morgan laughed. "Like me, for instance. Well, since I'm turning into a drunkard, it's lucky we can get hooch from Jane Forsyth." Mrs. Forsyth, one of Morgan's patients, was the very picture of New England rectitude. But she was happy to let her brother run a liquor store out of her basement—all very secret, of course. Jane was the one who called it "hooch."

"I, for one, will have a Coca-Cola," Addie said. "That's as

dangerous as I want to get, today. Who needs a drink after seeing Margaret Sanger up close and in the flesh? And she spoke to me. She asked me my name!" She fairly danced up the front steps.

The front door was unlocked, although Mulligan must have left long ago. That meant, to Morgan's relief, that Birdie was home, probably upstairs with her homework. At least she fervently hoped that's where the girl was. There was no telling, these days. Birdie was fourteen and her greatest ambition was to be a flapper. She wore very short skirts, and Morgan had also caught her with her stockings rolled to the knees a few times. She and her friends talked about boys incessantly, giggling and using slang that changed so quickly Morgan could not understand two words in ten. They also talked about "necking," but Morgan had never seen any of it. Birdie and her girlfriends all went to the tea dances at the St. George Hotel, in large groups, as did the boys in the Heights. And there, they danced most decorously, Morgan knew, because she'd gone several times to have a look.

She called up the stairs: "Birdie! Are you home, dear?"

"Sure thing, kiddo!" came the cheery cry. "Doing math with Jeanette!"

"Swell!" Morgan yelled, gratified to hear loud laughter from the girls. She supposed it was funny to hear someone considered so old use a word like "swell."

"Are you seeing Mr. S. later?" Addie asked in a casual tone. But Morgan was not fooled. Addie was very disapproving of Bill Seely. God knows why. He had loads of charm and knew how to use it. He was well-read and liberal-minded and could dance all the latest steps—well, that was no surprise, since he was a musician and music teacher by profession. He often sat at the piano in the front parlor and played and sang Addie's favorites by Jerome Kern and the Gershwin brothers. He had a beautiful singing voice—"something that comes with being Welsh," he claimed. But really, the nicest, most charming thing about Bill Seely was that when he looked steadily at you with his large warm brown eyes, you felt you were the only person in the world to him, in fact, probably his favorite person in the entire world.

It bothered Morgan that Addie became so tight-lipped whenever Bill appeared in the house, or indeed, whenever his name was mentioned. But it didn't make her unhappy enough to stop seeing him or even to confront her friend about it. She wished that Adelaide would find a man of her own, and then maybe she wouldn't be so jealous of Morgan's romance—if that's what it was. Morgan was not sure *what* it was.

Morgan had met Bill about six months earlier, at his sister's. The poor woman, Mavis, had died in childbirth through the stupidity of a so-called *real* doctor. The birth had been long and difficult, the woman was worn out, and the doctor, very elderly and forgetful, had neglected to wash his hands. When she became feverish and ill, nobody thought of childbirth fever—including the obstetrician. Everyone assumed such things had been eradicated. By the time one of Mavis's friends had called Morgan in, it was too late. Morgan barely had time to take Mavis's hand in hers and to say she was there to help, when the wretched woman breathed her last. Bill was at the bedside, as the man in the family. Mavis's husband had been killed in a factory accident. Distraught and weeping openly—his wife had also died during a difficult birth, and their child with her—Bill said he didn't know what was to become of this orphaned baby boy. Could he raise a child all alone, he a bachelor now and a musician with odd hours? He didn't think he could. Morgan had to agree.

She immediately thought of Mildred Logan, one of her patients whose child had been stillborn. It was the first child the woman had been able to carry to term and she was heartsick. Mildred would probably welcome this little boy, all alone in the world through no fault of his own. She still had milk in her breasts, and not being able to nurse was hurting her both physically and emotionally. Morgan told Bill Seely about the Logans, saying, "I could wrap him up and take him right over." The distaught man brightened at that.

"That would be perfect," he said. "A woman without a baby and a baby without a mother . . . Oh, my poor Mavis, to die so young and in such a way." He wiped the tears from his eyes without a bit of self-consciousness. "I'm just grateful our mother isn't alive to know about this."

Morgan called the Logans' home on the telephone and spoke with the husband. Both he and his wife were willing and eager to take the infant, as she had thought they might be. Morgan went back into the bedroom to say she'd be taking the child to Columbia Street, and would Mr. Seely like to come with her and see for himself where his nephew would be going? Yes, yes, he would.

Bill was so easy to talk to. He knew a great deal more than most men about childbirth, and did not think it beneath him to discuss child-rearing. They enjoyed each other; Morgan felt as if she were with an old and dear friend. Once the baby had been delivered to his new parents, and they were walking back toward Clinton Street, she realized that she did not want Bill Seely to disappear from her life. So she hired him to give Birdie piano lessons.

She always managed to arrange it so that she would be upstairs and just "happen" to catch Bill as the lesson was over. And then, what could be more natural than asking him if he'd like a drink.

"Just so long as it isn't illegal, Dr. Becker," he would say, with a twinkle.

After a week or two of some decorous flirting—many locked glances and heart-stopping smiles—she had decided that if he did nothing, she would. She didn't know what, but *something*. To keep eyeing each other this way was silly. The very next day, they were drinking sloe gin fizzes in her back parlor, sitting together on the love seat, their knees nearly touching, when without warning, he leaned over and kissed her on the mouth. She was surprised by the storm of emotions that took over her body, surprised at how avidly she leaned into him, welcoming his mouth and tongue. When they finally drew apart, they sat staring at each other in bemusement.

Morgan was the first to speak. "Now what?"

Bill threw back his head and laughed with delight. "I'm sure you know perfectly well what ... considering you're a doctor and all," he teased. "The only question, dear Morgan— you don't mind my using your given name?" More laughter. "The only question," he repeated, holding her chin in his hand

and kissing her mouth with soft yet firm lips, sending little shudders down her spine, "is, where and when?"

The question was answered that very evening: in his flat on Schermerhorn Street, not far from her house. He undressed her slowly, kissing each part of her as it was revealed, until she was fairly quivering with wanting him. Then, he removed his own clothes, but still he didn't embrace her. He grinned at her, saying, "Don't move. Let's just look at each other a bit." He stood a bit shorter than she, trim and neatly muscled, with black curly hair on his chest and surrounding his cock—which was, somewhat to her consternation, huge.

"Now don't you worry, Morgan darlin', I'll be slow and careful. You'll soon get used to it." Then he laughed at her blushing.

He took her, slowly and carefully, just as he had promised. She was so overwhelmed with sensations that she had to bite on a corner of the pillow to keep from screaming. She came to climax over and over, her eyes wide open, staring into his as he smiled down on her. "Oh, God, oh God, oh God," she moaned. Then he finally came to climax and lay holding her, breathing hard.

"There have been women who found me Godlike. But from now on, just 'Oh Bill, oh Bill' will do." They both laughed at that and almost immediately began to make love again.

That happened six months ago, maybe a bit more, and they were still avid for each other. He was a wonderful, tireless lover, who liked to take his time about it. He had beautiful hands and a lovely baritone voice. To hear him speaking or singing or whispering words of love was a pleasure. She often asked him to read aloud to her. He was an outgoing and amusing companion, and she liked him a lot. But marry him, as he sometimes suggested? She was not at all sure she wanted to give up her independence.

"Am I seeing Bill?" she answered Addie. "Let me think. It's Saturday, so yes, I'll be seeing Mr. Seely tonight. I think we're going to Harlem to hear jazz again."

"When are you going to *Abie's Irish Rose*?"

"That's next Saturday. You're sure you won't come? You know he's asked Birdie and she wants to go."

"Hmph. You could read your grocery list and Birdie would go to see it, just so long as it's on a stage and has footlights."

Morgan had to laugh. It was true. If ever a child could be called stagestruck, it was Birdie Grace Becker. She had been begging to see *Abie's Irish Rose*. "Everyone in the world except us has gone, Mama. It's the most popular play *ever*." It had opened three years earlier to horrible reviews, but nevertheless continued to play to packed houses.

"I suppose we should see it before it closes," Morgan had said to Bill, who responded: "Closes! Not likely! We'll be taking our grandchildren." He often slipped in something suggesting they would grow old together, snug and married.

"Well, Birdie will love it, no matter how bad it is," she said, ignoring his last comment. "I do hope she gets over this theater nonsense. She's always talking of becoming an actress."

"And what's wrong with that?" Bill asked. "If she's good, she'll have an interesting life."

"I don't want her to have an interesting life. I want her to grow up and do something worthwhile. Go to college, get a degree, go to medical school, and take care of people."

"Just like you. Not a bad idea, but daughters are noted for not wanting to be like Mama. Did you always do as your mother wanted?"

"Never mind about my mother," she snapped and then instantly apologized. Bill knew she had Indian blood—he thought it quite marvelous—but she'd told him few details about her childhood. She wanted to keep it that way. If she began to talk about Annis, Becky would be sure to come up and she definitely did not want to discuss Becky with anyone. Just the thought of her sister made her blood run cold with fear for Birdie.

Suddenly, Morgan realized that Addie was scolding her and she hadn't heard a word. Her thoughts had gone flying, a million miles away.

"Don't you feel awful, going to Harlem in a cab, slumming amongst the poor Negroes, and looking down on them?"

"Addie! You know I don't look down on Negroes. Besides,

those jazz musicians are so marvelous—so talented—*nobody* could look down on them. Their music is remarkable ... it makes you want to get up and do a dance, but no dance you ever heard of. We love the Cotton Club and Duke Ellington, his band always plays there. Bill says he writes a lot of the songs and they are as good as anything written by Jerome Kern or George and Ira Gershwin. Why don't you come with us? Bill always asks you and you always say no."

"Well, I'll say it again. I think it's awful that those clubs are filled only with white people from downtown, who drink too much and talk too loudly, while the Negro musicians play their hearts out."

"And how would you know that, since you won't even go?" Morgan tried hard not to smile.

"I read the newspapers and magazines, Morgan. I know what goes on. I've heard women at the clinic talk about going up to Harlem to 'hear the niggers.' "

"You know I don't talk like that! How could I call someone a nigger when I always so hated being called a squaw?"

"Anyway," Addie said, trying to cover her thoughtless words, "I find jazz—what a name!—loud and blaring and not at all nice."

"If you heard Bessie Smith sing the blues, you'd change your mind."

"The blues!" Addie repeated incredulously. "And you call that music?"

At that moment, the doorbell rang. "Oh dear, here I stand talking, and Bill's already here, undoubtedly looking 'spiffy,' as Birdie likes to say. Addie, would you let him in and ... Never mind, I'll go." It was amazing, how her heart speeded up when she knew he was near, how eagerly she anticipated the moment when he'd bend his head and put his mouth over hers. She was not in love with him, though. She was not about to be in love with anyone—not even Bill Seely, who some-times sang softly in her ear as he made love to her. Not even him.

27

May 1927

He was so wonderful. So utterly beautiful. So utterly talented ... the absolute berries. Birdie leaned forward in her seat, her eyes glued to the figure of Junius Justice Malone up on the stage. He was playing Robert, the younger son in *The Silver Cord*. She was seated next to her mother and Bill Seely, but Birdie hardly knew they were there. Her eyes and her attention were firmly focused on Junius Justice Malone. Thoughts of him had taken over her life. She just couldn't stop dreaming of him. She used to cut out every picture of him she saw in the rotogravure section of the paper, and tape them onto her bedroom wall over the dressing table. She even put his photo into a frame from the five-and-ten, and made an arrangement with the picture and a candle and a glass box from Venice that Jeanette had given her.

Then her mother saw it and sniffed and said, "A shrine, Birdie? To a man you've never even met?" Well, that ruined it; spoiled it utterly and forever. Birdie took all the pictures down and put them into a scrapbook, where nobody could see them and tease her. They filled only a couple of pages so far, but that was okeydokey. She intended to keep the scrapbook for the rest of her life. She'd seen him in another play last year, a matinee, and began writing little notes to him. She had a crush on him, sure, but that wasn't all. *She was going to meet him! Tonight! So there, Mother!* she thought. After tonight, he wouldn't be a man she'd never met.

Mother and Bill were going up to Harlem right after the

play, to Ye Olde Nest on 133rd Street. They went there a lot. It was a popular dive with old people, and Mother said you could see a whole cavalcade of cabs heading uptown from Broadway after every show. Somebody good was singing there tonight, but Birdie couldn't remember the name. She couldn't think of anything except Junius Justice Malone. She'd been carrying a torch for him for so long. He'd answered her letters, too, and he kept suggesting she drop by after the show one Saturday night and he'd show her the town. So, she begged and begged until Bill and Mother agreed to take her to an evening performance, although they'd already seen the play once.

They thought they'd be putting Birdie into a taxicab to go home, but guess what? She was going to have the taxi turn around and take her right back to the theater. He wanted to *meet* her, he said she should come to his *dressing room*. Anytime, he said. Anytime was going to be tonight! She just hoped he wouldn't give her the runaround. In his note, he had written that maybe they could go to a speak and make some whoopee with the gang. *The gang.* Just thinking of the words made her heart pound. Her palms had been wet with nerves all day and she kept wiping them on her hanky. Oh, if they shook hands, and hers was disgusting and clammy, she would die!

Of course, he didn't know she was still in high school and living with her mother and her old-maid aunt in Brooklyn. In *Brooklyn.* Actually, she'd be graduating next month and going to Syracuse University in the fall, to study liberal arts and be a co-ed. A co-ed was a lot different from a child in high school. Oh, God, what if he took one look at her and decided she was just a kid? She'd die, she'd absolutely *die* if he treated her like a baby and sent her home. She wanted to go to a speakeasy and have some hooch and maybe even smoke. "What if he makes a pass?" Jeanette had demanded this afternoon, as they lay on Birdie's bed discussing what might happen. "What'll you *do*, Birdie? I know I'd die, absolutely perish!"

"What'll I do?" Birdie had answered dreamily. "Melt into his embrace and as his lips meet mine, I'll hear heavenly music." But maybe she wouldn't. She didn't want him to think she was a pushover. Then she told herself to stop worrying.

She just had the heebie-jeebies, that's all, because he was so handsome and sophisticated. But she'd be fine; she had it all figured out, how to look bored and flapperish and grownup. That's why she'd put on her favorite dress. The shift, a pale green watered silk, was cut on the bias and clung, just barely, to her breasts and hips. She was wearing silk underwear, too, chemise and panties, and silk stockings. Nobody would take her for a schoolgirl, especially after she fixed up her eyes with kohl and put on the flaming red lipstick she'd bought at the five-and-ten-cent store. She'd do that in the taxicab. Jeanette had painted her nails with Chen Yu's Passionflower. Mother had glanced at the nail lacquer, but said nothing, for a change. So she was all set. Except for her damp hands!

Suddenly, it was intermission. Oh, God, and she hadn't heard more than three words of the play. They went out to the lobby, so Bill could smoke his cigarette, and of course, Mother asked her how she liked the play. "Oh, it's swell," she said, giving them both a great big smile. "I'm so glad you took me."

Her mother gave her one of her looks, the kind that made Birdie think her mind was being read. So Birdie widened her eyes innocently and looked right back. Mother looked away and began talking about Margaret Sanger. "I have a de facto birth control clinic operating in my own office, Bill. But Mrs. Sanger cannot get a medical license for her clinic! It's outrageous! She can't even get a license for the research clinic. What *ails* the men in this country?"

"It's not men, Morgan," Bill said, taking in a drag of his Camel, and blowing it out in big circles. "It's politicians. A whole different matter." He laughed.

"Everything is a big joke to you, Bill Seely."

"Well, the world's a funny place, darlin', and so are the people in it."

"There's plenty that isn't so funny. Going up to Harlem isn't funny and you know it. Addie's right. We never see a single Negro sitting at a table in any of the nightspots. It's their neighborhood! Where are they? They can't afford it! There's no work for them! And what are the politicians doing about that?"

"Now, Morgan, if we want to hear the Negro bands—and

we do, at least *I* do—that's where we have to go. I know it's a damn shame, the race situation, but there's not much you and I can do about curing it. Think of it this way: At least we're putting money into their pockets. And their music is getting more and more popular. You'll see, these bands will soon be downtown and everywhere."

Bill was a peacemaker, always trying to smooth everything out and make things pleasant. Birdie liked him a lot, even though it was embarrassing having a mother who wasn't properly married. Bill, a musician, occasionally played piano in a speak or someplace like that, which was pretty nifty. In his ordinary life, though, he was just a piano teacher, giving lessons to boys and girls in the Heights. He wasn't good-looking, not like Junius Justice Malone, but he had a terrific smile. And he treated Birdie like a grownup. That was copacetic. He was shorter than Mother, but they didn't seem to mind. *I* would, Birdie thought. I want my boyfriend to be taller so I can look up at him, the way you're supposed to.

'Course, Mother was pretty tall for a woman. Luckily, Birdie didn't have to worry about that. She was five foot two, just like the song. *Five foot two, eyes of blue* . . . Mother better not *marry* him, Birdie thought. The thought of Bill Seely being her father . . . well, it was just too too. Still, he was a lot nicer than some of the other men Mother had gone out with. Those others were always so sticky sweet with Birdie, pretending they just *loved* little kids. She knew it was all bunk, because even when she put on her brattiest act, they still pretended they liked her. Most of them she had hated.

Why did Mother have to go out at *all*? That's what she wanted to know. She was too old to really care about . . . sex and all that. Aunt Addie didn't date. Never. Aunt Addie was perfectly happy to stay home at night and listen to the radio— except for going to all her meetings, of course. It was embarrassing sometimes, explaining to the other girls at Packer that her mother had a boyfriend. That's not what mothers were supposed to do, in Birdie's opinion.

Just one more act to go. Birdie tried very hard to pay attention to the play once they were back inside and seated. But all she could do was think about him and what she would say and what he would say and what she would say *then*. Her heart was beating so fast it was hard to breathe. She was too jittery. She clapped louder than anyone, especially when Junius Justice Malone took his bow. Her hands stung. She thought she saw him searching the audience. Maybe he was looking for her! She longed to cry out, "Here I am! Right here!" But of course, she didn't dare. If her mother got even the slightest *hint* of what was going on, she'd kill her.

Everything went as planned after the show. Three blocks down Broadway, she told the cabbie she'd forgotten her gloves and asked him to turn around. When he offered to wait for her, she gave him her most dazzling smile and overtipped him. "No, don't bother. Really. But thank you *so* much."

She asked someone how to get to the dressing rooms backstage and was pointed toward the alley next to the theater.

That couldn't be the way, she told herself, hesitating. The alleyway was narrow and dark, just one dim bulb burning on the building, about halfway down. The way the click of her heels echoed and re-echoed was scary, and the streetlight made her shadow a long black shape walking in front of her. The place smelled of cats and urine. She got to a door where the lightbulb gave off a little light. Was it the stage door? It didn't say so. Metal steps led up to it, so up she went, the metal clanging loudly under her tread. She could feel the lipstick drying on her mouth. Tentatively, she tried the door. To her surprise, it opened without trouble, and she found herself inside in the middle of a hubbub.

People were running around shouting at each other, carrying props and pushing scenery. She was backstage; she knew backstage from the plays she had done at school. A gravelly voice asked, "Help you, miss?"

An old man with sunken lips and a white stubble on his jaws, sitting on a high wooden stool, had spoken to her. He sat in front of a warren of boxes, some of them stuffed with pieces of paper and envelopes. Was that where her letters had gone? "Mr. Malone," she told the old man.

"He expecting you?" He looked her up and down. Was he going to say "Go home, little girl, Mr. Malone doesn't want to see *you*?"

"Yes." She cleared her throat. "Yes, he is. He told me to come to his dressing room."

"Number three," he said, and, when she hesitated, gestured with his head to open metal stairs climbing up into the shadows behind him. "Up the stairs, one flight, to the left."

Clang, clang, clang. Birdie pulled herself up the rickety steps, afraid that if she looked down she'd fall.

At the top, she stood and stared until a young woman, naked except for a towel wrapped around her, came running by and asked, "Who you looking for, honey?"

"Mr. Malone."

The girl grinned at her. "Sure thing. He's number three. Over there."

The door had "Mr. Malone" painted on it as well as a faded numeral "3." She hesitated for a minute, while people ran back and forth behind her. Everyone seemed to be talking a mile a minute and calling each other "darling." The walls were the same pale green as the walls of the classrooms at Packer, only these walls were grimy and stained. The one window she could see was obscured with a thick gray coating of . . . what? She didn't think she wanted to know. Her heart was pounding so loud she couldn't even hear her own knock on the door.

"It's open!" called the thrillingly familiar voice.

Trembling a little, she opened the door and took a couple of steps into his dressing room. It was a small square room and, at the moment, he and she were the only ones in it. He was sitting at his dressing table, and, oh God, *he was naked.* Her heart began to race; her feet were rooted to the floor. She had to get out, but she couldn't move. He tossed a towel into a hamper, and then he looked into the mirror and their eyes met. She saw the expression in his eyes change rapidly: from blank, to pleasure, to something she couldn't name. It made her shiver in anticipation. *He thinks I'm pretty, really really pretty,* she realized. How lovely.

Everything seemed to happen so slowly: their eyes meeting, his delighted grin, the way he drawled, "Let me guess. You're my fine-feathered correspondent." Her speechless nod. His laugh was not a smug laugh but more a laugh of . . . well, happiness.

Then he got up. Since she didn't dare close her eyes, she was relieved to see that he wasn't completely naked. He was wearing shorts. She'd never seen a man in his underwear before and she didn't know where to look. He was very muscular, with no hair on his chest, and muscles even in his legs. He was handsomer in person than on the stage. She couldn't take her eyes off him. She couldn't move. She couldn't speak. She could hardly breathe.

He put out his hand and said, "You're beautiful, Birdie Becker, do you know that? You *are* Birdie Becker who's been writing letters to me, aren't you?" All she could do was nod. "Gorgeous," he went on. "Well, it's a pleasure, I'm sure. Won't you shake hands?" He grinned at her and said, "Beautiful Birdie, do you know, you look like a mongoose facing a snake. Oh. I see." He looked down and moved swiftly to a hook, took a ratty old silk robe, very stained, and belted it around his waist. "I'm really not a snake, although some of my pals will try to tell you I am. And here are some of them right now . . ."

Suddenly, the little dressing room was packed with people, and chatter, and a bunch of flowers. He handed the bouquet to somebody named Rafe to "take care of, would you?" His friends called him JJ.

Birdie was quite paralyzed. When, ever so casually, he draped an arm around her shoulders, she thought she would faint. It burned where he touched her. He introduced her. "Ladies and gentlemen, I want you all to behave because here's my new pash. Her name is Birdie. The hair is really that color, and never mind how old she is!" Everyone laughed— including to her amazement, herself. He squeezed her shoulder lightly and murmured, "Good girl. Just laugh at all my jokes and we'll get along fine."

If it hadn't been for all the people looking at her, she'd have pinched herself. She hoped she'd be able to remember every single second of this adventure. Jeanette would insist on a complete report. And anyway, Birdie wanted to remember this evening, wanted to hold it in her heart and her mind forever. Now that she was here and he was dressed—well, sort of— and all these beautiful people were crowded into the dressing room, it wasn't frightening any more. It was exciting. She knew now what people meant when they said they were in seventh heaven.

JJ Malone sat her in a little slipper chair and said, "Now don't you move. I have to change, but I'll be ready in just a shake of a lamb's tail." One of the men in the room snorted and said, "And we know the lamb whose tail will be shaking!" But JJ scowled and told him to "kindly keep it buttoned, would you?" To Birdie, he said, "Don't pay any attention to my rude friends. I'll be ready soon."

He sat down once more at the mirror and continued creaming off his makeup. Then he disappeared behind a screen and, throwing articles of clothing over the top, kept up a banter with the others.

When he came out, looking terribly elegant in his evening clothes, Birdie studied him. He was so handsome, lean and tall with thick dark hair and deepset eyes of a bright piercing blue. His nose was short and straight, his cheekbones chiseled, his mouth quick to smile. His chin had a cleft in it and his eyes a twinkle. He looked . . . devilish, in a way. The thought made her shiver a little.

She knew, from the reviews and articles she had clipped, that he used to play the juvenile but had moved up to the second male lead, which was what he was playing in *The Silver Cord*. Birdie was positive that one day he would be as famous as John Barrymore—more famous, even. And he was so nice! Every minute or so, he'd make sure to look at her, give her a grin or a wink or say something that included her. He was full of quips and funny comments that kept everyone in stitches. He took several sips from a slim silver flask, which he kept in his rear trouser pocket. A hip flask, an actual hip flask! Oh God, how romantic! He offered it to her and she took a little sip, trying very hard not to choke and cough when it went down her throat like fire. Someone asked him for the name of his bootlegger and he turned first to Birdie, asking her to keep mum about the name. She said she would, and he winked. She felt—she didn't know *how* she felt. Fizzy, sort of.

Everyone started to talk about jazz. JJ asked her if she liked jazz, and she was so glad she knew about King Oliver and

Duke Ellington and Louis Armstrong and the Chicago style. When she said she loved it, especially the blues, JJ came over and kissed the top of her head. They began talking about someone named Buster whose show was closing, wasn't that a shame, and everyone laughed and cheered. She had no idea who Buster might be, or why his show closing was funny, but what did it matter? She was here and she was a part of it, the exciting grownup world, for at least a little while.

Just thinking "grownup" made her suddenly uneasy. What if Addie didn't go to bed as early as she usually did? What if she was pacing up and down, *right now,* wondering where Birdie was? What if she called the police? Oh, God, the police! *I really have to leave soon,* Birdie thought, *and get myself home. I should just excuse myself sweetly. Say I have another appointment*—that sounded grown up—*and must be going.* But JJ was next to her chair, his hand resting on her shoulder, and she didn't want to spoil it. Then he lifted his hand to get his flask, took another little nip from it, and pulled her to her feet, beckoning to the others.

"Okay, everyone. Let's hie on over to the Pink Angel before all the tables are filled. Who's coming? Peggy? Andrew and Martha? Come on, Leo, say you'll join us, good . . . And, of course, the adorable Margarita . . ." He slipped on his jacket, and checked his hair in the looking glass. She stood there like an idiot, thinking, *What do I do now? Do I wait until they all file out of the dressing room? Do I thank Mr. Malone for seeing me after the show? Do I say good night to all of them or—?*

"You're coming, too, aren't you, beautiful Birdie?"

"Me? Oh, but I shouldn't."

"Oh, but you should. And you must. I can't lose you now that I've found you." A thrill coursed down her spine. "Say yes, come on, just open up that lovely rosebud mouth and say you will."

All thought of Addie, her mother, the police, the hour, fled. *That lovely rosebud mouth.* Oh God, wait till she told Jeanette! "Yes, I will," she said. "But, Mr. Malone—"

"Whoa! What's this Mr. Malone bunk? My friends call me JJ." He tilted her face up with one finger under her chin.

"And I have the funniest feeling," he mused, looking deep into her eyes and sending another shiver down her spine, "that you and I are going to be very very good friends indeed."

28

November 1930

Addie was tired. Bone tired. Maybe she was getting too old to be working so hard. She tried the door, and finding it locked, dug out her key from her large leather purse to let herself in. How she hated these dreary gray days of November. It hadn't snowed yet, just heavy icy rain and plenty of *that*, which made her feel damp clear through. She especially disliked coming home in the dark. She hated winter, that was it. Well, nothing to be done, since she was not going to join those brave souls— she thought of them as pioneers—who were going down to civilize the state of Florida. They might do it, if they ever managed to get rid of the mosquitoes and crocodiles and swamps. But that wasn't for her, not at her age. She went into the front parlor and sank gratefully into an easy chair. Just a moment to rest, while she waited for Morgan to finish seeing patients and come upstairs for their cocktail. And she would *not* fall asleep, like all the other times, and be caught, mouth wide open, snoring.

She'd spent a long weary day at the Birth Control Clinical Research Bureau, talking to woman after woman. The bureau was collecting case histories for a scientific study. It was hard work, because you really had to concentrate on what they were saying, and read between the lines of what they were willing to tell you.

A delicious smell wafted up the stairs from the kitchen. Mulligan had made one of her beef stews. Addie's mouth watered and she realized she hadn't had lunch. She was hungry, but she'd never eat without Morgan, who was still seeing patients downstairs. Both of them enjoyed their cocktail before dinner, and had become quite adept at playing bartender. They kept the whisky and wine hidden behind the ornate doors of a breakfront. Addie thought she'd mix them some Manhattans tonight. The bootleggers had brought in some fine whisky from Canada, and they had several bottles of it. She could do with a drink right now, but she'd wait for Morgan.

It wasn't just the gloomy November weather that had her down. Everyone was overworked at the bureau, mostly because male doctors refused to take orders from a mere woman, especially one without the "proper" credentials. The idea! Addie thought, getting up to take her coat and hat to the front hall closet. Dr. Hannah Meyer Stone had graduated from school as a pharmacist, true, but she'd spent many years practicing in the pediatric and gynecology departments of New York Hospital. So what if she was "irregular"! So was Morgan, and no better woman's doctor practiced in the whole city of New York, in Addie's opinion.

In any case, since so few men volunteered for duty at birth control clinics, they were always short of doctors. There were more women doctors now, but they were still being denied hospital affiliation. Women were always given second-class status! Mrs. Sanger had the right idea! She worked for what she believed in and did exactly as she pleased with her personal life. More power to her!

As she turned back to the front parlor, Addie heard Morgan's footsteps coming up the back stairs.

Morgan greeted her, and asked, "Did the Queen actually show up today? Or is she hobnobbing in Paris this month?" Morgan had stopped volunteering ages ago. She said that Mrs. Sanger was jealous of any other woman's expertise, particularly female physicians. When Van der Velde's book on sex, *Ideal Marriage,* outsold Sanger's own *Happiness in Marriage*, "that did it for the Queen," Morgan insisted. "Well, it was her own fault, really. Sanger didn't call a spade a digging implement, she called it a round object. She was so eager to offend nobody, she ended by giving no advice at all! Van der Velde was at least explicit—isn't that what all these women are dying for? Some straight talk? No wonder *Ideal Marriage* is *the* book people look for when they want a sex manual!"

"Now, Morgan, if it weren't for Margaret Sanger—"

"Please. Spare me 'if it weren't for Margaret Sanger.' There are other women fighting the good fight, too, Addie, and you know it. No, Margaret Sanger is a spoiled brat who was the queen of the movement for a long time. Now that others have joined the fight, she is afraid they might steal some of the attention."

"I wish," Addie said now, "you wouldn't always take that tone when you speak of Mrs. Sanger. It's so unfair! She works so hard, travels so much, talks to so many people . . ."

"Oh, hell," Morgan said. "Let's not fight about Margaret Sanger. What's important is that we, you and I, work to make sure women who need information, get it." Without another word, they walked into the front parlor, where Addie began busily mixing their Manhattan cocktails.

Morgan plopped into the easy chair. "You'd never know there was such a thing as a sex manual if you sat in with me all day. Some of my patients ask the stupidest questions! 'Is it true that if you stand up right after sexual intercourse, and let everything drip out, you won't get pregnant?' This, from a married woman with six children already . . . and now a seventh on the way. I tried to introduce her to the diaphragm, but she'd have none of it. Afraid her flesh would grow around it and then she'd never get it out. Thank you, I need that drink." They lifted their glasses to each other in silent toast, sipped, and sighed with pleasure.

A few moments later, Mulligan stuck her head in the door and said, "I'll be leaving now. There's a nice stew keeping warm on the stove."

"Thank you, Mrs. Mulligan. I hope you took some to feed Pat." Pat Mulligan, Agnes Mulligan's husband, had been sick in his bed for months with a wasting disease. He needed all the nourishment he could get.

"Thank you kindly, yes, I did. Pat does like his bit of beef, and Lord only knows how we'd ever get any without you, prices being what they are."

"You're so good to everyone, Morgan," Addie said after the housekeeper had left. "That's why I—"

Morgan, who had been idly leafing through a magazine, looked up. "That's why you—?" she prodded.

"That's why I admire you. And that's why your patients love you."

"Why, thank you, Addie, those are good words to hear. I do get involved with my patients—the way doctors are very carefully taught not to."

They sipped their drinks in companionable silence for a few minutes. Then Morgan got up and refilled both their glasses from the shaker.

"Let's take this wonderful elixir and go downstairs and get some of that good beef stew. I'm feeling a bit woozy," she said. They turned out the electric light when they left and went down the stairs to the big warm kitchen.

Addie dished out while Morgan sliced the heavy brown bread they both loved. Morgan brought the plate of bread and a dish of butter to the round table. "Oh, look at this. A letter from Birdie."

"Good. What does she say?"

Morgan read swiftly, as she forked her dinner into her mouth. "As usual, Addie, she writes a great deal and says nothing. Her classes blah blah, her teachers blah blah, the train she'll be taking blah blah. I can't believe such a beautiful young woman has no beaux! No girlfriends! It's as if she's having no life at all!"

She handed the sheets to Addie, blinking back tears. Could it be happening now? Were there voices in Birdie's head that kept her from making friends? Had those voices taunted her cruelly so that she couldn't fall in love? Morgan was never quite free of the worry. And this letter of Birdie's was so false, it was clear she was hiding something.

She recalled the night they saw *Strange Interlude*, Eugene O'Neill's new play. Just the three of them, Morgan, Addie, and Birdie, had gone on a weeknight. She remembered that because usually she was too weary after work to go gallivanting around Broadway. But Birdie had wanted so badly to see it— she must have been home on vacation—and of course O'Neill was always worth seeing.

Looking through the cast members, Morgan noticed a familiar name. Junius Justice Malone. "Haven't we seen this young man several times, Birdie? Didn't you write him a fan letter once?"

Birdie flushed deeply and stammered out something about wait a minute, did she? Oh yeah, maybe. She thought she never sent it, she couldn't remember. She was just a child, she had a kind of crush. "He *is* awfully good, Mother, he's written up all the time. 'Young Mr. Malone does his usual splendid job' . . . and so forth." She went on and on, and Morgan decided Birdie was behaving as if she'd been caught doing something wrong. But that fan letter had been written years ago; it shouldn't bother her at this late date.

The curtain had gone up then, and soon they were engrossed in the play, and Morgan forgot to pursue the conversation. She recalled the plot vividly, because the story had pierced her to the heart. Sam Evans—that was the part played by this Malone boy—is married to Nina. Sam's mother urges Nina not to have a child by Sam, because there is insanity in the family. So Nina has an affair with the family doctor and has a son, Gordon, by him. Gordon grows up hating the doctor, never knowing he is his true father. The secret is never let out.

Morgan had found herself mesmerized by the play. It reminded her of Becky, of course. That night, for the first time in years, she had dreamed of Bird, who looked very solemn and seemed to be giving Morgan a warning. Was it a warning that the bad spirits were coming for Birdie, her beautiful, brilliant baby?

"Morgan, for heaven's sake, whatever is the matter? You look like a thundercloud."

"I'm worried about Becky . . . I mean Birdie."

"Becky who? And why should you worry about Birdie? She's doing beautifully at school and she's been accepted by Cornell Medical, which is a great honor. And she'll be right here in New York for her training—at Bellevue, just like her father. I should think you would be very happy."

"Becky . . . Becky was my sister. Yes, I had a sister, an older sister. Birdie looks just like her, tiny and red-haired and beautiful." Morgan held her breath and then blurted it out. "My sister Becky was insane. She was a madwoman. So was my mother's sister, my aunt. Margaret, her name was, but I knew her as Quare Auntie. They both lived in the woods, at different times, like wild animals, and they both heard voices telling them terrible things. Schizophrenia, Addie. I know that now. Dr. Grace was the one who first told me. Until then, I always thought it was evil spirits. Our family was known to speak with the spirits, you see. I know, it all sounds so . . . primitive, and stupid. But it seemed very real to me. I accepted them, both Quare Auntie and Becky, and their strange behavior.

"My mother told me that odd behavior ran in our family, and that it was one way the Pequot people chose their medicine men. She also said that one of our ancestors had the shaking sickness and fell on the ground, foaming at the mouth. And when he awoke, he saw visions. He was just a boy, but his village knew he was special. They made him their shaman. And just once, my mother mentioned that she had had a brother, whom she loved. He also fell to the ground, quaking and twitching, and saw strange auras. But he hated it, she said. He hated being different, and when he was sixteen years old, he killed himself . . ." Morgan stopped talking then.

During a long silence, she stared into her past. Then, she added, "So you see, I have a real worry about Birdie. She is a woman of my family and we seem doomed, one in every generation, to madness."

"Oh, Morgan!" Addie's voice was thick with sorrow and pity. "I'm sure she's just fine! I've never known a young woman with such common sense. Birdie, mad? No! That's utter nonsense!"

"Perhaps. But sometimes—" She stopped. She was not ready to tell anyone about her Bird dreams, not even dear Adelaide, her best friend in this world. If she ever told anyone about Bird, they'd probably come and take her away. "I'm so afraid for Birdie, I'm so afraid!" Tears flooded her eyes.

Addie pulled her chair close and patted Morgan's back. "Now you just hush your fears. Look at Birdie, she's doing so well in school. A's in everything, she's so smart. And didn't she give up her ambitions to be an actress? Remember how relieved we were. Please don't worry. Birdie's probably too busy with her studies for much of a social life."

"You're right, of course," sniffled Morgan. She gave Addie a rather watery smile. "She's probably sitting at her desk right now, studying."

She was writhing like a snake, those beautiful green eyes wide open and fiery with passion, her hands grabbing at his ass, pulling him closer. He could feel himself swelling, getting ready to shoot into her. So he stopped moving and repeated to himself the seven times tables, the one he never could remember when he was a kid. But she was wild. "No!" she cried. "Don't stop, don't stop!" She began moving her rump from side to side. He tried to fight it but it was too much. He thrust into her, deeper and deeper, he couldn't wait much longer, and faster and faster and faster and NOW. He came like a bull, there must be a ton of it, and it wasn't the first time today, either. Christ, what she did to him!

He let his whole body relax, turning onto his side and scooping her satiny body close into his. She really was something! Looks like an angel, fucks like the devil. That's what he told his friends when they called him cradle robber. Looks like a schoolgirl, screws like a whore.

Loosening his hold on her, he braced himself on one elbow so he could trace her face and throat and shoulder with his finger. Slowly, he moved down to the curve of her breast and on to the pink nipple that hardened the minute he touched it.

"Nobody would ever guess what a wildcat you are in bed, Birdie Becker. You look like the Virgin Mary with that apricot hair and your smooth pink and white skin," he said. "Only *I* know what you're really like. I *am* the only one, aren't I?"

He tightened his grip, and Birdie cried out, "Hey! You're

hurting me!" and pulled away, annoyed. "JJ, you get rough sometimes, you know that? And I don't like it. So watch it."

"But I'm the only one, isn't that right? Just say it." He got ahold of her nipple again and pinched it tightly.

"Yes, yes, yes. Stop that, I mean it!" She rolled away, off the bed, and stood up to scowl at him.

"Oh, my little tough girl." He got up on his knees and grabbed her, pulling her back onto the bed, where they pretended to wrestle for a minute. He kissed her lightly, then more seriously, when he felt his cock stir and come to life. He was in the perfect position and he started to slide right in, but she wouldn't play. She pushed him away and got up, saying she had to go to the bathroom. "And don't you start drinking again, JJ! You already put away half a bottle of gin and it's only four-thirty in the afternoon!"

"So what? I'm not working right now. I don't have to be anywhere. Oh, all right, all right, lovey-dovey, I won't drink any more."

But the minute she closed the bathroom door, he got up and took a swig out of the flask he'd hidden in the desk drawer. They were in his room in a hotel, not far from the campus. They were very careful. Birdie insisted. She didn't want to get kicked out of school. JJ didn't think that was such a bad idea, but he didn't dare say so.

He intended to get some more pussy today before she started in on her goody-goody act about her studies and her classes and her grades. Why the hell did she have to be a *doctor*, for Christ's sake! Couldn't she just teach school or become a secretary like a normal girl? Not Birdie; she had to go to medical school, which meant another four years of having her say, 'No more right now, I've got to study.' He wanted what he wanted when he wanted it. And, goddammit, he wanted Birdie Becker in the worst way.

She was an obsession with him. He couldn't get enough of her. If he wasn't with her, he was thinking about her. He'd tried screwing other girls, but it was no use. No matter what they did or how gorgeous they were or how eager, they weren't *her*. He'd never been this way with any woman, never, and goddammit all, he resented it. Where'd she get this power over him, this kid who'd been a virgin before he got ahold of her?

Popping a peppermint in his mouth the minute he heard her bare feet coming up behind him, he turned around, grabbed her, and gave her a big juicy French kiss. She let out a little sigh of relief when she tasted the peppermint and then she heated up the kiss. He pulled her in tight, tenderly caressing the satin flesh of her backside.

"You can forget *that*," Birdie laughed. "I have a class to make."

He didn't stop. He kept on kissing her and, when he was good and hard, he took her hand and curled it around his penis. That usually got her. "Come on, baby, honey bunch, you can't leave me in this state. Come on, a quick one, something to remember me by . . ."

She pushed him away. "No, no, not a chance, JJ. So far, we haven't been caught and I intend to keep it that way. I'm sweet scholarly little Birdie Becker and that's how it's gonna stay."

"And they tell me *I'm* a good actor!"

Birdie eyed him. He was so beautiful, so sexy. She loved being with him, he was good to her, too, sweet and loving. But he could wait. She'd come back after class. Sometimes he was so greedy. Anyway when they were together in the city, if he had a performance or a rehearsal or audition to get to, there was none of this let's-do-a-quick-one sweet talk. No, *that* was *important* business, that was his work. There were three things that JJ Malone loved: acting, screwing, and drinking. Acting always came first. Did she even make the list? Did he love her? Did he even *think* so? He'd never said, so she had never told him what was in her heart. She was crazy about him. So madly in love, that if he ever got tired of her and left, she was sure she'd die.

Right now, he was standing in front of her, stark naked, and there wasn't a single inch of him that she didn't love and wouldn't kiss. But she was afraid of letting him know what power he had over her.

She began to put on her clothes, saying in a soothing voice, "Oh, JJ, you *are* a good actor, you know that! The best! It's just bad luck you're out of work right now. But you'll get a part soon, I just know it!"

"Well, in fact . . . look, Birdie, keep this under your hat, but Edna Ferber and George S. Kaufman are collaborating on a play. They hope to have it finished sometime next year and Artie says there's a great part in it for me. But he says I have to be a good boy," JJ sneered, "and come to rehearsals on time and stay sober and blah blah blah." He began to pace around the room, picking things up and putting them right back down, the way he always did when he was tense.

"It's not all blah blah blah, JJ. You drink an awful lot . . ."

"Just tell me one thing. Did you ever see me drunk and obnoxious?"

"Well, no, but—"

He put a finger under her chin and lifted her head for a light kiss. "You ain't a doctor yet, lovey-dovey. Mind your own beeswax, okay?"

"But, JJ, I only—"

"Yeah, you only have to go to stupid medical school, Birdie, so I'll never see you! Christ, Birdie, you don't have to be a doctor, even if *Mother* says so."

"I'm not going to be a doctor because my mother wants me to. I'm going to be a doctor because the women in my family have always been doctors." Seeing the look on his face, she said, "Well, it's true, JJ. And I made sure to apply to Cornell so I could be in the city. Close to you, JJ."

"Yeah, what happened to your idea of not even going to college, Birdie? Remember that? Remember how you were going to every open audition until you got a part in a show, no matter how small? Remember how I was going to show you the ropes and talk to Artie about handling you? You have talent, Birdie, you really do. So what happened to *that*?"

She laughed and said lazily, "One of us out of work from time to time is quite enough, don't you think?"

"I'm almost never out of work, Birdie, and you know it! What a lousy thing to say!" She actually thought he might cry; it was so strange.

"I was just kidding, JJ, honest."

"Is it my fault that two of the shows I was cast for closed out of town?"

"No, JJ, but you *were* fired from *Strange Interlude* for coming in drunk too often."

"Oh, that." He gave a little laugh. "I wasn't drunk, just a little tight. The producer is a prig and everyone knows it."

She didn't answer. He just wouldn't face how often he reached for a drink, and she couldn't ever tell him he'd been drunk. According to him, he was never drunk, just a little tipsy. Well, she didn't have time right now to argue with him about it. She had to get to Western Civilization; there was a blue-book exam today. Winter break was just ten days away. And then she'd have to get on a train. She shuddered at the prospect. She always thought of that train ride with Fa, where she caught the measles . . .

"What's wrong, honey bunch? Someone walk over your grave?"

What a poor choice of phrase, but of course JJ didn't mean anything by it. "I was just thinking, how soon I'll be taking the train down to New York. God, how I hate trains!"

"Trains? Why, for Christ's sake?"

"Nothing. Nothing. I just hate them, that's all." Without warning, she began to cry.

JJ instantly took her in his arms. "Come on, snookums, don't be blue. Dry your eyes and let JJ make it all better."

He rubbed her back gently and then his hands moved down to the curve of her buttocks, and when he pulled her in close, she could feel the hard bulge and she immediately got wet with wanting him. To hell with the test, she'd make it up. Her professors loved her, she could get away with anything she wanted. And, right now, what she wanted was JJ Malone.

29

May 1931

Indigo was one of Bill's favorite speaks, on East 21st Street in Manhattan. They went there often, for the music more than the thrill of illegal hooch. A trio was playing tonight, bass, piano, and saxophone, and Morgan really loved their easy sound. Sometimes, she found jazz too frenetic and loud, but these three men were kind of ambling through the tunes, light and easy and so smooth. She especially liked the bass player, a young Negro who seemed to be embracing and caressing his instrument. He had big hands and fingers but how lightly they flew over the strings and what rich sounds came from their touch. She was half in love with him; of course they had never exchanged so much as a nod. There was just something about the way he played, a sweetness that emanated from him.

She leaned close to Bill and said, in his ear, "Who's the bass player?"

"Milton Hinton's his name. He's great, isn't he?"

The trio finished their set, accepted their applause, and left for a break. Immediately, the noise level rose by several decibels. Bill signaled the waiter to bring them another round, and then grinned at her. "I converted you, by God. I've made a real music lover out of you."

She smiled back. "Not quite real, Bill. I've never taken to opera."

"Give me a few years. In fact," he said, after a tiny pause and in a different tone, "give me the rest of your life. How about it, Morgan? Don't you want to make an honest man of me? The neighbors are beginning to talk and I'm concerned for my reputation. Pretty soon, the word'll get out, that I'm easy."

That was just like him, making a joke even out of a proposal of marriage. It wouldn't be too difficult to live with a man who found life humorous. She did like him; in fact, she loved him. He was a good man, a funny man, an intelligent man. And a good lover, a very good lover. Even at fifty-seven, he was as eager as a boy, and as playful. *And even at sixty-three,* she reminded herself, *you're just as bad.* When she was younger, she'd always thought of a woman in her sixties as being elderly—certainly not interested in sex any more! Who was it said that youth was wasted on the young!

"Oh, Bill. Haven't I said no enough times to discourage you?"

He took her hand, playing with the fingers. "I'm Welsh-Irish and that makes me doubly stubborn."

"It also makes you think we're sinning."

"That's not why I want to marry you. Christ, woman, I love you. I want you for my wife. And that's all."

She smiled at him, saying nothing. A few nights ago, he'd burst out with it, after they'd made love. "It doesn't feel *right* making love to you and us not married . . . Not even engaged," he'd said. And then he'd tried to pretend it was all in jest. Morgan knew better, but she'd told him, many times, she didn't want to be any man's wife.

What she didn't tell him, and never would, was that she'd tried thinking of herself as Morgan Seely, and she just couldn't. It was silly, but Morgan Becker was who she was and would remain. She'd become accustomed to making all her own decisions and making her own way in the world. She'd done it twice and she really preferred it that way. Marry again? No, thank you. Even though they were good friends—even though Bill had only to touch her and she melted.

Lucky for her, the waiter came with their drinks and a little plate of tidbits to nibble on, and she could just babble on about them. A group across the room caught her eye . . . a familiar face that she couldn't put a name to.

"Bill, isn't that actor sitting right over there someone we've seen? Over there, in the corner, with a girl on either side. See? They have a bucket of champagne. Is it someone I ought to know by name?"

"Oh, sure, I've seen him on stage. Let me think . . ." Then he snapped his fingers. "I've got it! A couple of years ago, we saw him in something. *The Silver Cord,* maybe? Yeah, I'm positive that was it. Now I remember!" He laughed. "Birdie was just goofy over him, remember? She thought the sun rose and set on him. I remember thinking, only a young girl can fall in love like that, with an actor on the stage."

"Oh, yes. Of course. It's *him.* Birdie's been stuck on him since she was in eighth grade. As an actor, I mean. Well, she's nuts about the theater anyway, you know. She always used to pose in front of the mirror and pretend she was Sarah Bernhardt. What *is* his name? Whenever he's in a play, she's always crazy to see it. Hunh!" Morgan snorted, "Some hero *he* is, necking with two chorus girls at once! Just look at him. The man has no shame."

"Hey, what about the dames? They're not exactly discouraging him. And he's doing pretty well by the champagne, too. Just ordered another bottle. Whoa! Look at that, would you! Standing on his chair, waving the champagne bottle around."

The entire room had turned to look at the young man, decked out in evening clothes, calling for a waiter at the top of his well-trained voice. Bill said, "Drunk as a skunk."

"Waiter! Waiter! You can't snub me! I'm a star, goddammit! And I'm about to lose my freedom—"

One of the giggling girls with him tugged at his trouser leg. "What you're about to lose is your mind, buddy boy! C'mon, get down."

"Goddam waiter ignored me, Sally! *Ignored* me! Can't be done, hear me? Can't be done! Waiter! In the name of God, bring another bottle of the bubbly!"

The maitre d' materialized at the table. He spoke softly and soothingly, though Morgan could not hear what he was saying. The young man stood his ground. "Y'unnerstand? I gotta have more champagne, 'cause I'm celebrating! It's my last night as a bachelor!" he shouted.

People at nearby tables smiled and clapped loudly at his

announcement. As soon as he heard applause, the young actor stopped his ranting, grinned and made a deep bow, nearly falling off the chair in the process. A waiter appeared with a bottle in a bucket of ice, and the actor bowed again and sat down to more applause, which seemed to please him.

"What *is* the fellow's name?" Bill Seely searched his memory. "Something a bit odd . . . something to do with John Wilkes Booth."

"John Wilkes Booth? The man who shot Lincoln?"

"Yes, now what . . . ? Got it! Junius, that's his name, Junius Something Something . . . I'll have it in a minute. Named after Junius Booth, I'll bet. John Wilkes' father, also an actor."

"Junius Justice Malone," Morgan said, suddenly remembering. "And I just wish my stagestruck daughter could see him now! She'd forget *him* in a hurry! Look at him, French-kissing both of them . . . and I'd love to know where their pretty little hands are. Not around the stem of a champagne glass, that's for sure."

"Never mind them. All that petting over there has given me ideas, Morgan, my love. What do you say we go have a little nightcap at my place?"

He put his hand on her thigh and warmth flooded through her. He was a very skilled lover, and as usual, when he touched her, she wanted him. And she wanted him now.

"Your place? I say the faster the better," she agreed.

It was a beautiful day; she could see the sunlight through the cracks in the shutters. Morgan stretched languorously in her bed, thinking how lovely it had been to make love with Bill on Friday night—but how it was also lovely to wake alone in her own bed with a whole lazy Sunday to herself.

Well, not quite to herself, it seemed. Someone was banging on the door, making a racket, which was followed by giggling, feet shuffling, half-spoken whispers. And then Birdie's voice. "Mother! Wake up! Addie! Both of you! Wake up, wake up, you sleepyheads! I have an announcement to make!"

What had brought her down from Syracuse on a Sunday morning at . . . Morgan checked the clock ticking on her bedside table . . . 9 A.M.? She jumped out of bed, grabbed her robe, quickly smoothed her hair, and flung open the bedroom door. There stood Birdie and—Morgan's mouth dropped open, she could *feel* it dropping open—and that actor. Him. The very one they had seen absolutely ossified and carrying on with two women at once on Friday night. Junius Justice Malone.

Adelaide opened her door, and came down the hall. Neither said a single word. Morgan didn't know why Addie didn't speak, but as for herself, she had been struck mute.

Birdie was absolutely glowing. What's more, Morgan managed to take in, she was wearing a cream-colored silk dress Morgan had never seen before, a wide-brimmed hat in the same shade, and she was holding a somewhat wilted bouquet of creamy roses. What—?

"Mother. Addie. I'd like you both to meet JJ Malone. My husband."

"Your—husband?" Morgan was amazed that she had a voice at all.

"Yes, isn't it a wonderful surprise? We're madly in love and have been for simply ages. JJ called me Friday at school and told me to get ready for a wedding on Saturday. We met halfway, in Albany, he found the nicest justice of the peace and . . ." Still clinging to the young man with one hand, she held out the bouquet—at least Morgan thought that's what she was doing, until she saw that her daughter was showing her a gold band on the third finger of her left hand. She really *was* married to him. It wasn't a joke, or a horrible dream.

". . . So we did it," finished Birdie. "He begged me and begged me until I just couldn't say no any more. And now I'm Mrs. Junius Justice Malone . . . But you can still call me Birdie." She giggled. "Isn't it just too thrilling for words? And aren't you going to say *anything*?"

Morgan felt numb. All she could see was the drunken, sappy-looking young man in the nightclub, thrusting his tongue into first one eager lipsticked mouth and then the other. Now, he couldn't look more beamish and proud. She doubted he had told his new wife anything about his bachelor party on Friday. And obviously, since he looked at her with a clear-eyed gaze

and hopeful smile, he had no idea his new mother-in-law had
seen him behaving badly. She thought of several things to say
but rejected them all.

"You can't be married, Birdie. They won't let you graduate."

Birdie laughed merrily. "Well, Mother, we're not going to
tell them! Graduation's in two weeks, my finals are nearly
over and—" She gazed adoringly up at her handsome husband. "—And we just didn't see any reason to wait any more.
Is that *all* you have to say to us, Mother? Addie?"

Adelaide cleared her throat and said, "Of course. Much
happiness. But you have to realize, Birdie, this is quite a
shock. We had . . . well, we had no idea!"

"I know, isn't it just too thrilling? I actually kept a secret for
all these years. And you two think I'm so addlepated!" Birdie
laughed, delighted with herself.

All these years? Oh, my God, Morgan thought, all these
years, while I snuck out to make love to Bill, thinking she'd
never catch on, she was doing the same thing to me. Only,
stupid me, I *didn't* catch on.

Finally, trying to muster a smile, Morgan said, "Let's all go
downstairs. I think we could use some coffee. God knows *I*
could."

As they all clattered down the stairs to the kitchen, Birdie
prattled on and on, all bubbly and excited, about how they'd
been up all night, celebrating with friends on the midnight
train down from Albany, getting a suite at the Pierre . . . "just
waiting till we could come and tell Mother and Addie the good
news! Aren't we clever? And aren't you proud of us for saving
you the trouble of a big wedding?"

Morgan tried to make all the proper noises to indicate she
was listening, but she wasn't. She was busy thinking. She had
to call Bill, right away. He knew lawyers, lots of them. *There
must be some way we can have this thing annulled,* she
thought. They got married on an impulse; it was just the sort of
"romantic" thing to appeal to Birdie, especially the element of
surprise. Surprise! Shock was more like it. Shock and chagrin.
Birdie had made a dreadful mistake—she was young, she was
in love, she didn't know any better—but that was no reason to

allow the mistake to go unfixed. It was clear to Morgan that something had to be done, and quickly. Because her precious baby was not going to stay married to this drunken womanizer of an actor—not if she had anything to say about it!

SECTION FIVE

Birdie Becker Malone, M.D.
Morgan Becker, M.D.
Adelaide Apple
J J Malone
Alexander "Sandy" Malone
Robin Rebecca Malone

30

September 1938

The rain drummed against the windows and the wind howled. Trees in the garden bent low and swooped up as if attached to a string. Hurricane weather, Morgan thought. It was morning but you'd never know it by the sky, which was filled with dark, almost black, clouds. You could feel the barometer's inexorable fall. Oh, well, they were all safe here in the house. She decided not to worry about it, and went back to the morning paper.

Baby Sandy, propped into his high chair with several small pillows, picked up each neatly cut piece of toast Addie had put onto his tray and lobbed them onto the floor. Then, he complained, opening his mouth for more like a baby bird. When Adelaide frowned at him and said, "No, no, Sandy. Toast is not for tossing. It's for eating," he gave her a huge nearly toothless grin.

"Give him a zwieback," Birdie said, not lifting her eyes from the morning's *New York Times*. "That always keeps him busy." Adelaide got up obediently, but stopped.

"Birdie, remind me where we're keeping the baby food?"

"Addie!" Birdie said, impatiently, "It's gotten so you can't keep anything in your head. The end cupboard . . . no, not on the bottom. Up high."

"Oh, of course. I'm so confused since we got the new kitchen. I knew the old one like the back of my hand."

"After two and a half years, we can stop calling it new, can't we?"

"Birdie." Morgan gave her daughter a stern look and a little shake of the head. Addie was getting forgetful, true, but Birdie shouldn't be so blunt about it. It was cruel to keep reminding Addie she wasn't the woman she once had been. Who was? Morgan thought. Not even the oh-so-busy and ever-beautiful Dr. Birdie Malone. At twenty-eight, Birdie was still slender and curvaceous and as stunning as ever, but her milky porcelain skin was beginning to show tiny lines. She would wrinkle early. As Becky had. Morgan's heart stopped for an instant, as it always did when she thought about Becky. Still, she no longer worried that Birdie would suddenly become schizophrenic. She was too old, thank goodness.

Adelaide gave the baby a zwieback, and he rewarded her with another of his broad smiles. He was a sweet baby, no trouble to anyone. And a good thing, too, his grandmother thought with some asperity. If he'd been colicky, he'd have been left to scream by his mother, who didn't seem terribly attached to him, in Morgan's opinion. Although Birdie held Sandy and sometimes played with him, her mind always seemed to be elsewhere. It was a shame. He was a beautiful child, with his father's Irish good looks and Birdie's red-gold hair, and God only knew whose wonderful disposition. Birdie didn't seem to realize how lucky she was. She was not what you would call maternal.

Well, it wasn't as if she were lying around eating bonbons and reading novels. Anyone specializing in pediatrics had very full days—nights, too, sometimes. Birdie was not only an attending at Cadman Memorial Hospital, but she had a busy private practice right here in the house, down the hall from Morgan's offices.

Morgan regarded her daughter, who was so engrossed in the newspaper she was unaware of anything around her. Birdie really hadn't changed at all. The only other person, besides herself, who mattered to her was her husband. In Morgan's opinion JJ Malone was almost totally useless. He worked from time to time, in one play or another, but he never seemed able to hold on to a job. And when he was fired, it was always someone else's fault: the director had it in for him, the leading man was jealous of him, the leading lady had a crush on him and he wouldn't play. Always something, except the truth, which was that JJ drank too much. She wondered what he was up to out in California.

Birdie and JJ had been living with Morgan and Addie "temporarily" since Birdie began medical school. Birdie kept talking about buying a place of her own, but Morgan thought it would probably never happen. It was too comfortable here for either of them to do more than make noises about leaving.

That was why they had a brand-new, beautiful kitchen. The entire garden level had been turned into two medical office suites. Morgan's was only two rooms. But Birdie had to have her own X-ray machine and three different examining rooms, plus her office, a small laboratory, and a waiting room. They had moved the kitchen and dining room upstairs to the parlor floor, where the old second parlor and sun porch used to be, in the back, with a view over the garden. It had cost a bundle— Birdie helped, of course—and now she was eager to have a new outdoor stairway built, leading from the parlor floor to the garden.

Morgan often thought of describing to her daughter the two-room shack she'd grown up in, with her bedroom up a rickety ladder in a crawl space under the roof. But what was the use? Birdie would just look at her with that pleasant, bland stare, waiting for her mother to get to the point.

The kitchen was not as large as the old one, but it contained all the very latest equipment, including a new GE refrigerator and a brand-new gas stove. Wooden cabinets had been fitted into the walls, and the carpenter had found space for a nice little butler's pantry ... minus the butler, of course. The floor had the very latest asphalt tiles, green and cream in a checkerboard design, but Morgan had drawn the line at a matching checked wallpaper. "So I can look at it and get dizzy?" she'd said. "No, thank you. Just plain paint will do." She had won that battle.

A battle she'd lost was playing right now—a radio. Morgan had said it made too much noise and they could get all the news they needed by reading the papers. But Birdie had insisted and, finally, had just gone to Abraham and Straus and bought it. It sat on the shelf over the sink, cream-colored

Bakelite—horrid stuff!—with large brown dials and knobs, emitting the latest popular songs. At the moment, they were all being forced to listen to "A Tisket a Tasket" for the umpteenth time. At least it wasn't "Flat Foot Floogie with a Floy Floy." Although little Sandy seemed to love them both. Every time they came on, he twisted in his high chair, trying to discover the source of such enchanting sounds.

In a counterpoint to the radio, Morgan could hear the wild howling of the storm. The edge of a hurricane was battering Long Island and Fire Island. "Listen to this," Birdie read from her newspaper "an even worse hurricane has hit New England . . . Providence, Rhode Island, has been inundated by a tidal wave, causing thousands of dollars in damages, killing three people and flooding the surrounding areas! Wow . . . I hope we don't get flooded."

"We won't," Morgan said. "Remember it's called Brooklyn Heights. We're well above flood level. But the coastline . . . Does it say anything about Connecticut?"

"Lemme see . . . Yes, it says here that the Connecticut River has risen to dangerous levels. Say, Mother, wasn't that the river you canoed down, all the way to Brooklyn?" Her voice was tinged with amusement.

"You know perfectly well I didn't paddle a canoe all the way to Brooklyn. But I did go from East Haddam to Chester, and believe me, it wasn't easy. I was eleven or twelve and that's a wicked river in the spring."

"You sure you weren't eight or nine?" Birdie teased.

Morgan gave her daughter a hard look, but Birdie's eyes had already gone back to the newspaper. A sudden thought hit Morgan: Birdie thought the stories she had told of her adventures were fictional, or, if not purely made up, exaggerated far beyond the truth. It was a shock to find that Birdie felt her life was just a tall tale told to amuse children. If her daughter did not believe any of it, who would? Her life would just disappear when she died. All the things that had happened, all the knowledge she had gathered, all the heartache and joy and deep sorrow—all of it would just be gone, vanished like smoke in a breeze. It made her sad—and, truth be told, Birdie's superior little smile made her *mad*.

"It really happened, Birdie. I really left home when I was very young and paddled downriver in a dugout canoe, until a sudden storm came up and nearly drowned me."

Birdie looked up. "Yes, Mother, I know. And then Dr. Grace, who I'm named after, came out of the darkness and rescued you. I'm sure it all happened. But it was a long, long time ago."

Not so long, Morgan thought. *It doesn't feel so long ago to me.*

"Chamberlain is meeting Hitler," announced Adelaide in bitter tones, looking up from the *Tribune.* "Why does he waste his time? Hitler is just another Kaiser, greedy to rule all of Europe . . . Oh, and look here, fourteen new gas-mask stations have opened in London, preparing for the air raids they are sure will come. Of course. Everyone knows there will be a war."

"Except Mr. Chamberlain, apparently," Birdie said dryly.

"Exactly, exactly! Oh, I see, you're making fun of me. Well, we shall see, missie, we shall see."

"Missie?" Birdie reached over to pat the older woman's shoulder. "I'm not making fun of you, Addie, I'm just disagreeing. If Hitler lived near us, wouldn't you want to try first to make peace with him?"

Addie was not about to be mollified. She hated Fascists, wherever they were. "I'd know better than to try to make peace with a warmonger," she said.

Morgan decided it was time to change the subject. She had opened the paper at random and found herself looking at HOUSES FOR SALE and FLATS TO LET. She ran her eyes down the columns until she got to the Brooklyn listings. "Now's the time to buy a house in the Heights," she said. "They're going dirt cheap."

"Yes, Mother, but you know why. They've all been turned into rooming houses. I went on a call to a so-called flat in one of those houses and it was dreadful. Two pokey little rooms for an entire family, toilet in a corner, thin walls put up any old way . . . ugh! My patient had a horrible infection and small wonder—! This entire neighborhood is falling into ruin, if you ask me."

"Well, I'm not asking you. Brooklyn Heights will be rebuilt.

Some of the grand old houses have fallen on hard times . . .
Just look at all the families gone bust. All those women and
children left destitute by men who would rather kill themselves than face poverty!" She shook her head. "But never
mind. Someone will buy those old houses—they built really
well in the old days."

"We could still find a lovely place in the Village," Birdie
said. "JJ saw an ad for a mews house—"

"I know you and JJ love Greenwich Village, but Addie and
I are staying put. You, of course, are free to go." She knew it
wasn't fair to say that, when JJ was off in Hollywood, trying to
become a movie star. But why did he write Birdie about mews
houses, when he didn't have two nickels to rub together? He
didn't seem to be having much success out there, either. He
probably should have stayed in town and helped take care of
his baby. Instead, they had to depend upon absentminded
Addie and Mulligan as child tenders. Mulligan was well into
her seventies, her hands gnarled with arthritis. Still, she did
well enough with the baby.

But what was going to happen when Sandy began to walk?
He was already crawling everywhere and had to be kept in a
playpen. Lucky for them he was so placid. He didn't fuss, just
settled down in his cage and played peacefully.

"You mustn't feel obligated to stay here with us, Birdie.
Really. As much as we love having you here, you're free to
leave whenever you like," Morgan repeated. "But you'll have
to wait until JJ gets back, won't you?"

Birdie lifted her head from the newspaper and heaved a
great sigh. "I don't understand why Warners put him under
contract if they don't want to use him! It's not fair! Why
couldn't they either cast him in something or send him home?"

JJ had had a nice part in the play, *Brother Rat*, six months
ago, and actually stayed sober—most of the time. A Hollywood agent caught the Broadway production, liked what he
saw, and invited JJ to have a screen test. Of course, JJ being JJ,
he was convinced he'd get out to Hollywood and immediately
become the next Douglas Fairbanks. So far, he hadn't had as
much as a walk-on, and it was making his wife extremely
nervous.

"All those young starlets!" Birdie had said, one day not long ago, in a rare moment of candor. "All that free time! All the sunshine and swimming pools and all that booze!" And her eyes filled. She was obviously still crazy about her husband, whether he deserved it or not.

"I keep clipping items from the *Times*," Birdie said now, "about how busy the Broadway season is this year. I keep reminding him how much he always loved the theater. There are so many good plays around! Think of it! *Our Town. The Corn Is Green. Of Mice and Men. You Can't Take It with You.* So many shows, so many parts. He could find a role, I just know it! Don't you agree, Mother? I keep writing him to come home. The theater's in his blood. Sandy is growing so fast, and JJ's not even here to see him!"

Birdie bit her lip and blinked rapidly, pretending to become engrossed in the paper again. She thought Morgan didn't know how she worried about her husband, how JJ played around, how he drank too much. Morgan knew. Many was the night when Birdie, exhausted from a long day at the hospital, would sleep through his noisy fumblings at the keyhole, and Morgan would have to go downstairs to let him in. Often, she'd give him black coffee and douse his head with cold water before she sent him up to his sleeping wife. He'd be mumbling and singing, rambling on and telling all. So she knew all about the women, the bars, the after-hours clubs, the hotel rooms. Not that he ever remembered in the morning, except in the vaguest way. He seemed to recall that she'd let him in and poured coffee into him, but nothing more. He certainly never exhibited any shame about his amorous adventures. Morgan would call it their little secret, but that wasn't true. It was hers alone.

Oh, Birdie, she thought, looking across the table at her beautiful daughter—too young and bright to have a womanizing sot for a husband—*Can't you wake up and see what he's doing . . . what he's always done?* But her daughter constantly seemed ready to forgive her errant husband anything.

Morgan got up from the table to refill her coffee cup and caught a glimpse of herself in the windows at the back of the house. Her reflection always surprised her these days. She was seventy. She couldn't believe that, either. Seventy. She'd always thought seventy so terribly old, but it wasn't, not at all. Admittedly, she didn't look forty, but she didn't look like an old woman, either. Her hair was still thick and lustrous; she'd let it grow and was pulling it up, rolling it into a pompadour. Only that one streak of white ran right through the middle of her hair.

She'd dressed in black this morning—had done so for the past two months, ever since Bill Seely's funeral. Bill had keeled over in a cab, coming to pick her up for an evening of music and dancing. What a shock, when the doorbell rang and the cabbie, white as a sheet, said, "Ma'am, I hate to bother you but you better come down here and see for yourself."

"See what, driver? Where's Mr. Seely?"

"Passed out, ma'am."

"Passed out?" Her heart speeded up in alarm.

"Well . . . actually, ma'am . . . I hate to tell you this. But I think he might be dead."

"Dead!" She just stood there in shock, feeling the blood draining out of her face.

The cabbie reached an arm out to her. "Would you like to sit down? You don't look so good, ma'am. I'm sorry. But this is where he told me to come, and I figured . . ."

"Don't be silly," Morgan said, dismissing his offer of help. "I'm a doctor. Let me have a look at him."

Sure enough, he was dead. No chance of doing anything, except to get him to Cadman Memorial, sign a death certificate, find out why. Calmly, she went back into the house, called the hospital to say she'd be there in five minutes, and then told Birdie and Adelaide.

She had not wept at his funeral. She had felt emotionally frozen from the shock. It shouldn't have happened. He was healthy and active, still interested in sex, still teaching. But Starkman, the cardiologist, told her that many men suddenly died of heart attacks in their early sixties. Still, she grieved. Bill had been such a good friend and she sorely missed him.

The telephone rang. Morgan stopped staring at the rain-lashed window and went to the wall phone to pick it up. "Dr. Becker."

"Oh, Dr. Becker, thank God you're there." Morgan knew the voice. Alice Dowling, a twenty-five-year-old mother of five and wanting no more. She'd been in a week ago, to get something to end her pregnancy. "It's Bob, the pain is back and we're out of medicine. Is there something else I can do for him? I'm so sorry to be bothering you, but I do hate to see him suffer. A hot bath, maybe? Or ice? I just don't know what to do!" Her voice rose with every word.

"Take it easy, Alice. Of course you're upset. But don't you worry," Morgan said. "I have some samples of that medicine in my office. I'll get them over to you as soon as this rain lets up."

"Oh, Dr. Becker, young Bob'll come get it and glad to do something for his dad. He doesn't mind getting wet."

"Have him wait a half hour, will you? It may take me some time to put my hands on it."

"How can I ever thank you?"

"Just keep your spirits up. That'll help your husband as much as any medicine."

She put the receiver back on the hook, then picked it up again, dialing rapidly. "I hope the drugstore is open," she murmured.

"You don't have any medicine at all, down in your office. You're buying it for one of your patients. Again. Honestly, Mother—"

"Hush," Morgan said and then hung up again. "Damn this rotten weather. Mr. Goldstein isn't in yet. The Belt Parkway must be flooded." She turned to Birdie and said, "Please, Birdie. Call the pharmacy at the hospital and get some morphine sulfate for me, would you?"

"Morphine sulfate! They'll ask me why."

"Make up a reason. It's for Bob Dowling. You know the family, they live at 41 Willow Place in that big Greek Revival building that looks so elegant. Inside, though—! They don't even have heat, can you imagine? They use portable kerosene heaters. Anyway . . . poor Bob has multiple sclerosis and it's real bad. He's in such pain . . . I can't just let him suffer. There's nothing we can do for him except dope him up. Just get ahold of the pharmacy, okay?"

"Mother, really, you do too much for your patients. I know you try to hide it, but I know how often you 'forget' to charge for visits. I also know that some families find baskets of food on their doorsteps. You have to draw the line somewhere."

"Let's say I agree with you, for the moment. Would you like to tell me where I should draw the line? Shall I pay to have Chester Cook's club feet straightened or shall I let him grow up crippled? Shall I—?"

"Okay, okay. So you won't stop helping them. But I don't suppose you'd consider not going out on house calls at all hours of the day and night. No, I thought not. There's no reasoning with you. And don't worry, I'll get you your morphine." She got up from the table and took the receiver from Morgan's hand. "Why don't you finish your breakfast? If I know your patients, they'll start coming a full sixty minutes before your office hours start."

Morgan sat, but her eggs, congealing on the plate, hardly looked appetizing now. She poured out the cold coffee and refilled the cup. "I wonder if any patients at all will come today."

Addie, holding the newspaper very close to her face—her eyesight was getting worse and worse, but she was always misplacing her glasses—remarked, "They'll come."

"Do you want to give me the pamphlets now?"

"Pamphlets?"

"Yes, pamphlets. For the Lincoln Brigade."

Adelaide stared at her blankly. That was happening more and more lately. She'd have worried more, but Addie was still active with her usual causes and missions. Nowadays, she was flirting with the American Communist Party, all excited about the Popular Front and the brave new world of equality for all and sharing the wealth. The past few weeks, she'd been going door to door, trying to raise money for the Lincoln Brigade, which was fighting against Franco in Spain—but with few results. Even down on its luck and shabby around the edges, Brooklyn Heights was not the neighborhood to support any Communist or Socialist cause.

"You asked me earlier if I'd put out a stack of your Lincoln Brigade leaflets in my waiting room and I said I would."

The light dawned. "Oh. Yes. Lincoln Brigade. Now where did I put them? I know I brought them downstairs with me this morning."

Birdie, finished with her conversation with the hospital pharmacy, said, "I think I saw them on the front hall table."

"Oh, of course. Thank you, dear. I'll go right now and get them."

But she didn't get up because the Andrews Sisters singing *"Bei mir bist du sheine"* was suddenly silenced, and then the plummy tones of H. V. Kaltenborn said, "The war for which all Europe has been feverishly preparing was averted this morning, when leading statesmen of Britain, France, Germany, and Italy, meeting in Munich, agreed to allow Reich troops to occupy the Sudeten . . ."

"I told you! I told you! Chamberlain is an idiot. He thinks he can appease Hitler by letting him get away with murder. But he's wrong, dead wrong!"

"You should be happy we're not going to have a war!" Birdie snapped. "Instead of calling a genius like Chamberlain names!"

"Genius! Because he knows how to grovel? Hah!" Addie's cheeks were pink with excitement and her eyes sparkled. No sign now of the slightly addlepated elderly woman, Morgan thought with relief. It was the same old Addie, just a bit forgetful from time to time, that's all.

"Making peace is not groveling, for God's sake! And you sang a different tune when the Spaniards were forced to fight and—" Birdie stopped, as the downstairs buzzer was pressed over and over again.

Morgan said, "I forgot. I told Celia DiLauria to come over before regular office hours, so she could get to her job on time. Oh, she'll be getting *soaked*!"

She ran out of the room and down the stairs. When she opened the door to usher in her patient, the heavy, windswept rain put puddles on the floor. "Glad you could make it," Morgan said, pushing the door shut with great effort. As she and Celia walked to her office, Morgan could hear chairs scraping back from the table upstairs, then footsteps, then Sandy's gurgling, and Mrs. Mulligan's raspy voice. Another day had begun.

31

December 1943

Birdie handed the squirming infant back to his mother. "A fine healthy boy," she said.

"But, Dr. Malone, what about this diarrhea?"

"I've had calls all morning about it. It's going around, it seems. We'll take care of it, Mrs. Crumpacker. Scraped raw apple, mashed banana, and rice cereal. Make sure he doesn't get dehydrated." She fixed the young mother with a serious stare. "I see too many dehydrated babies in the hospital."

Mrs. Crumpacker's eyes rounded and instinctively, she held her child closer to her body, to protect him. "I'll make sure."

"Make sure the bottles are thoroughly sterilized." Birdie picked up her prescription pad and scribbled "scraped raw apple, mash ban., rice cer." on it. "A drop of paragoric after each movement—no more." She wrote that down, too. "It should be gone in one or two days." Birdie could see the tension in the woman's neck and shoulders begin to ease—and that reminded her of the nagging little pain in her own shoulders. She really had to get up to Orthopedics the next time she made her rounds at the hospital, and have Doug Wendroff take a look at her.

"I guess the war is nearly over now," Mrs. Crumpacker said.

"What? Oh. Italy's surrender. Yes. I certainly hope so." Wasn't the woman's husband in the Army somewhere? In the

Pacific though, if she remembered correctly. "What do you hear from your husband?"

"Not much." A nervous laugh. "V-mail is so slow sometimes. I noticed," she said, after a small pause, "that you have a star in your parlor window."

"My husband," Birdie said.

"But . . . I would have thought your husband would be too old for the draft."

Birdie laughed somewhat bitterly. "They didn't draft him. He's thirty-five but he felt he just had to join up."

"Isn't it awful . . . the waiting and all? Every time the doorbell rings—" The young woman shivered. "We all just sit there. Nobody wants to find out."

"You're sharing an apartment?"

"Three of us. They're your patients, too." She named two other young mothers.

"I know. It's terrible. But it can't be much longer. Hitler is running out of men."

"My husband's in the Pacific."

"Think how small Japan is. And we're such a big country. We'll beat them, too." On an impulse, Birdie reached out and covered Mrs. Crumpacker's hand with her own. She was rewarded with a radiant smile. *I'm not magical,* she wanted to say. *My touch does not work wonders. I'm only an overworked pediatrician who goes to sleep each night praying to God to please spare her husband.*

"I'd volunteer to be an aide at Cadman Memorial, but I have Eliot—"

"I'm sure your husband would much rather you stayed home to take care of your son."

"Well . . ." Proudly. "The three of us sharing the rent and everything, we have enough left over to buy a war bond every month. It's only the $25 one, but . . ."

"That's wonderful."

Enough conversation, she thought; she was dead tired. She showed mother and child out—they were the last patients this morning—and took in a deep breath. She'd have to hustle over to the hospital. Three newborns needed to be checked, plus the babies in the nursery, and there was only herself and Matt

Barstow attending. Then she'd have to get back here for evening hours. No wonder her shoulders hurt! But what could she do? A doctor couldn't say, "Sorry, I'm too busy to take care of you." She was exhausted, though.

So many male doctors were in the service that people were glad for any doctor they could get, even those who usually wouldn't come near a woman doctor. Her mother was pushing eighty and her practice was busier than ever. It was the same everywhere, not just in doctors' offices. Women were driving the buses and trolleys, and welding and riveting ships at the Brooklyn Navy Yard. With all the men gone, Birdie thought wearily, how come so many babies are being born? But she knew damn well how come. The night JJ came home after joining up and told her to kiss her soldier boy, with that strange combination of sheepishness and bravado he seemed to specialize in, they had quite a battle followed by a long sessions of stormy lovemaking. And didn't she miss her period the next month! But she had Mother give her something. No chance she was going to have another so soon after Robin!

She had to figure JJ really wanted to go fight for his country. The first time he tried to sign up, he was so drunk, they told him to go home and sleep it off. He made it the second time, though, even though she'd begged him not to do anything so foolish. "For Christ's sake," she'd argued, "we have two children, JJ!" Oh, he talked very earnestly about the evil of Hitler and Hirohito and it was up to every man to do his part, but she could tell by the sparkle in his eye that it was the adventure that appealed to him. It was a new part to play—and with the whole world as his stage. Men!

God, it was awful, him being gone. Sometimes she could hardly remember him; she had to look at pictures. Or at Sandy. Sandy looked so much like his daddy. And the army must have changed him. His letters home were very sweet and loving. God, she wanted him so badly—! Stupid, when he was unreachable. Where was he? They didn't know, but probably in Italy. He went first to North Africa, to Tunisia, and she knew the Thunderbird Division had been in North Africa and was now in Italy. At least he was alive. Wasn't he? Oh, sometimes her heart stopped when she thought of all the horrible things that could be happening to him in battle. But, she just knew no bullet was going to hit her JJ. He was going to come back to her, he was, he *was*. It had been weeks, though, since the last V-mail from him. She loved his letters. A lot was censored, but not his love talk or his descriptions of what he was planning to do when he got her in his arms. After the war. When will there ever be an after the war? It felt like this damned war had been going on forever!

She turned out the lights and headed up the stairs to the parlor floor. As soon as she opened the door to the kitchen, a small body hurled itself across the room and clung to her legs. "Robin!" she scolded. "I've told you and told you! Don't jump at Mommy!"

"Robin, come look what I have for you." That was Liz Markham, one of the two medical students rooming at 3 Clinton Street, in return for babysitting duties. It worked out quite well, and when both Liz and Linda were in class, Addie could fill in for a short time. Or sometimes Colleen, the house-keeper, was available. Colleen was Mrs. Mulligan's youngest; she had come to work for them after Agnes Mulligan's death two years ago. She came in the afternoons. "Robin, it's your ducky, he wants you." Liz squeaked the rubber toy, Robin's favorite, but Robin was not having any. She held on to Birdie's legs even tighter.

"That's okay, Liz. I guess it's her age. Although Sandy never did this." Sandy was in the afternoon session of kinder-garten. He was five years old. The teacher said he didn't want to play with the other children, and that worried Birdie a little. But he had always been a loner and somewhat shy. She'd wait and see what happened. "Is he mean to the other kids?" she'd asked Mrs. Smythe. "Does he push them or bite them?" "Oh, no," the teacher had said, "he's not at all like that. He's just . . . not interested. Whereas, the other children . . ."

Birdie had interrupted her at that point. "I try very hard not to compare children. They all develop at very different rates."

"Yes, of course, Dr. Malone. And he's a very *sweet* child."

Yes, he was. He was a very sweet child, and if JJ didn't get home pretty soon, he was going to be a stranger to his son. And his daughter, too, of course, she corrected herself, picking

Robin up. Robin would have changed even more. She was toddling all over the place now, and beginning to talk. When JJ had seen her on his last leave, Robin was a babe in arms. Dammit, why'd he have to sign up and leave her here all alone with two little kids? She missed him so much.

Oh, yes, he'd been very bad, back in '39 and '40, but that was just because he couldn't get good parts and was totally frustrated. They ended up fighting all the time after he got back from the coast, angry and nasty and drinking a lot, what she privately called his sneaky drinking, little nips all day long, not enough so he'd look drunk, but enough to bring out the worst in him. After one big battle, they hadn't spoken for a whole week.

Then, one night, after she'd put the baby to sleep, she opened their bedroom door to find JJ waiting. Without a word, they embraced tightly, kissing so hard their teeth ground against each other. He pushed her to the bed. They didn't even get undressed, really, just enough so they could do it. It was wild and wonderful. But Birdie had been through it all before. She lay there, her eyes closed, but awake, waiting. And, sure enough, she felt him bring his face close to hers, peering at her in the semidarkness. Then, apparently satisfied that she was sleeping, he quietly got out of bed, gathered his clothes, and tiptoed out. Birdie opened her eyes and stared blindly into the dark, tears leaking out of her eyes, as she listened to the front door open and close, downstairs. What was she going to do? What was going to happen to them? She tried to imagine life without him and felt as if she were about to fall from the top of a very tall building, breathless with vertigo. No, no, there *was* no life without JJ. And that was that.

"Come on, Robin, let Mommy go now." She looked down at the little face, so exotic, with the tilted blue eyes and Indian-straight hair, tipped up to her, so trusting. If only she weren't so clingy, Robin would be an adorable little girl. If her Daddy were home, maybe she wouldn't be so clingy. "Come here, baby, you want up?" The little girl smiled, held up her arms, saying, "Uppie uppie."

As soon as she was picked up, Robin held tightly to her. "Mommy, Mommy," she crooned. "Mommy no go bye-bye."

"Now, baby, you know Mommy has to make rounds."

"No, Mommy! No go bye-bye!"

Birdie was in a kind of despair. What on earth was she to do with this child? She was stumped, and she was a children's doctor! Robin was so different from Sandy, who, from the beginning, had happily kept himself busy. He'd even wake up from his naps and play happily in his crib until someone came in. Nothing ever bothered him, and he was still just as good as gold. But this one—! She just didn't have the time to spend on a whiner. She had patients, too many of them, and she had rounds at the hospital. She had important work to do. Then, feeling a bit guilty, she hugged the baby and kissed her on her chubby neck.

Robin was happily playing with Birdie's curly hair. In a spasm of love and guilt, Birdie said, "Look, baby, Mommy has to go to the hospital. How would you like to go with me?"

"Inna cah?"

Birdie laughed. "Yes. In the car." She had an old green MG roadster that she loved. She bartered for gasoline stamps so she could drive it. Everyone in the area knew Dr. Malone's sports car, so she never got parking tickets, never got stopped for driving too fast—which she did. She was Dr. Malone, and if she was speeding, it must be a medical emergency. She giggled to herself and Robin started to giggle, too. Soon they were both laughing like crazy. Over nothing. Maybe she should take Robin with her more often; maybe she'd feel closer to her.

She zipped into the parking lot, right under the gate, to the amusement of Marcus the gateman. Her car was the only one small enough and low enough to do that. She pulled into her space and picked up the baby. In the doctors' lounge on the ground floor, she found three doctors, two surgeons, and the new neurologist, Terry Snow. Terry had been wounded in Africa and had been sent back home. Why couldn't it have been JJ? Well, not that she wanted JJ to get *hurt*! But a wound in the leg, that wasn't so terrible. Birdie felt guilty about it, but she always had the same thought whenever she saw Terry.

Terry Snow was a nice guy, prematurely gray; his hair was white, actually. Startling to see that white hair with the young face beneath it. He was bent over a magazine, but when he heard noise and looked up, he grinned in a way Birdie recognized . . . in a way any woman in the world would recognize, she thought. He had a crush on her, but he'd never said or done anything about it. Not like some men she could name who figured if your husband had been away for a year, you were really hot for it.

"Hi, Birdie. Need a baby-sitter?"

"You free?"

He consulted his wristwatch. "For thirty-three more minutes."

"If she'll let go of me."

"Let's see. Hello, Robin, how are you today? You must be the nurse I've been waiting for. Are you ready to help me with an operation? I have a very sick teddy bear over here somewhere . . ." His voice was low and calm, and when he turned to walk away, Robin just toddled right after him.

For a miracle, Robin was having such a good time, she didn't notice when Birdie left to see her patients upstairs. The baby fussed so much every time she tried to go away . . . Maybe she *would* bring her to the hospital more often. If only she had more time.

It was a busy afternoon, and by the time Birdie got back down to the lounge, Robin was curled up in Terry Snow's lap, fast asleep.

"Oh, God, Terry, I'm sorry, I totally lost track of time. And you had an appointment, what? An hour and a half ago. How—?"

"I took her with me. I have only two neurology patients there, and they were very happy to see a cute little girl. They get pretty lonely, in bed all the time."

"I owe you, Terry. You're an angel." He smiled and handed the sleeping child to her, saying, "This little girl is the angel. But of course, you already know that."

Robin didn't wake up until they were home. As Birdie carried her into the entrance hall, she saw, on the table, like a bad dream, the dreaded telegram.

"Oh, God!" she said. "Oh God!" She put Robin down onto the floor and grabbed the horrid thing. With trembling hands, she tore it out of the envelope, whispering "Shit, shit, shit," when it refused to come apart. She was dimly aware that the baby had started crying. *He can't be dead, he can't be dead, please God, he can't be dead.*

... REGRET TO INFORM YOU ... oh, God, please ... YOUR HUSBAND SGT. JUNIUS JUSTICE MALONE HAS BEEN WOUNDED IN ACTION. Wounded! How wounded? Where wounded? But of course it didn't say. He'd already been wounded once. They were informed he had been awarded the Purple Heart. Also the Bronze Star. And the Silver Star. Oh, God, what if he'd lost a leg ... or something? She groaned aloud, and the baby clutched her around her legs, wailing.

Heart pounding, she reminded herself that he hadn't been killed, he was only wounded. Surely they'd send him home now. She bent down, picked up Robin, and rocked her. "Daddy's going to be okay, baby. Daddy's only wounded. Daddy's going to be just fine. And so are we—you and me and Sandy, all of us. Just fine."

32

March 1951

Robin knocked on her brother's door. It was a bright sunny day, a Saturday. Her best friend Carol was in the city shopping with her mother. Gran was at a birthing down near the navy yard. Daddy was sleeping; he slept all day just about every day. You didn't have to tiptoe around, though. Mom said nothing short of World War III could wake him up. Mom was at the hospital. She's *always* at the hospital, Robin thought. And if she's not at the hospital, then she's having office hours or some dumb mother is panicking because her baby is *crying*.

Don't they know, Robin thought with resentment, *that's what babies do?* They cry; that's their job, that's how they talk. She realized that Mom was a heroine to most people. She was looked up to and loved by everybody. But personally, in Robin Malone's opinion, it would be a heck of a lot better if Mom stayed home more and was a heroine to her own kids. *We're the last ones she ever thinks of,* Robin said, repeating a silent conversation she often had with herself.

She knocked on Sandy's door, again, louder. Still nothing. But she could hear his voice so she knew he was there. "Sandy!" she called. He didn't answer. She tried the doorknob. Locked. Why did he think he had to lock the stupid *door*? He was so weird! All the kids thought so; she heard them talking. And then if they noticed she was around, suddenly it got all quiet. She knew what they were saying: *Sandy Malone is a weirdo.* And they were right. Honestly, this family—! Everyone in it was strange. But if you asked her, Sandy was the strangest one of all.

"Sandy! You know Mom said not to lock the doors! Sandy! In case of fire!"

She heard the lock turning, then the door opened a tiny crack and one of Sandy's bright blue eyes peered out. "Come on, Sandy, you recognized my voice. I'm not here with an army."

"We're massing for a strike on Hill 47," Sandy whispered. He was always playing his stupid war games.

"Well, I'm unarmed," Robin said in a bored voice. "I'm neutral." Her sarcasm was wasted on Sandy, who took everything literally. Honestly, he had no sense of humor . . . and, if you asked her, he was getting worse. But of course, nobody ever asked her. She was only a *child*; she was only ten years old. Well, ten wasn't *stupid*. And she probably spent more time with Sandy than anyone else around here. Except maybe Gran, and she didn't want to bother Gran with it. Gran was a very good friend, but she was very old and Robin didn't want to do anything that would make her die or something.

Looking right and left down the hallway—as if there were enemies in his own house—Sandy finally pulled her in, grabbing her upper arm hard.

"Ow! What's the matter with you, Sandy? Who could possibly be on the fourth floor of our house besides us? Aunt Addie? She could care less about your dumb armies! She hardly knows who *she* is, lately." Her voice broke and she quickly turned it into a little cough. Aunt Addie was one of her favorite people in the whole world and it made Robin feel . . . squirmy . . . that Aunt Addie was getting queer. Sometimes she knew you, and sometimes she didn't. She could be reading you a story and all of a sudden just drift off and, when you poked her, look at you as if she never saw you before. Once, when she looked at Robin, she saw something that scared her and she screamed. That was the worst.

Didn't anyone else in this house *see* what was happening to everyone? Didn't Mom? Or Gran? Both of them were doctors, but they acted as if everything were just peachy-keen. She wanted to talk to her mother about Sandy, but her mother never listened to her. And Daddy . . . anything you told Daddy, he just shrugged and said, "What can you do?" Maybe she *would* talk to Gran.

"There are spies everywhere," Sandy explained, as he pulled her into his bedroom, closing and locking the door behind them.

Two armies, in World War II uniform, were laid out on his bedroom floor. The setup was elaborate, with every piece of miniature equipment you could imagine—the results of many Christmas and birthday presents. Daddy's war stories really stuck in Sandy's head . . . she got bored with them after a while. Especially since Daddy had favorites and kept telling the same ones, over and over. But Sandy always asked for more. Daddy couldn't tell a story too many times to suit Sandy.

"Who's winning?" Robin asked politely.

"Can't you *see*? No, I guess not, because you're only a girl." Sandy turned away from her. Sandy had never been a normal brother. Her girlfriends thought he was so handsome— well, he probably was—but they should only know what it was like to be in the same house with him. Robin sometimes felt invisible to him; he'd look right through her, and often, when she said something to him, he didn't seem to hear her. It was creepy. Every once in a while, he came up to her, wanting to talk. Usually, he wanted to know something or he wanted a favor from her. For some reason, he didn't like to talk directly to Mom; he was always asking Robin to do it for him. That was the other thing. Didn't Mom *notice*? Honestly, sometimes Robin felt like she was in charge of this entire family. The thing was, she loved Sandy; he was her big brother and he had taught her how to ride a two-wheeler. She just wished that he liked her more.

"It's a great day. Why don't you get out your bike and we can go for a ride?"

"Nah. I'm busy. If we let the Commies win even one battle . . ." He made the noise of a bomb dropping. "Curtains," he whispered melodramatically. "The end of the Free World as we know it."

Did he believe all this stuff? She couldn't figure it out. "It's really beautiful out. Look. The sun is shining. Come on. We could ride down to Union Street and get some cannoli at Mastropietro's." He loved cannoli.

"You get them. General MacArthur needs me right now."

"*General MacArthur* needs you. Oh, yeah, sure he does. Don't you know that General MacArthur isn't even in the army anymore?" She remembered the big fuss when he was fired by President Truman. That was all anyone talked about, for days.

But Sandy was totally involved in moving his tanks and artillery around on the floor, muttering about H-bombs and Commies conquering the world. A lot of baloney.

Okay. One more try. "Where's Addie, have you seen her?" Maybe she'd take Addie for a walk; it always pleased her so much, even though half the time, the old woman didn't know where she was or she'd wander off, and then Robin had to worry that a car might have run her over. She decided she wouldn't take Addie for a walk; it had gotten too scary. And anyway, Sandy actually answered her. "With Gran, I think. Or sleeping."

So Robin took her bike and went riding alone. She didn't really feel like riding down into Cobble Hill into the Italian section. Maybe she'd go over to the hospital. There was always somebody she knew hanging around the physicians' lounge.

She found four or five doctors, drinking coffee, gossiping, or whatever it was doctors did when they got together. Talked about their cases, mostly. They all knew her, of course, and they all thought she was looking for Mom.

"She's upstairs on the Peds ward, sitting with a little girl who nearly died from spinal meningitis," said Dr. Grad. He was one of the residents who was always nice to Robin. "The patient is getting better, but what makes your mother so special is that she's there even after the crisis is over."

Another resident said, "You must be very proud of your mother. Everyone just loves her."

"Yeah, sure, of course I am. We all are. But I wasn't looking for her. I was just out for a ride on my bike."

"And we're the best company you know, right, Robin?" That was Dr. Terry Snow. Robin loved him. She even loved his limp. He was so smart and funny, and he always had time to talk. Dr. Snow was two kinds of doctor. He'd started out as a neurologist and then went back to medical school and became a psychiatrist. He called himself a shrinker, although Robin had noticed that the other psychiatrists didn't like that. When people—they were so dumb!—asked if he had been wounded, he always said, "Yes, in W-W-two, in North Africa, where we weren't even supposed to be." He was always kidding.

Mom said Terry Snow was ironic, because he was bitter. "During the war, his wife left him for a 4F who made a fortune in scrap metal and he can't seem to get over it," Mom told her, and she laughed. Robin didn't think that was so funny.

"Does everyone here know Robin Malone, my bride-to-be?" Dr. Snow said. He was always kidding Robin, saying that they were going to get married one day, since her mother wouldn't have him. When she was really little, she had the biggest crush on him, and she believed that they were going to get married when she grew up. She knew better now. Today, for some reason, she suddenly realized that he really did mean the other part, the part about loving Mom. It made her very uncomfortable, so she decided to leave.

"Hey, Robin, you know I'm just teasing!" Dr. Snow yelled

after her. "Hey, don't go away mad! Come here and tell me what you've been doing in school." But she didn't want to look at him until she'd thought it over—what she had discovered.

Wheeling her bike out toward Fulton Street—woops, Cadman Plaza West now—she saw a familiar figure sitting on the curb, hunched over, shoulders shaking. It was Addie, looking even more disheveled than usual. Her hair was coming out of the bun and her slip hung below her hem. She was shivering, too. It was a beautiful sunny day, but there was still a chill in the air, and Addie didn't even have her old blue cardigan on. Robin hurried to Addie's side. Oh, God, she was crying. She was crying out loud, just like a little kid.

Dropping her bike, she sat down next to Adelaide and took her hand. "Addie, Addie, what's wrong? It's me, Robin. What are you doing here?"

Addie lifted a tear-stained face and said, "I don't know. I'm lost!"

"No you're not. You're very close to home. Come on, I'll take you there."

"Oh, thank you, thank you. That's very sweet." Robin helped Addie to stand, and wondered, *Did she shrink?* Because she suddenly seemed so small and light, as if a breeze could blow her away like a dried leaf. Addie gave Robin a real big smile, and said, "Thank you. I can't remember who are you, but I know I love you."

As they began to walk along together, Addie's hand on Robin's shoulder, Robin began to cry silently. She couldn't help herself. But if Addie noticed, she might get scared. Mom ought to be here, instead of taking care of a strange little girl who was getting better anyway. And then she heard, "Hey! Robin! What's going on?"

It was Dr. Snow, who must have come after her. She was so glad to see him. Sniffling and wiping her nose, she told him how she'd found her aunt sitting on the curb, lost. He gave her his big white handkerchief and said, "Go ahead. Blow. It's okay. In fact, you can keep it, as a souvenir." He was so nice, she didn't care anymore that he loved her mother, only that he was here when she needed him. "I don't have another patient until four o'clock," Dr. Snow said. "How about I just walk along with you guys?"

"Oh, yes. Yes. That would be neat."

When they got Addie up the stairs and seated at the kitchen table, with Colleen bustling around, making tea and talking a mile a minute, Robin relaxed. Addie looked very happy to be home.

Dr. Snow said he'd have a Pepsi with Robin; he even sang a little of the Pepsi-Cola song: "Twice as much for a nickel, too, Pepsi-Cola is the drink for you!" And then they both sang "Nickel, nickel, nickel, nickel" which made Addie laugh out loud.

Dr. Snow invited Robin to sit on the back stairs with him, since it was such a nice day. But the real reason was that he wanted to explain about senile dementia to Robin, and how it happened to a lot of old folks.

"And that's what Addie has?"

"I think so."

"I hate it when she doesn't know me."

"I know. That's the worst part. For us, anyway. I don't know what's the worst part for them."

"Sometimes when I talk to her, she doesn't hear me. Sometimes when she looks at me, she doesn't recognize me—" Robin broke off. *Oh, my God,* she thought. *I could be describing someone else.* "Dr. Snow?"

"Yes?"

"Can a young person, a really young person, like . . . like a teenager, for instance, could a person like that get it?"

"Senile dementia? Not unless he puts a lot of time into it." Dr. Snow laughed. "That's a joke, honey. Not funny, huh?" Then his face changed, just a little. "Why do you ask, Robin?" he said, trying to sound like he didn't care. "Got anyone particular in mind?"

But she was too scared to say Sandy's name. "No. No, of course not. I was just wondering." And she smiled, the phoniest, fakest smile of her entire life.

33

October 1953

They were all sitting around the breakfast table. Well . . . almost all. Addie was gone, poor dear. She had died two years ago. By the time she had finally let go, her brain had been as blank and innocent of knowledge as a baby's—maybe more so. She'd died peacefully in the nursing home, not knowing anybody, not even knowing where or who she was. Morgan's eyes still filled, thinking of the way bright, feisty Adelaide Apple had slowly faded away into nothingness. It had been horrible to watch.

Two years without her dear friend and companion, and it still wasn't much easier than it had been right after the memorial service. They had seen most of this century together; together, they'd observed all of the changes. It wasn't so bad, getting old, it really wasn't. You stopped looking so carefully in the mirror and you stopped thinking so much about your failings. What was dreadful was the loss of your dearest friends, your peers. With Addie gone, there was nobody who remembered what she remembered, nobody who had known Morgan as a young woman. *That's* what was frightening. In the end, Morgan had realized that Adelaide had been in love with her for all those years, and she knew, too, that Addie had kept it a secret out of love for her. It was quite a wonderful and sweet conundrum.

She got up from the table and walked to the stove to pour a fresh cup of coffee, waiting for Birdie to tell her she drank too much caffeine. But her daughter was engrossed in the morning paper. "President Truman says the entire Republican party is infected with McCarthyism, and I couldn't agree more," Birdie said.

"I don't like what's going on with that McCarthy," Morgan responded, glad to have something to think about that wouldn't bring tears to her eyes. "I think he's going to be trouble. I mean *big* trouble. Although . . . Harry Truman's pretty tough. He'll keep the senator in line." Suddenly, she raised her head, thinking she heard footsteps upstairs. But of course, it was just her imagination.

"You're always hearing Aunt Addie, Gran," Robin said. "Maybe her ghost is upstairs."

Morgan regarded her granddaughter. Robin was a sharp little cookie who missed very little. She loved Robin. Birdie had always been a mystery to her, but Robin . . . Here was another Wellburn woman, clear-eyed, insightful, brooking no nonsense. And she was still only a child.

"Ghosts!" JJ snorted. "What kind of nonsense are they teaching you at that fancy private school?"

"It's not fancy, Daddy."

"Ghosts! There's no such thing as ghosts!"

"How do you know?" Robin said, sticking her chin out. "You don't know everything."

"I'll know you right in the seat of your pants, Miss Freshmouth."

"Robin, apologize to your father," Birdie said, automatically, without looking up from her paper. Robin did no such thing. She never did. And JJ pretended not to notice. Father and daughter seemed doomed to mutual misunderstanding. What a shame. Birdie and her Fa had had such a lovely relationship.

Morgan sighed, and Birdie put down the paper. She said, "There wasn't a thing we could do about Addie, Mother. Senile dementia is an area where medical science hasn't moved one inch since the beginning of time. Much as I hate to admit it, we're still totally ignorant about it."

"I just wish we could have kept her here," Morgan said.

"Now, Mother, you know there was no way to do that. She was wandering away from the house. And remember how she accused Robin of stealing money from her? And she *adored*

Robin. No, there was no way to keep her at home, not with her unpredictable behavior. We'd have had to hire twenty-four-hour help, just to keep an eye on her."

"Gran and I would have kept an eye on her," Robin said in a shaky voice.

"I know you loved her, Robin. We all loved her. But there comes a time when a family cannot ignore what's right in front of them."

Birdie let the comment hang, and there was a thick silence as everyone at the table busied themselves with their food, carefully not looking at Sandy. He sat on a stool in the far corner of the kitchen, his back turned to the table.

He'd been eating all his meals that way for the past week. He never said why, and, Morgan thought, everyone was too frightened to ask him. Frightened of the answer. She, too.

Sandy's weird, Robin thought. *Just like Aunt Addie was. Why doesn't anybody say so? Why is everyone pretending it's not happening?* She sneaked a look at her brother. Weird. As usual. He'd cut his own hair, shaving it all off except for a long lock in the front. And he refused to wash, so he really smelled bad. Why didn't her parents say something to him? Mom was always going on about adolescent boys needing their privacy, but that had nothing to do with it. As for Daddy, he never paid much attention to either of them, unless they were in his way or making too much noise or something.

Earlier he had barked an order to Sandy to get back to the table and eat like a human being, but when Sandy didn't answer or even turn around, Daddy didn't notice. He was reading *Variety*, looking for his big chance to get back on the stage.

Suddenly Sandy turned around and said, loudly, "I want you to stop it! Stop it!"

"Stop what?" Mom said in that phony bright voice. "Nobody's doing anything, darling."

"Not you! Them! They're taking my thoughts. They must be right overhead."

Everyone at the table knew who "they" were. Her mother

gave a nervous laugh but, as usual, said nothing. Robin couldn't stand it any more.

"There are no flying saucers above Brooklyn, Sandy. You know that," Robin said. Sometimes, if she kept her voice very even and sure, she could stop his thoughts from flying off in all directions. Sometimes.

"How do we know they're not in Brooklyn Heights? They come from outer space. They could be anywhere," he said.

JJ looked up briefly from his paper and said, "For Christ's sake, Sandy, you keep talking like that and they'll come and take you to the funny farm!"

Robin watched Sandy's face as he struggled to come back to normal. Just like Addie, he could be okay and then, suddenly, not. Then he laughed. "It's a play. I'm writing a play about flying saucers."

"That's my boy!" boomed her father. "Writing and starring in it, too, eh, son?"

"Yeah, yeah." Sandy's eyes were darting around the room wildly. Pretty soon, Robin knew, he'd run upstairs, away from them, where he could be as crazy as he wanted.

"Maybe you should read something besides that science fiction garbage."

"It's not garbage! It's the truth!" Sandy stormed out of the room. Everyone sat and listened to him pound upstairs and slam his bedroom door. Please, would someone say, "There's something really wrong with that boy"?

But all that happened was Daddy said, "Jesus, Mary, and Joseph, it's a case of galloping gonads!" Mom gave him a dirty look—probably for the word "gonads"—but he always ignored her dirty looks. He got up from the table. "Well—time to get to work."

Robin eyed her father. He was phony, too. He did go to work once in a while. Lately, he'd been doing radio commercials, and she kept hearing his familiar voice talking about cars or Listerine or some other thing. But she knew he didn't have a commercial to do today. Sam, his agent, sent him out a lot for auditions, though. Her father even had an understudy part in a good play last year. She couldn't remember the name of it. He kept talking about how it was going to run for years. When

Tom Noonan got tired of the lead, then he'd have it, and *then* they'd see! But the play closed after the tryouts in Philadelphia. Mostly, when he went to audition, he'd come home without a part and smelling strongly of whisky. Her father's drinking worried Robin. She knew it worried her mother, too. Sometimes Robin heard them fighting about it.

"For Christ's sake, Birdie, do you ever see me drunk?" he asked, yesterday.

"The question is, JJ, do I ever see you *sober*?" her mother answered, in a calm, quiet voice. A minute later, Robin heard the front door slam hard. Oh, how she hated it when they fought and he left the house. When that happened, he *always* came back drunk, stumbling up the stairs, mumbling to himself or, worse, singing off key at the top of his lungs.

Robin pushed her poached eggs and toast around on the plate. Her breakfast was cold now, and disgusting. Her parents couldn't have believed what Sandy said about writing a play. They knew he was not writing any play. And yet, in some strange way, her mother did believe it. *Gran* believed it. They were *doctors*! She wasn't a doctor; she was only twelve years old, but *she* knew her brother wasn't normal. She just couldn't figure out what was wrong with him. For a while, she thought it was something that ran in the family because of Aunt Addie. But when she asked Gran if she and Sandy could catch what Aunt Addie had, Gran reminded her that Aunt Addie wasn't really a relative. Robin still worried that it might be something catching, like chicken pox. She decided she'd ask her grandmother. Gran never laughed at her or told her she was a silly girl—or got mad, like Mom did when she asked *her* a couple of days ago what was wrong with Sandy.

"What a stupid thing to say!" Mom had said, her eyes blazing. "I never want to hear you say anything like that again! There's nothing wrong with either of you!"

"May I be excused?" Robin asked, pushing her chair back. "I need to get to school." That wasn't quite true—she had plenty of time—but "school" was a magic word around here. You could do anything so long as it was educational. She did not go up the stairs to her bedroom to get her books, or even out the front door. Instead, she headed downstairs, sliding her loafers off so she wouldn't make too much noise.

Somehow, she had to find out what sickness her brother had. Telling them he was writing a play was a clever answer—sometimes he was very good at covering up his weirdness. But she knew that Sandy wasn't the least bit interested in the theater. He was only interested in what was inside his own head. It used to be his toy soldiers and war games; now, it was all space stuff. His room was stacked to the ceiling with science fiction magazines. He had scrapbooks full of newspaper stories about flying saucers. Maybe he *was* reading too much of that stuff and that was why he was getting so peculiar. But she had a sick feeling in the pit of her stomach that it wasn't reading that was bothering her brother.

Morgan went down the stairs slowly. She knew they weren't any steeper than they'd ever been; they just seemed that way because she was getting older. She twitted herself, "Older! There's a euphemism for you! You're *old*, that's what it is, and everything's beginning to fall apart." She was just grateful that, so far at least, *she* wasn't becoming senile. She'd already told Birdie, "If that happens to me, I want you to give me something to put me out of my misery."

Well, Birdie had a fit! *No, no, don't ask me to do that, it isn't fair.* So she'd grasped her daughter by the shoulders and looked down at her very seriously—sometimes it was damned convenient, being a big woman—and said, "Birdie, I'm begging you. When the day comes that I no longer know who you are, put me to sleep. Remember how awful it was to visit poor Adelaide." She made Birdie promise.

Morgan went to her office every day, although she was no longer seeing patients—not on a regular basis, at least. Every once in a while, a desperate woman would come knocking on the downstairs door, needing to be pregnant or needing not to be pregnant. Morgan always saw them and did her best. But she knew she probably shouldn't. At her advanced age, who knew what mistakes she might make.

She was deep into her own thoughts when she entered her office, so she was really taken aback to see Robin sitting behind her desk, poring through one of the big thick medical books, oblivious to anything else. She studied her granddaughter, noting the worried frown. The child was sharp. Poor Robin had been so sure she was to blame for Addie's decline because she'd yelled at the old lady and made her cry. It had taken a lot of talking to convince her that senile dementia wasn't anyone's fault, and certainly not Robin's. And she had only been nine or ten—very young; yet so sensitive, so caring. *She'll make a wonderful doctor,* Morgan thought. She laughed at herself for assuming that Robin was going to be a doctor. Just because the child looked so much like her, that didn't mean she was going to be like Morgan.

"What are you looking for, honey?"

Robin jumped, flushed, then got that determined look on her face that said she was not going to make excuses or apologies, and was just going to finish whatever it was she'd started. *Like me,* Morgan thought proudly.

"I think I found it, Gran."

"And *it* is—?"

"What's wrong with Sandy."

So. Robin hadn't been fooled after all, Morgan thought. Well, of course she hadn't. Nobody was fooled—except maybe JJ, who was too self-involved to notice much of anything. Birdie knew; she just refused to let it into her brain. Robin might be only twelve, but she had a way of looking at the world straight on, never flinching or turning away because something was too terrible to see. *Like me,* Morgan thought again. Looking into Robin's intelligent eyes, she decided it would be stupid to keep her secret any longer.

She told Robin the whole story. About her ancestors hearing voices and walking into the Sound, the epilepsy, the strange behavior—all of it. Almost all. "Now, Robin, you have to remember that some of the things I'm talking about happened three hundred years ago, two hundred years ago. Things that *supposedly* happened. They might not be totally true. Of course . . ." She hesitated.

"What, Gran? Now it's the important part. I can tell. Please tell me. I can take it."

She paused, then thought, *Why not.* "I had a sister named Rebecca. Becky."

"I know that, Gran. My middle name is after her. Robin Rebecca."

Morgan pressed her lips together. "I asked your mother not to use that name, but she always did precisely what she wanted."

"What's wrong with having your sister's name?"

"She was—she was insane, sweetheart. She seemed to be a perfectly lovely, good-natured child until, oh, ten or eleven, when she began having strange nightmares. Then they became waking dreams. And by the time she was sixteen or seventeen, she was hearing things and seeing things, sure that evil spirits were after her. Yes, we all believed in spirits in my family, Robin. Indians believe that everything has a spirit, even trees and rocks. The Algonquin Indians, the Pequots, which were my people, they believed that. It made them respect every thing on earth. But of course, there were evil spirits, too." She sighed deeply. "Most of the time, Becky saw and heard only the bad spirits. Poor Becky."

"What happened to her, Gran?"

"I don't know, honey. The last time I ever saw her, your mother was an infant, only a few months old. Becky spoke to me, said she was happy I'd had a baby, and then suddenly, she ran away from me into the woods. I'm sure she's dead now."

"And Mom still named me after her?"

"Oh, I never told your mother the whole story about Becky, only that I had a sister named Rebecca and that your mother looked like her."

"Why? Why didn't you tell her?"

Morgan paused, then decided what the hell. "I was afraid to tell her. I was afraid ... that she would get sick. I was so relieved when she didn't. I thought, now we're safe. I've had a female child and she's all right. I always believed it was a curse that struck only the women in my family ..." She stopped, her eyes filling.

Robin said, "But, Gran, it's not a curse. It's a mental illness. That's what it says in the book. Shiz—" She stumbled over the word.

"Schizophrenia. Yes. I know it's an illness. I knew it and yet I was still convinced that it was a curse put on us. I thought only females ... And now ... Sandy ..." Once again, tears threatened. She swallowed, willing them back.

"You think so, too. You think he's got schizophrenia."

"Yes. It's not quite the same as it was with Becky. But, yes, it *is* the same."

Robin stood up, looking very serious. "We have to tell Mom. We have to tell her right now."

"Sit down, Robin. I told her already. At least I tried. She wouldn't believe me."

Morgan wondered if she should tell Robin about Bird, who came to her in dreams. She'd seen her ancestress just a few nights ago, the first time in a long, long time. Bird was holding a baby in her arms, holding it out to Morgan, only Morgan couldn't reach it, no matter how far she stretched. She had awakened, in darkness, feeling panic. Why panic? She couldn't imagine. She couldn't even begin to understand what the message might be.

A telephone rang, down the hall in Birdie's office, and was picked up. No, Morgan thought, she would not tell Robin about Bird. Enough strange family history for one session. They both sat very still, waiting. After a short time, they heard Birdie's office door open and her heels click on the floor as she came down the hall. Morgan hoped that Birdie was finally ready to acknowledge the truth. For some reason, she just *knew* that the phone call had been about Sandy.

Birdie walked into her mother's office, looking pale and pinched. "That was Sandy's headmaster. He wants me to come in to see him. Sandy's been cutting classes, days at a time. *I* don't know where he goes. How am I supposed to know where he goes?" As she spoke, her voice rose higher. Her cheeks were fiery. "He said if Sandy keeps on this way, they'll 'have to let him go.' Kick my son out of school! Well, we'll see about *that*!" She didn't even seem to notice that Robin was sitting there, long after she should have been on her way to Packer.

"First things first. I'll go up and read the riot act to that young man. Then, out go all those junky magazines! It's time for Sandy to buckle down. If he doesn't, he'll be sent straight to military school."

Morgan stared at her, as did Robin. Neither said a word. Birdie didn't wait for them to speak. She spun around and ran down the hall and up the stairs as if demons were close on her heels.

34

June 1955

Why did they all want to believe, so badly, that Sandy was going to get better? For two years, they'd tried everything and nothing ever changed. *Except for the worse,* Robin thought. *It could always get worse, and it usually did.*

As soon as Mom discovered that Sandy was *really* flunking out of Poly Prep, she called Dr. Snow and asked him to please be Sandy's shrink. Of course he said yes. He could never say no to her mother. The school gave Sandy a second chance—and then another and another and another. He was smart, weird but smart. Recently, though, he couldn't concentrate on anything. He told Robin that the static in his head blotted out the words on the page. He saw Dr. Snow three times a week, but it never seemed to do much good. He still said weird things or turned his back on everybody or suddenly ran out of the room. Dr. Snow told them Sandy was always trying to escape the voices.

"There's no escaping those voices," Gran said. Everyone turned to look at her.

"How do you know that?" Mom said.

Gran opened her mouth, and Robin thought, *Now she'll tell about her sister Becky.* But she didn't. She just said, "He never does, does he? Surely you've noticed his lips moving, Birdie. No? The next time he turns his head away, look carefully. You'll see. He's talking back to the voices in his head. He thinks if he turns his head away, we can't see what's happening. Well, it looks like some of us *can't*."

Mom just wouldn't get it. She was totally stubborn. She kept saying he'd outgrow it, or that he was much better, didn't everyone think so. Nobody ever agreed with her, because nobody had the heart to keep telling her that Sandy wasn't getting any better. Last year, Sandy had begun to yell back at the voices nobody else could hear. He'd pace back and forth in his room at night, hollering. Oh, God, he sounded so . . . *tortured*. Robin always wanted to go and try to comfort him. But the few times she'd got out of bed and knocked on his door, he just screamed at her to go away.

The next thing was that he claimed his food was being poisoned. He refused to eat. Robin told him she would be his food taster, like the kings of yore. He liked that idea, and for a while, after she took a bite and didn't fall to the ground, dead, he'd eat the meal.

Even that didn't last. He began to accuse *her* of poisoning his food. She didn't die because she was immune; it was a special poison that would attack only Alexander Malone. Robin talked and talked to him but nothing convinced him. So Gran took over. She said she had special Indian magic and that she would shop for his food. She lined one of the kitchen cupboards with paper and said that cupboard was only for him.

Then he began to talk back to the TV, even after it was turned off. Usually he was careful and waited until he was alone in the room. But since he'd begun shouting all the time, the whole family couldn't help but hear what was going on.

You couldn't ever relax, because then Sandy would do or say something completely new and awful. He wouldn't believe there was anything wrong with him, either. Once Robin said to him, "Look, Sandy. You say there are voices yelling in the dining room. I don't hear them. Mom doesn't hear them and Dad doesn't hear them. Gran doesn't hear them. Even Dr. Snow can't. Don't you think it's at least *possible* that the voices are coming from your head?" She thought he was going to kill her; the look he gave her was murderous.

"You know, *you* could be the enemy, too, little sister!" he said, in a voice that sent chills down her spine. So she never said anything about it again.

Sandy's craziness was—well, crazy. Robin thought he'd hate her forever for saying the voices were in his head, but he didn't. About a month ago, she was the one who talked him into taking his meds again. He'd almost never take them. Naturally, since he thought everything in the world was poisoned. But that week, he was in a panic over Ernie Kovacs on the radio. "He's sending evil thoughts out to get me," Sandy said, and she could see that he was really terrified. Ernie Kovacs was so funny; his show was one of her favorites. But if Sandy heard threats instead of jokes, then it was bye-bye Ernie Kovacs.

She swore to Sandy that there would be no more evil thoughts coming from the radio, but Ernie Kovacs had said that first Sandy had to take his pills. Of course, Sandy would only take half—what did he think, that he would only half die if they were really contaminated?—but at least some of the medicine got into his system.

Thorazine. It really was good. After a few days, Sandy's lips had stopped moving all the time, which meant the voices weren't at him every minute. When Dr. Snow changed the dose, and the pill was a new color, Sandy just took it every meal without question. He began to sit down to eat with the rest of the family. In a couple of weeks, he seemed so much better that everyone kind of relaxed.

Sandy liked popular music—when he was healthy. He really liked "You Gotta Have Heart," one of the songs from *Damn Yankees*. He learned the words in about two seconds and even began singing along with the kitchen radio. That made them all happy, but Daddy became convinced that Sandy was "over that thing he had" and by God, he was going to end up a chip off the old block. Especially when Sandy said he wanted to see *Damn Yankees*. As far as Daddy was concerned, that was proof positive that Sandy was perfectly normal. There couldn't be anything wrong with someone who wanted to see a show! They went by themselves—"just us guys," Daddy said.

Daddy didn't get home that night until after midnight. The three of them were wide awake, Gran and Mom and Robin, worried and waiting. "If he's taken Sandy to one of those damned bars—" Mom muttered and then clamped her mouth shut and changed the subject. *As if I don't know he drinks too much,* Robin thought. But when Daddy let himself in, he wasn't even a little bit tipsy. He looked exhausted and scared.

"He loved it. As a matter of fact, he was singing along pretty damn loud, and I had to tell him to keep it down. But I don't think that was it . . ."

"What, JJ? What happened, for God's sake?"

"I'm trying to tell you, dammit! During the curtain calls, Sandy suddenly bolted and disappeared."

"Disappeared!" Gran said.

"Yeah. He was gone so fast—I ran all the hell over the place, but there wasn't even a sniff of him. Nobody had seen him. He must have been running like the wind. I called the cops and they went looking for him, but no dice."

"JJ, where *is* he?" Mom's voice was tight and angry.

"How the hell am *I* supposed to know where he is? I told you, he just turned and ran and none of us could find him. I think he'll come home. I mean where the hell *else* does he have to go? You'll see, sometime in the middle of the night, he'll be ringing the front doorbell, waking us all up."

But it didn't happen that way. Three long worrisome days went by and no Sandy. Dr. Snow thought Sandy might have come by his office, and he had people search all the closets and hallways at the hospital. No soap. Then one afternoon, Colleen Mulligan came running into the kitchen, shouting for "anyone, anyone who's home!" Robin was home. It was after school and she'd been upstairs doing her social studies home-work on American Indians, thinking how stupid the textbooks were. They didn't seem to know a *thing* about real Indians. When she heard Colleen yell, she ran right downstairs. Colleen said she'd gone out to dump the garbage into the can and she'd heard funny noises from under the house—under the back steps. There was a tiny crawl space there.

Robin rushed out and began moving the garbage cans, making a lot of noise on purpose. Then she knelt down and called: "Sandy! Are you there? I know you're there. What are you doing under the house, for God's sake?"

She couldn't see him, because it was pitch black, but he was there, all right. She could hear his teeth chattering, despite the nice warm day. "Come on out, Sandy. It's me, Robin."

"Can't."

"Why not?"

"The devil is after me. He jumped off the stage to get me. So I ran."

"You ran faster than the devil?" Robin said. "Good for you. Well, the devil's not here, so you can come out."

"The devil wants me."

Robin decided it was stupid to try to argue with him about that, so she changed the subject. "Aren't you hungry?"

"Starving. Can you bring me a sandwich, Robin?"

"No, Sandy, you have to come out before you can have a sandwich." When he didn't immediately respond, she asked, "What kind do you want?" and named all his favorites: "Egg salad? Tuna fish? Cold chicken?"

"Egg salad?" In a minute, out he came, all scrunched up and filthy, his eyes darting around. He was as bad as he'd been before the Thorazine.

Dr. Snow came to see Sandy later on that day, and he told Mom that Sandy should be in the hospital. But she insisted that she could take good care of him right here at home. After all, she was a physician; she'd make sure he took all his meds. Gran tried to tell her that it wasn't so simple, that she knew something about this kind of sickness, but nobody wanted to hear her. Including Daddy.

"Now, Mother Becker," Daddy boomed, in his big actor voice, "the boy simply has an overactive imagination. The curse of the Malones. Some R and R, and he'll be right as rain." Of course, Daddy was wrong. As usual.

Robin went to Sandy's room every day to see how he was doing, and she knew he was afraid of absolutely everything and everybody—even her. Day before yesterday, he stopped eating because the devil had got into all the food, and they had to order him Chinese takeout. Robin knew that, in a day or two, even food from the China Tea Cup would have poison in it, and they'd have to think of something else or he'd just starve himself to death.

This morning, Gran was still upstairs. It had rained yesterday, which meant that today Gran's knees were really bothering her. She didn't want to come down for breakfast because it hurt too much to negotiate the stairs. Robin took a tray up to her with toast and orange juice and coffee and three morning newspapers.

"If I find myself keeping to my room much more," Gran told Robin, "I'll have to move downstairs. Maybe we could put a cot into the old pantry."

"Oh, Gran, we can do better than that! How about a big featherbed in front of the stove?"

"Like I was the family pet? No, I think I'd rather bed down in my office." They joked back and forth about it. Gran was nearly eighty-seven years old—her birthday was in August—but she was still as sharp as a tack, reading the morning papers cover to cover and still getting all upset over injustice in the world. She was a neat lady. Robin gave her a big kiss and said, "I'll come up as soon as school's over and see if you need anything."

"Promise you won't tell anyone," Gran said, smiling, "but you're my favorite."

"Your favorite what?"

"Now that would be telling!"

By the time Robin got home in the afternoon and went up to check, Gran was feeling a lot better. "I think I can make it downstairs," she said.

"Well, I'm glad you waited for me to come home, Gran, because I don't think you should try it all alone. What if you fell?"

"I'm not going to fall, not with you there."

A little while later, Gran began making her slow way downstairs with her cane, Robin hovering above her. They were halfway down when Sandy, eating a peach, headed upstairs.

As soon as he saw Gran, he began shrieking. Then he cowered, covering his face with his arm, and whimpered. "Devil!

Please, no. I'll be good, just leave me alone. Please leave me alone!" He shrank back against the wall.

Gran kept moving carefully down, talking to him in a calm voice. "Sandy, this is Gran. Your grandmother. You know me, darling, I'm not the devil. I'll give you an Indian charm that will keep him away from you. It's a very strong charm. It always works."

Robin thought he was calming down. But as Gran came near him, Sandy shouted, "I see your pitchfork! Beelzebub! Prince of Darkness! Thought you could fool me?" Then he shoved her cane away, knocking it out of her hand. It went tumbling down the stairs and Gran lost her balance. Oblivious, Sandy gave her a shove and rushed past. Robin yelled, "No! Gran, wait!" She wanted to move but she felt frozen. Gran tried to grab onto the banister, but missed it and went bumping down the stairs. Robin just stood there screaming and screaming.

Sandy kept going upstairs, pushing Robin aside, too. He ran into his room and slammed the door. Robin, scared to death, made herself stop shrieking and ran down to Gran, who looked . . . broken. One leg was bent in a strange way under her. She lay very still, her head on the bottom step, her feet pointing up. But she opened her eyes when she heard Robin's breathing and tried to smile. "I think—hip's broken. Call your mother. Get Wendroff."

"Oh, Gran! You're hurt! I'll kill him! I'll kill him!"

"Robin. Hush. Call hospital. Please. Bring me three aspirin—water—pillow for head. Scoot!"

Robin scooted. She dialed her mother's telephone at the hospital because she knew it by heart. Mom was on rounds, but her secretary, Marie, said she'd send the ambulance and let Dr. Malone know what had happened—"and don't worry, sweetie, they'll move double-time when they hear it's Dr. Becker."

Robin brought aspirin, water, and a pillow to her grandmother, then sat with her until the front door burst open. It was Mom, all scared and pale and demanding to know what happened. Robin could feel her grandmother giving her a hard look, but she pretended she didn't notice. Her mother had to know. "Sandy pushed her," Robin said. "He *made* her fall down the stairs."

Gran said "Robin!" and, at the same time, Mom said "Sandy!" in almost the same disapproving voice.

"Well, he did, Gran," Robin insisted. "He did, Mom."

The ambulance came, but Gran refused to go to the hospital. She wanted to have her hip set by Dr. Wendroff, and then go to her room and be in her own bed. Mom said, "Do it! Do as she asks! There's a phone in the front hall."

Everything was crazy for a while. Robin called Dr. Wendroff's office from the house phone while her mother talked to Dr. Snow on her office line.

"We can't handle Sandy any more, he has to be hospitalized . . . Isn't that what you've been saying for months, Terry? Yes, dammit, there's a reason I've suddenly changed my mind. Sandy pushed my mother down the stairs, and I think her hip is broken, maybe a leg, too, and at her age—Okay. Right away would be fine. The sooner you can hospitalize him, the better."

Daddy came home in the middle of it all, and he shouted, "Oh, no, he is not! You're not going to put away my boy!"

Mom said, "Terry. As soon as possible, do you hear me?"

Daddy began pacing back and forth in front of her, shouting no son of his was going to the funny farm and get locked in a rubber room—stuff like that.

Mom paid no attention to him until she'd hung up. Then, she said, in a voice that you knew you couldn't argue with, "JJ. Listen to me. Sandy is sick. He pushed my mother down the stairs. He thought she was the *devil*." Her voice broke a little, and she stopped and swallowed hard. Then she said, "And he's going to the hospital to get this thing taken care of. And that's final."

"Does my opinion count for nothing around here?"

"JJ, for the love of God! Can't you hear? He nearly killed his *grandmother*. He's having hallucinations! Can't you *try* to understand what's going on?"

Robin thought her father would explode. His face got dark red and his eyes narrowed, the way they did when he was really mad. Then he turned and stormed out. Before he slammed the front door, he yelled, "If my son is not welcome in this house, then I won't stay here, either!" Bam!

So, Daddy wasn't around to watch Sandy struggle against the attendants who had ahold of him, one by his armpits and the other by his feet. Sandy wriggled like a large worm, yelling curses and begging to be set free, then threatening to kill them or crying that he was being attacked. Robin watched from the top of the steps. She wished he'd stop hollering; everyone on Clinton Street could hear him. She wished she could say a magic word and he'd be cured. She wished they would be gentler with him, even if he was hard to handle. He'd got very strong, suddenly.

But she was not sorry to see him go. Right now, she *wanted* him to go to the hospital. She was totally furious with him. She had been willing to put up with a lot of shit because she felt so sorry for him. But he'd gone too far, attacking Gran, the best person in the whole world! Robin knew he *needed* to be in the hospital. She was just glad that Dr. Snow had ordered the attendants not to put him in a straitjacket—"restraints," they called it. That would have been so humiliating and horrible! On top of everything else!

Terry Snow was standing behind her. He put a hand on her shoulder. "I know this is tough stuff, Robin."

She shook her head. "No, he's got to have help, Dr. Snow. I don't know why Mom—"

"Aw, Robin, your mother was hoping against hope . . . After all, he's her firstborn child, it can't be easy for her. In my business, we call it denial. But now, we'll be able to keep an eye on him. We'll make sure he takes his new meds, too. I have high hopes for Thorazine. I've seen it work wonders on some of my patients."

"As nutty as my brother?" Saying it out loud was like biting on a sore tooth—painful but a relief, somehow.

"Even nuttier, honey. But you just wait. He'll be a changed Sandy."

God, she hoped so. She watched the attendants strap him onto a gurney and push it into the back of the ambulance. At least he wasn't going to Bellevue. For now, he'd stay in the

Psych section of Cadman Memorial, where Mom could visit him every day. And where Terry Snow could make sure Sandy's meds weren't giving him terrible side effects. He said if the Thorazine didn't do the job, or if Sandy kept on refusing to take it, there was another new one, Stelazine. Dr. Snow felt that in the hospital, they'd be able to monitor him better, and then they could see exactly what was what.

Her mother came out of the house; Robin could hear her sniffling behind her. "Oh God, I can't believe this is happening," she said. Dr. Snow made comforting noises. "Are you *sure*, Terry?" she said, in a kind of desperate voice.

"That Sandy needs to be hospitalized? Of course I'm sure. I wouldn't put any of you through this if I weren't. But, Birdie, considering what happened—"

She interrupted him. Mom didn't want to be reminded of what had happened. "He could go into remission," she stated, as if Dr. Snow hadn't said anything. "Twenty to thirty percent of patients never have a recurrence of the original breakdown." She'd already said that about a million times. She just couldn't face it. *I'm acting more like the grownup than she is,* Robin thought. Despite her firm talk on the phone to Dr. Snow, it had taken *hours* to convince Mom to sign the papers for Sandy to be put into the hospital.

"Mom, he's getting worse and worse. You must see that. Even if he *does* go into remission, shouldn't he be in the hospital until he does?" She didn't dare add, "And now he's gotten dangerous," because she'd get killed if she said it.

The ambulance finally left, taking Sandy to Cadman Memorial's psych floor. Daddy was gone. And Gran lay upstairs in her bed with her hip and leg in a big cast. Gran's eyes were closed most of the time, all the life just drained out of her. It wasn't fair, Robin thought. Tears leaked from her eyes and her shoulders began to shake. Dr. Snow put his hand on her shoulder and said, "Don't worry, Robin. We're going to do our damnedest for Sandy."

But it wasn't Sandy. It wasn't Gran, either, although they were both part of it. It was everything. Terry Snow had always been her favorite doctor; she'd been so sure he was the smartest man on earth. She'd always planned to be a shrink, just like him, when she went to medical school. But Dr. Snow hadn't been able to help Sandy. The medication was no good, and she was sure the next medication wouldn't be any good, either. All of Mom's patients, all of Gran's, too, were always so in awe of them. *And so was I,* Robin thought. She had always believed that doctors were magic, but better than magic because they had science. She had really believed that doctors could make *anything* better. How stupid could you be!

And all her mother could talk about was Daddy. "Where do you think he went, Terry? I know him, he'll get drunk and get into a fight or be hit by a car— Oh God, what am I talking about? My mother is lying upstairs, maybe dying, and I'm still worried about JJ! Oh, God, what is wrong with me?" And she burst out crying. "What if he meant it? What if he never comes back?"

Gran was dying? Really dying? Robin turned, pushing past both of them, and took the stairs two at a time.

She tiptoed into Gran's room. Gran made no sign she had heard her. Robin walked to the bed and picked up her grand-mother's hand, crying hard. She was making a lot of noise, but she didn't care.

Then Gran squeezed her hand and said her name in a whisper as thin as a shadow.

"Yes, Gran."

"Death, Robin."

"Yes, Gran."

"Not frightening . . ."

Robin tried to say, "I'm glad," but no words would leave her throat, it was so clogged.

". . . Very tired, my sweet girl. So tired. My spirit wants to leave . . . See all my family . . . and my darling Alex."

"No, Gran, your spirit isn't leaving! Don't say that!"

"Too tired to mend this broken body. Too tired . . ."

She was silent for so long that Robin was afraid she'd died. "Gran? Gran!"

"I had a good long life. Healed many. Helped many. Good husband. Good daughter. Wonderful granddaughter. You. Just like me." She stopped and breathed hard, as if she had been climbing. When she spoke again, her voice was stronger, all of a sudden. "Never told Birdie about . . . Quare Auntie and Becky . . ." She was smiling and holding tightly to Robin's hand, although her eyes were still closed. "My only regret . . . except for . . ." Her voice was almost gone.

"No, Gran, wait!" Robin cried. "Wait! Don't go yet! Don't leave! It's too soon! I haven't *done* anything yet! You have to wait until I'm grown up!"

Her grandmother's lips moved in the shape of "You are" but no sounds came out. And then suddenly she stopped breathing.

"Wait," Robin whispered. "Just another minute." But she could see that Gran's spirit had flown away, like a bird, just the way she had always told Robin it would.

"No, no, no!" Robin shouted. Now everyone was gone! Everyone who cared about her. She was truly and completely alone in this world and would be, forever. Her head fell back, and she let out the dreadful sounds of grief.

35

August 1960

The climbing roses in the garden had gone wild and had traveled off the fence, sending shoots up the back of the house, over the porch roof and on up, clinging to the brick. Birdie kept saying it couldn't be good for the house, that they really should be cut back, but there was never anyone around willing to do it. Anyway, it looked so pretty, like a pink and red carpet. Colleen, who had long ago taken over the care of the garden, hated to cut any living thing—which meant the garden was usually a riot of colors. The crabapple tree, a pink cloud in early spring, now, in August, had started to form fruit, and its branches drooped a little from the weight. Colleen had also filled the four half barrels with red and pink begonias. They looked splendid in spite of the heat and humidity. She'd also hosed off the black iron furniture and swept the brick paths. Everything was neat and clean, as befitted a memorial service.

Birdie tried to feel sad, but she just couldn't. Her mind kept wandering. There was quite a little crowd here this afternoon. All the Mulligans, naturally, except for Jim and Brian, who would have been fired if they'd stayed away from the job. They were in construction and a good thing, too, since Brooklyn Heights was renovating and building like there was no tomorrow. This landmarks thing was going to be very good for the neighborhood—"and for the Mulligans, too," Colleen liked to say.

Standing way at the back were two teachers from Poly Prep, a man and a woman. The headmaster had sent his regrets. Colleen had had a thing or two to say about that, her lips pursed tight with her outrage. Birdie really didn't care. She just wanted it to be over. All the doctors from the hospital were here. Terry Snow, of course. Terry was speaking, in fact, and Birdie told herself she really had to pay attention. Sitting next to her were Robin and Pamela Boone, Sandy's favorite nurse at the Warrenstown Hospital for the Insane. Pamela looked to be about the same age as Sandy—would have been. *If I were Catholic, I'd cross myself right now, like Colleen does every time the subject comes up,* Birdie thought. *Too bad I'm not.*

Sandy is dead. Robin kept repeating the words, hoping to bring up a tear or two, but it was no use. Sandy had really died a very long time ago—maybe at birth, even though people kept telling her that schizophrenia happened all of a sudden in the late teens or early twenties. But they hadn't lived with her brother. As far back as she could remember, Sandy had been—maybe not nuts, but very goddam strange.

They were all gathered today for a memorial service, not a religious one, just Dr. Snow talking a little bit about Sandy's blunted and blasted life.

"There was no question about Sandy's intelligence," Dr.

Snow was saying. "Most of the time, it made him miserable, because he was acutely aware that he was not considered normal and would never live what is considered a normal life. But he knew enough to . . ."

Robin stopped listening. Obviously nobody was going to say that Sandy had committed suicide by hanging himself in the men's bathroom at Warrenstown. No, that would be a terrible thing, the truth. When Robin asked to say a few words about the real Sandy and how much he had suffered, and how terrible his medications made him feel so that he felt compelled to stop taking them—"all the real stuff"—her mother nearly had to be peeled off the ceiling. *Squawk, squawk, squawk.* Mom cared too damned much what other people might think. Like never letting Terry Snow stay overnight, even though they were going out together, finally.

Her mother never talked about where Sandy was, either. She almost never went to visit him. For two years, he'd stayed in the Psych ward at Cadman Memorial, so maybe Mom had seen him then, when it was easy to just pop in. But how about the two years he was in Bellevue? No, Robin was the one who went to Bellevue, even when he was really bad, so he'd at least know his family hadn't deserted him. A lot of the time, you couldn't talk to him; he'd think you were Joan of Arc or an alien from outer space. But Robin went, anyway.

She was standing right next to her mother, so she caught all the little turnings of Mom's head, all the nervous glances backward. Mom was hoping to see Daddy come in. What in hell did she want him for? He had walked out of the house five years ago, the day Sandy went into the hospital, and he'd never come back. Her mother eventually got divorce papers in the mail, from Mexico. Robin thought with great disdain that her mother was a fool, still loving a man who always drank too much and let her support him and then ran away at the first sign of real trouble. But Mom wouldn't give up; she kept hoping, waiting . . . Poor Dr. Snow, in love with her and so patient.

Robin wondered why Dr. Snow kept loving Mom in spite of how badly she treated him. He was a smart guy; he must know she was still waiting for JJ Malone; that the Mexican divorce wasn't quite real to her. It must be Mom's looks. She was beautiful. Robin thought it wasn't fair that her mother was tiny and curvaceous and delicate and gorgeous with a cloud of curly hair that had darkened to auburn. *I could've looked like her, but no. I had to be a giant with big feet and a big nose.* Although her straight hair was *finally* in style. Some people thought she looked a lot like Joan Baez, which she found neat, since she was part Indian, too.

If it hadn't been for Robin, poor old Sandy would have rotted in Bellevue. They didn't know what to do with him. Put him in straitjackets. Put him in cold baths. Put him in restraints. And it was such a horrible place, full of moaning and crying and other strange sounds. Every time Robin walked into the ward, she had to skip from side to side to avoid all the arms and hands that reached out to her. Some of them just wanted a little human contact, but some of them wanted to hurt. It was creepy.

When the doctor there suggested a frontal lobotomy, on account of Sandy's "aggressive behavior," Robin had put her foot down. "We've got to get him out of there, Mom," she'd said. "We've *got* to. Why can't he be someplace nice? There are all kinds of medications, now. Look, here's a list of mental hospitals. . . ."

To her surprise, Mom actually listened. She chose Warrenstown, which was in lower Putnam County, and not too far away, on the Hudson Line of the railroad. At Warrenstown, the doctors had put Sandy on Haldol, and his behavior improved so much, Robin couldn't believe it. He began to read again, and talk to other patients and stuff. The hospital suggested that Mom might like to try having him live at home, since she was a physician. Just on a trial basis, of course. But Mom became totally spastic! No, she was very busy with her practice, she wouldn't be able to properly watch over him. He'd need constant care . . . All that bullshit.

Robin said she'd take care of him. She'd always felt horrible about her brother's mental illness. She couldn't forget what her grandmother had said about thinking only the women in the family ever got it. The thought that somehow she got passed over, and that the illness meant for her had landed on Sandy instead, haunted her. She knew that was ridiculous, but she still felt that way. Or at least she felt responsible for him.

Her mother had said, "Remember what happened when you begged for a kitten and you said you'd take care of it?" Of all the stupid goddam things to say! "Jesus Christ," Robin exploded, "I was five years old, what did I know?" With maddening calm, her mother went on, "You still don't know what it takes to take care of a mentally ill person. He cannot come home. Period."

So Sandy had spent five years of his life in one hospital or another. And it was left to Robin to visit him, watching and hoping for signs of a cure, then for just a small sign of improvement. She finally realized that no improvement ever lasted for long. It didn't help that he'd sometimes refuse to take his meds, or he'd pretend to take them and then spit them out in the toilet. He hated the side effects so much. If they forced him, he got excited, and then they wrapped him up tight, usually in cold wet sheets, and put him in a room all alone. *No wonder he got violent, shut up in a nuthouse and treated like some kind of idiot.* If anyone did that to *her*, she'd get violent, too. She had tried to talk to his shrink about it, but Dr. Huffington couldn't hear what she was saying. He'd told her that kindness was beside the point.

"Your brother is suffering from a thought disorder, Miss Malone. He no longer goes logically from A to B to C. He flies from A to a letter in some other alphabet . . . omega, maybe. He'll be good for a while and suddenly, for no reason any of *us* can see, he'll accuse us of telling lies about him, or of plotting to kill him. I'm sorry," the doctor said.

And Robin said, between gritted teeth, "Did you hear what you said? 'He'll be good for a while . . .' Like he's five years old. He's a grown man. And even a nut deserves some respect, dammit! Especially a nut whose IQ is probably twenty points higher than yours."

That was the end of that conversation—and she was lucky, her mother told her, that it wasn't the end of her visits to Warrenstown.

"You really angered Dr. Huffington, Robin. Did you have to say that Sandy is smarter than he is?"

"I didn't say that. Well . . . not exactly. I just guessed that Sandy's IQ was higher than his." For a minute, she actually thought her mother was going to smile. But no such luck.

"Robin, grow up. Dr. Huffington is a well-known psychiatrist who could keep you from visiting your brother ever again. There's no point in annoying him. So, if you want to keep seeing Sandy, I suggest you use a little discretion."

"Dr. Huffington is a well-known jerk. Okay, okay. I'll behave."

She'd come to loathe doctors. Not Mom. Not Terry. But the profession. The only people, besides Terry Snow, who had ever treated Sandy with any kindness or any respect were the nurses—one in particular, Pamela Boone. She was just out of nursing school and Warrenstown was her first job. Robin was just starting CCNY; so they were more or less the same age. Pamela was a big tall girl, too, only she didn't seem awkward about it, the way Robin did.

"We're all that way, where I come from," Pam had said, with a laugh. "I guess it's the Scandinavian side of the family. My father always described me as a milkmaid. Well, he's a farmer, so maybe that's why." She was beautiful, Robin thought, with pink cheeks, big round blue eyes, and pale silvery blond hair in a long braid down her back or coiled into a neat bun at the back of her neck. And she was easy to talk to.

Pam liked her patients. She didn't mind that they were mentally ill. She wasn't afraid of their sickness. She thought if you really listened to them, even when they weren't making sense, and if you were nice to them, they would repay you by being nice back. That sounded right to Robin, and she was enormously grateful that someone in that place saw her brother as a person, not just a patient.

". . . Time to say farewell to Alexander Malone, better known as Sandy. He was chronically ill for much of his life and, in the end, this proved too much for him. But he told his nurse that he wanted to leave his body to Cornell Medical School in the hope that they might use it in their research, and perhaps find the answer that had eluded him. Or I should say, had eluded us, the doctors who tried to help him. Farewell, Sandy. Find us a cure."

Mom was absolutely pouring tears. "Oh, Terry, thank you. That was just beautiful. God, he was such a sweet little boy. And so good—! Never a moment's trouble! Who would've thought that—oh, God! Poor Sandy."

She really meant, Robin thought angrily, *Poor Birdie*. Even now, they couldn't say out loud that Sandy was schizophrenic, mentally ill, a nutcase, crazy. Why not? It wasn't *his* fault! Nobody was willing to mention, either, that he'd hanged himself because he couldn't stand the side effects of his medication: Haldol, the latest miracle antipsychotic drug. It had worked well on his symptoms. He stopped yelling at his voices. And he began to have actual conversations with people.

He was able to talk with Pam and tell her how he felt. She taught him how to play chess, and oh, God, how he loved it! He wanted her to teach him how to dance, but he couldn't do it because of the Parkinsonian side effects from Haldol. His legs were permanently stiff. His hands trembled so badly he couldn't even hold a spoon to eat. He told Pam he hated the trembling and the way his legs kept jerking. Also, it turned out that Haldol could bring out latent epilepsy, and all of a sudden, Sandy was having seizures.

Dr. Huffington didn't want to take Sandy off the Haldol because Sandy was "doing so well. He's so much easier to handle," he told Pam, and Pam, who had become friends with Robin, told her. Sandy could just keep on suffering, as long as he was easy for the doctor to handle. Robin was ready to kill Huffington. But Pam said don't bother, they'd only replace him with someone else just like him. "They all seem to be more or less like him."

To end the ceremony, two friends of Mom's, sisters, stood up and sang "Amazing Grace." Then it was over. Everybody began to stretch and chat, heading for the porch, where Colleen's sisters had been setting out food and drink on the big trestle tables.

Robin said, "You hungry, Pam?"

"A little, yes."

"Well, come on. We ordered all this stuff from Lasson and Hennigs, a terrific neighborhood deli, and it's really good."

"I liked what Dr. Snow said about Sandy—you know? That maybe his body and brain will help science cure schizophrenia."

"You know what, Pam? You're the only person in the entire world who will talk about Sandy—I mean, honestly, as if he were a regular human being."

"Well, Robin . . . he wasn't exactly *regular*, you know."

"And you can joke about it! That's because you accepted him the way he was! Most people would be too embarrassed to make a joke. You know what I mean?"

"Yes, Robin, I know what you mean. And I did accept him. He was interesting."

"For a nut," Robin supplied.

"Yeah. For a nut."

"It's so good to talk to you about him because you saw the same things I saw. And he must have loved you. He left you the note."

"Yeah," said Pam. "The note and all the Haldol he hadn't been taking. I thought I saw his lips moving a lot, but everytime I really looked at him, he stopped doing it. I never caught on, that he'd stopped taking his meds. He was awfully smart."

"For a nut."

"Yeah. For a nut." They smiled at each other. "And for a nut, he played a real good game of chess."

"He always loved war games," Robin said. "Isn't chess a war game?"

"It's supposed to be about strategy and planning ahead. But, just between us chickens? Yeah, it's a war game. Hey, you know what else he loved? This was just before—before—"

"What? Tell me."

"Monopoly. Isn't that a gas? A little kid's game. Except I love to play Monopoly. When I was in nursing school, a bunch of us used to play all the time. One of the girls had kept her set from when she was a little kid. It had the metal pieces. I always wanted to be the shoe. Isn't that strange? Other people wanted to be the ocean liner or the Scottie dog but Pam Boone only wanted to be an old shoe.

"I remember one day he was very agitated—your brother—

Sandy—and sometimes when his eyes began to dart around, I'd hold his hand and start talking to him. Real easy and low, you know. All I could think of that day was Monopoly, for some reason. So I described it to him and said what fun it was. He asked me to teach him. Of course I said I would. Hey, if the only thing I'd been able to think of was hootchy-kootchy dancing, and if he asked me to teach him that, I'd have said okay. If you ever get them to hear you, actually hear you . . . it's so great."

"Yeah," Robin agreed. "It didn't happen often, though."

"He really got into Monopoly. Made up people living in the houses and the big-time businessmen who owned the hotels. He talked in this Southern accent. I told him it was Atlantic City, in New Jersey, but he just ignored me. As far as he was concerned, it was a Southern town and it had a kind of life. He was really good at inventing stories while we played. If he hadn't been sick, I think he could have been a writer. Or maybe an actor."

Robin said, "Huh, my father should hear you say that. It was his great dream that Sandy would turn out to be another actor, like him."

"Your father? For some reason, I thought he was dead."

"He might as well be." She told Pam the story, as briefly as she could. "He went to the Coast again, looking for work in the movies. But the last I heard, he was teaching at an Arthur Murray studio."

"So you haven't seen him for—?"

"Five years. I guess. I try very hard not to think about him."

They helped themselves to salads and thinly sliced roast beef and turkey and Swiss cheese. Colleen had set up some small round tables in the yard, but nobody was sitting at them. The Mulligans were standing in a bunch, eating and talking. Her mother's colleagues from the hospital stood in another clump nearby.

"Come on, let's sit at a table."

As they began to eat, Pam said, "Now that you won't be coming to see your brother—what are your plans?"

"I wish I knew. Pre-med at CCNY was the plan. But I don't think that's what I want to do anymore. I was going to go to medical school and become a psychiatrist. Not anymore. I thought doctors really *helped* people, but look at poor Sandy."

"That's funny. I'm thinking of leaving Warrenstown—for almost the same reason. Sandy, I mean. I wonder if *anything* can be done for patients like Sandy. I wonder if I'm just wasting my time. But if I can't be a psychiatric nurse, I don't know *what* I'll do. If you don't want to be a doctor anymore, did you ever think of nursing?"

"Nursing! No, thanks! Woops, sorry, didn't mean to say it that way. But I think my mother would have a heart attack if I ever suggested nursing. She's going to be pretty fierce when I tell her I'm not going to medical school. But nursing? I think she'd rather I were mopping floors. I mean, she's a typical doctor when it comes to that." Pam nodded. "She's the other reason I'll never go to medical school, never."

"Robin, darling, perhaps you'd spread yourself around a little—as the co-hostess of this luncheon." Her mother had come up behind them without them knowing it. They both jerked around to face her, like guilty children. "Don't worry, I'll watch over Pamela." There was a tiny silence. Then Mom said, in a very different tone, "Wait a minute, Robin. What did I hear, just now? What did you say?"

"I've decided I don't want to be a doctor."

"You can't decide that. I mean, you can't decide anything just yet, you haven't even started college."

"Well, I might not do *that*, either."

"Robin, what in the world ails you? First, you refused to go to Cornell or Syracuse—both excellent schools—and insisted upon CCNY, of all the places. So go to CCNY. At least then, if you find you don't like it, you can always transfer. But not go at *all*? Is that what you're thinking? Give up an education altogether?"

Defiantly: "Yes."

"Well, I forbid it, absolutely forbid it. Don't bother to glare at me. I'm not easily intimidated. You are *not* going to waste your considerable intelligence, doing . . . What in the world were you planning on doing, if not college?"

"I don't know, Mom. Maybe I'll go on the road, like the Beatniks. Live in California. Or Spain. Yeah, that's it. I'll travel.

Go to Europe and wander around for a while, maybe to India or Nepal. Then maybe I'll know what I want to do. I might open a restaurant with some friends. We were talking—"

Her mother's voice had become very tight. "You'll do none of those things, young lady. This is part of your grieving for Sandy, but I can't allow you—"

Suddenly, cutting right through her words, Dr. Snow was there. "Now, Birdie, take it easy. Sometimes a year off is just what a teenager needs. Why go to college if you're not ready to decide what you want to study?"

"But, Terry, did you hear her? Nepal! Open a restaurant!"

He began to laugh. "Opening a restaurant? That wouldn't surprise *me*. Don't you remember, Birdie, when Robin was a little bitty thing and you used to bring her to the hospital and leave her in the Physicians' Lounge?" He turned to Pamela and continued: "Robin was everybody's pet. And she had a mouth on her, little as she was! I'll never forget the day one of the older doctors bent over her and said, 'Well, little lady, and are you going to be a doctor like Mommy when you grow up?' And Robin, here, shot back with, 'I don't want to be a doctor. I'm going to be a cooker!' Everybody laughed. Even you, Birdie."

"Just go say hello to everyone, will you, Robin?" Mom said, and walked away with Terry. Robin sat very still, feeling somewhat stunned. Unless she was as crazy as her brother had been, her mother had just set her free. Apparently, she wasn't going to insist that Robin start school in September. She could feel the smile spreading across her face.

As she got up, Robin said to Pam, "Don't move, please. Don't go away. We've got lots to talk about."

"Gotta get back to work." Pam rose and smoothed out her skirt. "But don't worry. We'll see each other sometime. We won't lose touch."

"Yeah. Sure," Robin said.

"No, really. I have a feeling we're fated to—I don't know— *do* something together. And my feelings always come true. You'll see."

SECTION SIX

Lt. Robin Malone,
Army Nurse Corps
Lt. Pamela Boone,
Army Nurse Corps
Capt. Harry Kaye, M.D.
Lt. Norma McClure,
Army Nurse Corps
Nguyen Ninh

36

Vietnam, October 1967

Robin Malone sat in the Huey, leaning out of the helicopter, looking at the countryside that flowed by beneath her. Her hair was whipping around her face, and she had to keep pulling strands out of her eyes and mouth. The familiar scenery sure looked good to her, eager as she was to get back to work and her friends. She'd just spent two weeks in Phu Bai, up the coast of the South China Sea, on loan from her regular assignment. Attacks on two of the firebases there had left a lot of wounded. They needed extra O.R. nurses, especially a senior nurse, and since she was charge nurse of the O.R. for the 161st Evacuation Hospital, that meant her. Phu Bai had been an interesting experience, to say the least, and it had helped put Art MacArthur out of her thoughts and her nightmares. You could not do your job in Nam if you let yourself get bent out of shape by somebody dying. Somebody was *always* dying.

She'd missed the One-Six-One, and was looking forward to seeing her friends at the compound by Moonlight Bay. Moonlight Bay wasn't its real name, of course; its real name was Deng Hua, but lots of things in-country got nicknamed. In fact, somebody had started to nickname her Birdie—until she frostily advised him that that was her mother's name. Her *real* name, the one on the birth certificate.

"No foolin'?" he'd said. "No foolin'," she'd answered. "Sorry, Robin. Sorry." He didn't even try for a joke about bird names running in her family; he didn't dare.

Looking down, she caught sight of the big white circle on

the ground with the red cross painted inside it. The white numbers, 161, stood out against the circle's dark blue rim. Robin Malone, R.N., lieutenant in the Army Nurse Corps, was back home. She remembered the first time she had arrived here, sitting in this same seat on a chopper. She had a vivid memory of looking down at the big bold numbers, and thinking, *Here I am. In Vietnam.* That was nine months ago. Nine months. Long enough to have a baby, if having a baby was what you wanted, which she didn't. Babies were definitely not in her life plans.

Today, sitting in the back of the Huey, were two Red Cross ladies—Doughnut Dollies, as the grunts called them. Girls, really; very very young, all giggly and excited. She wondered why in hell such nice young girls had chosen to put themselves into the middle of a war. For that matter, what in hell had compelled her to become an army nurse? Actually, she'd joined up to become an army nurse so she wouldn't have to stay at Harmony Hill Hospital, where she might bump into Mickey Aronson. Dr. Michael Aronson, who had supposedly loved her, only he really hadn't. Her eyes misted over and she cursed her own weakness. She had promised herself no more tears over Mickey.

The chopper was very noisy, very open, and the zoomie had a weird sense of humor. Right now, he made a sharp turn and a sweep, making her grab at the sides and taking her breath away. The sweep showed her the whole compound below, a mix of large Quonset huts, some of them joined together in a T shape, simple shacks, and a few real buildings. All of them had had parts blasted away. Close by, she could see the palm trees and that breathtaking curve of white sand beach with waves breaking peacefully onto the shore. Moonlight Bay. Then the zoomie made another sudden turn and they were going down, straight into the middle of the white circle painted on the ground, into the exact center of the red cross. A perfect landing.

Robin's ears were ringing when the engines were cut. "Here we are. The One-Six-One," the pilot announced, as if it had been a secret. "Okay, ladies," he shouted to the back. "Your home away from home! Welcome to Vietnam!"

One of the Red Cross girls looked quite green, Robin noticed. "Take deep breaths," she told her. "Swallow. That's right. The feeling should go away soon." The other one, a short stocky girl with dark hair cut so short she could have passed for a boy, looked grim but okay. The Doughnut Dollies in the compound would see to them. There were three of them, seasoned noncombatants—if there was such a thing as a noncombatant in this crazy war. They were standing with the rest of the group gathered in front of the hospital to greet the chopper today. So was Pam, with Dr. Jay Silverman and Dr. John O'Brien, two of the surgeons—and Joe, the bartender and *tummler*. Dr. Jay had labeled Joe "*tummler*," a Yiddish word meaning social director.

Joe was really Hubert (pronounced Hew-bear, French-style) Bisson, and he was a sergeant, but he had announced on his first day that bartenders were required by law to be called Joe. So he was called Joe. He'd been sent here for R and R; but he'd proven such a good organizer of volleyball games on the beach and contests of all kinds that the army, acting intelligently for a change, made him the manager of the rec center.

The minute her feet hit the ground, Robin felt the heat, moist and *heavy*, like a great weight on her back and shoulders. Whoo! She knew a grin was spreading over her face. She was so happy to see all these people. She really meant it when she said she was home. Funny, wasn't it? In the nine months here, New York, Brooklyn, Cadman Memorial Nursing School, the O.R. at Harmony Hill—yes, even Mickey, sometimes—all had faded into a dimly remembered background. This place, this motley collection of buildings with the beautiful beach, the dusty palm trees, the hootches and the bunkers, the recreation building with the big comforting bar, the stone building that used to be a rectory or a monastery or something else, and now served as her hootch—this lovely strange scarred place of beauty and fear, just a mile or so by dirt road from a real Vietnamese village—this alien place, halfway around the world from Brooklyn, had become *home*.

Robin grinned at Pam, who waved two bottles of champagne—good French champagne by the look of them—and grinned back. "Welcome home!" Pam called. "We have the makings of a real good reunion!"

Robin had never in her life been so surprised as the first day she'd come to the One-Six-One, and went to report to the C.O., Col. Barbara "Bingo" Batten. She'd given the colonel her smartest salute, announced her name, rank, and that she was reporting for duty, ma'am, when who walked in the door, looking at a bunch of papers and talking, but Pam Boone. Pam Boone!

"Colonel, these just came in from H.Q., and they thought you'd . . . Oh, I'm sorry, ma'am. The door was open and I didn't notice that you had—Oh, my God! Is that Robin Malone? Robin Malone from *Brooklyn*?"

"Pamela Boone?"

They both screamed, like two sorority girls, and jumped up and down, all military demeanor forgotten. Finally, they fell into each other's arms. Robin was so glad to see Pam, she couldn't believe it. Pam's promise to be in touch had not happened, of course. Robin hadn't thought about it much, hadn't been hurt or anything. Still—it was so great to see her!

"Pam, I don't believe it! Of all the places in the world—!"

"Ditto!"

Bingo Batten lit a cigarette and said, "I won't be too stupid if I assume you two know each other?"

In a rush, they both tried to tell her the story, talking over each other's sentences.

Finally, Bingo just waved them off. "Welcome to the One-Six-One, Lieutenant Malone," she said. "Lieutenant Boone will find you a hootch and fill you in. I'll see you later."

Pam had grabbed one of her bags and led her through the dust to a partly destroyed church rectory. "Or a monastery, or something, we're not sure." Six women lived there, three nurses and three Doughnut Dollies, each with her own tiny space. Robin thought it must have been a monastery, because of the tiny cells and little high windows cut in the stone. The cells had barely enough room for a narrow bed and some kind of storage for clothes and cosmetics and stuff. When other nurses were passing through, or U.S.O. girls, or new Doughnut Dollies, or whatever, they stayed there, too. Which meant the visitor got to sleep on the floor, but what the hell. The beds weren't much softer.

Every hootch had a bunker, in case of attack. Pam showed her theirs the first day, saying, "This is the important place. We have most of our parties in the bunkers. At least the ones that aren't on the beach or in the bar. If there's fighting anywhere—and there usually is—and if it's close—and it often is—you don't want to be outside."

Robin had looked around the low-ceilinged, dimly lit space. It was so bleak. "You party *here*?"

Pam laughed. "When it's lit by candles and the fireworks of distant, or not-so-distant, fighting, and stocked with bottles of wine or booze and glasses, courtesy Joe the bartender, it's terrific. Veddy romantic."

"Lots of—um—romance here?"

"You gotta be kidding! It's worse than a hospital!" She deepened her voice. "Hey, kid, this here's a war zone, you know. We could all be dead tomorrow. This could be your last chance."

"Yeah, yeah," Robin had agreed, laughing. Little did she know!

Anyway, they soon became best friends. They both hated the damned war and loved their patients. They were both smart and funny. And they were both topnotch O.R. nurses . . . the best.

The other nurse in the hootch was a gal named Norma McClure, a sturdy little body with blond hair cut Dutch-boy style and a narrow mouth that didn't like to smile. Norma was a good enough nurse, but she was so damned prissy and holier-than-anybody. She never let them forget she was R.C. and trained by the Sisters. Norma was the nurse they all loved to hate. Everyone liked to tease Norma because she'd been born without a sense of humor. On the other hand, she was quick to adopt the worst of the wounded. So, she was obviously a good person and couldn't be dismissed. She was from New York, too. She'd been at St. Francis Xavier as an O.R. nurse and she joined up because—"Can you believe this one, folks?" Joe had told them, laughing—"because she loved her country and wanted to serve it in its time of need. A patriotic nurse!"

To which Dr. Harry Kaye had remarked, "In this place? That's heresy!"

Dr. Harry Kaye had not been among the crowd waiting to meet the chopper. Harry was a surgeon and head of the O.R. at the One-Six-One. He was from Brooklyn—not Robin's part, he teased her, not the rich WASP part, but the *real* Brooklyn. Jewish Brooklyn. Flatbush. Canarsie. Greenpernt. Coney Island. Harry was savvy, sardonic, and very funny. She supposed he was cute: tall and skinny with flaming red curly hair and deep-set eyes the color of a stormy sea. He and Robin were buddies. They bantered all the time while working on patients, and they continued the wisecracks at Joe's bar after work. He was fun. And he was very helpful because he was an old-timer. "Why, I've actually been here a whole year and have survived to tell the tale," he told her.

When Robin first got to Vietnam, she became all involved with a pilot, a zoomie named Art MacArthur, a big drinker with prematurely white hair and a tattoo on his right bicep. One hot steamy night, when shells were falling close by, the two of them got hot and steamy themselves. For a short time, they were lovers. Then Art died—crashed his Huey into a mountain, reason unknown. Robin got herself very drunk, because she really didn't know what to do with her feelings. Okay, it was a war, dammit, and people kept dying because that's what wars were for—Harry explained that to her, very carefully. But not someone she knew! Not someone she'd slept with!

Harry had taken her under his wing, then. He talked her into drinking something other than bourbon neat—on the grounds that it had no vitamins—and kept appearing at her side whenever they had some spare time. Of course, it wasn't too difficult to find her, since she made a beeline for Joe's bar whenever she was off duty. Harry Kaye decided she needed to learn all the new dances. The snake. The monkey. The slide. The swing. After a while, she was sure he was making most of them up. But what the hell, he was a nifty dancer, and she felt wonderfully small and graceful dancing with him. He taught her the lyrics to all the new songs, too. Where he learned them so fast, she could never figure out. They did a whole lot of singing, she and Harry, loud and not always on pitch. They sang "Sugar Pie Honey Bunch" and "My Girl" at the tops of their voices—danced to them too, separately, eyes closed, each of them doing their own thing. Still, she couldn't sleep, and if by some chance, she fell asleep, she'd wake up crying. She dropped eight pounds in a couple of weeks.

Early one morning—early, as in 3 A.M.—Harry held her face in his two hands, and said, "Look here, Loot, you can't keep going this way, you know that? You'll be skin and bones. You'll ruin your career and your life. And then what'll I do for a charge nurse, answer me that?"

She began to cry, but he ignored her tears and told her that the hospital at Phu Bai had asked for O.R. nurses. "Why don't you ask Bingo to let you go up there for a while? You'll love it in Phu Bai. I hear it's the garden spot of Vietnam—or was it the Garden *State*, in which case it's just like Jersey and I won't let you go!" He always made her laugh. So, that's where she went, and where she was coming back from today. Dr. Harry's R and R. It had worked. She hadn't had a bad dream in a week, and she was feeling human. So where was he, the miracle worker?

A minute later, he ran out of the Quonset hut—late as usual, she thought—searching with his eyes. When he saw her, his face lit up, and she felt such a jolt in her belly, she almost grunted out loud. *Oh, my God,* she thought, with some surprise. *He loves me. And I love him.* She was amazed; the thought had not occurred to her before. *He loves me. I love him. We love each other. Well, what do you know?*

She grinned back at him and gave him the thumbs-up. He rewarded her with a wink so tender, it made her heart stop for a minute.

Just then—wouldn't you know!—a corpsman came running up, saying, "Dust off just called, and they're bringing in twenty wounded. Mass-cal. Let's get going." Mass casualty situation. They all got moving, double-time. Robin and the

other nurses ran into the hospital, and throwing extra tourni-
quets around their necks, got ready to clamp off blood vessels.
Stretchers were prepared. The nurses ran down each row with
practiced precision, hanging IVs all plugged and ready to go,
like a production line. The IVs were for that moment when the
doctor or the nurse said, "This one is saved." Expectants were
another matter. You made them comfortable and let them die
because there was nothing to be done. Expectants were usually head wounds, with brain damage.

During a mass-cal, Robin was always in charge, and she led
the way. She knew she was considered tough. Good. She'd
made herself that way. Her motto was *I never cave in: I never
give up; I save everyone I can.* And that's why she always did
triage: she was very good at it. She was also good at other
stuff. She'd done shrapnel extractions and closures, when
Harry was too busy, and it was often her voice in the O.R.
saying, "We're not going to lose this one." The doctors paid
attention to her. It was very satisfying. Every once in a while,
she thought that maybe she should have listened to her mother
and gone to medical school. But hey, done was done and who
cared? She was saving lives. That's all that mattered.

She heard the frantic chop-chop-chop of a Huey coming in,
saw the swirls of dust it kicked up. They were waiting and
ready as the gurneys were unloaded. Robin ran alongside the
first gurney, taking charge as she went, her eyes on everything
at once. She listened while the medics yelled out the vitals,
examining and judging on the run. She called out what was
needed, and then moved back to the next patient.

Harry was there, too, and Pam. Their voices crisscrossed
each other.

"This guy is full of frags. Back of the bus!"

Chest wound, but the grunt's eyes were open and he was
able to talk to her. Not too much blood. "Let's have an X ray
and a prep!"

"Three doing critical, two lower extremities, one lower
body . . . Harry, have a look!"

Bad head wound and the dressings were soaked in blood.
"X ray! I need a skull series! Set up an IV!"

"Chest X ray here! Prep him and give him blood."

"Head wound!" Harry shouted, spotting a bad one. "Front of the line! Prep him! And quick!" The medics rushed the gurney inside.

"Get me a trach tray!"

"Expectant. Over there." Pam directed, calmly. The soldier was carried off and laid down, none too gently. There wasn't time for the niceties.

A grunt, bleeding heavily, grinned up at Robin and asked for a date. "This one is saved!" Robin cried. "Get him in! NOW! AB neg!"

Everyone was working very, very fast. There was no time to feel bad, no time for sadness or regrets, especially no time for tears. Nurses in-country did not cry.

When the wounded had been separated, it was time to go in and fix them up. But first, Robin did what she always did: went to the expectants, the boys who were going to die, lying in a row on the ground. She wanted to look at them. Actually, what she wanted was a miracle, but she almost never got one. So she bent down over each man and looked into his eyes, if they were open—if he *had* eyes. Sometimes they looked back. Sometimes they smiled. Sometimes you could hold a hand for a minute, or a shoulder, and feel them respond to you. She felt very strongly that they shouldn't die without the touch and sight of another human being. They were so young! Most of them were black, most looked like high school boys . . . It was horrible, horrible. But she was not allowed to think that way, feel that way.

The last boy was wide awake. Why was a mystery, because there was practically nothing left of his face. She forced herself to look him right in the eye—which was just about all there was left of him. One eye. She made herself smile. He barely had lips but he was able to talk, and she could understand it.

"Hi," he said.

"Hi," she answered him, fighting tears.

"Nurse, don't you remember me? Buddy Nielsen? I was in a couple weeks ago with a busted femur."

Now she remembered. Freckle-faced tow-headed kid. A flirt.

"Of course I remember you, Buddy."

"You take care of me, okay? That way I know I'll get better."
His voice was getting weaker and weaker. Robin leaned over,
examining him more closely. The back of his skull was mostly
gone. Her eyes filled again. How did they keep right on going,
sometimes, when they were really already dead?

"I'll take care of you, Buddy," she said. "That's a firm!"

He repeated it. "Affirm." By the time his lips closed on the
"m," he was gone.

She got up from her crouch and turned, aware that she was
being called, rather urgently. "Malone! I need some help here!
Give this guy a trach while I start on his friend here." It was
Harry, all doctor right now. She was relieved to focus on her
job, on *doing* something, instead of thinking about poor Buddy
Nielsen who might not even have been laid yet. Or about
Harry Kaye, who almost certainly was going to be, before the
night was over.

37

November 1967

"Malone! Nurse! *Malone!* I need you!"

Robin finished adjusting the IV's flow, gave the young
Marine in the bed a smile, and ran to answer the desperate
voice. It belonged to Asa Watson, "better known as Ace"—as
he had informed her when she first met him, a couple of weeks
ago. She had adopted Ace Watson. It happened. You tried very
hard to be evenhanded, to treat every patient exactly the same.
But it didn't always work. There was always some grunt who

touched you where you lived, and when that happened, he got adopted.

She went to his bed, and smiled at him. "Here I am, Ace. What can I do you for?" Ace had come in with about a thousand pieces of shrapnel in his chest and belly, and she'd spent a lot of time picking it out of him. But that was two weeks ago. Now he had healed enough to return to duty. Physically, he was healed, that is. Mentally was another thing altogether.

"Malone, you gotta help me. They're going to send me back out there. You gotta tell them. You gotta tell them I can't. I *can't.*" And he began to shake. Robin held both his hands tightly and said, "It's okay, it's okay," over and over, like a prayer. It didn't stop the shaking; it almost never did. Ace's whole body was quaking, and his sad brown eyes looked up at her, pleading.

She felt so bad for him, because he was suffering such mental anguish, but mostly because of his age. Ace had lied to get into the army, and even after ten months in-country, he wasn't seventeen yet. It was obscene! How could they let this happen? He was a baby, and they put a weapon in his hands and sent him out to kill people, in a war where you couldn't tell friend from foe? Here, the friendly villager who gave you a drink when you were thirsty could turn around and shoot you the next time you saw him. All rules were off, in Vietnam. It was a big free-for-all with real bullets. No wonder the poor kid lay there, shaking and begging her to make sure they didn't send him back out.

"Ace," she said, leaning close to him. "You have to make yourself stop the shaking, okay? Or how can we talk?" Sometimes that worked. It worked today. He was sweating as if he'd run ten miles, and he'd wet himself again. He whispered to her, "I can't go back out there. I can't. I'll die, Malone. I swear, I'll kill myself first."

"Don't talk like that, Ace. Think of your mother back home in Kentucky, waiting for you. She wants her son to come home. You don't want to disappoint her." Blah blah blah. The kid couldn't listen to reason. Anyway, what in hell was so reasonable about telling him he was ready to go back to his unit? It wasn't true. He wasn't ready to go anywhere, except home to his mother. Or maybe to a shrink. He was so fragile. He was afraid to go to sleep because every time he did, he had horrible nightmares from which he awakened drenched in sweat and urine and, sometimes, shit.

Ace clutched her arm. "The worst part—about the shelling? the sudden attacks?—is you never know when to expect it. It could come any time. Day. Night. When you're in the crapper. I can't stand it. I vomit all the time. I can't go back. Don't let them send me back. Please, Malone, I'm begging you. You're the only one who understands."

She wanted to tell him that she really understood on account of having had a brother who suffered mentally, too. But she didn't dare. Only Pam knew about Sandy, and it was going to stay that way.

"I'll talk to Dr. Ostereicher, he's the company shrinker," she promised.

Ostereicher had already been contacted but apparently was too busy to make his way to the One-Six-One. Even if he did manage to see Ace, she wasn't so sure he'd send the kid home. Ostereicher was a colonel and, according to all reports, a hard-nosed SOB.

"He's Regular Army," Harry had told her, "You know the type." "Uh-oh," had been her comment, and Harry agreed: "Uh-oh."

She'd just got Ace calmed down when a truck came roaring by the hospital, screeched around the corner near the commissary, and backfired. At the sound, Ace flung himself out of the bed in a bellywhop onto the floor. Unfortunately, she was standing too close, and he managed to knock her over on his way. She went sprawling, all the wind knocked out of her.

"Lieutenant Malone, how many times do I have to warn you—No fraternizing with the patients. And you, soldier, have you no shame?" As he spoke, Harry Kaye held out a hand to the boy. "This is not a woman. This is an army nurse, an entirely different species." His tone was utterly casual, man-to-man banter.

Ace, who was in a kind of fetal curl, his arms wrapped around the top of his head, peeked up. Then, for a wonder, he grinned. "Gosh, Doc, I dunno why I did that. I thought I heard enemy fire."

"Backfire, that's all." Harry helped him up, and said, "You want to take a walk or something?"

"No. No. I can't."

"Okeydokey. You want to kiss Malone's booboos and make them all better? That's the one *I'd* pick."

Ace crawled back onto his bed, tears leaking from his eyes. "Aw, Malone, I'm sorry, I didn't mean—"

"I know you didn't. It's okay. Just close your eyes and relax."

"Don't leave me. Please."

"Let me check out the rest of my patients and I'll come back. Deal?"

"Deal. You will come back, won't you?"

"I'll hurry."

Harry waited and walked with her for a minute. "You got pretty dusty there, Malone. Can I brush you off?"

"Dusty? Where?" When he tenderly rubbed the curve of her buttocks, and a lot of the grunts began to hoot and whistle, she finally caught on. "Dirty old doctor! And in front of the patients!"

His answer was to go into his imitation of Groucho Marx, complete with leer and imaginary cigar. Then, in a lower tone, he said, "What time you get off, sweetheart? Meet you at Joe's Place?"

"I'll be the one with the rose in my teeth," she said. She watched him go down the ward, joking as he went. He was like a big ship that left a wake of laughter. What the guys didn't know was that he was looking them over as he went, and making mental notes. He had sharp doctor eyes, that Harry.

Robin continued on her rounds in the Post-Op section, which was not so hectic. She chatted, she checked, she gave meds and she gave advice. But all the time, her mind was on Ace Watson. She wasn't sure why, but he reminded her of Sandy. He certainly didn't look like Sandy. How could he? He was black, like most of the grunts. It must be because he was so afraid, the way Sandy had been afraid—of everything.

She hadn't been able to save Sandy, but she hoped to do better for Ace.

Her heart squeezed, as it did any time she thought of Sandy and how she had failed him. It was bad enough that their narcissistic father walked out on them because JJ Malone couldn't stand to see that he had sired anything less than perfect. Then Mom turned her back. The truth was, Mom had been ashamed of Sandy; they all had been. Robin had gone to see him, not only because she really cared about him, but also because it seemed noble and she liked thinking of herself as virtuous.

She was aware that she always kept a certain distance from everyone and everything. Well, she couldn't help being who *she* was, either, what with her mother always putting everyone else's kids first—and then her brother going crazy—and Gran revealing their family's frightening mental history—and her Dad abandoning them. *I mean,* she would tell herself, since she had nobody else to say it to, *who could blame me for hardening my heart with all that garbage in my background?* Of course, that was before she'd been in-country, where you were ordered to be heartless. She'd done pretty well at becoming tough all on her own, long before Vietnam.

Before she joined the army, when she was a surgical nurse at Harmony Hill Hospital in Manhattan, her father had tried to see her. He came in from the Coast and called her.

"How did you find me?" she demanded, her voice frosty.

"Jesus Christ, Robin, your mother told me!"

"I want you to leave my mother alone! You've hurt her enough!"

"I know, baby, I know. But, listen—"

"No," she had said. "No. I won't listen to you. You abandoned us. You abandoned poor Sandy." She could hear him, on the other end of the line, spluttering and trying to interrupt her. But she was strong in her righteousness, and implacable. "You can't just decide one fine day that you'd like to reclaim the family you deserted. You can't abdicate as husband and father, and then come back and be welcomed with open arms. You bastard! You didn't even come to Sandy's funeral!"

She didn't wait to hear what he might have to say. She banged down the receiver as hard as she could.

Since she was madly in love with Dr. Mickey Aronson, she told him about it. She did not get the sympathy and support she had expected however. Like many surgeons, at least in her experience, Mickey didn't have a helluva lot of heart. He tended to be too reasonable, which was maddening—especially if she was being irrational. Which she certainly was about JJ.

"You don't understand, Mickey, he walked out on us. Get it? Left the house without saying good-bye."

And Mickey's response? "He's your father. He deserves your respect. And he's trying to make amends."

She wanted to tell him what a total shit JJ Malone was, how he was a drunk, and how he played around with other women. She wanted Mickey to understand, especially, that there was no way the man could make amends for deserting his insane son. But of course, she couldn't tell him that. She couldn't tell *anyone* about Sandy. She was afraid people would pull away from her if they knew her brother had been crazy, so crazy he was institutionalized—so crazy, he killed himself.

"You're right," she agreed, and promised Mickey she'd see her father if he ever called her again. She was lying. She was crazy about Michael Aronson. He was so smart and so damned good-looking—actually gorgeous—tall, muscular, dark-haired, a bit scowly in a sexy kind of way. He looked like Marlon Brando. All the nurses swooned over him. And he had chosen *her*, Robin Rebecca Malone, too tall, too bony, too distant, too smart. The first day, after she had worked with him in the O.R., he'd come up to her in the cafeteria. He'd actually sought her out! He sat down opposite her, and waved off the other nurses around the table. Without saying a word, they all scattered like leaves in the wind. She realized later, much later, that she should have been insulted on their behalf; it should have been a warning. But that day, she'd just been impressed. Impressed and smitten. He could have done or said anything, and she would have agreed. What he did say was, "You interest me. What's your name again?"

What's your name again! If any man did that to her today, she'd spit in his eye. But back then, she was young and dumb. Besides, Mickey Aronson was not just handsome, he was the hot new surgeon, which made him a bit higher on the scale than Jesus. So she told him her name, and he bought her a cup of coffee. Later, she went home with him, where they proceeded to screw each other's brains out. And she was his slave ever after. She knew she would never fall for anyone in quite that total way again. Which was probably a damn good thing.

When she promised Mickey she'd give JJ a chance, she thought she'd heard the last of her father. He wasn't that interested in any of them. But she'd figured wrong. One afternoon, on her way out of the hospital, she ran into him in the lobby, looking for her. She glared as he put on a big grin and called to her in a phony Irish brogue.

"Robin! Robin, me darlin'! It's the bad penny!" She wanted to kill him, but at the same time, she was struck with how old he looked. Still handsome, of course, but a bit fat, the classic features a bit blurred. His hair was pure white although still thick and wavy, still with an adorable lock that fell onto his forehead. It was the one youthful thing about him.

She felt herself go rigid with anger. When he took her by her shoulders and planted a kiss on her cheek—he was aiming for her mouth but she turned her head—she felt nothing. He backed off then and said, "Aw, Robin, come on. This is Daddy, here, pleading for forgiveness. How can you refuse a sorrowful man forgiveness?"

"You ran away. You left us when we needed you most."

"I know, darlin', but—"

"Don't you *dare* call me darling or anything like it."

"Robin. I'm your father. I love you."

"Oh, really? I think not."

"Try to understand," JJ said, his hands spread out in supplication. "He was my son, my firstborn son. I had so many hopes and dreams for him, and I saw them disintegrate . . . I had to stand by, helpless, while his mind rotted. Robin!"

"JJ, we all had to watch that. The difference is, some of us stayed. You ran. Please. Don't beg me, and don't call me endearments and, particularly, don't try to explain yourself. You're a shit and you know it. You *must* know it."

The blood drained from his face but he stood his ground. "I'm your father, for Christ's sake, Robin."

"He was your *son*, for Christ's sake. And speaking of Christ, wasn't he the one who cried out to his father to ask, 'Why hast Thou forsaken me?' Why did you forsake Sandy? You bastard!" To her horror, he began to cry.

"You know what, JJ?" she said, loving every moment of it. "You and your crocodile tears do nothing to me. You're disgusting!" She turned away from him and found herself face to face with Mickey Aronson.

By that time, she knew Mickey was the only child of Holocaust survivors, and to him, family was sacred. No matter what. Even if she had been able to explain what had happened, it would have made no difference to Mickey.

So she stood there in the lobby of Harmony Hill Hospital, watching as Michael Aronson stopped loving her. It happened in an instant. An hour before, he had talked about them getting married. Twelve hours ago, he had made love to her four times in a row and said he had never felt like that, never. Now, she looked into his eyes and saw . . . nothing. Emptiness. A blank. The end. His eyes went vacant, then cold, and he turned away. Without a single word, he left her forever. They continued to work together, of course, but he never again looked at her with the slightest bit of recognition. The days that followed had been hell on earth.

Robin shook herself. No sense thinking about that now. That was a long time ago. It didn't matter anymore. She rarely thought about Mickey. She didn't even see him in her dreams, the way she had in the beginning, waking to find herself weeping. He was the past. Right now, she had to do something about Ace Watson. *Someone* had to care about him. He was so scared and so helpless.

The very next afternoon, Colonel Ostereicher finally showed. She knew the minute he walked in that he was trouble. First of all, he looked perfect and military, everything about him crisp and pressed, correct uniform—the works. She would be willing to bet he spent most of his time behind a desk and in meetings. Everyone here dressed for the heat, and for the messes they kept having to clean up. She saw Ostereicher eyeing her with distaste, and knew he disapproved of her olive drab pants and T-shirt. He probably expected her to be all starched and white and wearing a skirt—or, at the very least, to be in her dress blues. Well, tough shit. She looked right back at him, not giving an inch.

"I am Colonel Ostereicher," he said.

"Yes, Colonel. Lieutenant Malone," she answered, all very proper and military.

Even so, he kept calling her "Nurse" in that particular tone of voice she had come to recognize only too well. It said that he was a doctor and therefore on the right hand of God, whereas she was only a nurse, somewhat lower than a worm. This guy was a doctor times shrinker times Regular Army, which equaled dirty no-good heartless SOB in her book.

She walked along with him, as he checked out the patients, moving from bed to bed. Actually, she walked a little behind him. He never turned to ask her a question. Hell, what could a mere nurse tell a *doctor*? As they moved along the double line of beds, she got angrier and angrier. What a jerk! He spoke in this false-hearty voice to everyone, calling the men "Son" and stuff like that. When he got to Ace and read the chart, the look on his face made her heart sink.

"And what have we here?" That disgusting phony voice. "Healed, but still in the hospital? Corporal—ah—Watson, what seems to be the problem?" Ace looked at Ostereicher with suspicion. "You can tell me, I'm a psychiatrist."

"Well, Doc . . ."

"Colonel."

"Yessir. Well, Colonel, sir, I've got the shakes."

"The shakes?" False laugh. "The *shakes*? You'll have to forgive me, son, but that doesn't really tell me anything."

"I shake all over. I vomit. I shit my pants. I can't move."

"You mean . . . now?"

"No, sir. I mean, in combat."

"But here, in the hospital, you're fine?"

"He has terrible nightmares, Colonel," Robin said. "Palpitations. In my opinion—"

Ostereicher didn't even bother to turn around. "I will tell you when I want your opinion, Nurse."

"But, Colonel, this man has been my patient since he was brought in. I took the shr—"

He turned, a tight false smile on his face. "I'm sorry, did I not speak loudly enough?"

They stood staring at each other. It wasn't a fair fight, of course. He was going to win, no matter what. The smug fuck. "Yes, Colonel, I heard you loud and clear."

"I won't be needing you any further, Nurse. This man and I need some privacy, to talk."

Ace's eyes pleaded with her not to desert him. *I won't,* she promised him silently. *But right now, I'm forced to leave you with this piece of shit. Just hang in.*

"Certainly, Colonel, sir." Robin wheeled and marched out. She had to find Harry, to tell him about this unbelievable imbecile of a doctor. She needed to enlist his help. She had a horrible feeling that Ostereicher was going to lecture Ace about bravery and not letting his buddies down and then he would send the kid back out there.

Harry had already locked horns with Colonel Ostereicher. He hated his guts, too. After the evening meal, instead of heading for Joe's, she and Harry went into the ward to talk to Ace Watson. He wasn't there.

"That fucking doctor!" Robin exploded. "If he's had Ace sent—"

"Hold on, Robbie baby. You know it doesn't happen that fast. This is the army. There are papers to be filled out in quadruplicate. No, our Ace has decided to get the hell outta here before Ostereicher kills him. Ace's got combat fatigue, all right, but there ain't nothin' wrong with that boy's brain."

"Where is he? What are we going to do? What if he steps on a land mine?"

"Easy, easy. We gotta think like a scared but smart grunt and then we'll know where Ace went." A moment later, he snapped his fingers. "I think I've got it! The one place our shrink friend would never think of!"

"Where? What?"

"Just come with me." Harry grabbed her hand and began to walk rapidly, chuckling to himself.

"Where are we going, Harry?"

"You'll see." He led her past all the hospital buildings, out past Joe's Place, where a half-drunk group was singing "Heard

It Through the Grapevine" at the top of their voices, mostly off-key. She could see a couple of campfires on the beach and even smell hamburgers cooking. She couldn't hear the waves hitting the sand, but she knew they were. It was a beautiful night, with millions of stars. Too bad they were in Vietnam, and she and her boyfriend were looking for a runaway grunt with psychological problems.

When they got to the Quonset hut at the edge of the camp, Robin nodded. "Oh. Of course." It was the Graves Registration Unit. Boy scared of dying? Where better to hide than among the dead. It made a weird kind of sense, she supposed.

He was there. They could hear him, in the darkness. He was sobbing and shivering. "Ace!" Robin called softly. "It's me, Malone, and Dr. Kaye. We're here to help you. Harry's going to turn on the flashlight, okay?"

They waited and, finally, Ace's strangled voice said, "Okay." He was huddled into a corner, knees to chest, head bent, as if there were enemy fire. Well, he wasn't far from wrong.

They talked him out of the corner and onto his feet, and then they talked him back to his bed. On the way, they spotted the tall form of Ostereicher marching purposefully toward the C.O.'s quarters.

"Uh-oh," Robin said.

"Yeah. Looks like the good colonel has discovered your absence, Ace."

"Don't let him find me! Malone, don't let him find me! He says I'm a malinger—something or other and he's gonna send me back. Don't let him find me!"

"We'll fool him," Harry said. "Get back in your bed. When the C.O. goes running around trying to find you, you'll be there where you belong. We'll tell her the colonel is imagining things." He chortled. "We'll all keep a straight face and insist that you were never gone. Can you do it, Ace?"

"Yeah. Sure. I can do it." Ace's voice was shaky but game.

"Good guy. Okay, now's our chance."

As soon as Ace was back in his bed, he curled himself into the fetal position and began to shake. Harry gave him a shot to calm him and help him sleep. He whispered, "Come on, Robin, there's nothing more we can do."

But she couldn't leave the boy like that, so alone and miserable and scared. "No, I'll see you later, Kaye, all right?" She stood looking down at Ace, thinking, *What can I do? What can I do?* And then, she knew what she could do. She lay down next to the boy and curled her body around his, placing her arm over his, so he could feel her warmth and her touch and know he wasn't alone. Pretty soon, he stopped shaking, and his breathing became even. Soon, it got slower—and deeper—and slower—and deeper—

"What *is* this? Nurse! What's going on here!"

Robin's eyes flew open to darkness. For a moment, she didn't know where she was, or whose voice had awakened her. But the moment the bright beam from a flashlight bored into her eyes, she knew.

"Hey!" she protested.

"On your feet, Lieutenant!"

Now he calls me lieutenant! Robin thought. She wanted to laugh—which was stupid, because she was in deep shit with Colonel Doctor Ostereicher. She uncurled herself and rolled off the bed with care, trying not to disturb Ace. She needn't have worried; Harry's injection had done its work well. Ace was fast asleep, hands tucked under his cheek, mouth slightly open, like a small child.

"Explain yourself, Lieutenant Malone."

"I don't have to explain myself to you, Colonel. My boss is Colonel Batten."

Her eyes had grown accustomed to the darkness and she could see the expression on his face change. His tone changed, too. "Of course, Nurse. But I don't think Colonel Batten would approve of you sleeping with the patients."

She took in a deep breath, and reminded herself that killing a colonel would probably put her in front of a firing squad. "I don't know what you said to Corporal Watson, Colonel, but he ran away and hid with the corpses in GRU."

"He *what?*"

"That's right. He's in bad shape, Colonel. Combat fatigue."

"Huh! I don't believe in combat fatigue. There's no place in Vietnam for cowards and slackers."

"Ace is no slacker! He lied about his age so the army would take him! He's not even seventeen!"

That cut no ice with Ostereicher. "He wanted to fight. His wounds are healed. He should go back to his buddies and fight."

"This kid won't leave the hospital until Dr. Kaye says so," Robin said firmly. She was becoming truly angry.

"Very well, where is Dr. Kaye?"

"Off duty."

"I'll speak with him in the morning, then."

"Fine," Robin said. But this time, she knew better than to walk away from him. She stood there, waiting until he finally turned and left.

Bright and early the next morning, she hurried back to see how Ace Watson was doing. Norma McClure, who had taken the night shift and was just leaving, said "Good morning," paused, started to continue on her way, then changed her mind. "Robin? Dr. Ostereicher was in an hour ago."

"Six in the morning?" Her stomach tightened. "To see Corporal Watson?"

"Yes. He was in at midnight, too." Robin could see that Norma was torn. She was a person who went by rules and regulations. She was also in awe of doctors.

"What did he do that was evil?"

"Well . . . it wasn't *evil*, Robin. You do tend to dramatize, you know."

"Yeah, yeah, but what did he do?"

"Well . . . he gave Watson Thorazine."

"He did, did he? Excuse me!" Robin turned and went running, to find Harry.

"Wait, Robin, he came in to talk to Ace and—"

But Robin didn't wait to find out what. She knew it was no damn good for Ace. She stormed into Harry's "office," which was a space outside the O.R., to find Dr. Jay Silverman typing out a report on a patient.

"Harry? He left around five ay-em with one of the French doctors. A village up the coast whose name I have forgotten was attacked last night. Lots of wounded. Can I help?"

"No, dammit! Sorry, Jay, but— Oh, never mind. If he should come back, would you send him to Post-Op?"

"Sho' nuff!" Jay went back to his two-fingered labors on the battered typewriter.

On her way back to the tent, she heard the familiar sound of a chopper coming in and the shouts of "Wounded coming in!" She ran.

The next time she thought of Ace and Colonel Ostereicher, it was five o'clock in the afternoon. They had stitched together three guys, lost one on the table, and then tended to five Vietnamese from the bombed village, who had come back in the truck with Harry. In fact, as they walked outside to breathe some air, it was Harry who said, "Let's go see if Ace is aces, okay?"

"Oh, God, do you believe I forgot all about him? And, listen—" She filled him in on Ostereicher's midnight visit.

"That dirty rat!" Harry said, in his best Cagney imitation.

Ace was not in his bed. Someone else was. The two of them just stood there, staring down at the new occupant. When Robin looked up, Colonel Ostereicher, a smug look on his face, was heading toward them.

"If you're looking for Corporal Watson, he decided to join his unit," he said.

"What did you do to him?" Robin demanded. She didn't care if he ordered a court martial for her.

"We had a nice long session, and he realized that was what he really wanted. There was nothing wrong with him."

"He was terrified," Robin said.

"Well, so am I. Aren't we all. If we weren't frightened, we'd be crazy. Am I right, Captain Kaye?"

"Colonel, that young man will have a breakdown out there," Harry said.

"He's not going to have a breakdown. He was suffering with an acute situation reaction, not a psychosis . . ."

"Oh, really?" Robin interrupted, furious. "Is that why you were pumping him full of Thorazine?"

There was a dangerous silence. Then, "You have to remember, Nurse—"

"*Lieutenant.*"

"Lieutenant, then. You must remember this is an army Evacuation Hospital. You are here at this hospital to maximize the odds of every soldier and get him back out into the field. That is your job. I suggest you stop becoming emotionally involved with every scared boy and *do* your job."

Robin stood very still, pondering her options. She had none, she realized. So she left and went to the rec hall, where she sat at the bar and waited while Joe, without a word, poured her a shot of something. She couldn't even taste it, her mouth was filled with the metallic tang of rage. She tossed it back and nodded for another. But as she picked it up, a hand from behind her reached out and took it from her. It was Harry. Without a word, she wound her arms around his waist and buried her head in his chest. Harry gently extricated himself and pulled her off her stool. "Here's my promise to you, my sweet Robin. If I ever hear that Ace died, or even that he cut himself shaving, I will personally go and murder Colonel Ostereicher."

She gave him a wobbly smile. "Slowly? Painfully?"

"He will die the death of a million cuts."

"Okay. And now, will you make love to me?"

"Endlessly. You will die the death of a million thrusts."

"Oh, God, Harry, what would I do without you to make me smile?"

"Let us not find out. Instead, let us find out how long we can keep screwing. The first one who cries uncle buys the drinks. Deal?"

"Deal."

When they walked away, arms around each other, they were actually laughing.

38

January 1968

Oh, no, not again! Robin hugged her knees to her chest and swallowed hard, willing the nausea to retreat. That's right, go back down, down. She hated the feeling—especially since she never seemed to have anything to throw up. She could *not* be sick. She could *not* take time to stay in bed with some weird stomach thing.

"You okay, Malone?" Pam peered over at her.

"Yeah."

"You don't look so good."

"I'm fine, okay? Must've been the hot dogs. Sometimes they disagree with me."

"You've been sick to your stomach every day for a week," Norma McClure said in that definite way she had. "Maybe you ought to see a doctor."

"I see a lot of a doctor." Robin tried to leer, but the sick feeling rose in her chest and she shut her mouth. Just in case.

"When symptoms last more than a week—" Norma started.

"I'm *fine*, McClure. Get off it, will you?"

But she wasn't fine and Norma was right. She should go talk to one of the docs. Trouble was, they were all too friendly with each other. And Harry, the one doctor she felt comfortable telling her problems to, was up the coast at the surgical hospital in Phu Bai, to learn a new surgery for skull wounds. Harry had been gone for three days and wasn't due back until the end of the week. Her urpiness could wait, Robin decided, until he got back. She missed him, missed his wisecracks and

413

the way he spooned around her in bed at night, missed waking
up in the middle of the night to find that they were making
love. In their sleep, for Christ's sake!

The sand on the beach was still warm from the day's sunshine, and a magnificent purple, orange, and pink sunset was
in the making, right in front of them. Happily, there was a
cease-fire, so business had been slow. That's why Harry had
been able to take a week. The three nurses had come down to
the beach this evening, separately, wanting to see the stars and
listen to the gentle hiss and thump of the waves hitting the
shore. Robin liked to imagine that these waves had started on
the coast of California, and silently, she greeted them: *Hi, San
Francisco . . . Hi, Santa Clara, Santa Barbara, San Diego,
Santa Cruz.* She wasn't even sure they were all cities on the
coast, but the names were flowing and liquid, like the ocean.
Like the bile that was rising in her throat, dammit! Again, she
swallowed hard and willed it away.

The three of them didn't often sit down together. She and
Pam, of course—well, they were best buddies. But Norma
was so prim and proper. Robin always felt McClure was judging her, scornful of her sex life and her drinking. Norma could
go to hell. What she thought didn't mean squat. But it wasn't
particularly comfortable to be around her. Robin stopped letting her mind drift and focused on the conversation.

Pam was talking about how much she'd been forced to
say yes sir and no ma'am when she'd worked at the mental
hospital in upstate New York. "I couldn't make a single decision on my own. It was my first job, and I began to wonder
why I ever thought nursing was the best career in the world."
There was a tiny pause at that point, and Robin held her breath.
But Pam didn't say, "And then one of my patients committed
suicide—oh, and by the way, McClure, he was Robbie's brother."
She wouldn't. *Silly of me to worry,* Robin thought.

"So I switched to O.R. nursing, figuring that would be
better," Pamela went on. "I didn't realize that surgeons were
even more coldblooded than shrinks. Not Harry, of course,
Rob, but you guys know what I'm talking about. Back in the
real world, there's no power in nursing. You belong to the doctors. You're a fucking slave! Sorry, McClure. Here, it's so dif-

ferent. I love my work. Isn't that awful? These guys—I could have been dating any one of them. They come in and they're hurt so bad! With such terrible wounds. There was a grunt in here, last year before you two came, and a booby trap had got him. Both arms, both legs! I wept over him. How could I send him back to his mother that way? To his family? But even so—the ones you save—I feel I'm doing something *real* . . ."

Robin said, "Wait. What happened? To the quadriplegic? Did you send him home? My God, what did his mother *do*? Can you imagine the first time she saw her boy?" She shuddered.

"He died," Pam said, in a funny flat voice. Norma crossed herself. "Yeah, well, he wanted to die," Pam went on. "He begged— Never mind."

"No, what? What? Come on, Boonesie! Tell us the story."

"There's no story. He was miserable. He was badly wounded. He didn't want to live, and he died. That's all."

Robin eyed her friend, who, in spite of two and a half years in-country, still looked fresh-faced and healthy. Like the milkmaid her father had called her. Robin wondered if the flaxen-haired milkmaid had accidentally on purpose given the boy without arms and legs an overdose of something so he could die.

That was not something you could ask, though, particularly not in front of McClure. Norma was saying, "I worked in a Catholic hospital. I trained in a Catholic hospital. When I joined the army, everyone said, 'Oh, Norma, you've led such a sheltered life. The army's gonna be too tough for you.' But they'd never worked and trained under the good Sisters!" She laughed, sounding a lot more human than usual. "You worked until everything was *perfect*, and if you were sick, why, working harder would just push all that fever right out of you. I'm telling you, after the Sisters at Good Mercy Hospital, and then St. Francis Xavier, the army was a snap!"

They all laughed about that, and then McClure said, "What about you, Malone? What's your story?"

Robin fought down her nausea again and recited: "How to bandage a war: You do it a wound at a time. A person at a time. With all your skills as a nurse. With all the cheerfulness in your heart. You do it because you want to. You do it because you're an army nurse. The Army Nurse Corps.' Ta-DA!"

"I remember that one," Norma said. "It was pretty good."

"Pretty good!" Robin protested. "Hell, it was a great recruitment poster! It brought me here, and I don't even believe we should be in this country fighting a war!"

"You don't want the Communists to win!" Norma said, sounding shocked.

"You believe all that? I don't. I hate this damn war. Think it's stupid. Hate all the pro-war propaganda—which you, McClure, have bought. But, see, after I joined up, I trained for the E.R. in a V.A. hospital on the Coast. I saw the vets who were being shipped back home in pieces. This war is hurting young men, kids really, robbing them of arms and legs and eyes and, sometimes—" She paused, swallowing. "—their sanity." So many of them were just as crazy as Sandy, saying the same kind of things, not knowing what was real and what wasn't. They were the ones, the walking wounded, the ones with the shattered minds, that had made her decide to sign up for a Vietnam tour.

"You can't make an omelet without breaking eggs," Norma said, back to her usual style.

"Listen, McClure, do you even know why we're here? I don't mean the three of us, but the United States. You know why we're fighting with the Vietnamese against the Vietnamese?" Pam asked.

"Well, Boonesie, there's a thing called the domino theory. We let one country go Commie, pretty soon they'll take the next and then—"

"Oh, McClure, spare me! That's just an excuse to get the country into a war and beef up the economy!"

"And *that's* unpatriotic and un-American!" For a moment, no one spoke, and then they all burst out laughing. "Pretty corny, huh?" Norma added. But Robin knew she had really meant it. Norma bought the whole thing, swallowed it whole, and regurgitated it whenever the subject came up. A lot of nurses were like that. Lots of doctors, too. Hell, there were lots of *grunts* who still thought they were fighting for something!

Anyway, why talk politics when it was a beautiful, tranquil

night with a zillion stars. They could hear the juke box in the rec hall playing, and everyone singing: "I'll be there" and "Take a good look at my face." They sang along, too. Some-one played "Shout!" and they could hear the gang at Joe's Place singing and shouting and laughing. Dancing, too, probably. Nearby, a couple of grunts on R and R had built a fire and were barbecuing hamburgers. The greasy, familiar smell drifted her way and, suddenly, Robin had to vomit. It happened so fast, she couldn't get very far. So everyone got a good look at her bent back and heaving shoulders.

She heard one of the grunts yell, "Can we help?" Pam yelled back, "We're nurses!" Pam was at her side, holding her head until it was over. Then Pam took a wet scarf Norma had dipped into the ocean and wiped Robin's face and neck.

"I think I have solved the mystery," Pam said. "Come on, come back. I'll bury your mess in the sand." When they were all sitting comfortably again, Pam began to tick items off on her fingers. "You're tired. You're nauseous. You think you're getting fat—"

"I am! My pants won't go around my waist!"

"Shush up, Malone, and listen, for a change. Now, where was I? Oh, yeah. You think you're getting fat. You want to fall asleep every afternoon. And get this: You just told me a few days ago, your period is very late. You're a nurse, Malone, so you tell me. What's with you? Huh?" She made a dumb face. "You wanna guess?"

The light bulb lit. "Oh, Christ! Oh, shit! Oh, no! Sorry, McClure. Oh, shit!"

"What?" Norma wanted to know.

Pam groaned, and Robin said, "Oh, for Christ's sake, McClure. I'm pregnant." Oh, God, she was pregnant and she couldn't have a child. Not with her family history. She wasn't going to love and care for a child, only to watch it disintegrate into madness. Never. After Sandy died, she had made herself a promise. The schizophrenia in her family was going to end right there.

Norma said, "How could that happen?"

"Surely the good Sisters didn't keep you in the dark about that."

"No, of course not. But how——? Oh."

"Not 'Oh.' Harry," Pam said.

"Listen to me, Norma," Robin said. "I don't want him to know, do you understand? For reasons which I cannot divulge, I am going to end this pregnancy. You breathe a word of this near him, I will kill you."

Norma sniffed, insulted.

Pam was doing a lot of talking, about it not being fair for Robin to make such an important decision all alone. After all, the father might have other ideas . . .

Robin rounded on Pam, fierce and fiery. "It *is* fair. In this case, it's more than fair, it's the only way! As you damn well know!"

"Nothing is absolute," Pam said. "Nothing is certain."

Robin just stared at her, frustrated and miserable. She knew what her friend was trying to tell her: that this child might not develop schizophrenia. After all, *she* hadn't, nor had her mother. Nor Gran, for that matter. But how could any sane person take that kind of chance with an innocent baby? If Pam couldn't understand, Harry wouldn't either. Nobody could! This was something she was all alone with.

Seeing the misery on Robin's face, Pam started to go over to her, to put an arm around her and tell her she understood. She knew very well what Robin was afraid of. But before she could move, Robin got up and ran off, heading, no doubt for the safety of the rec hall bar. But, later on, when Pam walked into Joe's Place, Robin was not there. Joe said she'd been in, grabbed a bottle, and left. So Pam went to the hootch to stop her before she drank herself into a stupor and a rotten hangover. Robin wasn't there, either. Pam went back to Joe's Place. A really cute Marine who'd been making eyes at her ever since he got to the One-Six-One was there, and she wanted to find out if he was as interesting as he looked. And what do you know——he was. So she danced a little and drank a little and made out a little——well, more than a little. She figured, by the time she stumbled back into the hootch at about dawn, she'd find Robin passed out on her bed. Only Robin wasn't in her bed. So where the hell was she?

Like the deed following the thought, Robin walked in just then, bleary-eyed and looking like death warmed over. Pam hoped to God Robin hadn't thrown herself at some grunt, just to forget. Pam liked Harry Kaye a lot. He was a bit of a wild man, or anyway, he liked to talk as if he were, but she'd seen the way he looked at Robin. He was crazy about her. Pam knew Robin had been jilted by some jerk of a doctor, Stateside. "Dumped like a load of bad-smelling garbage" is how Robin put it one time when they were exchanging war stories. "Without a word. And then I had to keep working with him, while he acted as if I weren't even there."

An experience like that could make you really leery of men, and Robin had put a wall around herself about a mile thick. But Harry was getting through and he was good stuff. He seemed to genuinely like women, which was pretty goddam unusual. Pam was mad at Robin, on Harry's behalf. "Where the hell were you?" she demanded.

"I slept in GRU, with the dead guys."

"You *what*?"

"Well, it's nice and quiet there, and I knew I was going to wake up with one helluva hangover." From her brittle tone, it was obvious Robin didn't want to answer any questions, or even talk. At least she hadn't fallen into bed with some stranger, just to add to her anguish.

Robin pulled off her clothes and went outside to take a shower. Pam was headed there, too. As they soaped themselves, Robin said, "I want an abortion. I know you don't agree, but I'm going to do it."

"So why are you telling me?"

"Because, Pam, I'd like you to be with me, okay? Because I don't want to be alone. Because I don't really want to do this, but I have to—" Her voice choked and she stopped talking because she was crying. God, it was awful to watch your friend cry and not be able to do anything about it. Still, Pam was glad to see that Robin wasn't quite as tough as she liked people to think.

"We'll ask Li Chi," Pam said, pretending she didn't even notice the tears. "If anyone will know where to get an abortion, she will."

Li Chi was their servant. While they were showering, she'd come in, riding on her old bike from Bu Huy, the village down the road. She bustled cheerfully around the hootch, cleaning up and gathering the dirty clothes to wash. Li Chi was a mystery; all the Vietnamese were. They spoke French and most of them had already picked up English, so obviously they were smart. But here they were, waiting on a bunch of nurses and Dough-nut Dollies and the occasional U.S.O. singer. It couldn't be wonderful for them, and yet, Li Chi was always polite and smiling, always ready and willing to do or take or find or bring whatever the hell you wanted. She was good at listening, too, but Pam had noticed early on that the Vietnamese woman never offered any information about herself, her life, or what she thought. She was a mystery; Pam just hoped she wasn't Viet Cong, too. A lot of them were.

The servant didn't bat an eye, just listened thoughtfully, and said, "Certainly. In my village, we have an abortion center."

"An abortion *center*?" Robin looked half-amused, half-shocked.

Li Chi delicately cleared her throat and said, "Many girls are becoming pregnant by American soldier and Marine." *Of course,* Pam thought, *how stupid of us.* She felt somewhat ashamed. Li Chi did not elaborate, but Pam was well aware that children of mixed blood were ostracized in Vietnam. So, many of those babies were abandoned by their mothers. Around here, the infants usually ended up in the orphanage run by French nuns at the hospital in Bu Huy.

Of course, some Vietnamese women fell in love with their American lovers, lived with them, and reared whatever chil-dren resulted. Pam always felt sorry for them. They really thought these guys were going to take them back to the U.S. Or stay and settle down in Bu Huy or some other hamlet. Yeah. Sure. Like that cute Marine who fucked her so well last night was Prince Charming and would appear tonight with a wedding ring!

That afternoon, Pam commandeered a Jeep and the three of them—Pam, a white-faced Robin, and Li Chi—went bumping down the dirt road toward the village. Pam, who was driv-ing, kept glancing sideways at Robin, who looked paler and sweatier with every moment. Finally, she pulled over to the side and stopped.

"What's wrong?" Robin said. "Don't tell me we're out of gas!"

"It's you, Robbie. You look awful. In fact, you look scared to death. If you've changed your mind, just say the word and we'll go back."

Robin stared at her for a moment, looking blank, and then she began to shriek with laughter. When she was able to speak, she said, "Change my mind? No. It's your driving, Pammie. That would scare anyone!"

Pam refused to laugh, although she couldn't help smiling a little. "My driving isn't *that* bad. Well, it *isn't*. You're sure you want to go through with this?"

"Positive." Robin took a deep breath. "Look, Pam, I know you mean well, but—my grandmother was a doctor and she gave abortions and ended pregnancies with herbs and stuff. . . . We're part Indian, you know, and all the women in her family were healers and witches . . . No, really. She said her people never had more babies than they wanted. They had many ways, sometimes herbs and sometimes—magic." She slid Pam a quick look, but Pam wasn't about to laugh. *She'd* grown up with a grandmother who believed that if you sang before breakfast you'd cry before supper, and stuff like that.

"Anyway—no, I'm not scared," Robin finished. "And yes, I'm sure. Okay?"

So Pam started the engine again and headed for Bu Huy. Bu Huy consisted of an odd collection of huts, shanties, and large, solid houses, plus the hospital and a sprawling compound where the nuns lived and kept their orphanage. The ground had all been beaten into dirt but some trees still stood, shade for the chickens scratching under them. Children squatted in the dust, playing games, and an occasional woman came by, carrying water or food. The place looked strangely lifeless to Pam, although she was sure there was plenty of living going on where the "big noses" couldn't see.

Li Chi took them to a small building behind the hospital. An elderly Vietnamese man came out, listened to what she said, and bowed them inside. Pam was scared to death because it didn't look antiseptic to her: Where was the autoclave? Where were the IVs? There wasn't even any water on the boil.

She took Robin aside and said, "Do you really want to do this? Maybe we should go into Saigon, to an American hospital."

"No. This is fine. They give abortions to Vietnamese women, don't they? Stop, Pam. You know better than to think that Vietnam is in the Dark Ages. There's always *le docteur* Racine if something gets complicated."

She meant the nice-looking older French doctor who ran the hospital and the orphanage, and who certainly talked the same medical language as their own docs. So what, Pamela asked herself, was her problem? In a flash, she had it. Her problem was, she wished she was in love with a nice, funny guy like Harry Kaye and was carrying his baby. *She* wouldn't get an abortion. She'd get on a plane and go home. But Robin had her reasons, and—Pam reminded herself—*This is Robin's pregnancy, not yours, dammit.*

So it was arranged. Pam told them she was a nurse and she'd be glad to stay, but they kicked her out. She began pacing back and forth, like an expectant—*oh, shut up, Pamela,* she told herself. *Just shut up.* Later, driving back to Moonlight Bay, she went very slowly, because Robin looked awful, as if her own life had been sucked out of her, instead of just a small collection of cells.

Robin could have killed the woman! Norma had been sworn to secrecy and she had *agreed*, goddammit! Now, Norma insisted, "No, I didn't agree, I would never agree to anything like that. Abortion is murder, it's a mortal sin."

Robin wanted to take a knife and stick it into her. Her head buzzed, she was so fucking mad.

"I will never, never speak to you again, McClure. That may mean nothing to you, but I'm telling you, you are number one on my shit list. Forever!"

"It was murder and a mortal sin," said Norma, smug in her certainty.

"McClure, I'm not Roman Catholic. I don't believe in mortal sin. I'm Indian. It's not a mortal sin to me. Get it?"

"You could be Hottentot. It's still murder and a mortal sin."

Robin had had it. "Get out of my sight, McClure. You hear me? I have *real* murder on my mind! Out! *Out!*"

But what good did it do? Norma, the bitch, had told Harry and Harry was *pissed*. They had had a lovely, loving, love-filled night together when he got back. She had stayed in the circle of his arms for a long time after he'd fallen asleep, listening to his deep even breathing, smelling the wonderful smell of him. She felt as if she were floating, she was so at peace. *I love you, this is it. I really love you,* she told him silently, knowing this was the closest she'd ever been to pure happiness.

Then, the next day, while she was checking the patients, he strode in, no smile, no wink, just came over to her and in a tight low-pitched voice, said, "Outside. Now."

Was she stupid? She couldn't figure out what might be wrong. It just never occurred to her that Norma would rat on her. "What's the matter?" she asked when they were outside.

"Come on," he said, "Let's walk." He started in the direction of her hootch and she said, teasing, "You planning on a matinee? Aren't you even tired?"

There was no answering banter. He was holding her hand but not looking at her. His eyes were on the ground. Finally, he said, "What the hell did you think you were doing, killing our child?"

"Harry . . . listen." She stopped walking.

"No, babe, *you* listen and you listen good." He pulled at her to continue walking. "I'm the one guy around here who doesn't throw bullshit to women. I don't say I love you when I just want to fuck you. I don't lie about being married or engaged. Do you realize how fucking lucky you are? What the hell were you thinking, Malone? You had no right to do that. Not until you talked it over with me."

"Harry, you don't understand—"

He stopped and turned, his eyes boring into her. "Damn well told I don't understand. How *could* you, Malone? I thought you loved me."

"Harry, I do, I do."

"I sure as hell love *you*. I figured we'd get married when

this mess was finished and have a couple of kids. Jesus, I'm a surgeon, you crazy nurse! I can afford to send ten kids to college with what I'll be making! Why? That's all I want to know! Why?" He was trying to keep his cool, but she could tell he was deeply disturbed. He began walking again, so fast she had to scamper to keep up with him.

"Why? Because I'm the woman and I'm the one who gets to bear the children. I think that gives me a few extra points. I didn't want to have a baby right now, okay?"

"No. Not okay. It was *my* baby, too, Malone. *Our* baby. We were both in this thing, both of us."

"Yeah, but only one of us was pregnant, Harry. Only one of us was nauseated from morning until night. Only one of us couldn't—."

"Malone, Robin, Robbie, baby. Don't you realize that if you'd only told Bingo you were pregnant, she's have sent you straight home?"

"Oh, right. And how am I supposed to do my job if I'm in California, barfing all day and getting as big as a house?"

They had reached her hootch and he went in, heading for her little room. She followed him. Neither of them sat; both leaned against a wall, arms folded.

"Precisely!" Harry said. "You'd be in California." Now he smiled. "You'd be out of this fucking war—which you hate, remember? You'd be home and pregnant, waiting for me. Right where I'd like you to be. Where you belong."

That did it. "Where I belong! Dammit, Kaye, I should have known that under your facade of good guy who admits that women have brains, there was just another man who thinks his wife should be barefoot and pregnant, and that nurses are slaves. You want me Stateside, where I *belong*? Where I wouldn't be able to make any decisions. Where I'd have to go through the head nurse and the doctor and the patient's grandmother before I'd be allowed to take out an IV that's causing an infection!"

She could see that he was trying to interrupt her. She also realized that she was completely off the point, but she didn't care. "Here, I close. I get to decide who can pull through and who can't! Here, I'm a real person with a real brain. But I don't suppose that appeals to you, oh, no. You only want me home so I'll *behave*. Well, fuck you, Harry Kaye!" She began to cry.

"Robbie, you know that's not true. It's just—well, it was my baby, too, and now it's gone and I'll never h-hold it and—" Goddammit, now *he* was crying, with horrible gulping sobs.

"Oh, God! Harry! Oh, God, don't! I'm sorry! I'm sorry!" She ran to him, wrapping her arms around his waist and thought, for one wild moment, that she would tell him the truth—about Sandy and her family history and everything.

But just in the nick of time, they heard the sound of intense shelling. They rushed outside to see where it was coming from. It wasn't too close, not close enough to run for cover, although buildings were exploding in cascades of red light and fiery sparks. The sight was eerie and beautiful, and she remarked how unreal it seemed. "Hell, did you ever notice how unreal this whole war is?"

"Except out there. And in the O.R.," Harry said. And then the shelling stopped and all that was left was a soft red glow in the sky. The soft red glow was probably people's homes, burning, or the French hospital, or the abortion clinic, Robin thought with a shudder. She could have been blown to bits. Still could be. It might look unreal but it was realer than hell.

She opened her mouth—she really was going to tell him about the family curse. It seemed such a puny, stupid secret to be keeping in the face of all this destruction. But he put his hand over her mouth as she began, and said, "Not now, baby. Whatever it is, it'll keep. God, we're so lucky to be alive and to have each other. I just want to love you. Who knows when those shells will fall over here instead of over there? I just want to love you, and for Christ's sake, love me back, Robbie. Love me back like crazy!"

"Like crazy," Robin promised. She'd tell him some other day. They had their whole lives for her to tell him. Plenty of time.

39

February 1968

The moment the chopper landed, corpsmen began racing toward them with the wounded, shouting the bad news as they ran into the triage area in front of the hospital. "We have five from Firebase Whiskey. Doing critical . . . Both lower extremities . . . frags . . . head injuries . . ."

They bellowed the vitals while Robin and Dr. Jay Silverman went running alongside, eyeballing, examining, deciding who could be saved and who was expectant, yelling out orders. They were right in the middle of triage, when the sirens began to wail. Another attack! Robin looked up in weary disbelief.

"Holy smoke!" Dr. Jay said. He was famous for never swearing. "What's with the Cong? Don't they know it's Tet, for Pete's sake?"

"Chest wound! Set up an IV!" Robin shouted. To Dr. Jay, she said, "It's not Tet the holiday. It's Tet the offensive, haven't you heard? Uncle Ho wants to win."

"Gosh, I wish he'd give it a rest! Two weeks of this and no signs of stopping." He shook his head and shifted the cigar that was always in his teeth. Usually, it was out, but that didn't seem to matter. "Let's have an IV and a prep here!"

The night of the thirtieth of January, they'd all been relaxing at Joe's Place after a big cookout on the beach, getting ready to party. There was a cease-fire on; furthermore, Tet, the Vietnamese New Year, was a very important holiday. Everyone thought the whole country would be celebrating. Surely, not even the VC would start in during Tet, right? Wrong. Not only did the sudden, intense shelling catch everyone off guard, but it started everywhere at once, sparing nothing and nobody. There was always some shelling close to the hospital, because this damned war, unlike any other, had no real front and no behind-the-lines safety. Fighting went on everywhere, but, usually, hospitals were spared.

Not this time. Every day at Moonlight Bay, at least two or three times, they heard the screams of the sirens and the noise of incoming mortars. The patients, of course, knew that sound only too well. They'd start yelling for their weapons or shake their fists and scream at the invisible enemy, "This is a *hospital*, you blind bastards!" The landing pad had been hit twice in two days. Luckily, the Chinooks could still land with wounded. Some places had been so badly hit, the staff couldn't work at all. The Second Surgical Hospital in Phu Bai had been attacked so often, everyone had to remain confined to quarters. "Cornered and shut in," their radio message had said. In Cam Ranh Bay, sapper squads swam to shore and machine-gunned the doctors' quarters on the beach, blew down a water tower, and shot some of the ambulatory patients as they ran for cover. No one was safe. They found that out quick, when they tried radioing for help and supplies, only to learn that everyone else was trying to call *them* for help and supplies.

Robin glanced at the next gurney and almost turned away. How the man was still breathing! His chest was a bloody hole. As she watched, he stopped breathing. *I'm sorry,* she thought at him, *but you wouldn't have wanted to live. If we'd been able to save you, which I doubt.* "He's gone," she told a nearby medic. "Take him away. Who's next?"

She heard Dr. Jay yelling, "X-ray! I need a skull series!" Then he aimed his voice at her. "We're finished here, Malone, let's get inside!" The corpsmen were still unloading the chopper, but the rest were the dead. They were always the last out. Later, Robin would go over to GRU, or send one of the other nurses, to decide which wounds should be covered up and prettified before the bodies were shipped back home. It was the least they could do.

"Coming!" She ran because she had to. She also stayed awake because she had to. She was so damn tired. The heat made the air feel like a thick blanket. And the wounded just never stopped coming. Yesterday, one of the corpsmen had come into the O.R. to tell them they had piled up fifty legs so far this week, "and that's not counting arms, that's just legs." One of the doctors told the medic to get lost, they were too busy for statistics. No time to take a deep breath, even. She hadn't seen anything like this since she got here. It was a nightmare.

The first day of the attacks, the hospital had been hit several times, but luckily, not too badly. So had the recreation hall, which had been packed with people, and all decorated with tinsel and crepe paper, and whatever else Joe the bartender could dig up for their Tet party. They were dancing and drinking and singing, and in one corner, there was a hula hoop contest, when *boom!* from all sides. Bombs, shells, grenades, noise, flashing, crashing, explosions. Rockets, mortar, artillery. The entire invisible enemy, all at once. The sky was stained red from the constant explosions.

And there had been no letup. Yesterday, a new nurse, outside in the triage area, had been badly wounded—she was still unconscious—and two corpsmen had been killed bringing in wounded. There were plenty of wounded right here at Moonlight Bay, but the Chinooks were landing as often as they could and they were *loaded*. It was mass-cal times ten.

Something always went wrong. Today, it was the lights in the O.R. They kept going out. Everyone would groan and curse and then, a minute later, they'd come back on. But even as Robin thought about it, the lights went out and stayed out. Surely Dr. Jay, who was in the middle of sewing some grunt's guts back into his abdomen, would be moved to curse. Instead, he shouted, "Every live body, anyone who can hold a flashlight, to my side! Dollies, on the double!" The Red Cross girls were running all the errands, bless them. They didn't have to be told twice. They just kind of disappeared while Dr. Jay kept talking to the patient, who of course was sedated and couldn't hear him telling him to hang on. Two minutes later, the flashlights were delivered. Then, five or six patients who were ambulatory, plus a couple of guys on R and R, gathered round to shine light on the patient's middle. One light-holder made a retching sound, but he quickly said, "No, no, I'll be all right. It was—a surprise, that's all. I just won't look." It worked fine, and Dr. Jay said they were all hired for the next patient.

"What's wrong with the emergency generators?" someone asked, and Robin answered, "We save them for really important stuff, like respirators. In case someone stops breathing." For some stupid reason, that got a big laugh.

Hours, or minutes, or maybe weeks, later, Dr. Jay straightened up, his hand on the small of his back, and groaned. "They didn't tell us in medical school there'd be days like this. I'd give my fortune right now for a cup of coffee."

Two doctors, one on R and R at Moonlight Bay and the other a visiting woman doctor, part of an observing team from the States, were working with the nurses and corpsmen. The guy volunteered to get some and was cheered. Pam called to him, asking him to marry her after the war. He shouted back that he'd be glad to discuss it. "My place or yours, Nurse?"

"Lieutenant Nurse to you, Doctor!" There was a chorus of boos.

"Now," Dr. Jay said, "my life would be complete if Harry Kaye would get back from his errand of mercy."

"Mine, too," Robin muttered. Harry had gone out in a Jeep, two days ago, to treat wounded who'd been attacked while on patrol. They were supposed to be about two miles down the road, but he still hadn't returned. She was thoroughly spooked, convinced that he'd been killed. She kept having weird dreams full of dancing women and a huge white bird that flapped in circles around her and filled her with apprehension. Thinking about that bird made her shiver. One of the men said, "Someone walking over your grave, Malone?" and she felt a wave of panic sweep over her. It was time to take a nap.

She returned from a restless sleep a couple of hours later, not at all refreshed, and told Pam to go get some rest. Pam refused. "You didn't sleep for thirty-six hours, and I'm just as good as you are," she said. So Robin walked through Post-Op, smiling, giving pats and drinks of water and other small comforts to the recovering grunts.

The beds were three deep and very close together. Some of the men were in pretty bad shape, but Robin kept that bright smile on her face and hoped she showed nothing. Especially not the anxiety that sat, like a great lump, in the bottom of her stomach. Inside, she was frantic with fear for Harry. Goddammit, where was he? Please, God— And then she stopped herself. It was pretty disgusting to start praying when she didn't even believe in a god.

One of the patients was moaning in his sleep—his whole left side had nearly been torn away—and she checked his IV. He needed more morphine. She glanced at his chart, then bent over him and said, "I'll be right back, Lewis. I know you're hurting but I'm going to help you. I'll bring you something to kill the pain, okay?" In back of her, Pam said, "You think he can hear you?"

"Maybe. Maybe not. I don't care," Robin replied, and went to get the morphine. She was determined to concentrate on her patients and stop worrying about—

"Harry?" she said, almost unable to believe her eyes. Suddenly, there he was, his clothes torn, sporting a scraggly red beard, looking as if he was ready to fall over. Shaky, but definitely alive. "Harry! It *is* you, isn't it?"

"Watsamatta, baby, you don't recognize John Wayne when you see him?"

That was Harry for you, but he was walking ever so carefully and he seemed to be all wrapped with bandage. Still, he was on his feet, he was alive, he was okay. She rushed to him, weak with relief, tears pouring from her eyes.

He stood very still, and said, "Would you mind giving me a hug, Robbie baby? Just to make sure I don't fall over." When she embraced him, she could feel him sway with fatigue, and she shouted for help.

Out of nowhere, it seemed, two Vietnamese men appeared, one rather elderly and one very young. They bore him to a chair where he promptly passed out, still wearing that goofy wonderful smile on his face. The men bowed to Robin, and the younger one explained.

Dr. Harry's Jeep had been hit—boom! The kid pantomimed an explosion and showed how Harry had been thrown out.

Robin was listening intently but she made a mental note to ask Harry how come these villagers knew him well enough to call him by name. He had several broken ribs and lacerations all along his arm, which they had patched up. They said they hoped their efforts had not been too amateur, and apologized for anything they might have done wrong. Members of their family had found him and brought him back to their village. They brought him straight here, as soon as they could.

She thanked them, and began to unwind the bandages carefully. Not bad, for amateurs. Still bowing and smiling and wishing good health to Doctor Harry, they left.

After Harry came to and got some food into his stomach, she began to rebandage his ribs. "You know those guys?"

"What guys, baby?"

"The two villagers who wrapped your wounds and brought you home to my loving arms in one piece?" Her tone said, *And don't bullshit me, if you don't mind.*

"Oh, yeah. I treated one of their children last year. Every once in a while, I go over there to make sure they're doing okay. They live a mile or so outside of Bu Huy, kind of isolated. Christ, am I happy to see you. When I was blown out of the Jeep, I wondered if I ever would again. The driver was blown to bits."

"So that's where you go, all those times you take off."

"What're you talking about, Robbie?"

"About once a week, you disappear and I've been wondering—"

"For Christ's sake, Robin, I take off many times a week. I'm a doctor, remember? I make house calls."

"They seemed to know you very well."

"The kid, he was just a baby, he needed bowel surgery. The family camped out nearby and came in to see him every day. We got to know each other. Why are we talking about this instead of how horny I am?" He took her hand and placed it over a rather rampant erection. The thought of his big stiff rod pushing into her turned her to liquid. She fought off a smile and said, "No making passes at the nurses." But she was wet and ready for him, and she had to concentrate to keep her hands from shaking as she finished taping his ribs. He pulled her toward him and kissed her passionately. She sank into his arms, her heart knocking against her chest. She wanted him so bad. And he knew it. When he pulled away from her, he was grinning ear to ear.

"Well?" he said. She whispered, "Yes, you bastard, yes, yes!" He threw his head back and laughed, and then cried, "Ouch! Hey! At last, I can truly say it only hurts when I laugh."

"Oh, Harry!" She leaned over, carefully, and kissed him again.

"Just one little problem, baby, you'll have to do all the work."

"Believe me," Robin said, helping him to his feet, "that won't be a problem."

When the Army Surgical Hospital at Da Nang called him for a consult, Robin protested. Loudly. "Oh, Harry, don't go. It's not fair. You just got back."

"Yeah, but I've spent the last three days doing nothing but screwing you, baby. That counts as R and R, you know. Army regs."

"Your ribs haven't healed."

"I don't need my ribs to look at a guy and give my expert opinion, Robbie."

"Harry. Don't go. Please."

"I'll bring you back something really neat from Da Nang. A skimpy black nightie maybe."

"That's a present for *you*, goofus."

"A skimpy black bikini for me, then."

"Oh, Harry, you really should rest."

But she knew it was no use. He loved his work, and he was awfully good at it. Why should she gripe if he wanted to save some poor soldier's life? Wasn't that what she liked to do?

So the next morning, they smiled into each other's eyes, and kissed lightly. He said, "Be true to me, Robin, while I'm gone." They laughed, because he'd be back tomorrow. He climbed aboard the Huey and waved. The day was horribly hot and sticky, but she stood out in the sun until the chopper was well out of sight. Being in love was wonderful.

A few hours later, Pamela came into the O.R. where Robin

was checking supplies. "Robin," she said. When Robin turned and saw how white and drawn her friend's face was, she nearly stopped breathing.

"What's happened?" Her voice sounded far, far away, like someone else's voice. "What is it? It's Harry, isn't it. It's Harry. Oh, Jesus, what? What? *What?*"

Then Pam's face twisted up and she began to cry.

Robin ran outside. A Huey had landed and she'd never even heard it. She saw right away it was not the chopper Harry had left in. And there were three gurneys lined up. She ran, thinking, *No. No. No. No, no, no, no, no. Please.*

When she saw him on the gurney, she knew immediately that he was dead. She knew, even though there was no blood, no missing arms or legs, no gaping holes, no shattered head, no vacuum pants. She looked over to the other two bodies. The same thing. They looked unhurt—strange, but unhurt. When she got up close and knelt down she saw that their arms and legs were at funny angles. She reached for Harry's hand and it didn't feel like a hand. Every bone in it had been broken. She could not breathe. There was no air. She was going to pass out.

The zoomie standing nearby said, "Their plane collided with another one. The other guys burned up. But these guys . . . It was so weird, like picking up an empty suit of clothes."

Robin found her voice. In a monotone, she began to explain, even as her brain was in meltdown.

"The impact must have ruptured everything. Respiration must have cut off because of herniation of the brain." And then her thoughts left her. She began screaming, just screaming. No words, not even his name. Just the terrified sounds of unthinkable loss and unknowable grief.

40

April 1968

Five weeks. No, six. Was it really that long since—? Robin stopped the thought midway. She could not allow herself to finish it; she couldn't bear it. So she kept her mind occupied by keeping very, very busy. She was checking the patients in Intensive Care when she spotted an officer—all neat and uniformed—who didn't belong there, moving among the beds, peering at the occupants. *What the hell?*

She marched up to him and said, "Excuse me, Captain, can I help you?"

"No thanks, Nurse. I need to talk to whoever's in charge."

"Lieutenant, if you don't mind."

"Excuse me. Lieutenant."

"I'm in charge of this unit. So I ask you again, how can I help you? What are you doing here?"

"I'm aide to General Roscoe," he said, so proudly that she expected him to salute. "I'm checking out your unit. To see if there are really gross wounds—you know, things that might, like, upset him. I don't want the general upset by anything he sees."

She blinked at him. Was he stupid, or just R.A.? "And just why is General Roscoe coming here?" she demanded. She knew there was only one reason generals came to the One-Six-One.

"Why, to give the men their Purple Hearts."

Robin motioned the aide over to a corner where she whispered intently to him, "Now, listen up, Captain. This ward is full of young men who've put their lives on the line for your General Roscoe. You see these brave young men? They're badly wounded, some of them dying, and I *want* General Roscoe to get upset when he sees them. Let him see what happens when he orders troops to move out and engage the enemy."

The captain, who was quite young and looked a little scared of her, scurried away without comment. A minute or two later, he came back with the general, a tall heavy-set older man, who ignored her completely. He went briskly from bed to bed, pinning medals on the patients' blue pj's, looking as if he wished he were somewhere else. Maybe, Robin thought acidly, he should be up at one of the firebases. Maybe he should see some action, some blood.

She stood at the other end of the room, wondering if he was ever going to look up and acknowledge her. Then one of the patients called, "Malone!" in a tone that said something was very wrong, so she hurried over.

When she got to his bed, he was fine. But he gestured to the next bed. "Do something," he said. The other man was gasping for breath and she could hear the terrible rattle that usually meant death. Swiftly, she bent over him and breathed into his mouth, ordering silently, *Come on, don't give up on me, come on.* But there was no life left in him. He'd come in dressed in vacuum pants, and that was always touch-and-go because the minute you took off the pants, which were holding him together, the guy was likely to bleed to death. They'd managed to pull this one through, but he hadn't really been responding well. He hadn't even opened his eyes since the operation.

She leaned over again and pressed a kiss onto his forehead. Then she straightened up, pulled the sheet over his face, and jotted down the name and time of death on her pad. She blotted out any feelings she might have. It was important to feel nothing at all.

Bingo had called her in after Harry . . . Anyway, she'd called her into the office.

"Robin, I know you're mourning Dr. Kaye. We all are."

"Yes, Colonel."

Bingo leaned forward across her desk, peering closely at

Robin, who stood even straighter than usual under her scrutiny.
She was determined to be properly military. Colonel Batten
had told her staff often enough that nurses were not allowed to
have feelings, and since she was the C.O., she should know,
right?

"Let me remind you that the enemy has not let up."

"Yes, Colonel."

"Let me further remind you that there's no time for
grieving, not when you're an army nurse."

"No, Colonel."

"No time for crying."

"You needn't be concerned about me, Colonel."

"Good."

She'd hadn't yet cried over Harry. She didn't understand
it. She should have shed gallons of tears, but she was empty
and dry.

She was still standing by the dead grunt, pad in hand, when
General Roscoe came to the bed and pinned a medal on the
sheet. Horrified, Robin said, "Don't you think it's a little late
for that, General? Considering he's dead?" She couldn't believe her audacity. Neither could General Roscoe, apparently,
who turned to her with a baleful glare. But something in her
face changed his expression. To her surprise, he did not demand her name or dress her down. Instead, he mumbled something about how stressful this duty must be for a woman, and
then handed her the rest of the Purple Hearts. "Here, Lieutenant," he said brusquely. "You do the rest of them." He
turned on his heel and left, his aide close behind.

Robin announced to the room at large, "I have Purple
Hearts for everyone. I want you all to know that our country is
eternally grateful to each one of you. When you get back
Stateside, you will get the heroes' welcome you all deserve."
She proceeded down the room, bed by bed, saying, "Thank
you," to each man.

Robin knew she was lying. One of the U.S.O. gals, a singer,
coming through a week or so ago, had bunked with them for a
couple of nights. She'd told them that, Stateside, there was a
lot of ugly feeling about this war and that went for the soldiers
who were fighting it, too.

"Hell, the *grunts* didn't start this!" Pam cried. The singer, Susie, said she knew that and they knew that, but the men should be prepared when they ended their tours. "They won't be welcomed back," she said. "They won't be considered heroes. Nobody will ask them what it was like. Everybody will stay away from the whole subject. Believe me," she finished. "I'm old enough to remember other wars, and this one is *different*."

Well, at least I thanked them, Robin thought. And who knew how many of them would actually make it back to a V.A. hospital?

Still deep in her thoughts, she turned around to see, standing patiently the way they did, a *mamasan* holding a little girl, a baby of about a year. The child was really cute and obviously the child of a G.I. She hardly looked Asian at all. The woman, who was maybe fifty, though it was often hard to tell with the Vietnamese, was quite lovely. She bowed politely and spoke in French, slowly, using simple words. Robin, who'd taken four years of French, was amazed to find that she understood most of what the woman was saying.

"Pardonnez-moi, Lieutenant. Je suis Madame Chiou. Cette enfante, elle est la fille de ma fille qui est disparue ou, peut-être, morte—et la fille aussi du Docteur Harry." She pronounced it "Airy," but Robin knew who it was, and her heart began to hammer. Madame Chiou went on, asking if it were not true, that *le docteur Airy* practiced at this hospital *ici*, at the 161st.

At this point, Robin could no longer hear anything, much less translate from the French. She interrupted the woman and sent someone to get Joe the bartender. He was Canadian French, but the language couldn't be that different from Vietnamese French. Anyway, she hoped not. She motioned Madame Chiou to a seat and stared at the little girl who stared right back. What kind of scam was this, Robin wondered. If you were poor and your daughter had deserted her baby, maybe it was really intelligent to pretend one of the doctors had fathered it. After all, doctors had power and money, right?

Suddenly, the child smiled at her, and Robin gave an involuntary grunt of pain. The baby had Harry's crooked smile, exactly. Then she saw that she had his cleft chin, too, and the same curly hair, only it wasn't Harry's bright copper. More like chestnut. Some of the G.I.s' kids looked less Asian than others, but this child had only the merest hint of it, around the eyes, which were almond-shaped and dark. Harry's baby. Oh, God.

Joe came sauntering in then, pulled up a chair, and began parleying. After much nodding and bowing amid polite phrases, Joe began a simultaneous translation. Robin closed her eyes. It was really astonishing, what pain and anguish this was giving her. But the inexorable conversation went on: first the woman's soft, high-pitched French and then Joe in laconic English, with lots of uhs and ums between phrases.

Madame Chiou gave Robin a shrewd look and began to speak to *her*.

"Malone, she wants to know if the Doctor Harry was, um, your lover."

Numb, Robin nodded.

"Moi aussi . . ." she heard the woman say, and then Joe's voice took over. "Me, too, my man, er, husband, I guess, well, maybe not—my man was a doctor, a French doctor. He was, uh, already married, you understand? Married and Catholic. It was not, um, possible, but, er, I wished to keep our child. My daughter. *Alors . . .* See, Malone, there's no real translation for *alors*, I guess we'd say, oh, well." Madame Chiou gave a woman-of-the-world shrug.

Through a kind of haze, Robin said, "Ask her what happened. To her daughter. She told me she either disappeared or was dead. Anyway, I think that's what she said."

A brief exchange. Then, Joe said, "She was Viet Cong, her mother thinks. She needed to prove she was true Vietnamese . . . wait." The woman spoke rapidly. "The villagers were cruel to her, because of her mixed parentage. But Madame was, um, determined, I guess, to keep her daughter. Li Minh, that's the daughter's name. And now Li Minh has left, without a note, without a word, left without her child."

"Sans l'enfante," Robin repeated. "Yes, I got that."

"You okay, Malone?"

A really bright smile. "Perfect!"

"I don't think so, Malone. Hey! I get it! You didn't know, did you?"

"No. Did *you*?"

"Well—yeah. Now wait, Malone, don't look at me that way. When Harry fell in love with you, he swore me to secrecy. He said he was going to tell you himself, as soon as he was sure you really loved him. It ended between them, I think, as soon as he laid eyes on you."

"Christ, I—" Robin began, angrily. But Madame Chiou had begun to talk again, and she was looking at Robin pleadingly. "What does she want?"

"She asks—um—to see—uh—Harry, Malone. She says he was always very generous to Li Minh and now that she is gone, surely he will want to take his daughter home with him. To the States, where nobody will hate her and call her names and, um, throw dirt at her."

"Oh, God." What was she supposed to do? What was she supposed to think? It was all too much to take in. Although it did explain certain of Harry's absences, certain silences. She found she was furious with Harry, dead or not. Dammit, why hadn't he ever told her, the coward? Despite the little voice in the back of her head that said, *Whoa there, kiddo, you weren't going to tell him about the abortion. Yeah, but. Oh, the bastard! The bastard!*

Finally, she looked the older woman straight in the eyes and said, bluntly, *"Le docteur Airy . . . il est mort."*

"Mort . . . ah . . ." The woman gave her a look of such tender sorrow that Robin had to turn away.

She watched woman and child leave, and then walked out of the ward herself, without thanking Joe. She walked away quickly, almost at a run. Trying to get away from her thoughts, which were chasing each other around and around in her head. Why did she kill his child, leaving her with nothing of him, nothing at all? She had been so stupid! Didn't she realize that this was a real war, a war that killed men? She was so full of sorrow, so full of grief!

He had made a baby with some other woman! Oh, God, how that hurt. He had slept with this Vietnamese woman's daughter, had held her the way he used to hold Robin, had grabbed handfuls of her hair when he was about to climax, had spooned around her in the night. Robin clenched her fists and let the tears come. Harry's child. The little girl looked so much like him, too. And the mother was gone, probably for good.

She walked out of the compound and down the dusty road on her way to nowhere. As the sun was setting, she was still walking, her T-shirt soaked with sweat and her feet sore. It was a relief to hear the sound of a Jeep coming up behind her. Sure enough, as she had guessed, it was Joe and, next to him, looking worried, Pam Boone.

"Malone, you're too damned old to run away from home," Pam said. "And you're limping a little. I told you those shoes were too small."

"You did no such thing," Robin said, climbing into the back of the Jeep. "I bought these shoes in San Francisco."

Joe turned around. "Where to?" he inquired.

"Home, James. I'm too damned old to run away."

He swung the vehicle around in a circle and they headed back for Moonlight Bay. Robin was ready to go back. An idea had come to her and, the more she examined it, the more excited she became. Why shouldn't she, Robin Malone, become the orphan child's mother? Why shouldn't there be something of Harry Kaye left when this damn war was finally over? Her tour was ending soon. She would take his little girl home with her. Adopt her. Yes! Harry's baby and now hers, too. Yes!

She leaned forward and grabbed Joe's shoulder. "Stop!" she ordered.

He stopped. "What's the matter? You sick?"

"No, no, not sick. In fact, I'm very well and getting better all the time. I want you to drive us to Madame Chiou's village."

"Now?" Pam said. "It's almost dark."

"Yes, now. Can we, Joe? Please?"

"Nope. Sorry. Harry never said where it was. He just used to wave a hand vaguely north and west."

"Well, someone's got to know where they came from. I've got it! The kid! The kid with the bowel obstruction! I'll look through all the records. Okay, Joe, sorry I made you stop. Let's go back. I'm going to find that village if it takes me another tour to do it!"

As it turned out, it took three days of searching through all the patient records. Even when the three of them headed out again in the Jeep, they weren't absolutely sure they were heading for the right village. It was called Ca Binh—they thought—and it wasn't too far from Qui Nhon—maybe. But a young woman named Li Minh, surname Chiou, had come in to the One-Six-One almost two years before, with a gun-shot wound in her thigh. Sniper fire, she said. Her chart was scribbled in Harry's spiky hand. It seemed right. Besides, it was all they had. So, they headed to Ca Binh.

Joe was driving too fast, as usual. Pam and Robin had elected to sit in the back, where they could hang on to each other. At one bend in the road, sniper fire zinged past them, and Joe made an about-face with the Jeep, nearly tipping them out onto the road and splashing water into the Jeep as he went plowing through a deep puddle. The rainy season had begun.

"Back we go, ladies."

"Now, wait," Robin insisted. "You promised we'd go to Ca Binh and see if Madame Chiou is there. You *promised*. You said scout's honor."

"Malone, you want to get *killed*? Those are not little boys playing war games out there. That's Uncle Ho and he means it!"

"According to the map, we're almost there. Come on. We've been here in plain view for five minutes now and they haven't fired again. Come on, Joe. Let's find Ca Binh. And if Madame Chiou isn't there, that's it, that's the end."

"Scout's honor?"

She held up two fingers, but he only laughed and said, "The wrong two, Malone. Didn't you have Girl Scouts in Brooklyn? Oh, never mind. I give up. I never could resist a pretty face. Onward and upward to Ca Binh!" He reversed the Jeep, going from zero to fifty in about two seconds. The speeding car sent up huge dirty sprays on either side, like the wake of a boat. The two nurses wiped mud from each other's faces, glad that at least it wasn't pouring rain.

A mile or so later, Robin spotted light glinting off water—

Ca Binh was situated near a small river—and in a minute, they could see smoke coming from houses. They cheered, and the Jeep continued bumping down a road that had been built for oxen. Or built *by* oxen, most likely. When they got to the village, they were instantly surrounded by about a hundred small curious children, all of whom wanted to touch the Jeep and try everything. Then the adults, women and old men, for the most part, appeared.

Joe had some Vietnamese and a lot of French, and when that failed, he used sign language and pantomime. When he finally made himself understood, there was much head-shaking and hand-waving and acting out. Robin got it; they all did. Madame Chiou was not there in the village. She had taken the baby and gone. To Saigon? No. To Bu Huy, to the nuns.

Robin groaned. "All this way, and she's practically next door to us?"

"That's the way she goes," Joe said philosophically. He produced, as if by magic, candy and gum, which he proceeded to hand out. When they left, the villagers were smiling and waving and shouting in Vietnamese—"wishing us luck," Joe explained.

So back to Bu Huy they went. At least there, they could find someone who spoke English, in case Madame had once again flown the coop. The orphanage was run by French-speaking Vietnamese nuns, with one or two French nuns who spoke English. When they pulled into the big bare yard in the middle of the compound, it had started to rain, but that didn't bother the orphans. Most of them were all but naked, anyway. Robin spotted the little girl, sitting calmly in the middle of some sort of ball game, studying a bug. Oh, God, the expression on her face, that total concentration, the drawing down of the brows! So like him. Robin gazed at the child, feeling her heart contract, and she knew that she really had to become this baby's mother.

She said so to Pamela, and Pam said, "How? Your tour is over in three weeks. You're going home. And anyway, you're not married. They never let unmarried women adopt."

"Who is this 'they'?" Robin said smartly, but she knew it would probably be an uphill battle. A G.I., at the One-Six-

One, a sergeant, head of the M.P. unit, had fallen in love with his Vietnamese girlfriend, and when she was killed during a shelling, he tried to get their child sent back to his mother. Robin had heard how frustrated he'd become. The Vietnamese government was strangely unwilling to let any of the mixed-race children leave, even though they would be disdained and isolated for the rest of their lives if they stayed here. She also had a good idea of how strict adoption regulations were in the States. If you were Jewish, you had to find a "Jewish baby." The baby born of a Catholic mother was considered Catholic, and only a Catholic family could adopt. The same for Protestant. Adopting a child of a different race? Impossible. Robin thought it was crazy. Hell, if they asked her what her religion was, what would she say? She had no religion! Maybe she should tell them she was part American Indian; weren't they supposed to have come from Asia originally?

"Don't worry," she said to Pam. "I figure we can beat the system. We haven't been in the army for two years for nothing!"

"What's this *we*?" Pam said. "No, no, only kidding. Of course I'll help. But I don't think there's anything I can do, Malone. Now Joe, here . . ." She turned to him, grinning. "He could *really* help out."

"How?" Joe was genuinely puzzled.

"You marry Malone. They're much more likely to let a couple adopt."

"Hold on a minute. I'm willing to drive you anywhere, anywhere in the world. But—marriage?"

"Don't worry, Joe." Robin was laughing. "It's not such a good idea, anyway."

Shyly, Robin knelt in front of the little girl and held out her arms. "Wanna come to me, sweetie?" The child smiled and held out her pudgy arms. "Aw—"

Robin stood up, holding the baby, suddenly aware that her diaper was not only covered with dirt, but was soaking wet. "I'll be right back," she told her friends. "She has to be changed and I have to be introduced."

Inside, she found a very young Vietnamese nun who was obviously attached to the baby. Without hesitation, the nun took the little girl from Robin's arms. "Wet!" she said, wrinkling her nose. "Thank you for bringing her to me."

"What is she called?" Blank. "Her name."

"Ah. Name. Nguyen Ninh. Ninh, we say."

Silently, Robin tried "Ninh Malone." Fairly ridiculous. And "Ninh Kaye" sounded even worse. She didn't want the kids making fun of *her* little girl! And then she had it. Nina. Nina Malone. Yes! Perfect!

"Please," she said to the nun, holding out her arms. "May I? *Un moment, seulement.*" Wow! Where'd that French come from? She was impressed. So, apparently, was the Sister, who reluctantly gave up her charge, saying, "Wet, wet," as if Robin didn't already know.

"Un moment," Robin repeated, taking Nina into her embrace. She walked up and down the reception room, murmuring to the child, telling her about Brooklyn and New York: ". . . and there's a big green lady called the Statue of Liberty, I'll take you on a ferry boat and you'll see her. . . . My gran and my aunt Addie used to take me on the Staten Island ferry a lot, and I loved the Statue of Liberty, and that means you will, too, because by then, I'll be your mommy, won't that be nice?"

Robin patted the silky, almost auburn curls and kissed the round cheeks. The baby listened, very good-natured and obviously interested in the sound of this new voice. She put her fingers into Robin's mouth; she patted her face and stared into her eyes. She was so cute! She was absolutely perfect.

Soon, too soon, the young nun came to get Nina. Robin kissed the baby, loath to let her go. When she went back outside, Madame Chiou was standing with Pam and Joe and a tall, elderly nun who, Robin soon learned, was the Mother Superior. "Mother, I want to adopt Nina—Ninh. Nguyen Ninh. Madame Chiou's granddaughter." The two older women talked briefly. Then Madame Chiou turned to Robin with a brilliant smile, and spoke in rapid French, of which Robin caught only one word: *"Merci. Merci."*

"No. *Merci à vous!*" There were smiles all around as they left. "Well," Robin said, settling back into the hard back seat of the Jeep, "that's that."

But of course it wasn't. She started with H.Q. and, after fif-

teen phone calls, finally found a Lieutenant Carville who seemed
to know something. "First thing, the child must have a medical clearance," he told her.

"Fine," Robin said. "It just so happens I'm in a hospital. I'll
have one of the doctors here do it."

Lt. Carville cleared his throat. "I only wish it were that
simple, Lieutenant Malone. See, it takes six months to a year
to get medical clearance from the Vietnamese authorities. And
then you'll have to have a visa for the child."

"And how do I do *that*? Who do I see?"

"Well, since 1959 in the States, any foreign child needs to
meet state adoption requirements before she can be issued a
visa by the Immigration and Naturalization Service. Where
you from, Lieutenant Malone? New York? Let's see, in New
York State, the requirements include a provision that a licensed
adoption agency be held responsible for any child brought into
the country for adoption. So you'll have to find an adoption
agency in New York."

"You wouldn't have any idea how I do that, would you?"

"Sorry. No. Why don't you try a Vietnamese adoption
agency? They might know."

Unfortunately, there was no such thing as a Vietnamese
adoption agency. Not a single professional organization in
Vietnam dealt with orphans. In fact, the whole concept of
adoption had been virtually unknown in Vietnam until 1960,
she found out, and then it had only to do with Vietnamese children being adopted by Vietnamese families in Vietnam. Inter-
country adoptions were almost nonexistent. She learned, by
calling everyone under the sun, that war orphans were not a
top priority for anyone. Not for the U.S. Army—which had
provided most of the fathers, Robin thought angrily—not for
the Vietnamese government, not for the United States government. Nobody could help her; nobody knew anything. Officials all threw up their hands and said, "Sorry. I don't know
anything about this."

"I'm so damned frustrated at all the uncaring shrugs from
uncaring bureaucrats," she complained at the rec hall bar, one
rainy night. "I swear, I'm going to fake the necessary papers. No, I'll lie and say she's mine." Jerry Marx, one of the

new doctors said, "Yeah, sure. You ever hear of kidnapping? They'll get you for that!"

"What are they going to do to me?" Robin said. "Send me to Vietnam?"

They laughed, but it was becoming distinctly unfunny. And who had unlimited time to deal with bureaucrats and get the runaround, time and time again?

Robin had thought she might sign up for a second tour, but now it was obvious that she'd have to go home and get the adoption accomplished from there. She elicited a promise from Madame Chiou and Mother Superior and the French doctor that the medical clearance business would be started immediately. And that they wouldn't let anyone else take the child Robin already thought of as her own.

The gang threw her a farewell party, complete with hamburgers on the beach, volleyball game, and drinks on the house at Joe's Place. Nobody mentioned Harry's name. Nobody ever did. It was an unspoken rule: We don't talk about our sorrows. Hell, we don't *have* sorrows. We have strength, instead. Robin wanted to cry; she wanted to mourn her lost love, especially now that she was leaving the place where he had died. Why were her eyes so stubbornly dry? Because once you started crying, how could you stop?

She pounded her glass on the bar and called, "Barkeep! Another one of your fine Old Grandads, if you please!" A zoomie in for a couple of days R and R, a nice guy named Roy, was making moves on her. Maybe she'd give him a break. Maybe not. Everyone danced and sang along with the jukebox. The popular song of the moment went "We gotta get out of this place, if it's the last thing we ever do." They played that one over and over. She had another drink; she danced with Roy and she sang along. She danced with all the doctors and all the patients, including one guy in a wheelchair. At some point, the zoomie found a better deal and disappeared. She didn't care. Something big and important, maybe the biggest most important thing in her life, was about to end, and she needed to be there for every last minute of it.

Dawn found her with Pamela and Joe, sitting on the beach, watching the sun rise over the South China Sea while the tide went out. Then it was time to go. The Huey that would take her to Saigon was standing in the middle of the big red cross. Her eyes blinded by the morning sun, her dress blues already wilting on her body, Robin suddenly felt she couldn't say good-bye. Couldn't speak at all.

She climbed into the chopper and, as it lifted straight up off the ground, she leaned out and waved to everyone. To everything. To what she had lost. To what she had found. The chopper rose into the sky and turned, heading south to Saigon. She leaned way out, hoping to catch a glimpse of Bu Huy, but they were going the wrong way.

She waved good-bye, anyway, and made a silent promise to the baby. *"I'm going to be your mommy, if it's the last thing I ever do."*

41

September 1969

It was a madhouse at the International Arrivals building at JFK Airport—especially in the area above Customs, where you could look down and try to spot the person you'd been waiting for since the beginning of time. That's how Robin felt: as if she'd been waiting since the age of the dinosaurs for the plane to land. The plane that—finally, at last, at last, finally—was carrying Nina to her new life in the U.S.A.

Nina and four other orphans. That was the latest wrinkle. The Vietnamese government would not release any orphan until there were at least five of them. Then they were sent as a group. Why five and not six, or four, or seventeen, nobody could say. It was a rule, period, end of discussion. Until it got changed, suddenly, one day without warning.

A fat loud woman with a Queens accent, yanking her two obnoxious children behind her, pushed past Robin, yelling. Robin thought of saying something smartass that would silence her; then she decided to hell with it, it wasn't worth it. Her nerves were shot, as it was. She might as well get out of here. You couldn't tell one person from another from the viewing area, especially not a small girl who had grown and changed since the last time Robin saw her. Robin wasn't even sure she remembered what Nina looked like.

So, instead of giving a piece of her mind to the rude woman and her brats, she backed away and walked over to her parents, who had taken seats on a bench. They were tired and nervous. She was tired and nervous. The waiting seemed endless. She had told them not to come with her. "I'd rather be alone," she'd said. "I'm nervous enough as it is."

But Dr. Birdie Malone, that no-nonsense pediatrician, beloved of all the young mommies in Brooklyn Heights, would have none of that. "Don't be ridiculous," she'd sniffed. "Nobody should be alone at a time like this. Don't worry, we won't bother you. We'll stay in the background. But we'll be there if you need us. And, anyway, we're her grandparents now, and she'll want to meet us."

There was no arguing with Mom. There never had been. The only way to escape her was to make a break for it and go somewhere else. Unfortunately, Robin thought ruefully, she couldn't do that until her life was more settled. Until Nina was finally here and had made the adjustment. Then, she'd think about moving out of the big house at 3 Clinton Street, and leaving her stupid job at Cadman Memorial. She was working in the O.R., one of the more exciting and satisfactory nursing jobs in the hospital, and hating it—chafing at having to bow and scrape and behave and obey.

Her mother couldn't understand her unhappiness. Robin had tried to explain how, in Vietnam, she had worked side by side with the surgeon, not behind him. "I was trusted, Mom, looked up to. I was head of the O.R. and no patient was admitted without my say-so. Yeah, me, a nurse. But it was so different, there. I had everyone's respect."

"But you were not a doctor."

Robin had blinked at that. Then she got it. "No, I'm not a doctor, and if you want to say, 'I told you so,' go right ahead. And, yes, the doctors had the final say-so. First of all, they were captains and the nurses were lieutenants, so they out-ranked us. But, Mom, I'm not saying there was no difference between doctors and nurses. It's just that . . ." She searched and searched for something that would make it clear to her mother, who was looking at her expectantly. "It's just that the difference wasn't so *great*. The nurses weren't there to serve the doctors. They were there to take care of the wounded." She stopped talking, because she could see it wouldn't do any good. Her mother was polite but puzzled.

"Never mind." Why mention that she used to work in her army greens—T-shirt and pants, with her dog tags around her neck—when now she had to wear a goddamned starched white dress and stupid winged cap that made her look like she was about to take off? How to explain that she'd made deci-sions every single minute, life-and-death decisions; whereas now she was back to being a handmaiden, asking permission for every goddam thing, not allowed to think for herself, only to follow orders.

She was always getting into trouble at Cadman for doing more than she was allowed to, for using her brain more than she was allowed to. Her supervisor had actually gone to her mother, for Christ's sake, as if Robin were six years old.

"You're taking too much upon yourself, Robin," Mom had told her. "In Vietnam, they may have let you play doctor. You can't do that here. If you wanted to be a doctor, you should have gone to medical school when I offered it to you. But, no, you had to 'find yourself!' So now you're a nurse. Act like one instead of a poor imitation of a physician!"

Robin was breathless with that "play doctor" comment. It was so unfair. "How am I supposed to just forget everything I learned in-country? I can't! I know how to put in chest tubes. I know how to close after surgery. I can do a trach and I can triage with the best doctors at Cadman Memorial. I can't go back to being the kind of nurse I was before!"

Her mother's response: "Well, my dear, I'm afraid you'll just *have* to." There was a pause, and then she added, "And, Robin ... people are not ... comfortable with the Vietnam War. It was not a popular war, you know."

"Well, it was even less popular with the boys who lost arms and legs and lives fighting it!"

"I think our conversation is over. Your supervisor asked me to talk with you and I have done so. The rest is up to you."

Fair or not, she had to have a regular job. Nursing was at least well paid. It was better than starting all over again as an office temp or God knows what. She was a mother now, she reminded herself—or would be, as soon as Nina arrived.

Her parents were sitting patiently—at least Mom was, leafing through a magazine. Her father, as usual, was all nervous energy. His foot tapped and he cracked his knuckles while he looked around. In a minute, her mother would say, "JJ, for the love of heaven! Stop *doing* that!" And he'd stop for a minute or two, while he was thinking about it, and then he'd start up again.

Robin had come back from Vietnam amazed to find JJ in the house. At first, she was wild. What the hell did he mean, just walking back into their lives as if he'd never walked out?

"How can you take him back, after what he did to us?" she'd demanded of her mother; who had calmly replied, "The relationship between your father and me is personal and private, Robin. And as it happens, I love him."

"Are you crazy?" The moment she said it, she regretted the words.

Her mother looked at her calmly, then said, "And you, Robin. Do you consider what you're doing sane? Adopting a child who isn't in any way related to you? Cutting yourself off from any possibility of marriage and a normal life?"

Her mother had a point. It was a totally insane idea, totally. And the craziest part of it was, she'd done it, despite a year-long nightmare of lies and evasions and changes in the rules and changes in the laws. But she'd stuck with it and she'd won. Suddenly, it struck her that maybe her mother felt that way about JJ—that she'd been patient and stuck with it and had finally won.

Robin studied her parents sitting on the bench. What if she didn't know them? What would she see? A good-looking middle-aged couple who seemed totally comfortable with each other. The woman, petite and slender with strawberry blond hair—you couldn't tell if the color was real or not—cut to just below her ears, neat in her crisp white blouse and slim skirt. The man, his handsome features sagging, but with a full head of thick blazing white hair. JJ was going to the gym and had actually become quite muscular. He'd had a couple of bit parts in movies being shot in the New York area, and he was pleased with himself.

When he'd first come back, he was still a heavy drinker. In fact, he'd always taken a thermos of orange juice to the gym each morning, liberally spiked with vodka, until her mother had finally caught on. She had put her foot down. Stop drinking or get out. Now he was in AA and driving Robin crazy, telling her she ought to join. She snapped at him to mind his own business. "If you'd been in Vietnam, you'd know why I drink!"

"Hey, Robin, didn't I drink my way through Sicily and Italy in 1943? I know damn well why you drink. I also know guys who never stopped. And the way you're going . . ."

She told him to shut up. "I'm in control of my drinking, don't worry about me. I don't need AA." It was true that occasionally, when she'd had a particularly bad day at the hospital or memories of Harry came flooding back suddenly, she'd take sips from a bottle until it all fuzzed out and she could fall asleep and forget. And, yes, sometimes on weekends, she'd go to a bar she liked in Park Slope where veterans tended to gather. More than once, she'd awakened in the morning in a bed she didn't remember getting into, with a guy she didn't remember going home with. That was pretty scary.

But she always made it to work. It wasn't interfering with her life. In fact, she was more efficient now than she'd ever been, even working on a Ph.D. in psychology in night school, a few courses at a time. Once her little girl was here with her,

she'd just stop drinking. She could stop, she told herself, anytime she wanted to.

As Robin stood there, staring at her parents, her mother
looked up from the magazine and met her eyes. She raised her
eyebrows questioningly and Robin shook her head. *No, I
didn't spot her.* Odd: Mom insisting on being here with her
when, all through her childhood, everyone else had come first.
But Robin said to herself, *Oh shut up, will you? You had Gran
and Addie. You had more mothering than a lot of people get.* If
only she didn't keep losing people she loved.

But now she was getting someone she loved. A little bit of
Harry. Harry—who still haunted her dreams. The adoption
battle had taken over a year. There were so many holdups,
so many stupid people who wouldn't budge from their rules
and regulations. She had needed dozens of damned documents
from the orphanage in Vietnam: Ninh's birth certificate, a release from the orphanage, photographs. A social worker's
report on the child's emotional condition, a doctor's report on
her physical condition. An exit visa from the government. A
background report on Ninh's parents. That had been a tricky
one. With trepidation, Robin had contacted Harry's parents in
Florida. She made a date and flew down to see them, to tell
them about Ninh.

The Kayes were great. She sat down in their Florida room
bright with citrus colors, hemmed and hawed for a while and
then, just blurted it all out. She and Harry had been "engaged,"
he had fathered a child with a part-Vietnamese woman, and
Robin now wanted to adopt that child. They didn't faint or
anything. His father said, "Let's have that again? Slower?"
and he smiled at her. It was Harry's smile, crooked and ap-
pealing, the head tipped slightly to one side.

"She smiles like that, too. Ninh. She looks like Harry. She
has his curly hair, it's reddish brown, and she has his grin.
She's so bright."

When Robin finished there was a brief silence. Then, Harry's
mother, with a slight wobble in her voice, asked, "What do
you need?" Mrs. Kaye immediately went to dig up Harry's
school records, his medical records with everything about his
chicken pox and mumps and vaccinations, and his report cards.

By the time Robin left Fort Lauderdale, she and the Kayes were good friends. When she thanked them for being so understanding, Mr. Kaye said, "Look. I'm not going to pretend that we weren't a little shocked to learn that Harry, um— you know. But to find out that he isn't completely . . ." His voice cracked and he stopped speaking.

Mrs. Kaye finished for him. "We hope you'll let us be grandparents to the little girl. Nina." Of course she promised and she intended to keep it.

Madame Chiou did her part, writing a voluminous report on her daughter, who was still missing, according to letters from Pam. The Mother Superior was enlisted to write a report on Ninh and agreed to release her from the orphanage when the time came, her mother being presumed dead.

When it had all been pulled together, Robin realized that the papers couldn't be delivered to her personally. They had to be given to a recognized international social service organization. She got on the horn to Pam at the hospital immediately. The only social service group in Vietnam was ISS, International Social Service. "Well, if it's the only one," she said to Pam, "then I guess it's the one I want."

She called ISS in Saigon and they put her through to a woman called Marjorie Crandell. Miss Crandell said, "Oh, dear, we don't handle individual placements, Miss Malone. We locate and process foreign children for licensed adoption agencies."

"Oh, God! Another problem!" Robin moaned. "It never ends! I can't believe what a hard time I'm having trying to get one orphan child out of Vietnam." To her horror, her voice began to shake as tears started.

"I'm so sorry," said Miss Crandell, and she actually sounded sorry. "And I know just how you feel. But, look. . . . Just because we haven't had any luck yet, doesn't mean it can't happen. Let's give it another try, Miss Malone. I'm willing. How about you?"

What a question! Of course she was willing. She would never understand why adoption was made so impossibly difficult. You'd think everyone would be delighted that an orphan would have a real family, that someone would love her and take care of her and send her to school. But every obstacle that could be put in Robin's way, was put in her way.

For instance, it took months to get all the documents finished and stamped and sent over from Vietnam. Thank God for Madame Chiou, who really wanted to see her granddaughter in a safe place, and for Marjorie Crandell at ISS, who had a wonderful collection of official-looking stamps that she was willing to use with great abandon on all the reports.

"Well, they're all ready. I think. You never know, around here," Marjorie had told her during one of their dozens of phone conversations. "And now, I'm afraid you'll have to come here."

"Here?" Robin echoed stupidly.

"Yes. To Saigon. You'll have to collect all these reports and put them together. Then there are a few government officials who have to look at them and stamp them, so—"

So she went. It felt awfully strange to find herself in Saigon without the protective coloration of her uniform. Being a civilian was a little like being naked. She met Marjorie in person and was surprised to find her a young, pretty woman. She'd been picturing a librarian type, middle-aged, graying hair pulled back in a bun. Marjorie invited her to bunk down in her apartment, but Robin already had a reservation at one of the big hotels. Anyway, she was planning to spend as much time as possible at the One-Six-One, where she could get rides to Bu Huy.

She spent a week smiling at thousands of anonymous looking men with eyeglasses and glassy stares, trying to hold her temper, and willing them silently to use their goddamn stamps. They kept finding things missing and she'd go back to ISS and tell Miss Crandell. Quite a bit of benign forgery went on and she didn't care. Finally, it was all done. Really, Marjorie? Yes, really, Robin. Whoopee! Let's have a drink to *that*! Let's have two!

Then she hopped a ride on a chopper and went to see the old gang. Pam, who was getting ready to go home, was really glad to see her. So was Joe. Even Bingo Batten smiled and offered her a drink. Every chance she got, she spent with the little girl she now thought of as Nina. Nina was crawling and pulling herself up to stand and trying to talk—and Robin wasn't going to be there to see most of it. It drove her crazy. She was madly in love with the bright little charmer. She had a lot of Harry's mannerisms and, in one hour, learned several words in English. "Mommy." "Hi." "Bye-bye." "Brooklyn." Well, she sort of mangled "Brooklyn," but Robin was sure that Nina was the smartest baby in the entire world.

As soon as she got Stateside, Robin went to the offices of Immigration and Naturalization in downtown Manhattan and plunked the pile of documents down in front of an agent. The agent, a bald man with the face of a sad hound dog, whose nameplate said he was Mr. Golden, spent endless time humming over the papers. When he finally looked up, he said flatly, "You're missing a preadoption certificate from New York State and a home study report, an investigative report from us, and a birth certificate for the child."

"Missing her birth certificate? It's right there." While she went through the pile, he watched with a blank face, utterly disinterested. She found the paper and waved it. "There it is."

He shook his head. "That's not a birth certificate. That's a registration of her birth, a notification of the date and so forth, from the place where she was born. But that's not the same as a birth certificate."

"What in hell's the difference? This says she was born, where, and when! What more do you people want?" She was beside herself with fury.

"Screaming at me won't get you a birth certificate, Mrs. Malone. The regulations call for a stamped, sealed birth certificate from the country of birth and that's what we must have."

A phone call to Marjorie in Saigon brought a very legal-looking birth certificate in the next overseas mail. Another ten days down the rat hole. Robin thought that was the end of it. She was wrong. She had found a good adoption agency, Gladwin-Howell, to sponsor her and Nina, and now the real pain in the rear began. Petitions and forms had to be filled out, in triplicate of course. Documents had to be copied, verified, and reverified. She was fingerprinted, Birdie was fingerprinted, JJ was fingerprinted. Not one, but two home studies

were done. Home studies meant two mean-looking guys came
and looked into every nook and cranny of the house on
Clinton Street. They also snooped into everyone's lives. Even
a doctor, a nurse, and a real live bit-player in the movies didn't
mean beans to the tight-lipped, frozen-faced investigators who
studied the food in the cupboards and the sheets in the linen
closet, the garden and the neighborhood—everything.

After that, the Immigration people made their own investi-
gation, questioning the neighbors and colleagues at the hospital, checking to make sure that Robin hadn't been converted
to Communism over there, asking if anyone had heard that the
child to be adopted was Viet Cong.

"My God, she's just a baby! She doesn't *have* any politics!
What's *wrong* with them?" Robin screamed. But who was she
yelling at? The guys in the bar in Park Slope. *They* couldn't do
anything except agree that bureaucrats were the pits and buy
her another drink.

No sooner was that nightmare over when, about six weeks
ago, the situation in Vietnam suddenly changed, again. The
new Minister of the Interior did not favor foreign adoptions.
Immigration called to say they could not get an exit visa for
Nina. They sounded bored, as usual. So what did she do in her
hour of need? Called Saigon. Marjorie Crandell sounded worried over the telephone. "I'm not sure what's going on, Robin.
The rules have changed again."

"Oh, fuck."

"Indeed," Marjorie agreed. "I wish there were something I
could do. But unfortunately, there's nothing to do but wait.
And hope."

"Yeah. Wait. And hope. My usual. Oh hell, Marjorie, it's
not your fault. You've been super. I guess I just expect you to
pull rabbits out of your hat."

"Sorry. All out of bunnies. But things could change again,
overnight."

Why did she tell Larry Underwood? Who knew? She had
been dating Larry for a few weeks, on and off. He was an
assistant district attorney with the Manhattan office and, like
most of the young men who worked there, hyperactive and
super-aggressive. He drove a Jaguar, a beautiful car which she

was sure he loved more than any human being, and he drove it like a madman. One day, when she asked him, as casually as possible, to please stop playing chicken on the FDR Drive before they got totaled, he grinned at her and said, "My car is my *weapon*, sugar." He was a good lay—his cock was his weapon, too, and he used it aggressively—but hardly the person she would pick to tell her troubles to.

Nevertheless, one evening at the Embers listening to George Shearing, mellowed out on extra dry vodka martinis, she found herself telling him about the shits who worked at Immigration. Well, it turned out that Larry knew people in every government agency, loved throwing his weight around—especially, if he could do it to her applause.

"Immigration's giving you trouble? Give me a couple days, sweetheart."

Like magic, two different agents from Immigration called her, and what a difference in the tone! They'd had a call from Underhill and could they help her in any way? Maybe she should tell them what the problem seemed to be. And lo! A week later, there appeared in the mail a visa for Nina, still called Nguyen Ninh. Shortly after that, New York State in its wisdom sent a preadoption certificate. By that time, she had lost interest in Larry Underhill, whose predatory nature was beginning to wear on her, but she slept with him a few more times anyway, out of gratitude. She felt she owed him *something*.

That was all in the past now. And in a few minutes, she'd have her baby, her Nina, and her real life could begin.

Finally, only two hours late, the passengers from Flight 542 began to trickle out. Robin's heart started to thump. She called to her parents and the three of them crowded around the doors that led out of Customs and Immigration. Robin was expecting the baby she'd seen half a year ago, carried in somebody's arms. And then her mother said, "Is that her, coming out? With curly auburn hair? She doesn't even look Oriental!"

"Where is she? Her father wasn't Vietnamese, remember? He was Jewish . . . just like yours. And her mother's half-French. That makes her about as Oriental as you are Indian."

"Over to the left. Way at the back, with a stewardess and some other children."

Robin pushed forward, feeling as if she were plowing through water, looking for a baby with dark red hair.

Finally, there she was: Nina, a much taller and thinner Nina, walking just like a person—well, just like a toddler—holding a stewardess's hand. She was clutching the teddy bear Robin had brought her when she was in Nam, and looking around with great interest. She'd been overdressed by the orphanage, in her very best clothes, velvet dress and heavy cotton stockings. Poor thing, she must be sweltering. It was very warm. But what was she thinking? The child had spent her whole life in South Vietnam. The temperature was probably around one hundred degrees there now.

"Nina! Nina!" The little girl turned to the sound of her voice. For one horrible moment, Robin was afraid that Nina no longer recognized her. Then Nina gave her that Harry Kaye grin and a little voice piped: *"Maman! Maman! C'est moi!"* in perfect baby French. Nina shook free of the stewardess's hand and came toward Robin at a run. No doubt in *her* about where she was going or where she belonged!

Robin ran to grab her little girl, hugging her fiercely, holding her tight, crying like an idiot from love and excitement. When she felt the little arms going around her neck, hugging her back, she knew it was really over, at last. She sent a silent message: *Okay Harry, now I've got her, and she's mine, she's ours. You'll see, you'll be really proud of her. And that's a firm.*

Epilogue:
Nina Malone Crane, M.D.
Charles Dancing Crane, Ph.D.
Harry K. Crane
Robin Malone, N.P., Ph.D.

Old Saybrook, on Long Island Sound near the Connecticut River, Summer 1997

"It's about time you sold that big old house on Clinton Street, Mom. I mean, you're not exactly getting any younger."

"How kind of you to remind me, Nina," Robin said dryly. But she was not bothered by the comment. It was true, wasn't it? She was fifty-six years old. When she looked at herself in the mirror these days, she was always surprised. Shocked was more like it. She was shocked to see the face that stared back at her, with its sagging flesh and eye pouches, a face that, more often than not, looked weary. Good-looking still, she supposed, but different. Worn down.

Well, she felt worn down. She'd just come back from five months in Menlo Park, California, at the recovery center for combat nurses, particularly those who had been in-country. They'd been mere girls in Vietnam, most of them, not much older than the broken kids who were flown in to be taken care of. They had looked death in the face twenty times a day, day after day after day, had dealt with horror for twelve hours at a stretch with no respite, and were expected—ordered—to remain calm and stoic.

When they got back home, to a hostile country that wanted only to forget that damn war, nobody wanted to hear what the nurses had been through. The army insisted they hadn't really been through so much. After all, they hadn't been in combat.

That was Big Lie Number One. She remembered it—she remembered it only too damned well!—and if dealing with blood and gore all day and night, dealing with death and with terror and with constant loss wasn't combat, then what in hell was?

She'd lost so many people, so many hopes and dreams. She was so angry. But she was a nurse and nurses don't cry, don't mourn, and don't get mad. So, for years, she drank to cover up the rage at having lost her lover and then her best friend. Sweet, good-natured milkmaid Pam Boone, killed by sniper fire the last week of her final tour. Died instantly. Not to mention all those boys who came into the One-Six-One to be put together who, no matter how much you did or how hard you tried, didn't make it. She was mad at having had to say "expectant" so many hundreds of times but never being allowed to scream about it.

Nurses who screamed were considered crazy. Nurses who screamed lost licenses or their children. So most of the army nurses who came back from Nam kept it all tucked away. They didn't lose their licenses or their children; they just lost their minds.

All of that rage had been hidden so deeply that Robin hardly knew it was there. For nearly thirty years, she kept active, occupied. She raised her daughter. She did volunteer tutoring. She took graduate courses. After she became charge nurse in the O.R. at Cadman Memorial, and was asked if she'd like to head up the nursing school, she thought about it and said no. She was sick of being meek and mild and always in the background. She certainly didn't want to train other bright girls, only to have them end up in the same dead end. There was no way to change doctors' mind-sets—including her own mother's.

She went back to school full-time and finished her Ph.D. in psychology and became, of all things, a therapist. There she was, advising and comforting, when she was herself a walking time bomb of rage and sorrow, drinking herself to sleep most nights.

Getting up from the lounge chair, she walked to the far end of the deck, overlooking Long Island Sound. The day was clear and bright with a steady breeze, so the water was dotted with little white sails.

"Can you ever tell which of those boats is Charlie's?" she asked.

Nina shook her head. "Never. But if he asks if I saw him out there, waving, I always say yes. Otherwise, he's so disappointed. Charlie is a true romantic."

"You're lucky," Robin said.

"Don't I know it! He doesn't even mind that I'm smart." They both laughed, remembering all the boys who *had* minded when Nina was a teenager.

"I told you, didn't I? I told you it would get better."

"And it sure did," Nina said, with a glance at the old cradle sitting in the shade of the overhang. She got up from her chair and bent to coo at the baby.

He was two months old, his name was Harry K. Crane, and yes, he had red curly hair. Robin was madly in love with her grandson. She hadn't realized that such a thing could happen again, but it was very nice. She walked over to admire little Harry, sleeping on his back, his tiny hands lightly fisted, the red-gold fuzz of curls clinging damply to his neck. He was beautiful. Robin hoped fiercely that he would look like his grandfather. His grandfather! It was strange to think of Harry, who would forever remain thirty years old in her memory, as a grandpa. She blinked back tears.

Something must have shown on her face, because Nina said, casually, "You know, we meant it when we said you could come live with us here."

"Me? Out in the boonies? No thanks, honey. I'm a city girl. I still can't believe you and Charlie turned down a chance to own 3 Clinton Street."

"I loved growing up in the Heights, Mama, but the first time Charlie brought me here, to meet his parents, he took me to Hammonasset beach and I fell in love. Remember? I told you when I got back, 'That's where I want to live. Right on the water, watching the gulls swoop around, seeing the sun set right into the water.' And now that Charlie's doing all that Native American research, it's even more interesting to me. His people knew an awful lot of good medicine, Mama. The original settlers appreciated it, too. Everything they wrote says the Indians were a lot cleaner and a lot healthier than they were. They borrowed a lot of Indian remedies. And I'm doing it, too."

"What do you mean?"

"Well, for instance, the Pequots, really the Mohegans. They lived around here . . ." She waved in a circle, encompassing the beach and everything behind it. "In the summer, they camped on the beach and in the winter, they walked north into the hills. They planted corn and squash and beans and they caught seafood. They had a really healthy diet—none of the sugars and fried stuff that's making this country so fat and diabetic and prone to heart disease."

Nina was a graduate of Harvard Medical School, but she had become fascinated early on with alternative medicine. On a trip to China, she saw that acupuncture worked there the same way anesthesia worked in the West—which is to say, most of the time. That was the beginning, for her, and she had become an active debunker of a great deal of modern medicine's revealed wisdom. She thought there was far too much dependence upon drugs and not enough on the mind's ability to help heal. A great believer in the healing properties of proper nutrition, Nina loved to quote some doctor, whose name Robin could never remember, who had said, "The cure for cancer will not be found in the laboratory; it will be found on our dinner plates." Nina had begun, during her pregnancy, to write articles that, so far, had been published only in alternative medicine magazines. But she was unfazed. It took a lot to discourage Nina.

"And, Mama, this is amazing, the natives usually only had two, maybe three children. They got pregnant when they wanted to be pregnant. They knew how to abort a fetus—which they must have done with herbal medicine because they didn't have the tools, back then, for surgery."

Robin smiled. "Of course it was medicine, honey. My gran, Morgan Becker, knew how to brew it up."

"She did?"

"I must have told you about that."

"You told me she was a beloved and successful doctor. Oh, and that she started out as a midwife."

"I never told you about *her* mother? Well, her mother was a healer. Not far from here, as a matter of fact, somewhere near East Haddam."

"You're kidding me! My family comes from right around here? Wait till Charlie hears! Tell me! You've been holding out on me, Mama!"

"Not at all. And I think I *did* tell you—when you were a little girl. Oh, all right. All right. Now, remember, I don't know how much of this is really true, but Gran used to tell me stories about her mother—Annis, her name was, Annis Wellburn. She was the local midwife and the midwife became perforce the local gynecologist, too. And because she was so skilled at all that, people began coming to her about everything. Gran said it was just common sense, plus some secret potions passed on to her mother from *her* mother. But people thought that she was magical. A witch." Robin decided not to tell Nina the stories about casting spells. It was just too unbelievable. "You know, I'm not even sure I remember the stories right."

"Well, you'd better. That's half the reason Charlie began looking into them, Mama."

"What's the other half?"

Nina laughed. "Well, he's hoping that the Mohegans—they're his people—will fund some of his research into native magic and medicine . . . now that they're so rich, from owning Mohegan Sun Casino. And he says if they won't, he'll go to the Mashantucket Pequots—they're the tribe that has Foxwoods."

"Well, I hope one of the tribes gives him some dough. I've always thought magic and medicine were close cousins—I mean, look at what I do. What's therapy if not half and half?"

"Didn't your gran tell you other stories? She must have!"

"Actually, now that we're talking about it, I'm beginning to remember other things. Supposedly, my gran—and that means my Mom and me, too, I guess—we're all directly descended from a healer woman named Bird. That's why Mom was named Birdie and why she named me Robin. Well, it seems this Bird—"

"Wait!" Nina interrupted. "Listen, Mama. What's my name?"

Robin was puzzled. "Your name? Nina, of course." Then the penny dropped. "Oh. Oh dear. Crane."

In a hushed voice, Nina repeated: "Crane. My name is Crane. A water bird."

They looked at each other, and Robin felt a little chill go down her spine.

"The healer woman, Bird," Nina said, her eyes wide, "she was a Pequot, right? Well, what if this Bird actually lived right here, on this very beach?" She paused, dramatically. "What if my wanting to live here was the spirit of Bird, speaking to me?"

Robin laughed and said lightly, "You aren't really of Bird's blood, honey."

But Nina looked solemn and said, "But her spirit would know that I belong to this family. And remember, Charlie's part Mohegan."

Another shiver. Robin had got a sudden, very quick flash of the large white bird who appeared in her dreams occasionally. But no. It couldn't be. Her daughter might be crawling around the edges of New Age beliefs, but not she, not Robin Malone, psychotherapist. She was saved from having to answer Nina by the baby's cries, as Harry awakened and demanded to be fed. Nina picked him up at once and, settling into a rocking chair on the deck, offered him her breast.

Robin excused herself and went into the house to get a cold drink. Seltzer, these days, seltzer with lime, rather than cranberry juice liberally laced with vodka. Her drinking days were over. A lot of destructive stuff was over now, thank God. No, thank Menlo Park. Without the help of those women who were taking care of combat nurses with post-traumatic stress disorder—PTSD—out in California, she would still be on her downward spiral.

She'd had to get shrunk, in order to become a shrink, but, like the song said, the medicine never got anywhere near where the trouble was. Civilian therapists either wouldn't or couldn't listen to what she was saying. During her training, she'd had two shrinks. The first, a man, found her very angry and hostile and thought she had taken on the problems of the soldiers she cared for. She told him no, they were *her* problems. She had lost so many people, even boys whose names she didn't know. And he said, "You're dramatizing yourself, Robin. You came back. They didn't." It went on like that, with her trying to tell him what was bothering her, and him telling her it really wasn't bothering her. Finally, one session, she lost it. She screamed at him, asking why in hell he couldn't for Christ's sake *listen* to her. His reply was, "How can we continue with your therapy if you're so angry, Robin? How can you counsel other people? Perhaps you should think of another career." She blew up, left, and got herself a woman therapist. Who also didn't have a clue. But by then, Robin knew enough to keep her mouth shut and behave. She got her Ph.D. and her certification. But she didn't get herself taken care of. She was still deep into denial.

Robin walked into Nina's big beautiful kitchen, resplendent in brushed stainless steel. Everything was cool and open, with floor to ceiling sliding windows that opened to the other side of the deck, the side that looked out on the salt marsh. She spritzed a seltzer from the old-fashioned bottle into a glass, squeezed in a little lime and took a long sip.

All those years, even through Nina's medical school, Robin had seemed fine. She was Dr. Robin Malone now, her daughter was Dr. Nina Malone; what else could she ask for? On the surface, she was cool and calm and rock-steady. Her patients loved her. Then, last year, her father died. And then her mother died. Suddenly, she was alone in the house and alone in the world. She came down with a flu that had put her in bed for ten days. She got so weak she couldn't even get up to go to the bathroom, and finally had to hire a nurse to take care of her.

While she was limp, sick, and helpless, without even the strength to hold a newspaper, it all came rushing back. Sometimes in dreams, but often just out of nowhere. The sudden flashes of Harry lying on the gurney, looking all right, though she knew that every bone in his body was broken. He was dead. Dead. Dead. The stacks of arms, of legs at the end of the day of a mass-cal. The boys who came in for R and R, bold and brave and boisterous, and who returned to be sent out in body bags.

Standing at her daughter's smooth granite kitchen counter, Robin started to cry. It was amazing, how easy it had become to weep, since her time at Menlo Park. The therapists there said that the Vietnam nurses had all held in their tears too long, and they were right. She should have cried, years ago. But she was so cocky. Even after she heard about Menlo Park and what they were doing there, she thought she didn't need it. Hell no, not Robin Malone! Now, at the oddest moments, she'd have a memory flash and find her eyes filling. But that was okay; it was time to cry, to grieve and mourn for everyone she lost in that war. Including her own baby. She was only sorry she'd been so blind to her own pain for so long.

Imagine, who did she see, on her way into the recovery center at Menlo Park, but Norma McClure, looking pretty much the same: same Dutch-boy haircut and all. Only older, of course. She was on her way out, and she annoyed the hell out of Robin, as usual.

"You're going to hate it, Malone, especially at the beginning, but in the end you'll be grateful. I know I am. Good grief, a few months ago, they found me praying over a patient. I said he was 'expectant' and that I couldn't find the priest. He wasn't my patient at all. I was in Family Practice and the man was in the surgical unit for an appendectomy, and wide awake. I scared him half to death. I thought I was back at the One-Six-One." She eyed Robin, not unkindly, and said, "I'll bet you've never mourned Dr. Kaye properly. Oh, it'll be hell, Malone, but you'll be better for it."

You needn't be so fucking superior, Robin had thought. *I haven't been praying over anyone.* No, but she had freaked out at Thanksgiving two years ago at Charlie's parents' house in Killingworth, Connecticut. Suddenly the turkey leg on the platter became human and the gravy turned to blood. She got up from the table quickly and ran for the bathroom, stuffing her white damask napkin into her mouth so she wouldn't scream and frighten the Cranes, or vomit all over their beautiful carpeting. She had needed Menlo Park, all right, even though it took her awhile to admit it. Norma was correct, on both counts. It had been hell, and in the end, she was grateful for it.

However, it would be nice if she didn't puddle up quite so often; that was pretty inconvenient. She didn't want to worry Nina and Charlie or scare the hell out of her patients. She refilled her seltzer glass, threw a couple of ice cubes in, and strolled back to the deck.

"So what do you think, Mama?" Nina said, without preamble. "About the spirit of Bird?"

"I don't know," Robin said carefully. "What do *you* think?"

Nina laughed. "Oh, don't worry. I'm not quite over the rainbow. Charlie says that Native Americans thought everything had a spirit, even trees and plants. It's a nice idea, don't you think? We're all so careless with the so-called inanimate things in this world. Maybe a tree *does* yell ouch in tree language, when you nail something into it or cut off a limb. Don't look at me like that. I'm just thinking out loud. I'm not going to come all over strange and start wearing crystals and do channeling. Although . . ." She broke off, bursting into laughter. "If you could see your face!"

"Never mind my face. You've reminded me that I found something when I was cleaning out the house. I found two somethings. One is a notebook that my gran kept her herbal recipes in."

"Mama, you're kidding!"

"Nope." She couldn't resist a pleased smile.

"Great! Then I can try her herbal remedies and see if they work. And I can check them against the remedies Charlie's research has been turning up. I wonder if they're the same? I hope so. That would be so great! Then, maybe I can get someone at Yale–New Haven to set up an experiment. If I weren't feeding Harry, I'd come over there and kiss you! I'm so excited! And the other something?"

"This." Robin dug into her handbag and pulled out a small plastic bag. She handed it to Nina, who turned it over and over with her free hand.

"This is . . . a bead, right?"

"I believe it's like wampum, a long tubular bead cut by hand from a clam shell. I *think* it's a clam shell."

"Charlie will just love this."

"Well, I hope you will, too. It's an amulet. It wards off evil spirits. Or something like that. Anyway, it's magic. It belonged to Gran. Her mother gave it to her. Her mother told her that it had belonged to the original Bird."

"No way!" Nina's head came up, her eyes wide with wonder.

"I remember seeing it when I was little, and hearing stories about it. That's the one, all right. The bag's not an original." They both laughed. "I'm really so sorry you never knew my gran, Nina. Morgan Wellburn Becker. She was some great woman."

"As great as Nanny?" Nina countered, somewhat defensively, her voice trembling.

Robin went to her daughter's side and touched her shoulder. Nina had loved Birdie. And, she had to admit, her mother actually had been the mother to Nina she hadn't had the time to be for Robin. They'd been quite a pair, Nina and Nanny. While Robin was keeping herself too busy to think about her grief and her rage, Nanny had watched over Nina. And now Mom was dead. She hadn't lasted long after JJ died, no more than three months. Well, she'd always said she felt like less than a person without him. There was something admirable about that kind of loyalty, wasn't there?

"I'm sorry, baby, I know you miss your Nanny. She was great, too. She was a better mother to you than she was to me. I'm really glad you had her, because I have a feeling that a lot of the time I was pretty damn useless."

Nina squeezed her hand and said, "Never useless, Mama. But it's so nice to see you smiling and, yes, crying so much. You think we don't notice? It's so much better than being frozen—you know?"

"Nina . . . ?"

"Yes?"

"You ever dream about a big white bird?"

"A big white bird? Like a heron?"

"I don't know. Just big. And white. And a bird."

"Not that I remember, but I'll be on the lookout. What does it do, in your dreams?"

"Flaps its wings and flies around in circles. Maybe it was a substitution for my mother. You know—Birdie. But, somehow, I don't think so. Somehow . . ." She stopped.

"Somehow what?"

"I don't know. I seem to remember dreaming about it when I was in Vietnam. Maybe it has something to do with ... Harry? His accident? Oh, forget it."

"You really loved him, didn't you?" Nina said, shyly.

"I really loved him," she said. There came those damn tears again. To hell with them. She wiped them away with her hand and kept talking. "We were going to get married when we both got back."

"I know, Mama, I'm so sorry."

"Hey! Don't be! I know of a few couples who thought they were madly in love when they were in-country, but when they came home, it just wasn't the same. The danger wasn't there and the feeling of comradeship wasn't there. It's hard to explain. What I'm trying to say is, Harry Kaye and I might never have made it up the aisle anyway. But I still miss him."

"Charlie and I know a very nice man—our stockbroker—a man about your age. He's a widower—"

"No, Nina! No! I'm too old to be fixed up."

"He lives in Old Lyme, and I invited him to drop by any time this weekend."

"Nina, I'll kill you, I swear."

"Don't worry," Nina said, laughter in her voice. "I won't tell him my great-great-great-a-hundred-times-grandmother was a witch."

"Healer, honey. Midwife. Nurse. Shrinker, probably." She paused and laughed. "And a witch, I guess. All those things."

"A physician, in other words."

"In other words."

"You know, I've been looking at Charlie's notes and copying down the names of plants the natives always used. I've been trying them with my patients. Nothing that might be dangerous, of course. Highbush cranberry—you brew tea from the bark and it really does help ease menstrual cramps. A couple of the midwives I work with say it's good for easing the pain of labor, too. Or black cohosh, it does pretty much the same thing. Blue cohosh is great for arthritis and boiled slippery elm bark turns into a kind of mucilage, very good for burns . . . Oh, I don't think we've even begun to look into the old ways nearly enough. Do you think I'm totally nuts, Mama?"

"No, honey, I don't think you're nuts. But I think you're very brave to try these things. Or maybe it's your patients who are brave."

"All I know is, they work. There we go. He's fast asleep." Nina burped the baby and brought him to Robin. Happy to hold him, she buried her nose in the sweetness of his soft neck. Nina sat down next to her, and said, "I wonder . . . do you suppose those teas and decoctions I've been making are the same as the ones a-hundred-times-great Grandma used? That we've managed to carry on a medical tradition for generations?"

They looked at each other. They both shook their heads, saying together, "Nah. Couldn't be!"

*Look for these other poignant and
sweeping novels from
the pen of Marcia Rose.*

Published by Ballantine Books.

HOSPITAL

Heart-wrenching, engrossing, and always entertaining, HOSPITAL opens the door to the tumultuous lives of the men and women who make an urban medical center run. Marcia Rose has crafted a compelling story of hospital politics, sexual and otherwise, and brings to vivid life a cast of characters who wage a daily battle between life and death.

NURSES

Marty Lamb is a smart, savvy nurse practitioner who is the director of New York City's first and only nurse-run inner-city clinic. Heading a staff of tough, tenacious nurses, she fights daily to keep the clinic running and makes the hard medical choices that come with serving a poor community. NURSES captures all the crisis, chaos, and craziness in the lives of the dedicated healers on the front lines of a big-city hospital.

LIKE MOTHER, LIKE DAUGHTER

LIKE MOTHER, LIKE DAUGHTER is the sweeping saga of four generations of passionate and indomitable women, played out against the backdrop of the most important events in twentieth-century America. From "free love" in Greenwich Village in the 1920s to the Summer of Love in 1960s San Francisco, from the Triangle Shirtwaist Factory fire in New York to the fires of the London Blitz, here is the unforgettable story of a family of women led by Leah Vogel Lazarus and of American life in the twentieth century.

Published by Ballantine Books.

Ask for the novels of Marcia Rose
wherever books are sold.

Visit Marcia Rose on-line at:
http://members.aol.com//~mrosebook

The novels of
Marcia Rose

Published by Ballantine Books.